UNDER
WESTERN
EYES

PERSONAL ESSAYS
FROM ASIAN AMERICA

UNDER
WESTERN
EYES

edited and with
an introduction by
garrett hongo

ANCHOR BOOKS/DOUBLEDAY

NEW YORK LONDON

TORONTO SYDNEY

AUCKLAND

AN ANCHOR BOOK

PUBLISHED BY DOUBLEDAY

a division of Bantam Doubleday Dell Publishing Group, Inc.

1540 Broadway, New York, New York 10036

ANCHOR BOOKS, DOUBLEDAY, and the portrayal of an anchor
are trademarks of Doubleday, a division of Bantam Doubleday
Dell Publishing Group, Inc.

Acknowledgments for individual essays appear on pages 333–34.

Book design by Claire Vaccaro

Library of Congress Cataloging-in-Publication Data

Under western eyes : personal essays from Asian
America / edited and with an introduction by
Garrett Hongo. — 1st Anchor Books ed.
p.   cm.
1. Asian Americans—Biography.   I. Hongo,
Garrett Kaoru,   1951–.
E184.O6U47   1995
920′.009295—dc20   94-44594
                                            CIP

ISBN 0-385-47239-0

1 3 5 7 9 10 8 6 4 2

CONTENTS

UNDER WESTERN EYES

TO MAXINE HONG KINGSTON,
GOLD MOUNTAIN HERO

EDITOR'S ACKNOWLEDGMENTS

I enjoyed a good deal of support and encouragement on this project. Two years ago, T. R. Hummer, then editor of *New England Review*, allowed me to serve as guest editor of an issue of that magazine so that some of these essays could be initially published in periodical form. At Anchor Books, Martha Levin and Charles Flowers were generous with their time as well as swift and incisive with their editorial advice. Carol Jane Bangs, Director of the 1994 Centrum Writers' Conference, and Sherri Hallgren, Director of the NAPA Writers' Conference, asked me to give craft lectures there, which allowed me to present some of the thinking that led to my written Introduction. A residency at Villa Montalvo gave me the opportunity to finish editing several of these essays and begin writing the Introduction. David Mura, T. R. Hummer, Li-Young Lee, W. Lawrence Itogue, and James D. Houston read drafts of the Introduction and their comments helped me clarify and develop several issues I had raised. John Higgins worked as my editorial assistant in the final phases of preparation and did a commendable job. My thanks to all for their kindness and enthusiasm.

Garrett Hongo is a poet born in Volcano, Hawai'i, where he recently completed a memoir entitled *Volcano* (Knopf, 1995). He was educated at Pomona College, the University of Michigan, and the University of California at Irvine, where he received an MFA in English. He is the author of two poetry collections—*Yellow Light* (Wesleyan, 1982) and *The River of Heaven* (Knopf, 1988), which was the Lamont Poetry Selection of the Academy of American Poets and a finalist for the Pulitzer Prize. Among other awards are two NEA Fellowships and the Guggenheim Fellowship. Recently, he has edited *The Open Boat: Poems from Asian America* (Anchor, 1993) and *Songs My Mother Taught Me: Stories, Plays, and Memoir by Wakako Yamauchi* (Feminist Press, 1994). He is a professor at the University of Oregon, where he was Director of the Program in Creative Writing from 1989 to 1993.

UNDER WESTERN EYES

Since the publication breakthrough of Maxine Hong Kingston's *The Woman Warrior* in 1976, an increasingly higher level of success and diversity has been emerging in Asian American literature. During the eighties, Amy Tan's novel *The Joy Luck Club* was a runaway bestseller and David Henry Hwang's play *M. Butterfly* had a hugely successful run on Broadway, winning several Tony awards. Young poets like Li-Young Lee, Marilyn Chin, David Mura, John Yau, and Cathy Song rose to national prominence, winning awards and appearing in standard textbooks and anthologies. During the nineties, both Tan's novel and Hwang's play were made into commercial films, and mainstream commercial presses and regional and literary small presses have stepped up the publication of even more novels, memoirs, volumes of poetry, and collections of short stories by Asian Americans. A list of recognizable American literary names might now include those of Gish Jen, David Wong Louie, Wendy Law-Yone, Ben Fong-Torres, Sylvia Watanabe, Frank Chin, Gus Lee, Joy Kogawa, Philip Gotanda, Jessica Hagedorn, Fae Ng, and Le-Ly Hayslip. Newcomer novelists Chang-rae Lee and Julie Shigekuni will be recognized very soon. Poets Li-Young Lee, David Mura, Kiyoko Mori, and myself are now publishing memoirs and autobiographies with commercial houses. It feels like a storehouse of cultural riches has been filled, and that there is a lot of literary goodwill in the cultural bank.

Yet, alongside the recent rise in prominent national publications by Asian American writers, some troubling confusions and disputes have arisen concerning the public role of the Asian American literary artist, particularly with regard to questions of politics, community, social justice, and the representation of Asians in mass culture. There is an extremely divisive cultural war going on, made visible recently by the newspapers, that has sparked debate on university campuses and served as a hot academic topic for symposia panels across the country. Structurally speaking, the war is taking place on two ostensibly different fronts—in the mainstream culture and within Asian American academic and literary communities themselves—on the one hand pitting the Asian American writer against mainstream cultural perceptions, and then, on the other, pitting the Asian American writer against a political agenda defined as organically arising from out of diverse Asian American communities. Recent events like the academic panel at the Asian American Studies Association's 1990 convention, which featured several scholars presenting papers denouncing Ronald Takaki's prize-winning book *Strangers from a Different Shore: A History of Asian Americans,* have demonstrated that, despite what any single author might wish, this cultural war constantly engages the Asian American writer, marginalizing and censoring individual consciousness, playing out political arguments in a social arena, and absorbing the multiple meanings of any given work into oversimplified interpretive systems regarding the relationship between ethnicity and power.

There have been critics who demand that writers serve as political instruments to bring about social justice. Claiming to act as spokespersons for the Asian American community, these critics argue that Asian American literary artists have not done enough to curb or eliminate certain exotic or negative portraits of Asians in our culture. They have even gone so far as to allege that the artists themselves have perpetuated these negative images. From the mainstream front there are yet others who feel that Asian American writers have been treated well by the culture and have little reason to argue with it and no ground for advancing political critiques. I would say that many academic colleagues, white liberals, and assimilated friends have tacitly but consistently required that we writers be silent about our outrage for the dearth of that justice being visited upon our lives. I feel that *both* of these perspectives are patronizing and proprietary and work to perpetuate the twin crimes of limiting artistic freedom and infantilizing the consciousness of the Asian American writer.

The Japanese American poet David Mura once wrote an article for *Mother Jones* about the Actors' Equity protest against the casting of British Jonathan

Price, a white male, as the Eurasian lead in the Broadway production of *Miss Saigon*. The point had to do with the fact that no Asian was given an audition for that role, that, yet again, a *white* was playing in yellowface. Mura's article also exposed the breakup of his friendships with two white artists—a painter and a poet—as a result of his arguing with them over the legitimacy of the protest. His friends argued against reverse discrimination, against Affirmative Action with regard to art, against Mura's classifying them as recipients of white privilege. They insisted that they themselves had experienced discrimination, that they knew what prejudice was, that he had no point to make with them regarding their social privilege, that they were *the same* as he was. They wanted to depoliticize the racial question, setting aside the issue of representation and defusing his very political challenge to the freedom of art. But Mura would not relent, to the point that the friendships were strained past mending.

After the article was published, there was even more difficulty. Though their actual names were never used, Mura's erstwhile friends felt that their privacy had been violated, that Mura had exploited them by including the breakup of their friendship in the article. They felt betrayed. And their social group—a goodly number of liberal, white artists in Minneapolis–St. Paul—took up their cause, creating a huge burden of social pressure upon Mura, making him feel isolated, unsupported, and reviled by the very group that had been his circle in the past.

Other writers, who may have been neutral or mildly supportive of him, began to bash him publicly, speaking disparagingly of him as an "ethnic Johnny-Come-Lately," as a traitor to his white friends, as a "self-righteous convert" to radical ethnic politics who had been so mild and acceptable in the past. The criticism came from a group of local artists that was uniformly white and middle-class, a group that had previously authorized his work by including him in their circle, affording him various literary opportunities, and generally paying attention to his work. His crime was not only a conversion of consciousness, say (I would describe it as actually the *development* of consciousness), but the violation of privacy among former friends, the public report of their difficult conversations, the exposure of these very delicate and powerful maneuverings around the issues of race, representation, art, and politics. Mura was ethically faulted for exposing the discussions, for revealing things and mischaracterizing positions others took. Ultimately, to my mind, he was criminalized for breaking culturally imposed and socially policed silences surrounding the issues of race and culture in our society.

There are strong taboos against this kind of silence-breaking, and they are enforced at the level of the unconscious, disguised as ethics, protected by notions of privacy, enforced socially, and suppressed within the individual psyche as the territory of the forbidden, even at the level of thought—we dismiss what we experience as "out of bounds" to the point that we often deny their occurrences even after they've erupted.

It is often this way whenever a writer breaks a culturally imposed silence. Once he protested the ventriloquism and cultural appropriation enacted in the production of *Miss Saigon*, Mura was further victimized. In attempting to suppress his protest, Mura's liberal friends were committing a kind of cultural infantilism, trying to invalidate the authority of his perceptions and perspective on the issue, failing to respect his emerging consciousness, trying to persuade him that his hurt regarding their dismissiveness of this racial and political issue was delusionary and unrealistic. Yet, Mura persisted, pursuing his point of view, reporting on these discussions, breaking the cultural silence regarding how issues of race, art, and politics are negotiated at the levels of the interpersonal and policed by social groups.

For this outspokenness, Mura had to contend not only with the loss of friendships, but with the social mechanism of ostracism and demonization that ensued. In essence, he was *shunned*—excluded from society in a manner metonymic of the Japanese American relocation itself. Moreover, he had to endure the realization that this shunning would have economic as well as social consequences. Around literary whites in the Twin Cities, he'd forever be known as a troublemaker, likely costing him consideration for an academic job, curbing his invitations to contribute to local literary publications. He became widely known for a controversial political position with regard to art, and, once he became racially identified, he was cast out of his former circle. Very rapidly, he became friends with people of color, who seemed to rally to him.

Though our culture often claims that art is a separate category not entirely subject to the principles of political fairness our democracy might impose on elections and businesses, it is nearly impossible to ignore issues of representation, white privilege, and freedom of expression when we examine the images of peoples of color authorized by our culture. African Americans, Native Americans, Hispanics, and Asian Americans have long been subject to the power of the stereotype regarding their portrayals in the cultural mainstream. "Miss Saigon" is simply one of the most recent misrepresentations regarding Asians promulgated by our culture.

In protesting the producer's refusal to consider casting an Asian in the lead role, Mura opposed a long-standing tradition of white cultural privilege to represent the Other—whether Arab or black, Asian or Native American. This idea arises, perhaps, out of a primitive delight in spectacle, in seeing exotic things displayed for public delectation. It plays on cultural and psychic fear of the unknown, on susceptibilities to the sublime (dread mixed with fascination), and on the relationship between ignorance and the imagination. It is the essence of theater. Yet it falsifies, for reasons of spectacle and entertainment, the cultural and interpersonal identities of the very peoples it purports to represent.

During Shakespeare's time in England, the costumer Inigo Jones was famous for dressing actors in false beards and headdresses; in gowns, robes, and outsize pantaloons; in thick makeup and jewelry so as to create in the appearance that they were Moors, Jews, and Spaniards. The plays and masques of Renaissance England took white actors and created Orientals and Indians, blackamoors and rajas, gypsies and khans. In nineteenth-century America, white singers and dancers engaged in the practice of blackening their faces to make farcical the illusion that they were black minstrels. In this way, white performers colonized an African American tradition for white audiences, furthering the European tradition of white displacement, substitution, and usurpation of the ethnic in cultural practice. Later, during the 1920s, white musicians copied the styles and took the innovations of African Americans from New Orleans and made a reputation as musical originators themselves. Al Jolson—a Jewish entertainer—then made blackface an American icon in *The Jazz Singer*, the first "talkie," a motion picture with recorded dialogue, made in the late 1920s. In the silent film *Broken Blossoms*, a story of forbidden love between the races, a white actor played a tragic Chinese. Charlie Chan, the Chinese detective of the 1930s and '40s movie serials, was always played by a white actor in makeup that made him appear slant-eyed. During and shortly after World War

II, English-speaking Chinese and Korean actors started appearing in American commercial films like *Back to Bataan* and *The Flying Tigers* as Japanese military villains—more realistic updates of Ming the Merciless, a thirties pulp fiction and comic book character who was brutal, clever, and completely maleficent. The stereotype was again transformed in the 1950s, when white actors Marlon Brando and Mickey Rooney played slurred-speech, buck-toothed Asian males in movies like *Teahouse of the August Moon* and *Breakfast at Tiffany's*. Brando's Sakini was a sidekick buffoon, a procurer and helpmate to Glenn Ford's lead, a Caucasian army officer stationed in post-war Okinawa. Rooney's character was the salacious Japanese landlord to ingenue Audrey Hepburn. He suggested sexual favors in lieu of rent. Sexual threat to white women, emasculation, physical brutality, and social buffoonery are all part of the Asian male presence in American popular culture.

The stereotype was thus so firmly in place that, when television began to portray Asians, the characters, this time played by *Asian* actors, had to conform. "Bachelor Father," a half-hour comedy series, featured a Korean cook who spoke in fractured English and wrote indecipherable notes to star Jon Forsyth in a kind of pidgin phonetics. "Bonanza," an NBC western, had its Chinaman, Hop Sing, yelling to the Cartwrights, his masters, in mixed Cantonese and chop-suey English. Thus, first-generation Asian American creoles became identified with farce and buffoonery, invalidating the heroic languages of our pioneering ancestors.

Historically, the image of the Other produced by mainstream culture has flattered white supremacy, diminished ethnic dignity, masked the ethnic origins of certain art forms (i.e., jazz), and usurped creative opportunities for ethnics to represent themselves in a manner independent of the operating stereotypes. There is a tradition of *mis*representation with regard to the Other, and people of color sense it acutely, particularly when confronted with new outbreaks and hugely popular manifestations of it such as *Miss Saigon*, where the usurpation and stereotyping is so blatant. We have been appearing, for far too long, under Western eyes.

I once struggled with a similar issue when reviewing Gretel Ehrlich's novel *Heart Mountain* for the *New York Times Book Review* in 1988. The novel's setting is the concentration camp in Wyoming that housed 18,000 Japanese Americans during World War II. The principal characters are four Japanese

Americans and the ranchers, sheepmen, waitresses, and itinerant cowboys of the area. The hero is a white rancher who falls in love and has an affair with a beautiful Japanese American woman who is a painter educated in Paris. But she is married—to a Nisei who beats her, a political dissident who rages against the government and its racist policies. The other two Japanese Americans are benign and ineffectual—the painter's kindly father who carves Noh masks and seems to approve of his daughter's extramarital affair, and a young reporter for the camp newspaper who masturbates nightly, fantasizing her body joining with his.

In my review I pointed out that the Japanese American male characters are portrayed as menacing, emasculated, or mystically benign while the principal Japanese American female character is portrayed as lissome and exotic, sexually available to whites. I said this was still the production of the Other, that Ehrlich's novel, however well-intentioned and politically sympathetic, still suffered from unconscious stereotyping and some historical ignorance regarding the Japanese American characters and their experiences. I found it unreasonable to condemn the book, as I enjoyed its narrative flow and its affecting portraits of ranch life. Yet, in good conscience, I had to raise an objection regarding what I felt to be an almost laughably racist treatment of its Japanese American characters. My criticisms came in a single paragraph in a review that, overall, praised the book for its portrait of Wyoming ranch life and its aesthetic loyalties to a magnificent landscape.

During the year that followed, I was occasionally accused of having acted like an "ethnic hit-man," policing the work of white writers who dared to approach treating the lives of people of color. I was characterized as holding to the "politically correct" position that a white writer could not and *should not* write about people of color, that a white writer should not presume to speak *on behalf* of oppressed peoples, that a white writer who did so was colonizing the experiences of minorities who should be allowed to speak for themselves. This criticism was itself an act of cultural ventriloquism, as my published position asserted nothing of the kind. A system of cultural fear, a complicated manifestation of backlash, had appropriated my review and re-characterized me as radically ethnocentric. Somehow, the report of literary gossip held more authority than the printed words themselves.

Here, my own experience mirrored Mura's in the aftermath of his *Mother*

Jones piece. The reactions in both are typical of a society based upon an idea of cultural "centering" that unconsciously appropriates the experiences of racial minorities and interprets for them what their identities and consciousnesses shall be. When this process is criticized, particularly by anyone considered to be a racial or cultural "Other," the culture erupts in a backlash that takes a variety of forms, ranging from social shunning to active discreditation and persecution. Cultural conservatives perceive both the critique and the presentation of alternative interpretations as a threat to cultural stability and their own prestige. The view from the center is powerfully resistant to the incorporation of diversity, to any attempt to "de-center" its primary aesthetic and cultural beliefs about itself (e.g., that "culture" itself is universal and is empowered to absorb, flatten, and erase political and racial differences). The writer who comes from the margin, from minority enclave communities, from suppressed histories, from lifestyles not in the mainstream of society, generally has an extremely difficult time persuading audiences—even an audience of intimates who might share the same suppressed histories—that presentation of the new narratives brought to our culture by critical voices, often of minorities and women, is beneficial and not as destabilizing as so many feel it is. To speak *about* a trauma or social prohibition, to speak against silencing, can initiate further acts of trauma, silencing, and prohibition of the speaker.

For example, most adult Americans now seem willing to acknowledge the injustice of the Japanese American relocation during World War II. In 1989, Congress made a kind of national festival of its formal, legislative apology to those who had suffered internment, creating an entitlement program to make a small financial redress for every living survivor of the internment. But this was not always the case. Not too long ago, during my own childhood and adolescence, the mere mention of the Japanese American relocation invited controversy and vilification.

I once wrote a poem about a man who makes *shakuhachi*—the eight-holed, end-blown Japanese flute made from the base of a stalk of bamboo. Its music is that of the monkish, reclusive, and meditative Buddhist tradition, and it accompanies the *shamisen* and *koto* in an ensemble music something like a classical repertoire of passionate Japanese melancholia. The maker is an amateur—he is really a dirt farmer and gardener by trade, an immigrant to this country from southern Japan who endures hardship, some real racial humiliation, and stern losses during his lifetime. He was sent, along with 120,000 other Japanese Americans, to one of the relocation camps made for them during World War II after the bombing of Pearl Harbor, when the country suspected all persons of Japanese ancestry of collaboration and worse. He loses his farm, and he burns his flutes in a small fire by the bathhouse on his property, in the vain hope that eradicating all items and traces of Japanese culture will spare him from suspicion and persecution. It does not. He is sent off to the California desert—it was in the western deserts of California, Utah, Arizona, Colorado, Wyoming, and Idaho that most of these camps were built—where he is haunted by the ghosts of his old instruments that "wail like fists of wind/whistling through the barracks." He comes out of camp and rebuilds a life, becoming a more patient and less opportunistically minded man, allowing for reflection and privileging more mental acts of consolation than he had before. He becomes something of a philosopher, a poet sitting among tall canes in a bamboo grove at the edge of his property, and, near the end of his life, calling forth the music of his lost flutes to absolve him of history and its bitter losses.

It is a poem, in one version or another, that I had been trying to write since I was a child, when my maternal grandfather first told me about World War II and what it did to him and to our community. A child of nine, I thought it was a made-up story when he first told me about the camps. I asked, "How could they do this to you? And why did you go?" And then I remember talking to my parents and our neighbors and being silenced from the questioning. When I was fourteen, my grandfather told me the story again, and I went to my teachers and asked them—I was in junior high in Los Angeles—"What about this? How come we're studying World War II and you say Saipan and Okinawa, Pearl Harbor, the Battle of the Bulge, the Marshall Plan, the Berlin airlift. What about when they put 120,000 Japanese Americans into prison?— that's not in the book." My school in South Central L.A. was made up of about a thousand black students, a thousand Japanese Americans, and a thousand whites. I was marched to the back of the room and told that we would talk about this later, that I shouldn't bring it up. I asked my schoolmates in the schoolyard, "What about this?" Since I'd grown up in Hawai'i, I didn't know that you couldn't talk about it. One of the guys in my group punched me in the stomach and said, "Don't talk about it. We're not supposed to talk about it. Our parents said not to." Later on, when I was in college, I wrote a poem about this, and I showed it to my creative writing teacher—a man from a desert town in California who had gone on to Harvard for a fine education. He said, "This is a militant poem. You know, you've always been a good student. You're not here on any kind of minority admission program. You're here on academic scholarship—you don't have to be writing this sort of thing." So I took my poems back, cursing him under my breath.

About ten years later, when I was near the end of completing my first book of poems, I wanted to write about this same subject again, but in a way that wasn't like any of the ways I'd been hearing. During this time—the late seventies—there had been the Asian American movement, different kinds of student activism, and the idea emerged that we could create our own courses in Asian American Studies at places like Berkeley, UCLA, Long Beach State, and San Francisco State. But the student protest work I was seeing, the poetry from these places, was very much styled in the manner of the Last Poets, a group of urban blacks who took a revolutionary stance. Their approach was very street —bardic and insolent—characteristics I approve of socially, but somehow not in poetry. I wanted something other than that for myself, for my poetry. I wanted to write of the pain that I'd seen in the people who raised me, and their silence, their stoicism, and their reticence—in some ways their very real *dignity*.

There is a strenuous generational silence in the Japanese American community—in fact there is a two-generational silence—not only about the camps, but about an idea of an emotional life. When you have to be silent about something as cataclysmic and monumental as the relocation camps were, it tends to govern your willingness to live in *any* emotion at all. You feel your exclusion quite acutely. You feel your *difference*, your perception as an outcast *Other* in your society that is hostile to you. And you begin to internalize this hostility as self-hate—the inability to cherish your own inner life, your own social history, your own status as an individual and member of a community. At the level of the unconscious, you begin to perform an internalized silencing of your own perceptions and to rewrite your story according to patterns other than those of your own life. You uphold what is *not you* and live as if your own experiences were of little value. It's kind of a censorship or handicap—an illness. And this illness lasted for two generations—the generation of the Issei, the first generation of immigrants who made a place here, and the Nisei, the second generation, native borns who grew up as teenagers in the relocation.

My generation, the third (actually I'm fourth, but in terms of age bracket I'm of the third generation), called Sansei, didn't understand this. We tried to recapture the history and talk about it, but we were angry that we were denied, not just the facts, but the emotional experience, the report, the *parenting* of knowing about our parents' and grandparents' lives. The generations before us weren't telling us their story. Without that story, we grew up cipherously—as if everything behind us was a zero and we were the first. To be without history, to be without an emotional life, to be without the ability even to *imagine* the emotional lives of the people who came before you, is an incredibly damaging thing, an ache that hurts in a way that you don't even realize hurts.

The anger we Sansei felt, and felt empowered to express, was immature of course—we simply were unable to appreciate the group stoicism in the face of the generational tragedy, to understand the curious mix of heroism and self-hate from which this stoicism emerged. Because it was for a kind of *protection* that the Nisei and Issei were so quiet. There had been so much pain, losses so incredible, that to acknowledge them might have withered hope completely, and our elders wished to spare their children this kind of despair. *Kodomo no tame* is the phrase in Japanese—sacrifice for the sake of the children—which I grew to admire as a generational code that grew out of these very real and deep feelings of shame.

When I finally understood this, after I finally became aware of and began to appreciate the very real heroism of the Nisei and Issei, I was able to write this *shakuhachi* poem from my principles as a writer—a verbal music, a simplicity and directness, the idea of cherishing the smaller things like these bamboo flutes, and an acknowledgment of history and its wanton acts. I broke through some aesthetic, political, and generational silences, and I felt like I had written something from the story of my people, telling the tale of the tribe, speaking from a mystery and a great unsaid, speaking from the ancestors and giving them a voice.

I think many tales must emerge in this way, whether they be in fiction, poetry, drama, essay, or memoir. The new ones come from something that has been held back, in a way, *prevented* by our culture, which is largely censoring and conformist, which produces a system that governs discussion—literary or otherwise—to the extent that all speech is "policed" and brought into a chain of relations dedicated to the upholding of *power* and the denigration of what is unempowered—in many cases, the stories of ethnic people, women, and other culturally underrepresented groups.

Often, the telling must break through multiple layers of misunderstanding and stereotyping in order to be told. Mistellings need to be identified, confronted, and evacuated of their prestige, their cultural authority. Frank Chin has been quite righteous and entertaining in his career-long skirmish against the stereotyping of Asians in American popular culture. In "Confessions of a Number One Son," published in *Ramparts* (the forerunner to *Mother Jones*, by the way) during the early 1970s, Chin angrily and humorously confronted the issue of the Asian stereotype, ridiculing and deconstructing paternalistic American culture for its Charlie Chan, for constantly emasculating Asian men as patsies, sidekicks, eunuchs, buffoons, and maleficent villains; for exoticizing Asian women as geishas, dancing girls, courtesans, and sarong-wrapped sirens. Like Mura, he was writing against the stereotyping and silencing of Asians in our culture and made a public call for outbreaks against it.

In *The Political Unconscious*, Frederic Jameson—the foremost proponent of Frankfurt School Marxism in America—writes about how our culture gives us certain master narratives, in essence *male* narratives, which tell a story that the culture is trying to endorse. The literature, media, and even gossip conspire to give us an idea of how a life should be lived and how lives should be described in story. These stories enter our unconscious, give us our ideas of human value and human organization to the extent that we rewrite and reimagine our own experiences to conform to these master narratives. Jameson points out how these narratives flatter the political agenda of power and proliferate throughout the culture at multiple levels. We who feel woe and misery are under the domination of this kind of power.

The kind of stories promoted on television, for example—if you think of the 1950s and the Eisenhower administration and programs like "The Donna Reed Show," "Ozzie and Harriet," "Father Knows Best"—endorse a certain idea of family values: stability, heterosexual union, stable middle-class life-styles, and the wisdom of the father visited upon his family—a very staid, repressive, conformist idea of life. These stories work in a way to devalue the differences and specificities in the more various kinds of lives we lead. If you happen to be Hispanic, for example, what can you find but your own self-hate after watching something like "Bachelor Father"? The ethnics are houseboys, gardeners, and the butt of jokes and recipients of the white male father's kind patronage. These kinds of things work at the level of the unconscious to the point that the individual of color, of cultural difference, feels marginalized, canceled, pushed to the edges of culture and society, feels *Othered*, feels raced, feels gendered, feels different. The story that you have from your own life, then, is thus canceled, and you have begun to hate it, you have begun to live in a silence that's unarticulated by our culture. This is part of what Jameson means about the nature of the political unconscious—it creates revolutionary alienation.

At the same time, Jameson suggests that the new stories are going to be coming from those who feel silenced, who feel othered, whose stories are not taken up by culture and society and proliferated throughout the system; that the new narrative will reorder experience in a completely unexpected way. In this context, I'm reminded of a book by Tillie Olsen called *Silences,* which is mostly about women and women's lives, and how they are not portrayed by our master literature as revealed by the high preponderance of male writers in the *Norton Anthology of English Literature.* As a child of the Asian diaspora, I felt that the master narratives of America were not open to me either, would not easily incorporate stories that I knew except as addenda to the grander tales of Manifest Destiny, white settlement of the West, and the idea of "civili-zation" being brought to Hawai'i by Christian missionaries and planters. For most of my adolescence and early adult life, I felt that there was no literary matrix in which I could address the histories of the immigration and plantation experience in Hawai'i, and my own stories went completely untold. But, slowly at first, I began to reexamine some of my misguided values about the folktales I grew up with—Jataka tales of the Buddha, Hawaiian supernatural tales, Japanese folktales, oral histories of immigrants and laborers on the Hawaiian sugar plantations—and I realized that, because of my education and my par-taking of the values of the mainstream culture, I'd seriously repressed my own cognizance of these tales to the point that I'd engaged in the process of deny-ing, even to myself, that these were worthy tales of human wisdom. I'd be-come *colonized*, and I needed to begin the process of mental *de-colonization*. I needed to acknowledge the specificities of Japanese American history, and I needed to recognize that there was great value in the oral histories and Asian folktales and even in the structure of those tales. I needed to repossess my own childhood, my own ethnic background. I needed to reverse the process of cultural self-hate. And it was that process that brought me into writing a poem like "Something Whispered in the *Shakuhachi*" and an essay like "Kubota," included in this collection, which partake of the traumatic history of the Japa-nese American relocation and try to give homage to the emotional lives of the generations before mine.

It would be marvelous if the normal response to this kind of outbreak against a culturally imposed silence were one of welcome and the acknowledgment of a fresh and contributive perspective, but this is not always the case. Quite often, the response can be social hostility, misunderstanding, and severe personal punishment visited upon the writer who has broken the silence. Once an initial breakthrough is accomplished, that is, once the censoring powers of the politi-cal unconscious of centralized culture are somehow thrown off or defeated, silence, as a cultural code, still carries within its operations a note of the sacred that undergirds and perpetuates its maintenance. Power constantly maintains itself and polices those under its domination. And power is insidious—it often masquerades as resistance to power, inverting principles, exchanging roles, proliferating in a cultural hall of mirrors that distort, multiply, and disguise its operations. Therefore, a secondary breakthrough still has to be made—this time one that is against the censoring powers of the *margin* rather than those of the center. If the cultural war is successfully fought on the first front and the censoring mechanisms of mainstream culture are overcome, then there is yet another cultural front, equally powerful, that arises and must be engaged. The literary speaker against silence can still be severely punished, this time by the ethnic Other rather than by centralized cultural power. The Asian American writer can be victimized by those who have themselves been silenced, by voices purporting to emerge from within ethnic communities, making exclusive claims to political truth and raising challenges against a given writer's ethnic authenticity. What follows are a few examples of what I think are instances of "internalized oppression"—manifestations of social oppression and the exercise of hierarchical political power that sometimes emerge from *within* the enclave cultures of peoples of color.

Back in 1971, the Asian American Studies Center at UCLA published *Roots*, the first Asian American reader. *Roots* contained academic papers, political essays, memoir, poetry, photography, and graphic arts; and there was also an extended piece of literary criticism in it. Written from a Marxist perspective by graduate student Bruce Iwasaki, and given the carefully worded title "Response and Change for the Asian in America: a Survey of Asian American Literature," the article surveys the history of Asian American literature up until that point and makes some provocative judgments regarding two pioneering Asian American writers—Frank Chin and Lawson Fusao Inada. In essence, Iwasaki criticizes them for being more interested in their own sensibilities and in the problem of developing an authentic Asian American literary diction than in the welfare of "the Asian American community" as a whole. Iwasaki accuses Chin and Inada of using the Asian American community primarily to give "local color" to their works, ignoring that their "artistic decisions are tied with moral and . . . political decisions." As a final pronouncement, Iwasaki writes that "Chin and Inada remain within the bounds that makes so much literature *safe*."

I was inspired by what Chin and Inada were writing then, so Iwasaki's complaints surprised, perplexed, and even angered me. He seemed to be chastising writers for not promoting his own concept of community needs, his own political and academic agendas. Chin and Inada, if nothing else, seem to me always to be about doing what they want as writers—like Walt Whitman, they are the perennial unwashed ruffians of culture. Which, I assume, was what bothered Iwasaki. He could not annex their work to his own ends, he could not dictate theme, tone, or agenda to them. Like Matthew Arnold and Plato, he elevates the critical mind over the creative, has a vested interest in engineering culture and society, and therefore had great difficulty tolerating the aesthetic independence and unpredictability of writers like Chin and Inada, who seemed to me heroic for that reason.

During the summer of 1989, on a book tour after the publication of her novel *The Floating World,* writer Cynthia Kadohata, a Japanese American, was making a routine appearance at Cody's Books in Berkeley. The crowd was unusually large for a first-time novelist, packed with interested Asian American students and some UC faculty too. Her book had been receiving good notices in the mainstream press, and a chapter of it had run in *The New Yorker* prior to publication. She read quietly but clearly, with a fine delicacy of voice and a minimum of physical movement. The audience seemed charmed. But in the question and answer session that followed, she was chastised for not writing about the concentration camp experience. Her novel, partially set during the time of World War II, tells the story of an itinerant family of Japanese Americans wandering through the West and South in search of work, doing without community except for each other. It never once mentions the federally ordered evacuation of citizens of Japanese ancestry from the West Coast. But there was a powerful faction among Japanese American intellectuals who felt it was illegitimate of Kadohata to have refrained from any overt references to the internment camp experience.

"You mean to tell me that you have this family of Japanese Americans running around through Arizona, Colorado, and Utah, and you *never* say anything about the camps!" a scholar shouted from the audience. "You should be ashamed of yourself for falsifying our history!" he yelled.

More shouting ensued as a few other Asian Americans joined this public castigation. Kadohata responded by saying that she didn't *intend* to write about the camps, that her novel wasn't *about* the camps, that she was writing about a family of loners and misfits, writing from *her* experience, and that was that. She was then criticized for abdicating her responsibilities as a Japanese American writer, denounced for not fulfilling expectation, for not writing from the public truth of the time.

She told me later that the whole incident puzzled and upset her. It hurt that people, especially other Asian Americans, felt compelled to attack her for what she *didn't* write even more than for what she *did* write. Kadohata was wondering why there was so much vehemence, so much anger, and so much "attitude" among Asian Americans *against* Asian American writers. She hadn't defended herself then, but the episode made a deep and lasting impression. She told me that the next time she was out there, she'd be ready. She wasn't going to get beaten up again without a fight.

I once remarked that Asian America is so immature as a culture and so unused to seeing cultural representations of itself that, whenever representation does occur, many respond with anger because of the pain released. It is as if they recognize *their* story in the outlines of the story one of the writers is telling, but feel even more alienated rather than absolved because that story isn't theirs *exactly*, or doesn't present the precise tone and tenor of their inner feeling regarding an experience they feel the writer, as an Asian American, should understand. It's like a bunch of family members at a holiday dinner sitting around, trying to tell a story about a maiden aunt, a matriarch, or a black sheep. One starts it up, and, before you know it, six others chime in, saying the first didn't get it right, that their version is the one that is true and has all the facts. It has to do with issues of primacy, proprietorship, a claim of proper descent and legitimacy, and a claim to specialized knowledge. It is complex. And charged with passion. Whenever someone singles out a certain storyline, an interpretive angle, there are always those who would dispute its legitimacy, even to the point of trying to erode the confidence of the story-teller.

During the summer of 1990, I was in Volcano, Hawai'i, making trips through the rain forest there, taking field notes for my book about the place. I was home sorting through files when the telephone rang. It was a woman who told me she was the West Coast reporter for the *Philadelphia Inquirer,* asking my opinion of Maxine Hong Kingston's literary contributions, asking whether or not she influenced my own work in any way. I said, "If it weren't for Maxine Hong Kingston, I wouldn't have my imaginative life. It was a great moment reading *China Men*. That book released human feeling for me. It humanized me, it released my own stories for me." I said that *China Men* gave me the inspiration to envision the lives of my own ancestors, particularly the men in my family, in a way that I had been blocked from doing. Her work was liberating, I felt, and it gave me my own grandfathers back.

Time passed, and I heard nothing about the piece. Then, about a year later, I started getting letters and postcards from writers, white and Asian, all around the country, mentioning some newspaper flap between Frank Chin, our pioneering editor of Asian American writing, and Maxine Hong Kingston, perhaps the most eminent Asian American writer. Friends in Honolulu phoned and mentioned it too. Some congratulated me for my "brave remarks." All wanted to know what I thought about the supposed debate. But I thought nothing, not knowing what everyone was referring to. I tried to ignore the whole thing.

But then a postcard came from Maxine Hong Kingston herself. It said something like this: "Thank you for your kind remarks about my work. It was the first time any Asian American male writer has said anything in print that was *positive* about my writing."

I was astonished and a little embarrassed. "How could *that* be?" I asked myself. How could an omission like that be possible? Her books had been around for about fifteen years by then. And everyone knows their huge impact. But there was that strange phrase in her note—"Asian American *male* writer." Why was *gender* important here? What could she be talking about?

I called James Houston, a novelist who is a mutual friend, in Santa Cruz. Houston is coauthor with his wife, Jeanne Wakatsuki Houston, of *Farewell to Manzanar*, the first book to treat the relocation camp experience that gained popular acceptance. I thought he might be able to illuminate things for me, being on the mainland and probably "in the loop" for this kind of writerly controversy. He told me that various articles had come out in the *Los Angeles Times*, *San Jose Mercury News*, and *San Francisco Chronicle* putting forward the story that there was a gender split between Asian American male writers and Asian American female writers. They put Frank Chin at the center of the argument, along with Maxine Hong Kingston and Amy Tan. They quoted Chin as saying that Kingston and Tan had won wide audience appeal because they pandered to white tastes and promulgated a stereotypical exotic image, particularly of Asian women. Chin used words like "traitors," "feminist assimilators," and "whores" when talking about Kingston and Tan, describing their work as "white racist art," then raging on about how Kingston, in particular, gets Chinese myth, language, and culture completely wrong. The articles collected opinions about the controversy from various other Asian Americans, me included, and the comments fell pretty much on both sides of the issue. Houston said that my remarks were some of the strongest, and he read me more of what I was quoted as saying.

"People are approaching ethnicity with a religious fundamentalism," I said in the *San Jose Mercury News*. "They want to discredit and repress certain works from the canon of Asian American writing. They want to be the arbiters of what constitutes worth in Asian American literature. The problem is they're trying to exert control over all the rest of us." Along with playwright David Henry Hwang and critic Elaine Kim, I came off defending the phenomenon of Kingston's and Tan's popularity.

This was my introduction to the social force that rocked throughout the Asian American writerly community for the next couple of years. Wherever I went, whether it was UC Berkeley or Williams College in Massachusetts, whether it was the Asia Society in New York or the Asian American Studies Center at UCLA, students wanted to know where I stood on the issue. Every Asian American literary event I was a part of took up the controversy as a central theme. Academics started framing scholarly presentations accordingly, devoting whole panels at the Asian American Studies Convention to the examination and discussion of the issues of the gender split and the debate between Chin and Kingston. The purported split was tone-setting and divisive.

White academics had identified a gender war in mainstream writing, African Americans had identified one in black writing, and, it seemed, we Asian Americans had the mimetic desire to define one among our own writers. Thereafter, discussion of our literature constantly proceeded from the assumption of division and divisiveness among the writers, based either on a gender split or another, even more pernicious dichotomy. Asian American students I met, either in large groups or individually, began to take it as an article of faith that there were "radical" and "authentic" Asian American writers, and contrasted these with those who were "sellout" and "inauthentic" writers. Chin and other somewhat underpublished writers would be in the "authentic" camp, while Tan and Kingston led the "inauthentic" camp. As I wrote in the Introduction to *The Open Boat: Poems from Asian America,* this kind of thinking led to the creation of a litmus test of ethnic authenticity. If a writer was adjudged successful in the larger culture, either by bestseller popularity or by virtue of certain awards, then this very success invalidated that writer as an *authentic* Asian American one. This judgment often licensed out-and-out rudeness toward some Asian American writers when they visited college and university campuses. Others could be excluded for "inauthenticity" or boycotted by the faithful if their visits arose from an invitation by an English Department rather than from Ethnic Studies.

Such divisions serve as a kind of *policing* mechanism of the ethnic culture, governing the range of allowable literary production. At the level of the un-conscious, then, the level of unspoken agreement, to be an "Asian American writer" meant subscription to a code of cultural and political values that ex-cluded certain mainstream literary practices—perhaps rhetorical eloquence, perhaps Anglophone tradition-based style and structure in poetry, perhaps mass-market success in fiction, perhaps subjective personal accounts as opposed to jargonized sociological treatises in nonfiction. Chin's criticism of Tan and Kingston and the subsequent public brouhaha had set up a kind of operating cultural myth that divided the small community of Asian American writers into easily distinguishable and, to my mind, grossly oversimplified binary opposites. This myth of opposition, unfortunately, was then readily taken up by the Asian American community of students and academics.

I'd witnessed this phenomenon before. I was a first-year graduate student at the University of Michigan in 1975 when a group of us raised some student funds to invite Native American novelist Leslie Marmon Silko, black poet Etheridge Knight, and Japanese American poet Lawson Fusao Inada to read on campus. We got monies from a coalition of minority student groups, and we arranged for the black fraternity on campus to host the event. The poet Robert Hayden, author of "The Middle Passage," an epic poem about the slave trade, and editor of *Black Fire*, one of the first anthologies of African American poetry, was a professor on the English faculty there at the time. Fiftyish, past six feet and large-framed, he wore thick, Coke-bottle glasses and always had a greeting for me whenever our paths crossed, usually in the poetry room of the English building. There weren't very many people of color around the poetry world at Michigan at the time, and Hayden was a sort of hero of mine, a quiet man who wrote delicate, sometimes mournful lyrics about his childhood in Detroit. He came from the same neighborhood as the boxer Joe Louis. He'd taught at Fisk University, an exclusively black institution in Nashville, Tennessee, and he had lived awhile enduring enforced segregation and de facto Jim Crow segregation. I looked up to him, and I invited him to join the group at the podium.

His answer surprised me. "While I want to honor you folks," Hayden said, "and while it flatters me to be asked, I'm afraid that I must decline your invitation, Garrett."

I was astonished. When I asked him why, he said, "Did you ever hear of the term 'Uncle Tom,' son?"

I nodded, shocked it could apply to him.

"Well," Hayden said, "I'm afraid the black students around here think of me as just another Uncle Tom—a corny, submissive Negro shuffling around the white folks. I am *obsolete*. And I am afraid that I am *persona non grata* around African American Studies. I think it would hurt your cause if I appeared on the podium with the other writers. Students might boycott, and that wouldn't help you build the kind of feeling or audience I think you want."

I held him in conversation for a little while longer. I may have asked him why the black students thought of him that way, but he didn't have to answer. I knew about the attitude. Hayden was professorial, learned, mild in his social personality. The model in play for the black poet then was what came out of Black Power and the Black Arts Movement. It was a brilliant, pissed-off male in a black leather jacket, wearing a Che beret and sermonizing about the revolution. I had heard Black Panther David Hilliard speak. I had heard black revolutionary poets Stanley Crouch, Quincy Troupe, and Ojinke read at the Watts Writers' Workshop. I had heard Amiri Baraka give a speech to black students at Michigan in 1974, exhorting them, excoriating them, sermonizing and hectoring them. It was an exhilarating performance. What ran as universal among all of these presentations was a stance that had emerged out of black patriarchy and black urban experience. It was Stagolee—the legendary black gambler who could get away with murder if he wanted to. It was black male defiance in proud opposition to dominant white society. And Robert Hayden did not fit that model at all.

Don't get me wrong. I *liked* the revolutionary stance. It was entertaining and empowering and, as a young Asian American male, I needed both. But I also admired Hayden and cherished the tenderness of his verses. I was troubled that the revolution could not move aside to make a space for him and his work as well, that learning, gentleness, and a soft social manner would be so rejected and condemned. In contemporary terms, I understood that Hayden was adjudged or, at the very least, suspected as being "white identified," and therefore ostracized from the mainstream of black student and literary life. As a poet and mentor for blacks, he was looked upon as a kind of oxbow lake in a meandering river of cultural evolution. And I was sorry about it.

Our multiethnic coalition went on with the event, which was a huge success, and Robert Hayden came, though he did not speak from the podium. A ripple went through the crowd, a mix of Third World students, as we called ourselves then, when he entered the room with his wife, people moving aside as his large frame lumbered through the aisles and down to the front row, center seats I'd reserved for him. I remember that Lawson Inada and Etheridge Knight both acknowledged him from the podium. Hayden meant something to them too. And the man did not speak a word to our audience that night. Among we students at the University of Michigan, Robert Hayden had been silenced.

For this anthology, I tried to choose essays written *against* social silencing, but emerging from deep personal silences dedicated to reflecting upon moral, political, and identity issues. They are written *against* cultural conformism, intransigent rationalisms, and convenient pragmatisms all vying for space in the mind, all making exclusive claims regarding the truths of our experiences. Their progress is toward a different kind of resolution than that made available by most other mechanisms of society—be they systems of justice, social welfare, or community organization. One of the central things these essays *are* about, it seems to me, is an *arrest* of the practical mind so that the mind of memory and imagination can then be engaged, calling forth the purpose of taking pure pleasure in the meditative act of writing itself. This is the exercise of symbolic imagination to no purpose but the achievement of a kind of resolution known as aesthetic composure or, to be sublime, rapture. One of the things writers try to achieve, perhaps even more than any kind of moral decision or political vision, is the moment of literary *pleasure*, a feeling that does not depend on any other logic except that dictated by the world of its own language, its recollections and interpretations of events, its need for or dismissal of practical resolutions to its inner problematics. To risk an even more venturesome statement, I would say that these essays are *written against power* to achieve a consistency of their own fictions—an otherworldly power of their own—so that the writing itself can stand separate from any sacerdotal class of interpreters (academics, intellectuals, political organizers) and undermine the ruling doxologies, be they of race or class or ethnic group, whatever ideology would claim itself to be the norm of thinking.

To varying degrees, I think important cultural stories that need to be told generally go this way. They emerge from long-held silences, and, with most cases, the storyteller has had to have spent a good deal of time mulling over the issues before breaking that silence. Sometimes the stories are received with welcome, but, too often, the stories meet with strenuous resistance, and the culture restricts their proliferation and tries to negate their authority. The writers whose essays I chose for *Under Western Eyes: Personal Essays from Asian America* each speak from this kind of acute silencing. They are trying to expose issues, authorize suppressed histories, and articulate experiences that, in general, have *not* been spoken to before. Many included here quest for stories of immigration and the hardships of acculturation, stories which have been silenced somehow, pushed to the margins by an idea of common culture, a homogeneity of belief in certain kinds of social and even spiritual values that push aside not only the new tales, but, in fact, even our means of perceiving and recognizing our individual experiences. The operating notion that there is such a thing as a common or universal culture, in effect, pushes aside very specific experiences that don't happen to flatter what is assumed to be the common agenda of the country. This notion devalues stories about women, for example, stories about people of color, stories of gender, stories that are somehow forbidden and tagged as aberrational, as militant, as depraved. This is the kind of silencing I'm talking about too—the kind of silencing felt by the Japanese Americans about the relocation. The kind of silencing that was enforced even *within* the Japanese American community.

For a writer, as you live in this kind of silence, in this kind of misery, not knowing quite what it is that the world is not giving you, not knowing quite what it is that your work cannot address as yet, you are at the beginning of a critique of culture and society. It is the moment when powerful personal alienation slips into critical thinking—the origin of imagination. It is this initial step of intellection that enables the emergence of new, transformative, even revolutionary creativity. It occurs at the juncture between the production of art and the exercise of deep critical thought.

It is in this way that the new stories emerge from the shadows and margins of cultural disapproval and come into a piece of writing. The personal essay and memoir, in particular, seem well-suited as literary vehicles for this kind of self-examination and historically recuperative storytelling. The personal history and the "ethnic" story, the giving of testimony, the journeys of consciousness, and the providing of witness to the operations of racism in our society—these come together in a piece of writing to create a complex literary substitute for the unconscious matrixes of cultural legitimacy and social understanding that exist for others who see themselves as more "central." Citizens comfortable organizing or deriving their personal identities under the codes of cultural centrality don't feel quite as strong a need to have an ethnic or racial history explained for them—theirs exist in the standard textbooks, in the movies, in TV commercials and prime-time programs. But those citizens who emerge from marginalized histories, from complicated and fractured loyalties, need a means to probe the inner life, the ideological conflicts, and the repressed communal histories in order to create identity.

In "The Faintest Echo of Our Language," Chang-rae Lee illustrates his intense love and gratitude for, and even loyalty to, the music and beauty in the Korean language his mother was hearing at the moment of her death. In "Mother Tongue," Amy Tan writes about how she took courage and inspiration from the way her mother spoke English, mixing it into Chinese syntax, transcending and beatifying its Anglophone roots. They sway our linguistic orientations and expectations, and honor the mixing of languages in our American culture; and, in the process, they honor the Asian diaspora and the mother tongue of our America. They search for a new way to see the spoken languages in our lives, how they bear remnants of culture and promises of great emotion, how, in speaking them, we writers express our need to seek new poles of narrative and cultural orientation rather than those more readily available, even in books.

I think each of the writers in *Under Western Eyes* has gone through a decolonization process, rejecting the master cultural narratives and, in their place, insisting on the new stories emerging from silence. "Silence and the Graverobbers" by Lillian Ho Wan and "Bad Blood" by Geraldine Kudaka assemble the fragments of suppressed and underimagined familial and cultural histories. They talk about stereotyping, prohibitions of identity, and the tyranny of social expectations based on race and gender. Memoirs like David Low's "Winterblossom Garden," a poignant tale of the struggles of his immigrant parents, and John Yau's "A Little Memento from the Boys," a fulminant and streetwise fable, are narratives that give testimony to the processes of urban acculturation and cultural resistance among Chinese Americans. Peter Bacho does something similar regarding Filipino Americans in "The Second Room," yet he also explodes the stereotype regarding one of the greatest macho myths of our culture. Bacho was a student of Bruce Lee's principal disciple in a kung-fu school up in Seattle, and his memoir gives dimension and a personal poignancy to the adolescent-quest narrative in place in our culture regarding the martial arts.

The personal essay, as a literary form, seems to lend itself quite easily to the kind of internal questing with which so many here have been engaged. Like the lyric poem, the personal essay is an intensely subjective genre, insisting on individual sensibility and consciousness as the final court of arbitration for issues somehow undealt with by society. It places the individual, its author and hero, at some contemplative remove from dailiness, providing a kind of "momentary stay against confusion" so that a certain obsession can be indulged, a troubling question can be wrestled with, an evanescent experience, as yet unchronicled by the culture, can be recorded. Yet, unlike the shorter lyric, the personal essay gives itself over to copiousness and development, incorporating anecdote, personal history, rumination, and discursiveness and allowing for extended reflection upon events which would have to be compressed or metaphorized in poetry, or made somehow less intimate and questioning in a fictional narrative. The development of a self becomes one of the stories embedded within the personal essay, and, in the selections collected here, the story of that development is one of Asian Americans arriving at a consciousness evolved within the fractures of available identities and elective affinities, whether literary or popular. It involves the *imperative* of having been *raced* by this culture, of the individual having to account for the social and cultural forces that threaten to marginalize or suppress both individual experience and the potential for collective identification with Asians in America. These narratives involve questions of race, ethnic history, and the interpersonal set against a backdrop of education and society resistant to the development of individual and ethnic identities.

It is interesting to note that many of the contributions here were written by poets. Li-Young Lee, a poet with two well-known books, contributes a fond and pained remembrance of his magisterial father who was a Presbyterian cleric for a poor parish in Pennsylvania, but who was also, prior to immigrating to America, the personal physician to Mao Tse-tung and a perennial refugee. Lee's memoir reports on a complicated history and on the development of an even more complicated aesthetic and moral consciousness. In "The Internment of Desire," Sansei poet David Mura tells the story of the development of his own sexual consciousness—a subject which has largely been silenced concerning Asian Americans, particularly males. His essay is frank and confessional, and it addresses the hidden relationship between the pattern of development of carnal desire and that of ethnic and personal consciousness. "Lalita Mashi" is Chitra Divakaruni's tragic portrait of a "No-Name Woman" back in her native India, a story of victimization that would be forgotten were it not for the obsessive loyalties of one who lives with a consciousness of diaspora—Divakaruni, standing on a BART platform in Oakland, sights the ghost of the dead woman going the other way on a train, and it is the incongruity that triggers her memory and imagination. As with so much poetry, it is a powerful and unforgettable image that compels the rest of the writing, the unfolding of the story behind the mysterious and symbolic image. Perhaps, feeling the lack of the kind of historical, emotional, and intellectual foregrounding provided for poets more identified with central culture, these Asian American poets have gravitated to the memoir and personal essay to fill this psychological absence. They must "explain" themselves beyond what is possible in a lyric.

Indeed, it is the job of an essayist to explain, and so we have story, history, recollection, and rumination bundled into one extended yet highly poetic piece of writing by Jeanne Wakatsuki Houston. Her "Colors" is a kind of compressed epic, an "explanation of a life." NPR reporter Nguyen Qui-Duc's "A Taste of Home" is a heartbreaking report on his return to Saigon years after having fled it. He struggles with feeling privileged and saved as he compares himself, in terms of body and mind, to those who stayed behind in Ho Chi

Minh City. Nguyen's portrait of an elementary school classmate he encounters on the street is tinged with pity and regret even as his catalogue of the physical surroundings and his profile of the typical, quite alcoholic life led by so many contemporary Vietnamese male laborers are somewhat hard-boiled.

"Telling Differences" by Debra Kang Dean and "Where Are You From?" by Geeta Kothari address the powerful inner conflict and soul-searching that goes on when one becomes aware of the subtle racism beneath the surface of so much of daily interaction. In seemingly innocuous events like Kothari's shopping for a dress in a trendy boutique and Dean's work as a student editor on a university literary magazine, the effects of racism within our culture conspire to repress their self-esteem as people of color. In Kothari's case, it is that constant feeling of being cast as an outsider, being automatically denied her status as an acculturated American because of her skin color. Dean can't abide the racist notions implicit in a poem being considered by the editor of the magazine she works for, and resigns in protest, which triggers a complicated sequence of events of social pressuring—her fellow student editors argue with her, try to persuade her against her own instincts, challenge the legitimacy of her protest, diminish the seriousness of the matter, and ostracize her for betraying the belief system of the social group to which she had once belonged. She talks about social trauma versus individual awareness, mutuality versus consciousness, and she chooses the path consciousness demands. Her essay chronicles the interior process of creating a complex social analysis with high personal stakes. Both Kothari and Dean struggle against the social silencing that tries to deny the legitimacy of their own interpretation of events. These writings are heroic in that they not only oppose the powerful pressures to uphold the legitimacy of mainstream values, even in its interpretation of events, but in that they also identify and carefully delineate what would otherwise be invisible pressures. They expose the operations of silencing.

A couple of years ago, I got a phone call at my home in Oregon from a reporter at *Newsday*, the daily paper for Long Island. Just the day before, Robert Olen Butler had been awarded the Pulitzer Prize in Fiction for his collection of short stories called *A Good Scent from a Strange Mountain*. The narrator of each story is Vietnamese, each a different survivor of the war in

Vietnam, most of them living in this country. The reporter wanted to know what I, as an Asian American writer, thought about the prize being awarded to a white male who wrote stories in the personae of male and female Vietnamese refugees.

I told him I was personally delighted that Butler had won the Pulitzer, that I was glad that the prize had finally gone to someone who was known as a dedicated laborer in the fields of creative writing, who wrote for long years in obscurity, who wrote well and without recognition except from his peers in the business, who taught a heavy teaching load at a regional branch of a state university, who was a single parent who gave to his community and to the community of Vietnamese immigrants. I stalled, wanting a little time to think.

"Yes," the reporter said, "but what is your opinion about his being white and writing in the voices of Asians? Of him *adopting* the identity of Vietnamese individuals in order to write his fiction?"

I had suspected there was something hot behind his questioning. On matters of race, American culture has the chronic habit of organizing itself in terms of opposition first, even with regard to a book that, to me, was a sincere attempt to create commonality.

On the one hand, there was the history of stereotyping and ventriloquizing Asians in this country. There was certainly a history of abuse there. And it was a history that was vague in the minds of most Americans who were not Asians —an "invisible" history, one that did not penetrate daily consciousness unless one were oneself Asian American. Butler's collection of stories, in the act of taking on the voices of Vietnamese people, could be interpreted by some as perpetuating that tradition.

On the other hand, there was my own feeling that Butler's book was kind of a breakthrough for American books on the Vietnam experience. Until Butler published his stories, most every piece of writing from Americans had to do with the tragedy of the American experience in Vietnam. Tim O'Brien and Larry Heinemann had written powerful fiction from the point of view of American soldiers. Michael Herr had published nonfiction from a similar perspective, while Yusef Komunyakaa had written a stunning book of poems—it, too, based on his GI experience. Very little had been published from the Vietnamese point of view, and almost nothing about the Vietnamese experience in America. Butler's book had created characters and described an ethos much unknown to mainstream America—that of the Viet Kieu, Vietnamese survivors of the war who had emigrated to the U.S. and were struggling over their losses, their identity, and the difficulties of acculturation. Sympathetic without being sentimental, Butler's treatment gave the outlines of their lives great human dimension and humor without ignoring the multiple tragedies of their having lost homelands, loved ones, and a certain continuity of cultural identity. *A Good Scent from a Strange Mountain,* though written by someone who was white and not Vietnamese, could not easily be seen as yet another piece of "minstrelsy" by the white culture ventriloquizing the ethnic experience and colonizing the mind of the Other for the purpose of reinforcing cultural dominance. It is a work which seemed to me at once more complex than that, and yet I could not say so within the simplistic framework in which the reporter was asking his question.

I told the reporter that I couldn't give him a short answer and gave him the long one instead. I begged off making any kind of *ultimate* political judgment. Since I am not from the Vietnamese American community, I couldn't presume to speak to the issue of whether or not his characterizations and tales infringed upon some "right" of theirs to define themselves in our culture. I felt uncomfortable being asked to speak "as an Asian American," knowing that we are an extremely diverse group in terms of generations, cultures of origin, and economics. I urged him to ask a Vietnamese American. I told him that, by asking me for my opinion, I knew he was operating as if Asians in America were one vast, homogenous category, and making the false assumption that any one of us, no matter that our ethnicities were different, could speak "on behalf" of the entire race.

He tried to press me, but gave up after a few more exchanges. He couldn't pin me down because I didn't want to be. Frustrated, the reporter thanked me and hung up. It was obvious I hadn't helped his story angle. He wanted a fight between Butler and Asians, and he wanted me either to defend Butler or to attack him. He wanted my answers to be *simple* and unqualified. On one side or the other. I guess, on that issue, I was sitting on a fence. The reporter's coming to me was itself another act of racism, and I worried about participating in that.

But I continued to feel uncomfortable about the incident. Why couldn't I have given the reporter something more definitive? Why hadn't I been more ready to give a strong opinion on the matter? What was it that made me speak on both sides of the issue? Was I, in fact, in being so equivocal, acting as an apologist for white colonization of ethnic cultural space? Was I—of *all* things—acting like a goddamn Uncle Tom? What are the issues here and how could I rethink myself through them? I questioned myself but hesitated to bring it up among my friends, whether Asian or not. I feared policing and I feared judgment. I wanted some space to think. I decided to look for other writers who could help me to do this kind of thinking.

There was indeed a political dimension to this issue, but it is not one regarding a given writer's "right" to represent a culture. There is a profound difference between the idea that any group has an exclusive right to engage in authorized acts of cultural representation and the idea that cultural representations are not open to criticism, whether by a group or an individual critic. Although our system of prestige can itself be seen as a kind of rule of unwritten laws, I myself believe that we cannot, finally, create legislation regarding cultural properties in the verbal arts—i.e., provide cultural laws empowering and licensing only certain individuals to do what we will prohibit others from doing with regard to language and the arts. At the same time, I do not think that anyone can be above being criticized for what they choose to do with this kind of liberty. I think we can applaud Mura for raising a political objection to a work of art, but we can also critique—though not silence—Butler on political grounds for the work of art he has produced. I think we can critique Mura as well, and we can praise Butler too—for his humanistic politics as well as for his powerful artistry. The confusions, then, have less to do with the practices of the individual artists and much more to do with the way general thought in our culture (as enacted by media and the ephemeral communal mind) tends to oversimplify complex social and artistic issues, with the habitual comminglings and false oppositions of matters of art with matters of social justice. The problem, ultimately, has to do with confusing and, finally, conflating the two realms.

I think David Mura was coming from a mainly *political* critique of *Miss Saigon* when he protested the casting policies of its producer. Empowered by his own rising ethnic consciousness and a fresh understanding of the operations of the racial stereotypes in our culture, he raised political and social objections to an instance of racism. That he protested its manifestation in a work of popular art was an attempt at critique of the *system* and not of the artists—not of the playwright, not of the actor. The casting of a white actor as Eurasian was an infringement upon Asian identity enacted systemically, through the coalescence of power assembled in the lack of political awareness in the play's producer coupled with the tacit, unconscious approval of the larger portion of American society culturally comfortable with the notion of a white playing a person of color. Yet, Mura did not ask that a writer be silenced or that political controversy dictate the cancellation of the play. He made a critique, a fairly modest, if socially powerful, literary objection. Mura was an individual expressing conscientious objection to a systemic cultural problem. He politicized an instance of unconsciously created racism manifested in a work of popular art. His protest occurred at the very line of collision between art and politics, but I do not believe he confused one with the other, nor did he mistake what the relationship was between a single writer and systemic power.

Yet, our culture often does. In contrast to Mura's objection to the casting of *Miss Saigon,* the political issue that the *Newsday* reporter raised around Robert Olen Butler's book of stories proceeds from the notion that an individual writer could be *silenced* or censured as somehow not representative of an ethnic group or improperly representative of an ethnic group. Behind this is the further notion that a given group could claim exclusive proprietary rights to all representations of itself created in the culture. A notion like this would establish that ethnic topics, ethnic identities, and the literary portrayal of ethnic voices were the *exclusive cultural properties* of a group that would somehow be deemed "authentic," licensed with the cultural "right" to represent itself as the ethnic *Other.*

Setting aside the enormously complex problem of identifying exactly *who* would constitute this authentic group and exactly *how* ethnicity is to be identified, it would still remain that this ethnic group would possess the right to silence any individual it deemed "inauthentic" or otherwise undesirable. This would grant the identified group the power of high censorship over an individual writer, thus creating yet another system of cultural silencing and, in microcosm of and mirroring the mainstream, reproducing the tyrannical situation of group dominance over the individual artist. It is yet another form of cultural centrality that would itself create margins within a cultural margin, that would reproduce cultural hierarchies and replicate, within ethnic enclaves, mainstream-like relationships of repressive group power over individual expression. It is system against individual and yet another manifestation of the conservative workings of the political unconscious.

The other instances I cite are acts of severe silencing that were attempts to create fear and acrimony around literary production itself, victimizing isolable writers with a damaged climate around the social reception of their work. Such efforts are attempts to capture, manage, and assemble social power and bring it to bear in censure upon an individual. This is a powerful, inevitably volatile encounter that encroaches upon artistic freedoms, asking art to play out politics and conscripting the artist to be an ally in the war to achieve a perfect social justice. When the artist refuses the conscription or is perceived to have refused, or when the artist performs in a manner that is perceived as inimical to the political agendas of an ethnic group to which that writer is perceived to belong, then critique of the writer can sometimes escalate into social and political censure. This is when the principles of artistic freedom become compromised. Mainstream fears of ethnic individuation and an ethnic group's agitprop suppression of an individual's consciousness emerge from such motives. The possessiveness felt by an ethnic group for cultural representations of its history too frequently results in authorizing unfortunate acts of literary tyranny. Those who see art primarily as an instrument of social engineering are allied, at an extreme, with thinkers like Joseph Stalin and Jesse Helms.

I myself think it's time to break away from debates couched in terms of opposition, which ask artists of color to make oversimplified choices between politics and art. We cannot adjudicate justice in society by infringing upon the freedoms of our artists. To oppose social responsibility to artistic freedom is itself a crime. The realm of art, what sixth-century Han Chinese called "the water margin," is where the dispossessed go when they have lost the possibility of getting justice in society. I believe one powerful justification for artistic freedom is that human judgment itself is first cultivated and refined in acts of imagination, and then applied to political and social practices. Wrongdoing cannot be made right until recognized as wrongdoing, until it is *perceived* as such. And the artist (along with the media consultant) is at least one of those citizens who can both create and change our perceptions.

The writers included in *Under Western Eyes* have been engaged in the project of trying to free these political, artistic, and personal issues from each other, carefully mulling over problems of consciousness, characterization, and political infringement not only of any given group but of any given individual, including the writers themselves. As subjective personal accounts and *not* pieces of cultural legislation (not even artistic decrees or manifestos), the essays included here are poised at the point of collision between notions of culture and the personal, and they try to negotiate the tricky mental ground between the twin imperatives toward the creation of an affecting human portraiture and the social wishes for the fulfillment of a necessary justice. Their enterprises have to do with finding the fine psychic strands of human intuition as they respond to the wanton acts of history and, based on the ensuing discoveries, writing new histories.

I think acts of imagination are precisely what *enable* just politics. As written acts loyal to extremely specific *ethoi* and eschewing reliance upon the complex of notions regarding central values and shared histories that would otherwise be known as *natural* (or, worse yet, as *universal)*, these essays have struck out into fresh territories of consciousness and ethnic histories in order to establish a new relationship with cultural power. Though art cannot itself bring justice about, yet it calls for justice to be done. Literature itself is always an outbreak of some kind, a turning away from social pressures and issues so that the writer can mull things over in a meditational space that might reorganize not only the issues, but, potentially speaking, society itself. In this sense, these essays are *foundational*, more primary perhaps than fiction, epic in intent if not in scope. They are about the making of new Americans.

—Volcano, Hawai'i

THE
SECOND
ROOM

PETER BACHO *was born in Seattle in 1950. He is a lapsed attorney, who has found a second calling in teaching and writing. Currently, he is the Student Recommended Visiting Professor at the University of California, Irvine, in English and history. His 1991 novel* Cebu *won the 1992 American Book Award.*

MARY RANDLETT

IN 1967 I JOINED THE JUN FAN GUNG FU INSTITUTE IN Seattle, more commonly known as the Bruce Lee school, and stayed for thirteen years. By then Bruce had left town for Hollywood. But the school he founded stayed open, left in the care of Taky Kimura, his good friend and former student, who carried out his mentor's wishes, like the decision not to advertise. Bruce was about fighting, not the size of yellow page ads. Although the school was open to the public, it wasn't advertised. Students learned of it by word of mouth. Nothing commercial, just the way Bruce wanted.

Consistent with that theme, the instructors weren't paid. Almost three decades later it's still the same. Neither Taky nor his assistant, Roy Hollingsworth, nor anyone else who taught there has ever made a dime. It was payment enough to be part of a legend.

And the style they taught—*jeet kune do*—wasn't pretty or mysterious, just simple and effective. Unlike in most Chinese arts, with their twirling, leaping choreographed forms, we kept our balance and stayed on the ground. Unlike in most Chinese arts, we never sought our higher selves; Zen was never spoken.

Back then, the school, because it was open, was always exciting, sometimes dangerous. A thirty-buck fee covered rent and equipment, but didn't include background checks or psych exams on the cross section of Seattle that showed up to train. The month before I joined, two senior students had been expelled for fighting each other. Their dispute, starting in class, was settled outside. One of them, a black belt judoka, later turned to amateur boxing. Within six months, he was the heavyweight runner-up in the Seattle Golden Gloves. His opponent became a cop who later found Jesus in the joint after he killed his wife, my grade school classmate. He was released, I heard, and killed again, Jesus' presence notwithstanding.

The expulsions governed our conduct. Because we wanted to stay we stopped just short of full-blown fights. But everything else was okay, which made the atmosphere electric, almost, but not quite out of control. In that sense the school resembled the African plain, its hierarchy denoting predators and prey. Rookies were prey—numerous, nervous, defenseless—expected to take lumps from senior students who stalked us and threw punches we couldn't parry, kicks we couldn't block. We were training dummies for action on the street, but better because we could react and show pain. Still, no one complained, not even the most abused rookie. Pain, we figured, was a small price to pay just to be here.

Although I stayed at the school for thirteen years, learning from Taky and others who taught me, and from those I later taught, the key block of time was those first few months during which Taky was mostly absent. His world was shaken by the back-to-back deaths of two older brothers. That meant the burden of the family-owned grocery, the First Hill IGA, fell solely on him.

In this formative period, Roy was my teacher and model, my *sifu*. I first saw him at the IGA on the day I went to meet Taky for the first time. As I searched the store, I passed Roy, who was wearing the mark of his trade, a butcher's bloodstained smock. He was standing in an aisle, deep in conversation. Although I didn't know who he was, I noticed him because when he spoke, his body moved to merge words with motion; his gestures brought attention to a pair of long arms at the ends of which hung thick, callused hands.

Roy taught me the basics: the salutations that begin and end each class, stance and balance, kicks and punches. What amazes me still is how simple and practical it all was. Like the stance: no contortions and exotic poses, no rigid stances or imitations of legendary animals. Just hands up with the right hand and leg forward, the latter covering the groin, body weight balanced. Simple.

"Like a boxer fighting southpaw?" I asked.

"Precisely."

Roy should know. He'd fought as an amateur in England, and later as a pro in Chicago; he carried the marks of his old trade, especially above his eyes and on the flat bridge of his nose. Although years from the ring, he still had a fighter's instincts and skills. Stints as a teenage British paratrooper fighting Malayan communists and as a professional soccer player rounded out his résumé. Roy didn't need Bruce Lee to be deadly. But Lee's talent was such that he converted all, even the dangerous ones. Until he met Bruce, Roy had dismissed martial artists as harmless. "Useless," he declared. "Can't slip a jab or block a hook, at least not mine. Ah, but that Bruce . . ."

Then there were the kicks. Nothing above the belt, movie fights notwithstanding. Kneecaps and shins were favored. Easy to reach, easy to hurt. Damn, I thought, why hadn't I thought of that? Finally, the punches. Short and quick —exploding in a crossing and recrossing motion through an imaginary lengthwise line splitting the body in half.

"Think in flurries, not a single big punch," he advised. "And when you throw, move into the man quick and hard. Beat him to that center line, take away his room to punch. That way he has to go around you. It's called 'closing the gap.' If you do that, you'll whip him every time."

At least that's what he said. Closing the gap with a straight punch was our basic style, one learned by every rookie during the first few weeks. You move onto the man and keep moving until you drop him. Simple and effective. But in watching Roy spar, I noticed that he didn't always follow his own advice.

To our orthodox straight-punch arsenal, he added boxing staples—hooks, jabs, uppercuts, crosses—all with deadly effect. After one such show, I asked him why he mixed boxing moves with the straight punch.

Roy smiled and shrugged. " 'Cause they work," he said simply. "That's one thing about Lee. He knows everyone's different, everyone's got a different strength. You figure it out and build your style around it. You'll learn the basics here, but everything else you pick up on your own. Just keep what works for you. Not for me or Taky, but for you. For me, boxing still works, like second nature. But for you, who knows? As you get on, you'll learn moves, techniques, but you gotta always ask, 'Does it work?' "

It was a hell of a question, an antidote for orthodoxy and smugness. Although Bruce Lee's physical skills dazzled the public, his skepticism moved me more. In surveying the ritualized attacks of the traditional Chinese fighting arts, he saw weaknesses, artificial moves that didn't work. Not on the street. His critique led him to rebel not just against these arts but against the weight of Chinese opinion and tradition that sustained them. His answer stressed simpler moves, functional in a crisis, aimed at addressing one question: Does it work?

I've carried that question with me since, and applied it first to martial arts

—training sessions, boxing rings, and street fights (short punches, uppercuts, hooks work)—and eventually beyond to religion, marriage, and careers. Asking the question can be lonely. There are few models to follow; in asking it, history matters less—so-and-so did it and you can, too—than personal experience and a short supply of wisdom. But each choice I've made has always followed the question, that troubling inquiry first raised almost thirty years ago.

I couldn't get enough. At home, I'd train with friends, family, alone, it didn't matter. I'd spend hours before a mirror checking for precision, position, and speed, trying to beat my image to the punch.

Learning to fight became an obsession, another way to gain respect. My neighborhood, the Central Area, was mostly black, but dotted throughout with pockets of Filipinos. In one of these pockets my family and I lived. The sixties hit the neighborhood hard; people started to draw lines and call each other down, just on race. Mostly, the conflict was black and white, but where did that leave me? For a while, I put it aside, confident in knowing that at least on my street I had respect. That's what mattered.

Some got it by fighting, others got it through sports. I'd chosen the latter, spending the summers at the outdoor hoops of Madrona playfield where every evening the best players in the city gathered. Most were older—college players, legends, could've-beens—and all were black, except me. In this world, respect could only be found in the lane, faking left and driving right, or reversing it the next time around. I'd ignore the outside j—a safe and sissy suburb move—and take it hard to the hole, defying big sullen brothers who enjoyed swatting trespassers back to their moms. If I survived, and sometimes I didn't, it was defense chest to chest, and grabbing boards in traffic. From the fellas at Madrona, I earned respect, but the playground was just a small part of the Central Area, not to mention the city and the world beyond. As Seattle grew more tense, I wondered: Off my street among those who didn't know me, would my record at Madrona matter?

Probably not. I figured then I'd better learn to fight. But from whom? My father, Vince, was a possibility, but we were too different. He was a tough man and, unlike me, quick-tempered, made that way by twenty-five years of migrant work. Although Dad had left the fields, the anger remained and drove his skill. As a kid, I hated to walk anywhere with him. Hard looks or insults, real or imagined, could set him off. Dad could've taught me, but how do you teach anger? I never asked him.

That left a variety of commercial martial arts schools, the last being one that taught a traditional Chinese style. Somewhere in the middle of futility—between that first mechanical punch thrown from a squat and rigid deep horse stance, plus thousands more—I realized this was useless, a point underscored by Sal, a neighborhood acquaintance.

He mocked my style with words and worse—quick jabs and hooks I couldn't defend. My moves were wooden, hands too low, too slow. I paid forty bucks a month and I couldn't stop a jab, not even when he told me it was coming. That day I blocked more than one with my face and forehead. Sal took pity.

"Remember Kato?" he asked.

I nodded. "Yeah," I said sullenly. Of course, who could forget?

By then Bruce was on his way to becoming the baddest man on film. Ever. He started with Kato, the only reason to watch the Green Hornet on the tube; Bruce didn't move as much as explode on opponents. Sure, the fights were staged. But no one could fake Lee's balance and swift, balletic fluidity—better, I thought, than Ali's best—or the speed of his kicks and punches, either hand. All of that was real enough. He was already a legend. As with Michael Jordan to another generation, the laws of nature that restrict and limit didn't apply, at least not to him. He was one bad dude.

"You're no Kato," he laughed.

What could I say? I quit the school and saved my money, swearing to spend it on something better.

It almost never came. Finding the Bruce Lee school was a fluke which turned on a tip from Rick, a high school buddy.

He worked nearby, a part-time checker at the First Hill IGA. One afternoon, Rick mentioned in passing that his boss, Taky Kimura, was Bruce Lee's friend and student and that Taky ran the school Bruce had founded. I begged him to set me up. He shrugged. No sweat. Simple as that.

. . .

Over time, I came to know other students, to gauge their skills and temperaments. Some were nice, decent folks. Some not, and of these the most dangerous were those with skill. They were older, bigger, stronger, a bad combination if you were new. Typically, we'd work in pairs matching rookies with senior students. For many of the latter, a training session was a green light for aggression. The most vicious was a stocky, powerful man that we rookies nicknamed Killer. If beginners were victims, he was our main tormentor who needlessly punished his unskilled partners, leaving welts on sternums, stomachs, and foreheads. Killer worked construction and to class he often wore his work boots, not tennis shoes, knowing full well his choice of footwear made blocking his potent kicks more painful.

Supervising our slaughter was Roy, who'd move from pair to pair, making suggestions, inspecting technique. His mere presence protected us, slowed the aggressor down. "Easy now," he'd say, a phrase that brought respite lasting until he moved on.

But even then, sometimes a predator would go too far. Maybe a head snapped back too hard, or a body doubled over—if Roy noticed, he'd intervene, talk to the suspect, tell him to cool it. "Come on," he'd scold, "it's too easy, you don't need to do that."

Sometimes, however, talking didn't work; the bully would remain unrepentant. We prayed for such defiance, barrels of it. Roy would then suggest a spar, an invitation designed to induce repentance. It gave us hope and underlined another lesson from the African plain: badness is relative. And Roy was the baddest of all. But unlike Killer and our other tormentors who beat beginners for sport, Roy never did. He didn't have to. Unlike our predators, he'd long since faced the pain and fear of the prize ring to become a man with nothing to prove.

At 185 pounds, Roy had a heavyweight's power and a smaller man's speed. That meant he could plow right through a foe or, if he chose, stay outside and pick his shots. Either would work; often, he'd do both. At the start, he might probe and play, and even drop his hands while slipping single punches or even straight-punch flurries. In this phase, he'd just defend with old boxing tricks— rolling with punches, tucking his cheek against his shoulder—all designed to show he couldn't be touched, much less hurt. A devastating display. Then, tiring of the game, he'd launch his offensive—boxing jabs and crosses, straight punches, grabbing and trapping techniques—with such precision, power, and malice it befuddled his foe, our tormentor, now weak and vulnerable, just like us.

If Roy was really irritated, he'd add short, punishing hooks, hard to defend against. These he threw with an open hand—so as not to kill, just plant a lesson—with brain-jarring slaps upside the head. First the right—bip—then the left—bop. Then maybe again—bip-bop—for good measure. After that, Roy wouldn't say much, didn't have to. Lesson learned, we were safe until the next class.

Although Roy was our protector, there were some tasks he couldn't do. The achievement of skill is, at its core, an individual prize. Unlike Roy, I was just starting out, unsure and a bit apprehensive. Fueling my doubt was a second room in the school, adjoining the main one. There, pairs of students— again matching a senior student with someone less skilled—went to spar— hard.

"In there," one student said, "almost anything goes. Long as it works." He said they fought on a board, about the size of a door, a primitive venue that forced flurries of quick and direct, explosive techniques. The action would stop only when a fighter was forced off the board. Roy and the other instructors rarely interrupted these matches, figuring a healthy dose of violence and fear were essential to progress, especially for rookies. From the main room, we could hear thuds and slaps, curses and screams. The audio of conflict made me nervous.

During a Friday session, a fellow who'd started a few weeks before I did had been taken to the room. He emerged shaken and bruised. "Rough," was all he said.

I knew I was next, probably on Monday when class reconvened. That left the weekend, too much time to nurse my growing fears, and doubt, for the first time, my nerve and dedication. Over the two-day break, my mind raced from scene ("You fought well," said one voice) to scene ("He's unconscious," said another). I wondered how others had faced it, had focused the mind and summoned the anger. In seeking an answer, I quickly skipped over Roy. He wasn't a model. He'd fought too long, both inside the ring and out, and had come to know violence well. It didn't scare him.

I wondered if it had ever scared Taky? Because of the sudden deaths of his brothers, I seldom saw him and couldn't say I knew him well. All I had was an impression, now months old, based on the meeting arranged by my friend Rick. One morning Rick said okay, Taky would meet me after class at the First Hill IGA. It was only three blocks from my high school. I'd passed it many times, but had never paid it much attention. It was a small box-shaped building buried in a valley of tall, aging brownstones and new high-rises. In this neighborhood abutting a bustling downtown, the IGA was easy to miss.

At the final bell, I raced out the door and down the street, stopping in the IGA parking lot to catch my breath and gain a semblance of composure. The semblance wasn't much, but having gone this far, I decided to enter the automatic door. I wondered how to introduce myself. What could I say to someone touched by legend?

Inside, I still wasn't sure. I stalled by strolling slowly through the store, practicing my introduction. Near the meat section, I first saw Roy, who was talking to another employee; as he spoke, his right index finger jabbed the air for emphasis.

I passed Roy and walked to the front. I felt as ready as I'd ever be, and asked a clerk for Taky Kimura. She pointed toward the produce aisle. There, a Japanese man was inspecting a table full of apples, oblivious to all but the apples themselves. He was of medium height and stocky, the perfect build for a judoka, which I later discovered he once was. Mid-thirties, maybe older, hard to tell.

My apprehension was unfounded. Taky saw to that. After my first few mumbled words, and his offer of an apple (quickly accepted), I felt at ease. A man lacking pretension, he answered all questions. I was stunned a bit by the contrast of Taky's humility and Bruce's explosive, arrogant image. It seemed an odd match. But yes, he was Bruce's student. And yes, he ran a small Chinatown club across the street from the Four Seas, a restaurant I knew well.

Our chat was going so well, we covered topics (like school) beyond the martial arts. His interest, I felt, was genuine. He liked young people, and seemed to like me. I felt so comfortable I almost forgot the purpose of my visit. Yet when it came time to choose and align the right words, I balked.

He acted as if he didn't notice that my face was starting to flush. "We'll meet again this Monday," he said. "If you're interested, come down about seven."

Taky's kindness touched me. Such a trait, I assumed, sprang from loving parents and protective older brothers who formed a precious core around him that violence rarely touched. Yet this gentle, considerate man was the head of a tough, rowdy school. He had Bruce's respect, Roy's too. Somewhere along the way, he must have faced a challenge similar to mine, and just maybe he had to beat down his fears. Just like I was trying to do. Taky had survived. Maybe I could, too.

My premonition was true. Monday marked the start of my fifth month of training. The session started innocently, exercises and then technique drills. During the break, Roy motioned for me. "You'll be working here tonight," he said, pointing to the doorway to the second room. "I'll get you a partner."

Silently, I entered the room for the first time. It was poorly lit by a single weak bulb that dangled from a cord on the ceiling. My eyes adjusted to make out the form of a door-sized board in the middle of the cement floor. Deep in my belly, I could feel a knot form.

I studied it, this tiny arena, and pondered techniques its dimensions would allow. Not much, I concluded, just straight blasts, and hope like hell I give better than I take.

Suddenly, a figure appeared in the doorway. Even without good light, I knew who it was. Just his build alone—starting with his thick, muscular neck—gave him away. It was Killer.

I hoped it was a mistake, that others would appear, and Killer would be paired with one of them. No one else showed. Hope disappeared when he took his position on the board, and motioned for me to do the same. The knot tightened. Killer was mine for the night.

Over the course of the next hour, the predictable occurred: he pounded me. I'd throw and occasionally land, which surprised me but only angered him further, prompting quicker and harder hand and foot barrages driving me backward, off the board. Again and again. Still, I'd return, resume my position, and begin once more, the last time determined to try something new.

Up until then, my attack had been an orthodox one. I moved right down the middle, technically perfect but foolish against Killer, whose build and disposition controlled this area via his straight-punch flurries, quicker and more powerful than mine. This time, however, as he started his rush, I stepped back and faded slightly to the right. I just managed to avoid his oncoming left, over which I threw a right hook, tight and fast like the bombs Roy threw. Bip. It landed hard upside Killer's head, surprising him. Surprising me, too, as I forgot to bop with the left. Killer, like any good fighter, pounced on this lapse to renew his bruising attack and drive me once more off the board.

Bent over, hands resting on knees, I stalled for time. The pain on my arms and chest throbbed in new spots to which I wasn't anxious to add. I glanced up and saw Killer pacing the board, hands on his hips, eager to beat me again. During the break, strategies raced through my mind—straight punch? (he was too strong), another hook? (it worked but he'd just seen it, wouldn't work now). Killer was still pacing, this time a bit quicker. I sighed. Although still undecided, I joined him on the board, ready for the worst.

"That's it," said a loud voice ending my torment. It was Roy standing in the dim light by the doorway.

As I passed him on the way to the main room, he pulled me aside.

"You're coming along," he said.

"Thanks, *sifu*," I replied.

"Nice hook," he said with a smile. "Keep it, it works for you. But you gotta follow up." He paused. "Not too rough, was it?"

I could feel the bruises on my arms and upper torso. My belly was tender, my thighs had taken so many kicks I could barely walk. "Nah," I lied.

"That's a good boy," he said.

I went to a corner of the room for the salutation marking the end of class. As we lined up, I looked around and studied the faces of those newer than I. I smiled. Food for their predators, a state natural as life on the African plain. Or the second room in the Bruce Lee school.

His brothers' deaths took a toll on Taky. Even as he mourned, the store stayed open, demanding more attention than anyone can imagine or pay. Something had to give; he eventually closed the Chinatown school. Temporarily. When Taky and Roy reopened the school, it was in a different locale—the spacious basement of the First Hill IGA—and had a different approach. It was now free of charge and informally run like a small private club, not a school open to the public. A few old students were invited back, including me. Killer and the other lesser predators and lunatics were gone; there was no second room.

In this new, less hostile environment, we stressed techniques and conditioning, and downplayed competition. We worked well together. Although some got hurt, the injury was always accidental, not the product of malice.

But even peace has its price. I began to miss the old days, the tension and sense of challenge, even the fear. I started to prowl martial arts classes and boxing gyms looking for spars, eventually settling on the latter. I respected boxing's functional nature, an art less concerned with style than result—that is, landing a punch that hurts the other guy.

In one bout, I fought a tall, rangy Navajo named Clyde. He was vicious and powerful, a raw talent who later turned pro. I'd seen him slaughter three other boxers; he played with them, hitting them just hard enough to keep them standing. When we hooked up, we were just supposed to spar lightly and focus on technique, nothing too heavy. That changed moments into the match as I slipped a hard straight right designed to slam my forehead into my brain.

The spar was off, the fight was on. I got under him and smothered his power. I counterpunched and held, bobbed and weaved, hit him wherever, whenever I could. Legal and illegal tactics blurred; Clyde was too dangerous. I did whatever worked.

In the second round, frustrated by my lack of sportsmanship and his lack of success, Clyde made a stupid move. He lunged at me and missed, tangling his long arms in the ropes. Before the coach could intervene, I rushed over and hooked him hard on the back of his unprotected head. It was a good punch; my wrist and hand tingled from the impact.

Near the end of the bout, I'd managed another illegal but effective move. Trapping both of Clyde's hands with my left arm, I pinned them tight against my body. I was hooking him with my free right as the bell rang.

I smiled as I left the ring, pleased with my performance. I'd fought well and had parried or slipped most of his shots, while landing almost all of mine. It was a great ratio, one I figured any fighter would've loved. Even Killer or Roy.

DEBRA KANG DEAN

TELLING DIFFERENCES

DEBRA KANG DEAN *was born in Honolulu, Hawai'i, in 1955 and received an MFA from the University of Montana in 1989.* Her poems have appeared in Tar River Poetry, *for which she is a contributing editor,* Ploughshares, Embers, Bamboo Ridge, *and other journals. Her work is also included in* Unsettling America: An Anthology of Contemporary Multicultural Poetry. *She lives in North Carolina with her husband and son.*

DO YOU SELL NEWSPAPERS?" I ASKED THE CLERK AT the Safeway store in Hamilton, Montana.

"Yeah," he answered, "there in the stands just outside that door." I walked in the direction his finger had pointed. Outside, in front of the *Ravalli Republic* stand, I realized that I didn't have the proper change. I went back into the store.

The clerk I had spoken with earlier was just finishing with the two teenagers he'd rung through. I waited in his line. "Be good," he said to the boys, then turned to me. "What, no ruck?"

"I need some change," I said.

Normally I would not even have mentioned such an exchange to my husband, Brad, who was waiting for me in the car with our thirteen-year-old son, David. Over the years I've come to expect a certain amount of discrimination, a recognition of difference, in my dealings with strangers in the continental United States. In Eureka, California, for example, a girl of about five once hugged me in a locker room, saying, "I love you because you're Chinese," and followed me out to the parking lot. I didn't have the heart to tell her I wasn't Chinese, and I'm glad that David, with whom I was registered in a toddler swimming class, was at the time too young to understand the dynamics of that situation. In a backwater town in Arkansas, during a cross-country trip Brad and I made, a teenage girl followed me around a convenience store as if I were a celebrity; I felt a little silly, trying to decide whether I should forgo a candy bar and Coke in favor of something good for me. More recently a woman stopped me in the hall of the liberal arts building at the University of Montana and asked if I was Beverly Chin, a professor in the English Department; when I said I wasn't, she told me I looked like her.

I had come to the conclusion that when I wanted to, if I talked enough I could convince strangers I was not a foreigner. But a trip to Japan had altered my perspective. Only three days before the clerk "no-rucked" me, Brad, David, and I had returned to the United States after spending almost three weeks in Japan, and we were on our way to the southern end of the Bitterroot Valley, the fourteenth residence we had taken up in as many years.

"No shit," Brad said when I told him. It was one of his three favorite reflex responses, the others being "fuck it" and "whatever." A vestige of the time he spent in the Navy, together they comprised his equivalent of their more civilized counterparts: yes, no, maybe. Though his father had been stationed in Hawai'i and we met in high school, we actually got to know each other through letters written over a period of about eighteen months. I was in the Air Force then, and he in the Navy.

"No, reary," I answered. It was a joke we'd shared since Brad began working as a communications consultant for the Japanese company that funded our trip to Japan, one reminiscent of a stereotype locals in Hawai'i had about Japanese tourists: "Take-ah pick-cha prease."

As we drove south on 93, I remembered what Brad had said as, probably from his perspective, I popped out of the Hankyu department store near the Umeda train station in Osaka like one of those numbered Ping-Pong balls in the old lottos: "God," he said, "normally it's easy to find you. I just look for your black hair." It is one of the few moments I remember from our trip.

In a letter to his publisher, Nathaniel Hawthorne wrote, "In this world, the best one can do is pitch a tent." I almost believe that. In the past fourteen years, the longest we have lived in one house has been four years—Brad, David, and I moving for a variety of reasons. This nomadic life probably has something to do with why I still call Hawai'i my home; if I feel rooted in any one place, surely that place is Hawai'i. I spent eighteen years there in the same house before I left and began doing my part to keep America moving.

It is tempting to regard the trip to Japan as a search for my "roots," but in truth the reason we went there was business—or, rather, Brad went on business, and David and I tagged along. And because of my mixed ancestry—my father is Korean, my mother Okinawan—and my own need to distance myself from the Japanese tourists who seemed everywhere in Hawai'i when I was growing up, I couldn't convince myself that my trip to Japan was a return to some sort of motherland.

For the Hawaiians, home is the place where one's ancestors are buried.

Both sets of my grandparents emigrated from their respective countries; of those four individuals, only my maternal grandmother is still alive. And she, like the others, will be buried in Hawai'i, as will my parents, as were my maternal great-grandparents, who followed their children to Hawai'i—and as I hope I will be. If I am buried there, perhaps Hawai'i may lay claims on David, who has spent his life up to this point, and will probably spend the rest of his life, in the continental United States. Though I hope that he, like his father, can feel comfortable saying to someone he loves, "Wherever you are is home," I want him to have a *place* that he can call home.

Though I never at any point felt at home in Japan, I confess that I was struck by how much I understood of the culture—even if as a woman I bristled a little in it. I suspect it is because as a child I spent a lot of time in the company of my mother's family.

When I was eight, my mother received a phone call from my grandmother. When we arrived at my grandmother's house, I followed my mother into my great-grandmother's room, which, until that time, had been off-limits to us kids.

In my mother's mother's house, my great-grandmother was an eerie presence. I cannot recall her ever leaving the house, and she seldom came out of her room. We'd hear her first, thumping her cane and, with her right foot, sliding her bedpan down the hall to the bathroom. She spoke no English, had no teeth, and had a full head of wiry, white hair cropped to shoulder length. She wore only *yukatas*. On a few occasions when the clan had gathered at my grandmother's house, however, she came to sit with us in the living room. I remember staring at her hands, the backs of which were blued as if heavily bruised. Because I was never close enough to her to examine her hands—I was afraid of her—and because I was too embarrassed to ask anyone about them, I reasoned that it probably had something to do with poor circulation.

My great-grandmother lay on her tatami mat on the floor, all but her face covered by a patchwork quilt my grandmother had made. She was breathing very slowly, and her lips had begun to turn blue by the time we actually saw her. I wanted to pull back the quilt and look at her hands. Instead, I studied the quilt, noting the triangles of fabric whose patterns matched a dress of mine or my sister's. My grandmother and mother shared the cost of buying garment factory scraps. My grandmother cut her strips into a host of geometric shapes and stitched the pieces into colorful quilts for herself, her children, and all of her grandchildren. My mother patched matching strips of fabric together and made dresses for my sister and me.

When the doctor arrived, I knew to leave the room. I sat on my grandfather's blue vinyl chair until my mother, grandmother, and the doctor came out of my great-grandmother's room. My grandmother, who normally bustled around her own house saying, *"Matte, matte* you," to any grandchild who got between her and her business, whatever it happened to be, was terribly silent. My mother called my grandfather at work to tell him that his mother had died.

It was not until three years ago, when I read about the immigrant Okinawans in *Uchinanchu: A History of Okinawans in Hawaii* that I discovered the reason for my great-grandmother's blue hands. Shortly after she was married, the backs of her hands had been tattooed—as was the custom. She was thereafter easily recognized not only as a married woman but as an Okinawan.

This I discovered in the context of stories old folks told about sailing to Hawai'i with the Japanese in the early part of this century. The Uchinanchu, as the first Okinawan immigrants called themselves, spoke of being treated badly by the Japanese, who regarded them as inferior. Influenced by the Chinese, who in the past had periodically gained political control over the Ryukyu Islands, of which Okinawa is a part, the Okinawans ate pork and spoke a dialect different enough from Japanese "proper" so that one man, who as a child immigrated to Hawai'i, said that other children on the ship asked each other if the language he spoke was Korean. Thus, those who were not visibly marked, as were the married women, were marked by their speech. Keeping silent must have seemed a good strategy to some.

Reading that book, I realized for the first time that there was a difference between Okinawans and Japanese. I thought the terms were interchangeable; on forms asking for my race, I had always written "Japanese," as my mother had done. Apparently, for many members of my grandparents' and even my parents' generation, marriage between an Okinawan and a Japanese was something akin to an interracial marriage. But for my grandparents, being Okinawan didn't seem to be an issue. Perhaps it was because they fully possessed the Japanese language—I had seen both of them writing letters, their script running top to bottom, right to left on the page. More likely, though, that new place, which rendered Okinawans and Japanese alike equally capable or helpless, had, to their way of thinking, a leveling effect. And perhaps because it was not an issue with them, it was never an issue with my mother— nor with me. How could it be when we thought nothing of it?

I was surprised by how easily I blended in with the Japanese—as long as I kept silent. I was eighteen when I left Hawai'i, where my nationality could not easily be pinned down by others. My maiden name, Kang, can be mistaken for a Chinese surname, and I have my mother's dark complexion and "double" eyes. People used to ask me if I was Hawaiian-Chinese or Filipino or what- ever. I suppose such fine discriminations come from possessing the greater range of possibilities that exists in Hawai'i's multicultural environment. That I could not be pinned down worked to my advantage on several occasions, one in particular that I remember.

During the first week of my first year at Kawānanakoa Intermediate School, I heard rumors that the girls from Stevenson Intermediate School were planning a visit that first Friday. Their purpose: to beat up on "all da Japs"— in particular, the new seventh-grade girls. At recess in the bathroom, where wads of paper towels dampened, balled, then flung at the ceiling hung above us, one unmistakably Japanese girl questioned another.

"You t'ink it's for real or what? You goin' stay?" one said, examining the Scotch tape she had trimmed that morning and stuck on her eyelids to alter her epicanthic or Mongolian folds so that her eyes would look bigger.

"No way. When da bell ring, I makin' it," her friend said, combing her long, straight, black hair. The consequence of being the wrong shade of brown had been made very real to us the second day of school. There, everyone was fair game.

During lunch recess, a huge crowd had gathered in a circle. Students were jostling each other and shouting, and the circle their bodies formed somehow managed to maintain its symmetry even as it shifted left and right, toward me and away from me. By the time I was close enough to see what was going on inside the circle, the circle was starting to break up. What I did see was an eighth-grader, her hair gone wild, one eye a little darkened—though whether the result of a blow or running mascara I couldn't tell—and a trickle of blood at the corner of her mouth. She jerked her head to flip her brown hair back, then smoothed it as she walked past me. Later I learned her name was "Boogie." She had a French surname and a capped front tooth. Circles formed around her several more times over the next few weeks before she was accepted and left alone.

Still, I took my chances and stayed after school that first Friday. Not fifteen minutes after the dismissal bell rang at three o'clock, the school was visibly emptier than it had been earlier in the week. I hung around near the safety of the air-conditioned music building. Nothing happened. The next-day news was that the Stevenson girls didn't show up—though the source of that report was as mysterious as the rumored event itself.

Many of those girls who were supposed to have come down from Stevenson lived in Papakōlea, an area near Punchbowl Cemetery that had been designated "homestead land" for people of Hawaiian ancestry. Kawānanakoa, on the other hand, was fed by families who lived in the Pauoa and Nuʻuanu valleys, districts largely comprised of middle-class families, many of them Japanese. I grew up between Papakōlea and Pauoa Valley.

Pidgin English, a language that developed under the exigencies of business, was my first language. The word "pidgin" itself is said to be a corruption by the Chinese tongue of the word "business."

Contact with Westerners beginning in the late eighteenth century had decimated the native Hawaiian population, and by the late 1800s sugar growers desperately needed field laborers for their booming industry. As early as 1852, contract laborers had been brought to Hawaiʻi from China, and under the rule of King Kamehameha V (the last ruling descendant of the legendary king who had unified the Islands), a Bureau of Immigration had been established in the 1860s. In 1881 King Kalākaua, the "Merry Monarch," embarked on a tour of the world, in part to investigate labor immigration, and he met with success in Japan and Portugal. In the latter part of the last century and the early part of this century, people from the Far East and the Azores and Madeira islands immigrated to Hawaiʻi, lured by the promise of a better life.

Pidgin grew out of the need for people who shared no common language to communicate, and those who acquired a command of English or pidgin English possessed more options, hence greater freedom: they might become *lunas,* bosses in the cane fields, or better still, leave the hard physical labor of the fields altogether.

These are the circumstances under which my grandparents immigrated to Hawai'i, and from what I can gather, my father was born on a sugar plantation in Kōloa, Kaua'i. I know little of his personal history, except that until he retired in the mid-1980s, he worked as a crane operator, helping stevedores unload cargo from ships at Pearl Harbor, and as a "truck chauffeur," driving flatbeds between the docks and warehouses.

His mother lived with us for about five years before settling for good with her youngest daughter. My grandmother bore thirteen children and outlived two husbands, both of whom died before I was born. She died at the age of ninety-two. As far as I know, she never wrote letters home to Seoul, Korea. Perhaps she didn't know how. In the seventy-five years she lived in Hawai'i, she permitted herself to speak perhaps a half dozen English words. The ones I remember most clearly are these: "Nancy, baby *kukai,*" meaning my younger sister needed a diaper change—words addressed to my mother. But more often I remember, when we kids were especially rowdy, her saying, *"Chibiga. Anja,"* which I gathered meant something like sit down and shut up.

In her mother's house, my mother was always called or referred to as Tsuneko in deference to my grandmother. Even so, as a child I believed my mother to be a one-dimensional character I called Mom or, more often, Ma. That did not change until, at the age of twenty, I had a child of my own. When David was five, we flew back to Hawai'i for a visit. During that visit, I asked my mother if it had been difficult for her having her mother-in-law live with her. "Yeah," she answered, laughing, "she used to tell your father Japanese girls no good."

My mother is the fifth of eight children: preceded by a sister and three brothers, followed by three sisters several years younger than she. My aunt, the oldest child, ran away from home to get married when she was sixteen, and so at a young age my mother had to help prepare meals and take care of her younger sisters. Over the years my mother and her younger sisters have extended their kinship into a network of supporting friendships. They enjoyed each other's company and drew their husbands and children into that circle of family.

We used to gather every Friday night at my grandmother's house, where the adults would stay up late playing cards, the men drinking beer. My grandmother loved playing a game they called Paiute, a game in which, as they bet, the winner collected between two and ten cents from all the other players, depending on what he or she was holding. Each player kept a jar of pennies with his or her name on it at my grandmother's house, but neither the jars nor the labels really meant anything. If a player ran out of pennies, someone would give over a handful; at the end of the night, anyone who won big filled up his or her jar, then put the remaining pennies in whatever jar was at hand. Often it would be late and the men would be drunk, and we would all end up sleeping at my grandmother's house, the adults on the floor in the living room and the children, herded past my great-grandmother's room, sleeping in my grandmother's sewing room.

On that same trip I asked my mother not only about her relationship with her mother-in-law but about her family as well. I even managed to get my mother to act briefly as an interpreter for my grandmother and me. My grandfather had died, my uncles had sold my grandmother's house, and my maternal grandmother was now living in the basement apartment of my parents' home.

Because my grandfather had been a resident-alien when he bought the house, he could not own property, so he had put the house in his sons' names. He did not bother to change that after he became a naturalized citizen in the late 1960s. According to my mother, my uncles decided to sell the house, and only one of the three had offered my grandmother a place to live. The sale of my grandparents' home was divisive, partly because the family had lost its long-standing gathering place, but mostly because in the eyes of my mother and her sisters, the sale itself by their brothers had been a violation of family they could not forgive. Despite my grandmother's insistence that my mother and her sisters put aside their grievance because seeing her family together mattered above all to her, a rift had opened, one that could be bridged but not closed.

The intimacy I had known with my extended family had ended, and now I wanted to know more than what I already knew about my grandparents' lives: that my grandfather had gone to English school and received the equivalent of a third-grade education; that he and my grandmother were married by proxy; that my grandfather had at one time been regarded as a very fine samisen player. I wanted my mother to get my grandmother to tell me things no one had thought to ask about. But all I managed to find out about my maternal grandparents was that in Okinawa my grandmother's family had made roof tiles, and that my grandfather's family made molasses barrels, and that somehow my grandfather's father, who opened the first Okinawan music school in Hawai'i, had retired at a relatively young age and put his sons to work.

These things didn't much interest my mother, whose whole life had been pointed in one direction—the future—and who had been so busy most of her life that she didn't have the time and leisure to look back. After about fifteen minutes my mother begged out, saying she had to cook dinner. The whole time my mother kept saying, "My Japanese not good."

Two years ago I again went to visit my parents. At that time, Masako, a woman about my mother's age who has lived next door to my parents for twenty years, came over to chat.

"Where you living now?" she asked.

"Montana," I answered.

"Ho, cold, eh?" she said, crossing, then rubbing her arms.

"It's not so bad," I said, wrinkling my nose and shaking my head.

"You still in school or what?"

"Yeah," I said, somewhat embarrassed, more for my parents than for myself because I was thirty-two and still in school, and studying something as seemingly worthless as poetry. (I had discovered "real" poetry at the age of thirty and had begun to try to write the stuff.) Perhaps even less comprehensible to them was the fact that, encouraged by Brad, I had chosen to leave him temporarily to go back to school, while he finished his own graduate program in Connecticut—and knowing that it would be two years before we lived permanently under the same roof.

"Well, you can't go wrong with education, eh?" she said.

"Yeah."

It's an old idea, one that many children of immigrants raise their children on. It was the vision my parents had of a better life; they were, like Moses, looking at a promised land they themselves would not enter. The word "education" was to them what the name Hawai'i had been to my grandparents, but they could only point me in that direction.

In the context of the larger American world, my parents occupied a middle ground, mastering neither the language of their parents—whom they often had to speak for and were probably sometimes embarrassed by—nor standard English. I can only believe that as children they *were* bilingual, but because they did not possess the same first language, pidgin was the language spoken in our home.

At the same time I was surrounded by models of standard English: in textbooks and through the example of my teachers, on TV, on the radio, in the newspapers and in the few books in our house. Though I was not by any means a bookish child—my idea of a good read was the *Reader's Digest*—I did listen to the language people spoke. I did notice the easy singsong quality of our speech and the droning speech of the newscasters. Though I was not bookish, I did notice that the language we spoke was an invisible language, for I never saw it in print.

Moreover, back then even people who spoke only pidgin English called it poor English or baby English, and as they entered the public sphere, the judgment cast on their language in relation to standard English must, in their minds, have reflected their condition. Confident and competent adults, the life drained out of their speech, apologized for their bad English in public, especially in the company of haoles (Caucasians)—or remained silent.

I can only believe that as a child I subconsciously perceived these things. Accepting that implicit judgment because I didn't know how to separate judgments about my language from myself, at the age of eight I began to correct the *bad* English I spoke—and my bad self—with no more guidance than what I heard on TV.

. . .

It is easy for me to imagine what it was like for my parents to meet my in-laws for the first time. Brad, David, and I were living in Connecticut at the time, and Brad and I had been married for nearly ten years. My father-in-law had retired from the Air Force and had settled in Spokane, Washington. That's when my mother-in-law finally convinced him to take her back to Hawai'i for a vacation. When they arrived in Hawai'i, my mother-in-law called my mother, and they decided to meet at King's Bakery.

My parents arrive a little early. They find a table and order coffee. They sit across from one another.

"What time?" my mother asks.

"Nine-t'irty," my father mumbles.

"What?" she says. He clenches his teeth together; his jawbones push through his jowls.

"Nine-t'irty," he says slowly as if she doesn't understand English.

It's the way they do or don't communicate with each other. They are both nervous and edgy, and they have no words of their own to express their anxieties to each other. Over the years that silence has created a gulf between them.

When I was in high school, my father bought Engelbert Humperdinck's hit "Release Me" and played it repeatedly as he drank a few beers before supper. As if in response, a month later my mother bought "Hey Jude." I like to think "Let It Be" was on the flip side, whether it was or not, because then through the songs I have a fleeting glimpse of their personal lives, the ones they kept hidden from me and guarded with silence.

My in-laws arrive, and my father-in-law instantly recognizes my mother. (All my life I've been told that I look just like her.) He goes over to their table. My mother stands up; my father remains seated. My father-in-law reaches over to shake my father's hand, then hugs my mother. Despite her effort to contain them, tears well up in my mother's eyes. My father-in-law tells my parents about David and me. My mother was afraid she would have to bear the burden of this meeting because she knows my father will not speak. And because my in-laws are haoles, she is terribly nervous and self-conscious.

My mother cried because she was relieved that my father-in-law made an effort to put her and my father at ease. My mother cried. It is the only thing I could not have imagined because I don't ever recall having seen my mother cry, however difficult her life has been. My mother-in-law told me about that.

I heard a story once about a famous African American poet who, suffering under the combined effects of drugs and despair, visited a friend and proceeded to fall apart. "A black man ain't worth shit," he repeated over and over and could not be consoled. Like my mother and this poet, I too was confronted with the brute fact of my body. If as a child I had failed to separate judgments about the language I spoke from judgments about myself, as an adult I had spent a good part of my life denying my body in favor of developing a self stripped of its attributes. In trying to remake myself, I guess I thought I could will myself "out of nature" and "never take / My bodily form from any natural thing." But the fact that I inhabited a particular bodily form was a fact I could continue to ignore only at a terrible psychic price.

However, acknowledging my body flew in the face of what I had been taught through ten years of "higher" education—namely, that objectivity is better than subjectivity; that in the pursuit of objectivity what I think and do could, and perhaps should, be separated from what I feel; that what I am is not a significant part of who I am—and exposed what seems to me now a contradiction inherent in the idea of assimilation. In my life in the continental United States, I had always been reassured that the facts of my existence didn't matter, and so I learned to accept as ignorance incidents that indicated they mattered to someone else. But now they mattered to me.

For six months I served as a member of the editorial staff for *CutBank,* the University of Montana's literary magazine, reading and offering opinions on poems submitted for publication. During the final stages of putting together the issue, the editor had asked me to look over and comment on the order he had established for the poems. It had been a while since I'd read the poems, so I decided to reread them all. Among the galley proofs I discovered a poem I had not seen before. Its presence bothered me a little, but I accepted that it was the editor's prerogative to include a poem of his choosing. Alone on the third floor of Corbin Hall, an old dormitory that had been converted into offices mostly for teaching assistants, I sat in the *CutBank* office sipping coffee and taking in this new poem. But soon my expectation of delight gave way—the way sometimes, for reasons we can't fully explain, an innocent joke someone tells goes sour on us or turns savage. I finished reading the poem, not sure what I felt. I read it again, and then again more slowly.

I could not get past certain elements of the poem: its use of "The Chinese" as a refrain of sorts; the woman with "small breasts," "dark hair," "butterfly hands," whose only words were "Stomping at the Savoy," words she uttered as she fucked the "I" of the poem. I read the poem again, trying to look at the content of the poem objectively—imaginatively casting off my yellow skin, my small breasts, my long, dark hair, trying to ignore how the author's representation of the woman, whether conscious or not, tacitly assented to the peculiar and disturbing confusion of the words "exotic" and "erotic." I thought about an intersection on Brooks, the main drag through Missoula. I always seemed to hit the red light there. Maybe twenty-five yards from the intersection is a brick wall on which, in fine black script across garish pink and yellow stripes, are the words "Exotic Dancers" and in block print "Private Booths, 6 to 8 Girls Daily." I thought about how much I didn't like to think about these things because neither "erotic" nor "exotic" seemed to bear any relation to me. I thought about the way the conflation of those two words had driven me further inward during my brief stint in the Air Force. About the way for years I had believed that if I hoped to establish an identity, I ought not to *look* at myself.

Perhaps it was a failure of imagination, but I could no longer be objective. Even when I tried to read the poem as an ironic commentary on the speaker's angst rather than as a sincere expression of it, I felt I was being asked to sympathize wholly with him. And I couldn't.

I finished my coffee. I made recommendations for the ordering of poems. Then I chose my words carefully as I wrote a note to the editor, saying that I thought some women in the Asian American community might find the poem offensive insofar as it trafficked in stereotypes. As I saw it, this was one of the few moments when I believed I could take my feelings and experiences as somehow representative.

Several days later the editor called me to ask what my note meant. I really had nothing to say because I hadn't quite explained it to myself. However, in the period between my having left him the note and his calling me, the implications of my own words were becoming clear to me. Publicly, I could no longer remain aloof. I had found an anthology of writings by Asian American women called *The Forbidden Stitch;* in her introductory remarks, one of the editors openly addresses the troubling effects of the confusion of "exotic" and "erotic." Her words confirmed my feelings, and that was enough to convince me to resign.

Whatever having my name on the masthead might have meant for my ego, I felt it unconscionable that my name should appear there. Though I'd always believed that my voice was my own, in this context I could not help but consider that my voice—my name on the masthead its visual equivalent— might be taken as representative acceptance of the content of that poem. My name on the page, perhaps even more than my public face, clearly identified me as a member of the Asian American community, whatever I might have felt about my membership in that community.

I told the editor I planned to resign and did not want my name to appear anywhere on the magazine. He pressed me for an explanation, and when I didn't answer, he became defensive and accused me of making a power play. I told him that if he believed that, he didn't know me. For a moment, there was dead silence on the line, and then he asked me if that was all I had to say. When I said it was, he hung up. At that moment, all I knew was that I felt as if I had unwittingly walked into and shattered a sliding-glass door.

A half hour after the editor hung up, the phone rang again. It was midaf- ternoon, and David was not yet home from school. I'd been sitting at my table, brooding—thinking, maybe, if one can think without words. I walked across the room and picked up the receiver. It was Brad. As soon as I heard his voice, I began to cry.

"What's wrong? What's the matter?" he kept asking, the concern in his voice slowly giving way to frustration and mild irritation. He was three thou- sand miles away and had called because he needed some information from the files I'd brought to Montana when I'd moved. I knew that because it was the only reason he'd call during the day. He hadn't been prepared for this.

"I'll call you back later, okay?" I managed to say between deep breaths.

When David came home, I was in bed. Through the door I told him I wasn't feeling well and that he could go outside for a couple of hours. An hour passed before I called Brad back.

"What did you call for?" I asked.

"Jesus," he said, his concern now expressing itself in anger. "You don't know what kind of things I was imagining—like maybe David got hit by a car or something."

"I would have told you that," I said after apologizing, then went on to give him an account of what had been going on since I'd last spoken with him the week before. In the telling I knew that the conflict I had internalized was generating some heat; what I felt were parts of my life, parts I had chosen to disregard or to regard only dispassionately for the past ten years, beginning to thaw.

"That's what I'd have done," Brad said when I finished. And, of course, "Fuck 'em."

"You mean it?" I said.

"Very funny," he said, and made me promise I'd call him in a few days.

It had not been my intention to have the poem withdrawn from the issue; in fact, that this might happen did not occur to me until I thought about the editor's accusation. I had assumed the matter was settled, and the poem would be published. But later, under pressure from the other readers, the editor reluctantly removed the poem. All my life I had avoided taking sides on racial issues, influenced by the fatalism that made life possible for my parents and grandparents: *shikata ga nai*—it can't be helped. I wondered whether my resignation was another manifestation of that fatalism. And yet artistic freedom, something I greatly valued, was also at stake, and resigning seemed to me the only way to preserve art's integrity and my own. Only later was I convinced that I had made the right decision. I had as much right to remove myself from those circumstances as to demand that the poem be removed. It was a choice not to participate in what I could only regard as circumstances that would, in effect, signal my full assimilation into white American culture.

For weeks afterward I feared that the slightest pressure from those who had heard about what I'd done would start me crying again. I avoided eye contact. I went home from school as soon as I could. At home, when I could not contain the pressure in my throat, I wept. I had no words, and the outbursts seemed as sudden and inexplicable to me as to my son.

"Are you okay?" David would ask.

"Yeah," I said. How could I tell him what weighed so heavily on my heart was the thought that a slant-eye ain't worth shit; that by accident I had been forced to call into question the way I had spent the last ten years of my life— nearly all of them in pursuit of "higher" education, fully participating in an institution where the benevolent color blindness of equal opportunity seemed to have turned on itself—and on me; that I had gone as far as I could with formal education, when I had barely begun to find the words to express those feelings?

Brad moved to Montana in May, and soon after I graduated in June, we moved from the Garden City south to the Bitterroot Valley. A month later, we flew to Japan. Looking back now, I understand why I remember so little of the trip to Japan. I was—and still to some extent am—both physically and emotionally disoriented. Yet the trip itself was sanative.

In *Mind and Nature: A Necessary Unity*, Gregory Bateson explains the value of what he calls "double description," two descriptions of the same event from different perspectives, by likening it to the way we see with our physical eyes: where the fields of vision of both eyes overlap, we perceive depth. My experience in Japan was an odd mirroring of my life in the continental United States, its photographic negative.

Before going to Japan I had not tried to learn any more Japanese than I already knew—which was and still is virtually no Japanese. I was tired of talking. As a result, I experienced that country without the mediation of language. I had to pay attention to body language and the sound of language and the context of utterances again, and, when I shopped for food or household items, to the way things looked through clear plastic or pictured on labels. That texture of Japan was as strangely familiar to me as my great-grand-mother. What was even more important, though, was that I discovered a way of looking at the seemingly disparate elements of my life at the National Bunraku Theater in Osaka.

Bunraku, an extremely refined form of puppetry, does not seek to conceal its illusions. Unlike the puppetry we are familiar with, where strings or hand puppets permit puppeteers to remain offstage, in Bunraku the puppeteers, hooded and dressed completely in black, appear onstage and manipulate puppets that are about half life-size. Three puppeteers manipulate each puppet that has a principal role in the drama: a master puppeteer operates the head and right hand, another puppeteer operates the left hand, and yet another puppeteer works the legs.

On a raised platform located to the right of the stage are the *tayu* and the samisen accompanist wearing elegant traditional costumes in muted colors. The *tayu,* or reciter, tells the story and chants, whispers, shouts, or sobs the dialogue for the puppets onstage. The samisen accompanist provides not only musical accompaniment to the *tayu*'s recitation, but also effects, such as wind and rain, that heighten the atmosphere of the scene played out on the stage. During the performance I attended, there were three samisen players and five *tayu* reciters—one narrating and the others lending their voices to the play's principal characters.

Watching Bunraku for the first time is an exercise in concentration, for the puppets, the puppeteers, and the *tayu* and samisen accompanist all compete for one's attention. It is only when you become engaged in the story that the puppeteers recede, and the reciter and musician claim possession of the mind's eye through your ears; only then do you give your attention wholly over to the puppets in whom life has been breathed.

So it is whenever I speak with someone face to face for the first time. The fact that I am an Asian American is as much onstage in the encounter as the hooded puppeteers in a Bunraku performance. Though this fact recedes with longer acquaintance, it never entirely disappears for either of us. Yet often I feel as if I'm being asked to suppress parts of myself by pretending it can disappear. What of it?

I am a visible minority who wishes to be asked neither to live in the illusion that it is a fact that makes no difference nor to believe that it is the sole determining factor in my life. My body is the necessary, the essential locus for events—in this respect, there are few differences between us, but those few differences are conspicuous. My personal history, which is a confluence of subcultures, is the animating force that colors my actions. And the voice I have acquired through training is, for good or ill, the bookish reciter somewhat removed from the action, attuned to the pulse of the samisen that guides the telling. Each part must be rendered its due.

In "Statements of Faith," Richard Hugo writes, *How you feel about your-self* is probably the most important feeling you have." Hugo goes on to say, "Not from birth and circumstance, but by virtue of how they feel about themselves and their relation with the world, as revealed in their poems, many American poets see themselves as (or really are) Krebs [a character from a Hemingway story] or Snopes [a character from a Faulkner story]." By birth and circumstance, Krebs is an insider, but as a result of a traumatic experience, he comes to feel himself alienated and an outsider. Snopes, on the other hand, is, by birth and circumstance, an outsider, but wants desperately to be an insider; he believes himself to be "a wrong thing in a right world."

My experience with the poem in *CutBank* made me face my own feelings about myself; the poem was simply a trigger. However, I believe that my being a visible minority made this self-reckoning inevitable. Moreover, in my case, I don't think it's possible to separate birth and circumstance from how I feel about myself and my relation with the world. I am a Snopes. Neither taste nor temperament nor the most vigorous exercise of will can entirely change how I feel.

I don't know what to say to people who tell me I'm lucky to have such "unique" materials at my disposal, or those who tell me they have no ethnic background to draw on and wish that instead of emphasizing differences minority writers would focus on universal experiences. I'm tempted to flip a coin: Heads, "No shit"; tails, "Whatever." Or maybe even "Oh, reary?"

In me those materials arise when I can no longer bear the pressures of existence; they are my life. And so when I do write, I am driven to it neither by force of habit nor by an obsession to be a writer, but by the need to create for myself "a momentary stay against confusion." Still, I am often tempted to be silent and to pay the price of silence. I am my mother's daughter. I am tempted not to try to find words adequate to my feelings because writing has become both a painstaking and often painful process of coming face to face with what I'd rather ignore, a process of recovering and rediscovering what I once knew but had long ago chosen to forget. For the moment, though, I value that process and persist in it, hoping somewhere along the line I may find my own words to echo that golden oldie—Whitman singing the body electric, declaring it sacred in every respect.

Victor, Montana
Fall 1989

CHITRA BANERJEE DIVAKARUNI

LALITA MASHI

Originally from India, CHITRA BANERJEE DIVAKARUNI *lives in the San Francisco Bay Area with her husband and two children and teaches Creative Writing at Foothill College. She is the author of three books of poetry and a collection of short stories. Her work has appeared in* Beloit Poetry Journal, Calyx, Chicago Review, Ms., *etc., and in more than a dozen anthologies. Her awards include a Pushcart Prize, a Gerbode Foundation award, an Allen Ginsberg poetry prize, and two PEN Syndicated Fiction Project Awards.*

DRU BANERJEE

THE OTHER DAY I SAW LALITA MASHI, MY MOTHER'S oldest sister. Suddenly, shockingly. But I should have expected it. In recent years she has always come to me this way.

I was standing on the platform of the Oakland BART station, my attaché case filled with slides and spreadsheets, on my way to the City, where a committee of heavy-jowled old men were waiting for me to try to persuade them to change the way they do things. Dressed in my power outfit—navy-blue skirt and jacket, deep red silk blouse, pearls, stiletto heels—I felt confident, ready for them. I knew my presentation would go perfectly.

Then I saw her. She was sitting by the window of a train going in the other direction, her hair caught back loosely in a knot, her chin propped by her palm. It was a posture I knew so well my breath caught in my throat. And suddenly I was six years old again, back in my grandfather's house in a tiny Bengal village.

"Mashi," I called, "Lalita Mashi!" although I knew she couldn't possibly hear me through the double-layered glass. I waved frantically, trying to make her look up. But she was intent on something in the sky that only she could see. The warning beeps sounded, the doors closed, the train began to pull away. I dropped my case and started running along the platform, the gleaming electric tracks separating me from her. People stared. Still I ran, stumbling in my high heels, throwing out an arm for balance. Perhaps that desperate movement finally caught her eye, because she looked up. She was too far for me to read the expression on her face—recognition? bewilderment?—but the face itself I knew without a doubt. It was her face, yes, just the way it had been the last time I saw it. Except, of course, it couldn't be, even if by some unaccountable magic she had remained unchanged by time. Because Lalita Mashi died twenty-four years ago, halfway around the world, in the village of her father, where she had lived (except for one brief year) all her life.

Still, I couldn't shake off the woman's face, the angle of her chin tilted toward a wonder in the sky visible only to her. It haunted me like no face has the right to. And now I was hearing her voice. *"Shona,"* it called, "golden child," the special name that Lalita Mashi gave me on those long-ago summers when I used to visit her. The voice caught in a sob—or was it a laugh? It tugged at me as I climbed onto my train. I knew it would stay with me for days, weeks. Forever.

Of the many women in my family that I've known and loved, who have shaped my life and thinking, whose legacies of pain and shame and courage I carry within, why is it I remember Lalita Mashi so clearly? I only knew her for a few years—she died when I was six—and after her death her name was never mentioned in the family. Perhaps it is the mystery that clings to her story, the faint odor of disgrace. Perhaps it is because I, the defiant daughter who left the protection of the family to come to America, who faced their bewilderment and fought their anger, know that she and I are two of a kind.

Mashi was born in the early years of the twentieth century in the village of Mashagram in Bengal, the first child of the Mukherjee household. Hers was a respected family; not only was her father—my grandfather—a Brahmin, but he also owned a good amount of fertile paddy land. His was one of the few homes in the village built of brick instead of black mud.

No one knows the exact year of Mashi's birth. Few people kept track of such things in those days, especially for girl-children. And her parents, who might have recalled it by the calamities of nature that marked most rural lives —the year the Basumati River flooded, the year the too heavy rains ruined the crops—have chosen to forget. So I am free to place her where I want—in the 1930s, when the Independence movement against the British was beginning to sweep the land.

It was the beginning, many would say, of women's independence as well. A lot of women came out of purdah to take part in the battle for their country's freedom. For the first time in their lives, they stood shoulder to shoulder with men (the threat of the British being considered more dangerous than the loss of tradition). They shouted *Jai Hind* and carried the bright new Indian flag, saffron and green and white. They faced the *lathi* charges of the troops and went to jail and died with smiles on their faces. They became national heroines, Sarojini Naidu, Matangini Hazra. Traveling minstrels made up songs about their courage and glory.

But back in Mashagram, my grandfather's village, the winds of change were slow in arriving. Maybe they were held back by the thick bamboo forests that surrounded the village on every side, where even in the daytime one might come across a wild boar or a cheetah. Maybe they spent themselves crossing the miles and miles of fields—mustard and paddy and jute—which farmers tilled and watered patiently, with the help of their buffaloes, as they had for thousands of years. At any rate, they did not ruffle even the edges of my aunt's life.

Lalita Mashi grew up in the big house surrounded by a high wall, like girls of good family were supposed to. I imagine she was taught needlework and cooking by my grandmother. Much like my own mother a few years later, she must have sat in the courtyard (under the thick shade of the pipal tree, so her skin would not turn dark) and stitched quilts decorated with the elaborate tamarind leaf design. On feast days she must have helped Grandmother cook the sweet *kheer* that took hours to prepare, stirring the thickening milk over the slow coal fire patiently, learning at once a skill and a womanly virtue. In addition—and this was unusual—she was taught to read and write by an old Brahmin, for my grandfather was a progressive man. For a while another old Brahmin came by every week to give her singing lessons—religious *bhajans* only, of course, not the modern *gazals* or *rabindra sangeet* that could give a young girl the wrong kinds of ideas. Mashi had a natural skill for song, a sweet clear voice that rose as unapologetically into the air as any bird's—I remember it from vacations I would later spend at my grandfather's. But the old women whispered it was too loud, shameless. And when she turned twelve, all lessons were stopped, for it wasn't fitting that a daughter of the Mukherjee household should be taught by a man, even if he was white-bearded and hobbled around on a cane. There might be talk, and it might affect her chances of making a good marriage.

Did Lalita Mashi cry when the lessons were stopped? Did she shout her anger at her mother (she would not have dared to do so with her father)? When asked to fetch water, did she throw down the earthenware *kalash*, smashing it to smithereens? Did she burn the curries so that the family would have in their mouths the same taste of bitterness that was in hers? But it is more likely that she put away her songbooks and grammar texts sadly but without surprise—for they were, after all, childish things which would not help her in her future life—and busied herself learning more appropriate skills. She knew what the true purpose of her life, the life of all women, was—she had been told it every day since she was old enough to understand.

And that purpose was fulfilled soon enough for Mashi. The flower of marriage, as they call it in our language, bloomed for her as soon as her menstrual blood proclaimed her a woman. My grandfather, a practical man, saw no point in waiting. A daughter was only born to a family as a loan. Unlike a son, she couldn't carry forth the family name. Nor could she, at the yearly memorial services, offer rice and water to the spirits of departed ancestors. One might as well return her to her true home, her husband's house, as soon as possible. Grandfather knew that a woman's fragile beauty tarnishes soon, her good name even sooner. A grown daughter in the house is more dangerous than a firebrand in a field of ripe grain. Besides, he had two other daughters he needed to find husbands for.

This does not mean my grandfather didn't love Lalita Mashi. She was a girl-child, yes, but his oldest, the first baby he had held in his arms, on whose forehead he had pressed the kiss of blessing. Perhaps he had walked up and down with her on nights when his wife was too tired to do so, whispering to quieten her crying. *Hush, my moonbeam, my little bird.* Even to an Indian father that would count for something.

I imagine my grandfather sparing no efforts to find Lalita Mashi a suitable husband, sending matchmakers to all the nearby villages to inquire after young men whose families were of the same standing as his, whose horoscopes matched his daughter's. And when he discovered such a man, he spared no expense for the wedding, inviting people from three villages to admire the style with which a daughter of the Mukherjee house was sent off to her in-laws.

I see Mashi being brought into the marriage courtyard, under the silk canopy where the bridegroom is sitting. Red-veiled, wrapped in a red-gold Banarasi silk (the color of married bliss), she keeps her eyes tightly closed, for it would be bad luck to see her husband's face before the priest had recited the proper mantras. Is she frightened at the thought of leaving her familiar world behind? Does she struggle to hold back tears as she walks around the fire with the stranger who is now her master, to whom society has given every right over her body and her spirit?

The next morning the bride and groom start on their journey home at the exact auspicious moment specified by the family astrologer. Conches sound, women strew their path with flowers and rice and prayers for strong sons, and five bullock carts filled with dowry follow their painted palanquin along the dusty village road.

But the old astrologer must have read the signs wrong. For soon my aunt is back again. Only this time she returns weeping, stripped of her jewelry and dressed in the coarse white cloth that widows wear. The servant who brings her back carries a letter from her in-laws. The letter states that they never want to see her face again, for surely it is her bad luck that caused their son to die of typhoid within a year of his marriage.

Back in the house where she was born, Lalita Mashi must have slipped easily enough into the grooves of her old life. Everything was still the same—the lowing of the cows at dawn as they waited to be milked, the blind *baul* who came by each morning to sing the 108 names of Krishna, the women gathered in the hot afternoons of the mango season on the downstairs veranda, salting the hard green fruit for pickles. Yet everything was different.

Mashi would have known—though her parents were too kind, I hope, to ever let anyone say it—that she was in her father's house on sufferance. From the moment her parents give her away at the wedding with a handful of puffed rice, a married woman's place is with her in-laws. This house with the familiar high ocher wall she had looked back at, weeping, from the bridal palanquin, the green shutters through the cracks of which the women could look out and not be seen, the cool marble-floored dining room where the men were served dinner (the women ate in the kitchen, afterward)—she had dreamed about it many times while in her husband's house. Longed for it when her mother-in-law scolded her for a task not done correctly, an imagined slight. But it belonged to her brothers, and their sons, and theirs. She had no real place in it, and every so often—in case she was in any danger of forgetting—her brothers' wives would remind her of it with the twist of a lip, a silent, meaningful look.

So Mashi made herself useful. She milked the cows and scoured the heavy brass and copper *puja* dishes with coal ash and did all of the vegetarian cooking (a widow was not supposed to touch meat). She picked the red hibiscus flowers that grew against the wall and made garlands every morning for the family deity, the goddess Kali. On auspicious days, Durga Puja or a wedding or a naming ceremony, she stayed out of sight so that her ill luck wouldn't taint the others.

She took care of the babies that were being born to her brothers' wives, dressing them in the tiny clothes she had hand-stitched, feeding them, bathing them, singing to them through the hot afternoons when their mothers slept. After the men had eaten, she served dinner to the women, and sat down to her cold, solitary meal only after they had finished. When I visited during vacations, it would be very late—the moon disappeared behind the bamboo trees by the pond—before she finished cleaning the kitchen and came up to bed.

She certainly didn't have to work so hard. No one ever asked her to, and there were servants. Perhaps she kept herself busy to stay sane, to not dwell on the fact that since the age of fifteen her life had effectively been over.

Was she unhappy? Most will say she had no cause to be. She was better off than many other widows who, not coming from such affluent families, are shunned as burdens by both in-laws and parents, who have to throw themselves on village charity and live by doing odd jobs—roasting puffed rice for festivals, making painted fans out of palm leaves—who in desperation run away to the cities and blacken, forever, the family name.

My actual memories of Lalita Mashi are few, and so many of my own feelings have been superimposed on them—hurt and hate and hope—that I am no longer sure that this is how it was. But here is one:

It is a June night in Mashagram, pitch dark and very hot. A girl of five, I have been sent to Grandfather's because a cholera epidemic is raging in Calcutta. Sweaty and fretful, I toss and turn under the coarse mosquito netting, push restlessly at the sleeping body next to mine.

"I'm thirsty, Lalita Mashi. I feel itchy all over."

"Hush, *shona*, don't cry. Mashi will get you water."

Through the haze of the netting, my eyes follow my aunt across the room, which is lit only by the sliver of moon hanging low outside the barred window. A glimmer of white in her cotton sari, Mashi bends over the earthen *kalash* in the corner of the room. (As far back as I can remember, she has always worn white, and always the same thick, cheap handloom that no one else in the house would touch. Even my grandmother, who seems very old to me with her crushed velvet skin, wears beautiful *tangails* with brilliant maroon and gold borders and *dhakais* so fine they can be pulled through her gold ring.) Mashi's long hair, which she pulls back into a tight bun during the day, as widows should, swings softly about her face. Before I fall asleep, I like to weave my fingers through its silky darkness, to press my face against it as I would never dare to with my own stricter mother. It smells faintly of hibiscus flowers, because although widows are not supposed to, sometimes Aunt puts the fragrant red oil in her hair. She does it at night after the others have gone to bed, after she has bolted the door of her room. But I know because I sleep with her whenever I come to Grandfather's house. She lets me rub in the sweet oil, shows me how to curve the fingertips to massage the scalp. *You have such gentle fingers, shona.* Sometimes she sings very softly, eyes closed, while I am rubbing. *O Krishna, I've given up all for your love. Don't forsake me now.* It is a traditional religious song, such as the traveling *bauls* sing, but Mashi transforms it with her longing. Mashi has the sweetest voice, I think, even nicer than Mother's. The note of sadness in it makes me shiver a little. If I had the words, I would say that it haunts me. I take great care not to pull on Mashi's hair, not to snarl its smoothness in any way. I would die before I give away Mashi's secret.

But Mashi is the one who dies, in between vacations, so I am not there when it happens. Mother looks up from a letter and her eyes are red-rimmed. A sob bursts out of her. It is the first time I remember seeing my mother cry. Lalita Mashi has drowned, she tells me, in the *dighi*, the women's lake.

I cannot believe it. I picture the *dighi*, its dark waters stretching all the way to the horizon. So many times when we've been there to bathe, I've seen Mashi swim toward the middle, where people say it is deeper than a ten-story build-ing, her powerful strokes parting the masses of mauve water hyacinths. She would swim until her body became a tiny bobbing speck, until I, waiting on the worn stone steps with the hand-spun *gamchahs* with which we dried our-selves, was afraid that surely this time she wouldn't be able to get back. But she always did, smiling and not even out of breath, her slim, gleaming body cutting effortlessly through the rippling water.

"It can't be," I tell Mother. I want to do something terrible to express the baffled rage I feel—throw myself at her, snatch the letter from her hand, take the edge of her sari between my teeth and pull until it rips. But of course I don't.

She wipes at her swollen eyes and tells me she doesn't want to talk about it. She tells me to go to my room.

No one at Grandfather's will talk about it either when I visit them next summer. They change the subject adroitly whenever I ask. "Have some of this nice *nimbu* pickle," they say. Or "Go see Mangli-cow's new calf, so cute you won't believe it." In the steamy afternoons when the women gather in the downstairs hall to sew and talk, Mashi's name is never spoken. Her photo-graphs have all been removed from albums. Her clothes have disappeared. Her room is filled with dusty old trunks that look like they've always been there. It is as though Mashi had never lived.

It is the ultimate punishment.

Death in our Indian culture is not necessarily a tragedy. Too much of it happens every day for us to think of it as such, if we are to keep ourselves from going crazy. We devise heavens for our dead—the seven *lokas* where they go to enjoy the fruits of their karma, until they are born again. And on earth we cherish them by keeping them in our thoughts. Even daughters have photographs hung in the corner of their parents' bedroom. On the anniversary of their deaths, jasmine garlands are placed around them, incense lighted. Food is offered to beggars and cows, and Brahmins are paid to pray for their souls.

But what when you are forgotten, deliberately, your name plucked out from the hearts of those you loved best and sent wandering over the void? I am not a believer in spirits, but sometimes I dream of my aunt, a tiny white wraith, palms outstretched, mouth open in supplication. She winds about the house, about her mother's bed, for surely a mother wouldn't want her daughter

—no matter what she had done—to be doomed forever to the terrible mists that are worse than darkness, where after a while even her own face is taken from her.

My grandmother too must have dreamed of her daughter. Startled awake in her high mahogany bed, under the thin mosquito netting, she must have lain in half-shadow, listening to Grandfather's heavy breath, and felt that wrench in her belly, that ripping of the umbilical cord that mothers know whenever their children are in despair. Perhaps she thought of going down to the *dighi* secretly, with a little boat made out of plantain leaves and filled with my aunt's favorite foods. Perhaps she could send money to a Brahmin in faraway Kashi, by the holy Ganges that cleanses all sins, to pray for Mashi? A small photo, hidden in her dresser drawer under the velvet boxes filled with jewels she would give to her daughters-in-law to give to theirs—who would know of it? But she did none of these things. For the sake of her other children, for the good name of the family she had taken as hers when she walked around the wedding fire—so long ago she hardly remembered she'd had another life before it—she kept hidden whatever was inside her. At *pujas* and harvest festivals she wore her red-bordered silks as always and smiled as she served scented betel leaves to the women who visited. Who can blame her? The choices a mother has to make are often hard, heartbreaking.

But they couldn't stop the mouth of rumor. Even I heard things when I visited—snatches of servant gossip, neighbor ladies whispering. Something about a man. A drowning that wasn't quite an accident. A too quick funeral. Family dishonor.

Here is another wisp of memory: I am playing out in the courtyard with the children of the neighborhood. Something happens and a girl yells that I'm a slut, just like my aunt was. I wrestle the girl, whose name I have long forgotten, to the dirt, claw at her face till the blood comes. Later, when Mother, shamed and angry, brings the switch down on the backs of my legs, demanding *why, why did you do it?* I stand tearless, silent with an animal stubbornness, unable to explain.

It would take me years to discover the circumstances of Lalita Mashi's death— to even begin to discover them—though perhaps "uncover" would be a more accurate word. I was handicapped by the double disadvantage of my youth and my femaleness. The questions I did dare to bring up, suitably polite, oblique enough not to offend anyone's sensibility, could always be brushed aside by adults. The foolish fancies of teenage girls, everyone knows, need not be taken seriously. Perhaps I could have pressed harder, but I think a part of me was afraid of what I might find.

It was only when I was done with college and the family was looking to arrange a suitable match for me—against my wishes, for I wanted to go abroad to continue my studies—that I got up the courage to confront my mother. Perhaps it was out of a desperation I didn't know how to put into words, a desperation that I was being pushed toward disaster, just as Lalita Mashi had been.

It is late at night, but the June air is still moist and heavy with heat. It presses down upon my sweating skin like a premonition as I watch Mother go through the bedtime rituals she must have learned as a girl. At the marble basin she sprinkles warm water on her face, then rubs in the lentil-and-turmeric-paste that is supposed to lighten the skin. When it dries into a yellow crust, she washes it off, first with hot, then cold water. She pats on a glycerine-and-rosewater solution from a bottle that I recognize because I have seen a similar one for years on Grandmother's dressing table. She takes the ivory comb carved with her initials and runs it through hair that is fragrant with *amla* and that is, even at her age, softer and thicker than mine. Unhurried and deliberate, her movements belong to a different generation, a simpler, more elegant age when women had the time to indulge in beauty. But I am wrong to call it an indulgence. The color of a woman's skin, the length of her silk-black uncut hair, the way her eyes glowed when underlined with *kajal*—these could make all the difference between a good match and a second-rate one. They could hold fast a husband whose roving eye might otherwise turn toward a second marriage, a younger wife. Is the age I live in that different?

As I observe the long, languorous strokes of Mother's comb it strikes me that Mashi must have performed the same rituals until widowhood deprived her of the right—and, according to all who kept watch on her, the reason. She was not even allowed to keep a mirror in her room. For what? people would have asked in genuine bewilderment had anyone suggested it. For birthdays she was given vellum-bound copies of the *Ramayana* and the *Puranas*, which assert that the body is a thing of vanity, a poor garment to be cast off at death. What accompanies us into the beyond are our virtuous deeds, our ability to sacrifice. If Mashi had any doubts as to how to achieve this, she had only to look at the examples of the many good women—Sita, Savitri, Gandhari—provided by the good books. I remember again how Mashi had to hide behind her locked bedroom door even to apply a little hibiscus oil to her hair, and suddenly I am so angry that the question I had rehearsed so carefully tumbles out of me, stopping my mother in mid-motion.

What really happened to Mashi?

My mother looks at me, then away. I wait for her to make the usual excuses. I am ready to fight them today—something in the air, the smell of a far rain falling on the great brown Ganges, the smell of my coming departure, gives me strength. Perhaps my mother senses it too, for she says with a sigh, "It's a long story." And as we sit on her high mahogany bed, where as a child I had spent many nights of illness, with her cool hand on my brow, soothing away my fevered nightmares, she tells me.

Mashi's story is ordinary enough—the story, I think, of many young widows of the time. She had the misfortune to fall in love. It was a misfortune because though in far-off Calcutta changes had begun to take place, in the villages a widow of good family would never be allowed to remarry—if marriage was at all what the man Mashi loved had in his mind.

Who it was my mother never knew. Lalita Mashi had whispered a few words to her on Mother's last visit, feverish and hasty, not making total sense. But it was Durga Puja, the busiest time of the year. New clothes had to be stitched for the children and dyed in auspicious colors, sweet coconut-and-jaggery balls to be ground and cooked, the floors decorated with traditional good-luck designs painted with rice paste. My mother's place was with the other married women, stirring enormous pots of *khichuri,* the thick lentil-rice soup with which all visitors would be fed, frying *brinjals* and yellow squash and fresh-picked sweet potatoes. She wouldn't have had much of an opportunity to be alone with her widow-sister—who was expected to keep to her room—to ask her questions, or even to warn.

"But who do you think it might have been?" I ask.

She shrugs. The identity of the man is not important. All that matters is the enormity of Mashi's crime, her betrayal of the family.

Nevertheless I imagine him—I need to—this man who charmed my aunt as bird catchers charm the red-throated bulbuls from their safe nests. He must have come from the city—Burdwan, Jamshedpur, maybe even Calcutta— wearing a white tailored kurta over his starched dhoti, the dark sleeveless Nehru jacket that the freedom fighters favored. Perhaps he sported a pencil-thin mustache like I've seen in the oil paintings of my uncles that hang along the dark corridors of grandfather's house.

The man stood outside the high ocher walls, singing one of the patriotic songs so popular at the time—*break the shackles, light the fire, the time for sleep is over*—exhorting listeners to join the revolution. Lalita Mashi would have peeped through the green shutters of her bedroom, felt that fervent young voice rising up at her like flame, stirring emotions she thought she was long done with. She fought them, for she knew that was the way to heartbreak—or worse. But when her brothers invited the man in to drink a glass of tea and tell them news of the big city, she couldn't resist joining the other women of the house behind the curtain to listen. At dinnertime—for he stayed on, this man with his magnet voice that held even the men in thrall—she served him the biggest, best pieces of dessert, the sweet, cloud-light *rasogollahs* she had spent all afternoon making. And when he looked up to thank her, she did not glance down as was proper, but held his eyes with the bright black flash in her own.

But I could be mistaken. He could well have been one of the village men, someone Mashi had known for years, a friend of her brothers who came by evenings to play a game of chess or read the Calcutta newspaper my grandfa-ther subscribed to. Someone who had helped to carry the *piri*, the ornamental wooden plank on which the bride sat, at her wedding. Someone she had called "older brother" as village custom demanded. Someone who had watched with pity as, her bowed, white-veiled head glimmering in the failing light, she now silently served them thin, salty *namkeens* and tall stainless-steel glasses of car-damom tea. Watched and pondered until one day the pity had turned to something else, and he had waited in the shadows of the plantain trees beside the pond to speak to her when she came to fetch water.

Finding a place to meet would not have been difficult, but arranging a time when she would not be missed by the household would take a lot of care.

Perhaps they met when she went to the women's lake for her bath, very early in the morning before the sun had dried the dew from the tiny blue moss flowers. She would look around to make sure no one was in sight, then turn into a dark bamboo grove—a different one each time for safety's sake—and there he would be, waiting, his kurta shining through the gloom of the trees as bright as the armor of any knight. They would come together urgently, lips seeking lips, fingers pulling at clothing, hot breath on naked skin that shivered with the cold and the excitement and the guilt, the knowledge that time was surely running out. For her sake I hope there was more. I hope they talked, sitting side by side, her head resting on his shoulder, his arm around her waist. He described to her life in the city—horse-drawn *tangas* driven by turbanned men from the north; the red-faced British guards standing at attention in their starched white uniforms outside the Governor's House; restaurants where you could walk in and order whatever you wanted to eat; the freedom of living on a street where no one knew your name. Promised to take her with him when he went—soon, soon now. She sang for him in a windy whisper that caught in her throat, *O Krishna, I've given up all for your love. Don't forsake me now.*

Lalita Mashi must have known how it would end. All the ancient tales of doomed lovers she—and I—had grown up on would have left no doubts in her mind. Why then did she rush toward destruction, like the rain flies that flung themselves into our kerosene lamps on monsoon nights? Why did she choose to bring shame on the family I know she loved? Why did she risk their hatred, their stern forgetting—not just in this life but even after, into the eternities? I cannot believe it was for the sex, or even for romantic passion. It was, I think, something more complex and deliberate, rising from a deeper, more urgent need. But for proof I can offer, once again, only a brief and tenuous memory:

Those nights in Grandfather's house, before we went to bed, Lalita Mashi would extinguish the oil lamp by pinching the flaming wick with her fingers.

"But doesn't it hurt?" I had asked her once, distressed.

Mashi had smiled. Only now, years later, I can gauge the sadness of that smile.

"Sometimes the pain is the only way I know I'm alive, *shona.*"

■ ■ ■

All that month while the family was trying to arrange a match for Susheela, her youngest sister, Lalita Mashi was restless and distracted. She would burst into tears for no reason at all. She burnt the simplest curries, scolded the children for the littlest pranks. Even her mother, busy as she was putting together jewelry and saris for the dowry, noticed the change in her and dosed her with the juice of *tulsi* leaves in case she was coming down with *kalajor*, the black fever. *Jealousy,* whispered the sisters-in-law behind their veils. *Pure jealousy of Susheela.*

Was Mashi counting the days with terror until it was well past her time of month, until the nausea and tiredness and aching breasts left no doubts in her mind of her body's betrayal? Was she trying to decide whether to wrench herself away from all that was loved and familiar for an uncertain future from which there was no turning back? Or was the man—tired with waiting or afraid of reprisal—gone already, so that she was contemplating the final choice he had left to her?

Sitting face to face with my mother as she braids her hair into tight obedience, I remember another day. It is late summer, almost the end of my vacation. Barefoot from play, I run into the dim living room decorated with old-fashioned oil lamps and clouded mirrors in mahogany frames. Heavy shades of *khush-khush* grass, dampened against the heat, cover the windows. Yes, here's Grandfather, just as I hoped, reclining in his favorite easy chair, immaculate in his ivory kurta, his hookah in his hand. Maybe I can climb onto his lap and get him to finish the story of the evil magician and the princess of the gold mountain.

Then I notice the young woman standing in front of him, twisting the edge of her widow's sari.

"Please, Father," she pleads, looking down at her hands.

"No," says the old man, his voice dispassionate. "I've made my decision already."

He closes his eyes and draws on the hookah as though the woman in front of him did not exist. Lalita Mashi makes a small, choking sound and runs from the room, holding her hands to her face. The rush of her white sari stirs the air of the room so that I can smell for a moment the faint, damp fragrance of the *khush-khush* curtains.

What could she have wanted so much? What could have been so forbidden that her father, usually so loving, would deny her this ruthlessly?

"Mashi," I cry, but there is no reply, only the British clock painted with happy shepherds and shepherdesses that ticks and ticks on the wall behind Grandfather's head.

It is the last memory I have of Mashi.

It is the memory that will finally give me the courage to leave Calcutta, to tear through the protective, suffocating cocoon of family in which we had both always lived, and strike out for the unknown.

Three weeks after Mashi disappeared, my mother told me, they found the body in the *dighi*. It had floated up among the *shapla* flowers on the far end, naked and bloated. No one was sure how long it had been in the water.

"There was a lot of bad talk," Mother said, "and the marriage the family had arranged for Susheela fell through." There is no anger in her voice, or blame. Only a mild sorrow.

Even now, years later, I dream of Lalita Mashi on that last night. The air is still, as before a storm, and only the cry of a lone jackal, eerily like a woman's, wavers along it. Before she steps over the threshold of the house to which there is no coming back, Mashi stops for a moment outside the new baby's room, listens for a cry. Hesitates, pressing a hand to the growing curve of her belly. Then she is running, her shadow long and trembly behind her, yearning backward to those ocher walls. At the edge of the lake she stops to pick up the stones, choosing the smoothest, roundest ones. The water gleams faintly in the light of the waning moon. When she steps in, it is not cold like she had feared but warm, warm, a lover's kiss. She pushes off without sound, as gracefully as though she were a white-plumed waterbird.

But what when her arms and legs grow too tired to carry her further, when the stones tied to her sari begin to weigh her down? And the water itself becomes a black hand squeezing her lungs, pulling her under. Does she struggle then, does she cry out her lover's name? Does she try to untie the stones and swim back to shore because the worst life is better than this breathless, choking end?

I am not sure. The dream always grows murky at this point, a swirl of rain and wind and dank, black lake mud, the smell of which will persist in my nostrils long after I wake. But her face—I sometimes see it in the last moments of the dream, framed by a bare arm flailing in wet moonlight, its mouth opening in a furious, futile cry. Sometimes it is my face.

One time when I wake, weeping, I call my mother in Calcutta.

"You killed Mashi, all of you," I cry, liberated from the usual filial courtesies by darkness and fear and pain. "You left her no other course of action."

A moment of silence at the other end. Then my mother's voice, calm as always. "She knew the rules, Lalita, the dangers." The edge of warning in her voice is meant for me too—the wayward niece of a wayward aunt. "She made the first choice. After that there was nothing anyone else could do."

Much as I wish to, I cannot deny her words, the truth in them. What is truth except that which we have made so by believing in it, generation after generation? And so a new dream is added to my old one. In it the wheel of karma rises, enormous, inexorable, the color of thunder. With a grating roar it rolls forward, gaining on the tiny figure of my aunt, who has set it in motion. She makes no effort to run, to escape it. She believes in it too.

But a few weeks later a brief note reaches me. It is in my mother's hand, unsigned—perhaps her attempt at consolation, for a mother must take part in the heartaches of her daughter, even a wayward one.

"There were no identifying marks on the body," says the note. "The face was completely eaten by fish. It could have been any young woman."

I've seen Lalita Mashi many times since then, in the airport as I rush toward my gate, in a crowded vegetable market, at the other end of a dimly lit restaurant filled with elegant diners. I no longer try to go to her. I know from experience that when I get close enough, she will turn into someone else and give me a polite, inquiring glance.

But it doesn't matter. Because I have another picture now inside my head to counter the dream of drowning, the dream of the crushing wheel. In it a young woman is leaving her father's home at night. She stops for a moment outside the new baby's room, listens for a cry. Presses her hand to the growing curve of her belly. Then she steps resolutely over the threshold and begins to walk. She is going to the station at the edge of the bamboo forest where a night train will stop in an hour's time. She will meet her lover there, and together they will travel to their new life.

Or perhaps the woman is alone. There is no man. He left a long time ago, as all men ultimately do. But the woman doesn't care. She knows now that she has always been alone. It is the nature of her condition, of being female, though throughout her life she has tried to hide it—in wish-dreams, in gossip, in frenzied activity—like her mother, and her mother, and her mother before her. The realization makes her feel translucent, weightless, as though she could lift off the ground at any moment.

The woman's arms swing freely by her side, for she is carrying no baggage. She knows that nothing from her old life will fit into her new one, the one she—and I—cannot quite imagine yet. Not the taboos, not the memories. She will have to create all anew, out of herself, as the mother goddess, Prakriti, does after the end of the world. The bamboo trees rustle like footsteps in the rising wind. She doesn't look back. She walks lightly, this woman, having shed her fears along with her hopes, and, as she makes her way across the moonlit land, I hear her sing.

SILENCE AND THE GRAVEROBBERS

LILLIAN HO WAN *was born in Oakland, California, in 1958. She received her JD from the University of California, Berkeley, School of Law and was admitted to the state bar of California in 1984. Her work has appeared in* Calyx, Industrial Relations Law Journal, *and* New England Review. *She and her husband, Bruno Leou-on, have two children, Yune Christopher and Vanina Clare.*

LORA JO FOO

I HAVE MY FATHER'S SUITCASE, YELLOW-BEIGE WITH metal reinforcements on the corners. He bought it in Paris in 1958, the year I was born. He and my mother were Hakka, the ethnic Chinese guest people, and they were accustomed to traveling.

The suitcase bears a destination label for Berkeley, California, but no indication of a home address. It sags with age, broken in the center, but I still keep it, stored inside my garage.

I was conceived in Paris and born in Oakland, California. My birth certificate labels me—first name to last name: Lillian Teng Lei-lan Howan. But these names are temporary, deceptive, and like my father's suitcase, offer no indication of the home address.

My mother told me the stories, how these names were not truly my name. She would talk to me in the afternoons as she washed her hair. "Boar's hair," she said. "So stiff." She would pull a section straight, the thick wire strands between her fingers. "Impossible to manage. I should cut it all." Saying this, she then combed her hair gently, untangling, rolling, and drying her hair in the afternoon sun. Her hair, opaque and impenetrable, would dry during the remainder of the day, the faintly detergent smell of shampoo evaporating through the rooms.

My parents selected Liliane as my Western name because of the sound, its similarity to my Chinese name, Lei-lan. When my mother gave birth, she had lived in the United States for two months and her English was minimal. She spoke a stilted and quaintly grandiose version of English, in accordance with her University of Paris textbooks. When the nurse asked for the name, my mother's reply was musical, romantic: Liliane. The nurse wrote Lillian, the English translation. My mother never recovered from the disappointment. The sound translated to English was wrong, she always explained to me. "So flat.

Too heavy." The creases between her brows deepened. "I did not choose Lillian."

My last name, Howan, was another mistake. "A paper name," my mother said. "A name given to your father's father by someone—a clerk in French immigration." The name of my paternal grandfather was Teng Yune. He was thirteen when he left his village in the Kwangtung province of southern China. His father had died when Yune was a child and his mother was a quarry worker who lifted and transported stones. She sent Yune, the eldest of her five children, to the island of Tahiti, where Hakka Chinese were working in the sugarcane and vanilla fields and as servants in French households. Yune found work as a groom. He brushed and fed horses, riding them through fields of coarse-velvet crabgrass, beneath rows of coconut palms. When transportation changed from the horse to the car and bicycle, Yune began working as a mechanic, a groom repairing and oiling the spirit inside the machine. He did not mount a bicycle standing still. He would give the handlebars a push and run alongside, leaping with sudden grace, his legs swinging over the seat. Yune, his name, meant luck, a wheel that turns, the movement of fortune.

My mother taught me how to write my father's family name: 鄧 "Teng. The same sound as light." She would point to the side: 阝. "This is a lantern." I thought it looked like the streetlight buzzing outside my bedroom window at night.

As the sunlight dried my mother's hair, I practiced writing in a spiral-bound notebook. "When you write, you must imagine a square," my mother said. "The character must fit inside this square." My characters rarely fit; they sprawled, lopsided, too long and too wide. My mother surveyed my writing. "Try again. No, don't squeeze the pencil." I bent over the notebook and began another column. When the sky was cloudy, my mother used the hair dryer, her hair submerged inside the aqua dome. We did not talk over the whirring of the motor. I waited then for the sun, the quiet, when my mother would tell me her stories again.

"Teng is not your true family name," she said once. "The true name was changed a long time ago."

"What was the name?" I asked.

"They killed everyone," my mother replied.

"Who? How come?"

"A Teng cannot marry a Yip or a Yang."

"Is Yip my true family name? Is Yang?"

"Why don't you set the table for dinner," my mother said. She disapproved of elaboration. "The truth is the truth. There's no need to get excited and make it bigger than it is." Whenever my mother thought I was embroidering on the truth, she would say, "Is that so? Or is that just you, being melodramatic?"

I would fall silent, avoiding her eyes.

But I was incorrigible. I preferred flourishes. I was unsatisfied with my one correctly given name—Lei-lan, my Chinese first name. "Complete lack of imagination," I complained. Lei—beautiful—and Lan—orchid—were commonplace in feminine names. Beautiful Cloud. Beautiful Shadow. Lovely Orchid. Pure Orchid. Many girls had these names. I felt that my name was the Hakka Chinese equivalent of Mary Jane, a combination of two ordinary overused names.

"Boys were never given their true name," my mother said.

I protested. "I'm not a boy."

"They were given terrible names," my mother continued. "Ugly Dog. Useless Crab. Or silly names that had no meaning. Big Crybaby. The names meant nothing. A child's name is not important, a child is too precious to name." She would touch her hair with the palm of her hand, feeling for the places that were still damp, turning her chair so that her hair would dry evenly. Around five in the afternoon, she stood and walked to the kitchen. After a moment, I would hear the water running and the sound of swirling grain, my mother washing rice.

Further questions were futile. My mother would be silent, sharpening the cleaver on the whetting stone in rasping strokes. "Have you finished your homework?" she would say.

She had told me all there was to say about my names.

I no longer asked—but I was certain, confident as only a child could be in the face of absence. I knew that my true name still waited to be spoken. One day I would say the word, the sound, and it would fit completely. The day would come when I would uncover my name, snatching it light-fingered from the silence.

. . .

I stole two trinkets when I was six. The trinkets were delicate and small and they felt perfect inside my hand. One was a porcelain white poodle standing on its hind legs, the way a dog jumps up when greeting a friend. A tiny pink rose perched on top of the poodle's head, a little red smile painted on its lips. The poodle was smaller than my pinkie finger and it stood with its twin and a much larger poodle mother, decorating a display of lamps in a department store.

I saw the porcelain poodle as I followed my mother shopping. There were many lamps for sale on top of a display table. The lamps seemed tall, their light reaching over my head, but right where I rested my chin on the table was the little poodle, looking at me, eye to eye. Its twin was uninterested, turned in another direction.

Looking up, I saw my mother watching me. Her face seemed blank, and even to this day, I cannot remember if she frowned or smiled. She was just silent and she watched.

I looked back across the table. The little poodle had clear-colored eyes and gold curls painted around its paws. I reached out and picked it up. It seemed happy in my hand. I took my mother's fingers with my other hand and we walked out of the store.

The second trinket was a miniature white wicker basket filled with rose-buds. The roses were plastic and pink, the color of my mother's powder puff that sat on top of the TV tray next to my parents' bed. Each bud was attached to a feathery green leaf. I stood in front of a store cart filled with a rainbow of artificial flowers, but only the miniature white wicker balanced lightly in the palm of my hand.

I remember that my mother had been cranky all morning. She was not smiling and I had dashed off to hide among the store flower displays. When she walked up beside me, I turned, offering the basket of roses. This time, I remember, she smiled. I remember the calmness in her step as we strolled away, the basket hidden, curled inside my hand.

The tiny porcelain poodle and the miniature rose basket became the prized procession of my childhood. I had dolls who lost all their hair, green plastic soldiers I misplaced every time we moved to a different apartment, crayons I broke and ate, but I never lost the tiny poodle and the miniature rose basket.

They slept in a corner of a shoebox beside my bed. I kept them wrapped, swaddled in Kleenex that I occasionally unraveled, placing the two trinkets side by side inside my hand.

Many years later, when I was twenty-eight, my mother passed away. Sorting through her possessions, I came across the poodle and the rose basket. I had long since forgotten about them—but there they were, inside my mother's china cabinet, displayed next to her favorite wedding gift: salt and pepper Limoges porcelain swans with tiny matching 24-karat gold spoons. My mother had taken few possessions when she had left Paris, but she had brought the swans. She had saved even fewer possessions from my early childhood. "Life is a voyage," my mother always said, and voyagers travel light.

Opening the china cabinet, I took out the two trinkets, one in each hand. I had been too young to know that I was stealing at the time. But my mother had been there and she had seen.

My mother and father always punished me for doing wrong—spankings followed by exile to my room. I was taught not to lie, not to talk back, not to stick out my tongue or make ugly faces, not to fight with my cousins. I said please and thank you in Hakka, French, and English. I was sent to Catholic school and every night I prayed to Our Father to deliver me from evil. And yet, I had stolen twice and my mother had not punished me. She had even saved my loot, displayed in the family china cabinet.

I placed the poodle next to the rose basket next to my mother's wedding swans. I closed the china door, the trinkets rattling slightly, a tinkling as the door snapped shut.

My great-great-uncles stole from graves. My mother recounted this many times and I always listened—graverobbing was my favorite story. During the end of the Qing Dynasty, at the turn of the twentieth century, the funerals of the wealthy were grandiose and loud. Public mourners garbed in white, the beating of drums, the bodies of the dead heavy with gold and jade. Hidden in the hills surrounding the town, my great-great-uncles observed the funeral procession winding its way to the cemetery and they waited, patiently, for night to fall.

A particularly lavish display of mourning accompanied the funeral of a young bride, betrothed to the only son of a prominent official family. At her wedding banquet, the bride had swallowed a small roasted bird and she had choked on a tiny bone. Restrained by elaborate etiquette and too polite to cough up the bone in front of her strange new family, the family of her husband-to-be, the bride had tried to discreetly swallow. Her attempts only lodged the bone still deeper, blocking her breath, until she coughed and gagged—too late. She fell to the floor and died.

The night following her funeral, my great-great-uncles climbed the walls surrounding the cemetery and began digging. They dug until they uncovered the coffin of the bride. Prying open the lid, they discovered the body, a pale silk gleam, adorned in jewels and gold. They laughed quietly, stripping the corpse of her finery, slipping rings from cold fingers, unfastening and unclasping necklaces, bracelets, and bangles. After they had stuffed all the jewelry and gold into sacks, one great-great-uncle propped the corpse up inside her coffin. "Thank you," he said. "Good girl." He patted the corpse on her back, a hearty pat.

There was a strange sound, a little *pop,* and then the corpse coughed.

Out flew the tiny piece of bone.

The corpse coughed again.

"Ai-ya!" the great-great-uncles shouted.

The face of the bride turned pink and the faces of the great-great-uncles turned white. They grabbed their sacks, scrambled out of the grave, and ran away, back to their village in the hills.

"Liang kong," my mother said as she ended the story. "They ran back to their village in the *liang kong."* The clear hills.

"Why were they called *liang kong?"* I always asked.

My mother was quiet, puzzled. Raised in the South Pacific, on the island of Raiatea, the ancient capital of Tahiti and of Polynesia, she had never seen the *liang kong,* the hills where the Hakka settled in the southern provinces of China. She saw them only in the words of her grandmother, my great-grand-mother, who had recounted this story to my mother. "Maybe the hills were bare," my mother said. "No trees. Maybe not much grew on these hills." She would smile, a restrained smile. "Perhaps that is why we lived there."

But I had already lost interest in the hills, bare and drab. I was wondering about the bride. I imagined her, enclosed in her coffin, before my great-great-uncles opened the lid. Was she asleep? Or was she like me—a poor sleeper, who lay awake, quiet, motionless in her small room, waiting?

I imagined the bride climbing out of her dirt grave, walking out of the cemetery, walking back to her house. Did she knock on the gate? Were they happy to see her?

"What happened to the girl?" I asked.

"She was not Hakka. She was *punti,*" my mother replied. *Punti* was the Hakka word for the Cantonese. "She lived in town and her husband's family was very rich. She did not live in the *liang kong.*"

My mother's family retained their original name. Mu. The name is old and not common. The ideogram is written 丛. "Simple to write," my mother said. "This is a person: 人. And another person: 人."

"What are they doing?" I scrutinized the two people. "And what is this? A tower? Two doors?"

"Why don't you look for yourself." My mother pointed to the ideogram, the image of her family name.

I scrunched over the paper, my elbows resting on the table.

"Sit up straight," my mother said. "Close your mouth." She tapped my lips. "No, don't hold your breath. Breathe in and out. Just look."

I did as instructed. I wondered if the ideogram was like some of those drawings in the cartoon section of the Sunday paper—stare at the drawings long enough and they would turn into something else. A hot dog, a smiling face. My science teacher called them optical illusions.

"This is a very old name," my mother sometimes explained. "It comes from the north, the place where we originated." The Hakka left the northern homeland over a thousand years ago when Central Asian peoples invaded north and central China. The Hakka became nomadic, moving in waves, south across China. Arriving in the southern provinces of Kwangtung and Kwangsi, they found that the fertile farmlands of the valleys and plains were already inhabited. They settled in the hills, the *liang kong,* where each family clan formed its own village.

"The Mu village had a teacher," my mother said. "When all the boys were around eight years old, they were sent to the teacher, to learn to be a Mu. Of course, they had to pass the test, and very few were selected."

"What happened to those who were not selected?" I imagined something terrible—a punishment for flunking.

My mother was gentle. "Nothing bad happened. They became farmers, or soldiers, or they had stores and sold things. Most boys did not pass the test—it was very difficult—and in the end, there would be only one or two boys who remained and studied with the teacher. And even then, they trained for many, many years—and there was no certainty that they would learn. They had to be very patient. They had to wait, sometimes for nearly their entire lives."

"How did they learn? What did they do?"

"They were silent," my mother replied. "They learned how to be silent."

"And what would happen?"

"The teacher would die and then perhaps it would start." My mother said this in the voice she used for emphasizing the important—a voice reserved to underline practical survival techniques—like always checking fruit one by one before buying ("old fruit is always on top") or never drinking water cold ("cold water makes a body weak") or always keeping your own mind ("they say that others will make your face, but this is not true—your face is your face and no one will make it for you").

"What started after the teacher died?" I asked.

"They would hear the voice of the dead," said my mother. "A boy learned how to be silent so that one day, when he became a man, the dead would speak through his lips."

I learned about the dead through my college textbooks. I took undergraduate courses in Chinese history and studied the uprisings, the rebellions, rarely successful, invariably brutal. The Hakka, isolated for a thousand years and relegated to the bare hills of China, had an ambiguous interest in the established order. The name Hakka itself means a guest, a temporary visitor, an outsider. The guests stole, they raided. They were vulnerable to recruitment into secret societies and comprised a large proportion of the casualties when a rebellion failed. I could follow my mother's lesson never to exaggerate and the numbers would still be staggering.

The leaders of the Taiping Rebellion were Hakka and at the end of the siege of Nanjing in 1864, three thousand of the leading officials committed suicide. A few drowned themselves, most burned themselves alive. Nanjing fell following the mass suicide of its leaders. The report to the Qing imperial court records that the one hundred thousand followers of the Taiping living in Nanjing either committed suicide or were killed by the invading Qing army. In all, forty million Chinese died before the rebellion ended.

A few Taiping leaders who were not at Nanjing were captured for execution. The punishment for treason was severe. They would be killed slowly, their bodies cut a little piece at a time.

But while they awaited execution, they were granted an exceptional opportunity. For this reason, some chose not to commit suicide—to await a far more painful and difficult death. In exchange for submission to capital punishment, they were given the opportunity to write. To tell what happened. To sit in silence and write down the words. The writing survived, preserved intact by the descendants of their captors.

Many years after my mother passed away, I asked my father about our family name. My father was visiting temporarily. He was always changing his address. Sometimes he lived with his brother, sometimes with my maternal grandparents, or in a house under construction—some months in the United States, some months in Tahiti. He rarely lived where I could reach him by phone. I had to leave messages with various family members and wait for him to call. When I gave birth to my first child, my husband left messages at the restaurant of my father's sister and then at the bowling alley of my father's brother. "He's around," everyone said. No one was sure of his exact location. Everyone promised to give him the message that his grandchild was born.

"Is Teng our real family name?" I asked my father when he came to visit. We were sitting in the living room, my baby daughter sleeping on my lap.

"No," my father replied. "The real name was changed."

"Is it true that a Teng cannot marry a Yip or a Yang?"

My father thought for a while. "A Teng cannot marry a Ship or a Yap."

When I asked why, he replied, "Because all these names are the same family. The names were changed, but they are always the same family." Tradition prohibited marriage within the same family name. My father sat, reflecting, and then he spoke again. "They killed everyone."

He had been drinking a cup of coffee and he stood up to bring the empty cup into the kitchen.

"A lot of people died," I said.

My father asked, his voice quiet, "Do you know when this happened?"

I opened my mouth to speak, but my father shook his head. "You must feel it. Inside." He pointed to his heart and then he walked away.

The perfume of my mother was L'Air du Temps—The Air of Time. She kept it in many forms: *eau de toilette* in scalloped glass, perfume in crystal flacons, milk-white lotion in creamy bottles of soft plastic.

I have saved her perfume, time distilled into liquid. Her fragrance smells different applied to my wrist—but it still evokes flowers, her favorite pink and magenta carnations. Again I am eating mirabelle plums with my mother in Paris. She eats without talking, occasionally passing her curled hand over her lips, her tongue, hidden, sliding the stone into the narrow funnel formed by her fingers and palm. The plums are golden, the size of cherries.

Or I am in Algeciras, in southern Spain, and there are honeysuckles and the flame-petaled flowers of pomegranates blooming outside the hotel balcony window. The heat is choking and only the subtle spice of my mother's perfume clears the air. She is sitting at a table, where she is writing our daily expenditures in a slender notebook. She knows exactly how much we have already spent and how much we still have saved. The perfume seeps from a thin wad of tissue inside her left blouse pocket. Earlier in the day, she had wiped the opening of her perfume bottle with this piece of tissue. I would have thrown the tissue into the wastebasket, but my mother folded the remnant into a small square, tucking it into her pocket.

Every summer, I traveled with my mother. We lived frugally all year, my mother clipping coupons and buying on sale, but in the summers we voyaged. By the time I was twelve, I could pack for both of us—one month's worth of clothes and toiletries into one suitcase and two carry-on bags. I could pack in less than an hour.

My parents traveled, but not always together. My mother remained with my father from the age of seventeen until the day she died, at fifty-three, but she did not always live with him. She lived in Berkeley and my father, a civil engineer, worked on a hydraulic project in the Central Valley. She visited her sister in Hawai'i while my father went to Tahiti to see his parents. I grew up with my mother telling me, "Your father will join us in Honolulu" . . . "in Paris" . . . "soon."

Travel was when my mother smiled more, ate desserts, and slept badly. She suffered from insomnia in strange rooms. "You move so much when you sleep," she complained to me in the morning. "You jump around, just like your father." My mother could remain without moving for hours, even when she was wide awake.

My grandmother was sixteen when she gave birth to my mother, her first child. My mother was premature, seven months, and looked like a hairless kitten. She was placed on a sack of rice and left in a corner, in the back of the store where my grandparents lived and worked. "I was born on a Sunday," my mother always said. "The busiest day for a store. Everyone had to work. It was December, the hottest month."

She remained on the sack of rice, among the cartons and crates. The day of her birth passed into night. My mother's grandfather, my great-grandfather, came to town to visit. He was sober, a rare occurrence. "Where is the new baby?" he asked.

He was told that the baby, a girl, had been born too early and had died. The body, curled and wrinkled, was somewhere in the back.

My great-grandfather decided to look for himself. He found my mother lying quite still. With a finger, he stroked her small body. Her arms twitched and her tiny mouth opened. My great-grandfather picked her up.

"She's not human-looking, a girl and nearly dead," the others in the family complained.

My great-grandfather was undaunted. He would not let go of her body, so small, it fit inside his hand. "She's hungry," he announced.

. . .

My mother liked eating squids. Her favorite dish was the Spanish *chiperones en su tinta,* squids cooked in their own ink. As students in Paris, she and her sisters traveled by overnight train each summer to the Spanish Costa Brava, where it was so hot, my mother spent her afternoons sitting in the bathtub— always empty because water for a private bath was too expensive. She traveled to Pamplona to watch the running of the bulls on the Feast of St. Fermin and she ate *chiperones* nearly every night. She described the squids to me—how unctuous, how silky.

I was disappointed when I saw the dish for the first time. We were sitting in a restaurant in Gerona and the waiter placed a plate filled with black before my mother. It was not an attractive black, not shiny or smooth, but grainy dull. There was no other color, no accent, no garnish, only black liquid and rolled black lumps of squid.

My mother beamed. I dug deeper into my bowl of fish stew. My mother picked up her fork and cut a piece of squid. When I looked up, she was waving the piece before me, skewered on her fork. Black sauce dribbled on my plate.

I shook my head.

"It's good," my mother said.

I kept my mouth closed. This was my mother's dish.

"Try a little."

I could not imagine digesting something so unrelentingly black.

"Don't look, then," she said. "Close your eyes and open your mouth."

She motioned toward my lips. I was silent but her fork did not budge. I closed my eyes.

The squid slithered into my mouth. The taste was sublime—smooth, subtly sweet, and nutlike. I opened my eyes and my mother was cutting herself a slice. She did not insist on feeding me squid again. I did not ask for more.

My cousins and I played with fire when we were children. I bought Ping-Pong balls at the variety store and we would hide in my uncle's garden, among the rows of Swiss chard and bok choy, and set the balls on fire. After depleting our supply of Ping-Pongs, we would look for twigs and light one end, daring each other—seeing who could hold the twig the longest as the fire burned to the end. We sneered at the losers, those who quickly dropped the fiery sticks to save their fingers.

I remember how still I stood, watching the wood burn. The slightest movement would make the fire burn more rapidly—and I was determined to win, to be the one who held on to the end, the one who came closest to the flame.

I burned my hand once, accidentally, over the kitchen stove when I was eight. I was warming some milk mixed with honey and, having spilled the honey, I tried to wipe the surface clean. The paper towel caught on fire and I carried it, walking steadily, across the speckled linoleum floor, into the sink. The resulting blisters—the one on my thumb was the size of a half walnut shell—filled with pus and took days to heal. At night the pain was agony and nightmares tormented my sleep, but during the day I ghoulishly squished my blisters, yellow sticky liquid squirting under the fragile new skin. My younger cousins were impressed; my mother was not.

"Don't show off," she said while my father drained the pus with a needle sterilized over a match flame. It was important to be humble, she insisted. "Making your own face is up to you, but don't go shouting and bragging about it."

She told me then about my great-great-uncle, a *mu* who had practiced in Raiatea. He led a simple life, spending most of the day sleeping or doing household chores. He wore wrinkled white sleeveless T-shirts and baggy shorts. His voice was toneless, but in the nights when he entered the spirit world, his words took wing and he sang.

My mother knew this because she was allowed as a child to stay up late, on occasion, and watch. Her grandmother thought such things were not appropriate for children, but my mother was the eldest grandchild and she wanted to see. Her grandmother relented. My mother could stay, but she was expected to remain quiet.

"Who was the hardest to find?" I asked. Was it someone who had died violently? Was it a child?

"A mother," she replied. "A *mu* can rarely find his mother among the dead."

. . .

Yang Xiuqing, the leading strategist of the Taiping Rebellion, claimed he was the true conduit, the medium for the voice of God the Father, all-knowing and omnipotent. He succeeded in manipulating the power of his trances to dazzle and intimidate—and to centralize the authority of the Taiping government in himself. Less concerned with spiritual truth than in maintaining power, Yang supplemented the scope of his visions with an extensive network of spies. He was not the central prophet of the Rebellion, but he became the commander of the Taiping armies and chief organizer of the government of its three million followers. He was called the East King and his administrative staff in Nanjing numbered over 7,200 officials.

Yang formulated detailed regulations governing areas ranging from military operations to medical care to the construction of weapons. Land was to be divided equally among all families according to size, with women as well as men receiving equal shares. The actual implementation of Taiping law, however, placed less emphasis on egalitarian land reform and a higher priority on maintaining rigid discipline and collecting revenues for the maintenance of its armies. Military discipline was strict, enforced without exception. Soldiers who retreated when ordered to advance or who hesitated in battle were killed by their officers.

As commander-in-chief, Yang was feared, but he was not popular. His family was Hakka and poor; Yang worked as a servant, a miner and a charcoal burner. He became East King of the Taiping Rebellion through intelligence and relentless cruelty. His military strategy and organization shaped the Taipings from a provincial Hakka uprising in 1850 to a rebel government that by 1853 controlled central China, maintaining power from the Nanjing capital for eleven years. Yang elevated himself, his family, and his culture from the barren hills to imperial splendor, but he succeeded through a system of centralized military rule, unbending and austere.

On September 2, 1856, a rival leader of the Taiping Rebellion assassinated Yang Xiuqing and ordered the death of his entire family and staff, killing over 20,000 in a single day. The few members of Yang's clan who managed to escape fled Nanjing and changed their family name. In this way, they managed to survive the defeat of the Taiping Rebellion, since they were no longer at Nanjing when it fell.

One of my older cousins traveled from France back to China, to trace the family genealogy. He lived for a month in my father's family village. Clan elders showed him written records of past catastrophe, widespread slaughter narrowly escaped. His father, my uncle, visited California one holiday season. I sat with my family at my aunt's table and my uncle recounted his version of his son's discoveries about the family history. We were descended from a highly placed official.

"He was important, very powerful," my uncle said.

"What was his name?" a cousin asked.

"We were always very smart," said my aunt. "Your grandfather could speak many languages."

Several of my cousins had left the table and were playing video games in the front room, among my uncle's voluminous suitcases packed with the spoils of his visits to every department store within a fifty-mile radius. The suitcases were filled with computer diskettes, microwave popcorn, pistachio nuts, bottles of whiskey—the number well exceeding the personal import limit.

"The turkey is too dry, I left it in the oven too long," my aunt complained. Another aunt protested—the turkey was wonderful, not dry at all. They cut my uncle another slice.

"Many, many were killed," said my uncle.

"What was his name?" I asked.

"No—don't give him yams," my aunt told her son, who was passing a platter to my father. "He hates yams."

"Give me one," my father replied. When he was an infant, my father had returned with his parents from Tahiti to the village in China, where he ate an unvarying diet of rice and yams. The way my mother described it, the Hakka in the *liang kong* seemed to eat nothing but rice and yams, supplemented with a dab of fermented bean curd swirled sparingly on the end of a chopstick.

"We're descended from officials," said my uncle.

I scooped myself more cranberry sauce.

My father started cutting the yam with the back of his fork. "How does anyone really know?" he said. "At Ka-san, all the families go to the cemetery." Ka-san, the feast for remembering the dead, occurs twice a year: once in the spring—one hundred days after the New Year—and once in the autumn.

"What was his name?" I asked. I spoke more slowly. "What was his name?"

"The family goes to the cemetery," my father said. "All the families." He pushed the yam to the side of his plate.

"I've decided to be buried," my mother announced. It was early evening and she was resting on her bed. Her hair was falling. I would pass through the rooms of my parents' house and find her hair, tangled in the corners, hidden behind the doors. She had always wanted to be cremated. It was cleaner, she had said.

"Are you sure?" I asked.

"I've decided to be messy," she replied. Even with the curtains drawn, I could see her one dimple, cleaving the bottom of her chin. "You should pick your name."

My mother had urged me to choose my name ever since I had turned twenty-one. Boys selected their true names when they turned twenty. The Ugly Crab became the Glorious Warrior, the Big Crybaby became the Piercing Lance. Times had changed, my mother explained—a woman should pick her true name too. She had many suggestions. "How about Claire?"

"You won't recognize me with another name," I said.

"Pick a name you like." Her voice was tired, a whisper.

I rested my head on the edge of the bed. "I already have my name," I said. "I've had it all along—it's the one on my birth certificate."

"I never liked that name." She lifted her hand in a slight flicker.

"I never liked it either. But it's my name."

My mother closed her eyes. I wondered if she was already asleep. She tilted her head toward me. "I've always kept my name. Sou-kin." A name that meant jasmine. "Mu Sou-kin."

■ ■ ■

My mother is buried in a copper coffin in the Chinese cemetery in Tahiti. The cemetery, on a hillside, overlooks the ocean. Tahitian families live on the border of the cemetery; their horses graze among the tombs, the grass so thick, their hoofs pass in silence. Only the sound of birds punctuates the quiet—the raucous call of seabirds, the subdued cooing of doves in the dense mango trees.

My mother always said that silence was the training of the *mu*, that if one listened to silence long enough, one could hear the voices of the spirit world. The *mu* apprentice waited in silence for the doorway to open—to enter the place of the dead, the forgotten, the lost. There were no sacred sites in traditional Hakka culture, for a people wandering, never certain that they could return. The doorway that dissolved the division between living and dead, present and past—this doorway, the entrance to names long forgotten, was carried within. It was difficult to uncover, but it could not be destroyed. Within lay the sound, the lure that invoked the scent of the soul, like the scent of perfume, breathing life to remembrance.

My father's suitcase is somewhere in my garage—among my mother's books, old appliances, my children's outgrown toys. My husband and I always say we will clean the garage—we have ambitious plans for sorting through piles of accumulation, deciding what to keep and what to give away . . . but the jumble remains, unsorted and undiscarded.

My husband ventures often into the junk in the garage, where he hunts for the remains of tools, machine parts, pieces of wire. The garage resembles the back of the general store where he was born in Tahiti—a store identical to all the Chinese-owned general stores in Polynesia and perhaps the world over. The back rooms of the stores are always crammed with cartons, sacks of rice, onions, flour, and potatoes, the floor littered with flattened cardboard boxes, newspapers, rusting bottle caps. In Tahiti, there is the scent of drying vanilla beans and skinny cats stalk the traces of furtive mice. I can never open the brown opaque bottles of vanilla extract without thinking of these storage rooms—the chaos, the near-darkness. It was the place where my mother waited, already born but not quite alive.

I have often wondered how her grandfather looked for her. There were endless places to look, hundreds of sacks of rice. She was quiet, dulled by exposure.

When I was a child, I pictured my great-grandfather walking, surefooted and heroic, to rescue my mother. As I grew older, the truer picture began to materialize. I knew that he did not go, direct and bold, to the place where my baby mother waited. He poked about, he was uncertain. Perhaps he walked past her, hidden in the unlit shadows. Perhaps he was thinking of the drink, the sweet fire of alcohol, his friends talking and reading the Chinese newspaper in the front room.

A web of sound would reverberate in the shadows of the back room. The rising and falling cries of fighting roosters scratching in the dust behind the store, the chatter of customers in the front room, someone asking for a fishing line, a half kilo of beans; the distant boom of the ocean, surging and crashing on the coral reef surrounding the lagoon.

Among the murmurs, the cries and echoes, one line of sound searched for my mother. The rustle of boxes pushed aside, the footsteps—the sound that my mother heard as she waited, and waiting within her, the infinitesimal seeds of her unborn, the seed that would become mine. It was the faltering, the shuffle of error, a flawed litany from beginning to end. It was the sound, named by its imperfection, of the one who would find her, lifting her, cradled in the palm of his hand.

GARRETT HONGO

KUBOTA

GARRETT HONGO, *editor of this volume, was born in Volcano, Hawai'i, in 1951. Author of three books, he has also published poetry and essays in numerous periodicals, anthologies, and newspapers. He lives in Eugene, Oregon.*

SHUZO UEMOTO

ON DECEMBER 8, 1941, THE DAY AFTER THE Japanese attack on Pearl Harbor in Hawai'i, my maternal grandfather had barricaded himself with his family—my grandmother, my teenage mother, her two sisters and two brothers—inside of his home in La'ie, a sugar plantation village on O'ahu's North Shore. This was my mother's father, a man most villagers called by his last name—Kubota. It could mean either Wayside Field or else Broken Dreams depending on which ideograms he used. Kubota ran La'ie's general store, and the previous night, after a long day of bad news on the radio, some locals had come by, pounded on the front door, and made threats. One was said to have brandished a machete. They were angry and shocked as the whole nation was in the aftermath of the surprise attack. Kubota was one of the few Japanese Americans in the village and president of the local Japanese-language school. He had become a target for their rage and suspicion. A wise man, he locked all his doors and windows and did not open his store the next day, but stayed closed and waited for news from some official.

He was a Kibei, a Japanese American born in Hawai'i (a U.S. Territory then, so he was thus a citizen), but he was subsequently sent back by his father for formal education in Hiroshima, Japan—their home province. Kibei is written with two ideograms in Japanese—one is the word for "return" and the other is the word for "rice." Poetically, it means one who returns from America, known as the Land of Rice in Japanese (by contrast, Chinese immigrants called their new home Mountain of Gold).

Kubota was graduated from a Japanese high school and then came back to Hawai'i as a teenager. He spoke English—and a Hawaiian creole version of it at that—with a Japanese accent. But he was well liked and good at numbers, scrupulous and hardworking like so many immigrants and children of immigrants. Castle and Cook, a grower's company that ran the sugarcane business along the North Shore, hired him on as a stock boy and then appointed him to run one of its company stores. He did well, had the trust of management and labor—not an easy accomplishment in any day—married, had children, and had begun to exert himself in community affairs and excel in his own recreations. He put together a Japanese community organization that backed a Japanese-language school for children and sponsored teachers from Japan. Kubota boarded many of them, in succession, in his own home. This made dinners a silent affair for his talkative, Hawaiian-bred children, as their stern *sensei,* or teacher, was nearly always at table and their own abilities in the Japanese language were as delinquent as their attendance. While Kubota and the *sensei* rattled on about things Japanese, speaking Japanese, his children hurried through their suppers and tried to run off early to listen to the radio shows.

After dinner, while the *sensei* graded exams seated in a wicker chair in the spare room and his wife and children gathered around the radio in the front parlor, Kubota sat on the screened porch outside, reading the local Japanese newspapers. He finished reading about the same time as he finished the tea he drank for his digestion—a habit he'd learned in Japan—and then he'd get out his fishing gear and spread it out on the plank floors. The wraps on his rods needed to be redone, gears in his reels needed oil, and, once through with those tasks, he'd painstakingly wind on hundreds of yards of new line. Fishing was his hobby and his passion. He spent weekends camping along the North Shore beaches with his children, setting up umbrella tents, packing a rice pot and hibachi along for meals. And he caught fish. *Ulua* mostly, the huge surf-feeding fish known as the jack crevalle on the mainland, but he'd go after almost anything in its season. In Kawela, a plantation-owned bay nearby, he fished for mullet with a throw net, stalking the bottom-hugging, gray-backed schools as they gathered at the stream mouths and in the freshwater springs. In an outrigger out beyond the reef, he'd try for *aku*—the skipjack tuna prized for steaks and, sliced raw and mixed with fresh seaweed and cut onions, for *sashimi* salad. In Kahaluu and Ka'awa and on an offshore rock locals called Goat Island, he loved to go torching, stringing lanterns on bamboo poles stuck in the sand to attract *kumu,* the red goatfish, as they schooled at night just inside the reef. But in La'ie on Laniloa Point near Kahuku, the northernmost tip of O'ahu, he cast twelve- and fourteen-foot surf rods for the huge, varicolored, and fast-running *ulua* as they ran for schools of squid and baitfish just beyond the biggest breakers and past the low sand flats wadable from the shore to nearly a half mile out. At sunset, against the western light, he looked as if he walked on water as he came back, fish and rods slung over his shoulders, stepping along the rock and coral path just inches under the surface of a running tide.

When it was torching season, in December or January, he'd drive out the afternoon before and stay with old friends, the Tanakas or Yoshikawas, shopkeepers like him who ran stores near the fishing grounds. They'd have been preparing for weeks, selecting and cutting their bamboo poles, cleaning the hurricane lanterns, tearing up burlap sacks for the cloths they'd soak with kerosene and tie onto sticks they'd poke into the soft sand of the shallows. Once lit, touched off with a Zippo lighter, these would be the torches they'd use as beacons to attract the schooling fish. In another time, they might have made up a dozen paper lanterns of the kind mostly used for decorating the summer folk dances outdoors on the grounds of the Buddhist church during O-Bon, the Festival for the Dead. But now, wealthy and modern and efficient killers of fish, Tanaka and Kubota used rag torches and Colemans and cast rods with tips made of Tonkin bamboo and butts of American-spun fiberglass. After just one good night, they might bring back a prize bounty of a dozen burlap bags filled with scores of bloody, rigid fish delicious to eat and even better to give away as gifts to friends, family, and special customers.

It was a Monday night, the day after Pearl Harbor, and there was a rattling knock at the front door. Two FBI agents presented themselves, showed identification, and took my grandfather in for questioning in Honolulu. No one knew what had happened or what was wrong. But there was a roundup going on of all those in the Japanese American community suspected of sympathizing with the enemy and worse. My grandfather was suspected of espionage, of communicating with offshore Japanese submarines launched from the attack fleet days before war began. Torpedo planes and escort fighters, decorated with the insignia of the rising sun, had taken an approach route from northwest of O'ahu directly across Kahuku Point and on toward Pearl. They had strafed an auxiliary air station near the fishing grounds my grandfather loved and destroyed a small gun battery there, killing three men. Kubota was known to have sponsored and harbored Japanese nationals in his own home. He had a radio. He had wholesale access to firearms. Circumstances and an undertone of racial resentment had combined with wartime hysteria in the aftermath of the tragic naval battle to cast suspicion on the loyalties of my grandfather and all other Japanese Americans. The FBI reached out and pulled hundreds of them in for questioning in dragnets cast throughout the West Coast and Hawai'i.

My grandfather was lucky, he'd be let go after only a few days. But others were not as fortunate. Hundreds, from small communities in Washington, California, Oregon, and Hawai'i, were rounded up and, after what appeared to be routine questioning, shipped off under Justice Department orders to holding centers in Leuppe on the Navajo Reservation in Arizona, in Fort Missoula in Montana, and on Sand Island in Honolulu harbor. There were other special camps on Maui in Ha'iku and on Hawai'i—the Big Island—in my own home village of Volcano.

Many of these men—it was exclusively the Japanese American men suspected of ties to Japan who were initially rounded up—did not see their families again for over four years. Under a suspension of due process that was only after the fact ruled as warranted by military necessity, they were, if only temporarily, "disappeared" in Justice Department prison camps scattered in particularly desolate areas of the United States designated as militarily "safe." These were grim forerunners to the assembly centers and concentration camps for the 120,000 Japanese American evacuees that were to come later.

I am Kubota's eldest grandchild, and I remember him as a lonely, habitually silent old man who lived with us in our home near Los Angeles for most of my childhood and adolescence. It was the fifties, and my parents had emigrated from Hawai'i to the mainland in the hope of a better life away from the old sugar plantation. After some success, they had sent back for my grandparents and taken them in. And it was my grandparents who did the work of the household while my mother and father worked their salaried city jobs. My grandmother cooked and sewed, washed our clothes, and knitted in the front room under the light of a huge lamp with a bright three-way bulb. Kubota raised a flower garden, read up on soils and grasses in gardening books, and planted a zoysia lawn in front and a dichondra one in back. He planted a small patch near the rear block wall with green onions, eggplants, white Japanese radishes, and cucumbers. While he hoed and spaded the loamless, clayey earth of Los Angeles, he sang particularly plangent songs in Japanese about plum blossoms and bamboo groves.

Once, in the mid-sixties, after a dinner during which, as always, he had been silent while he worked away at a meal of fish and rice spiced with drabs of Chinese mustard and catsup thinned with soy sauce, Kubota took his own dishes to the kitchen sink and washed them up. He took a clean jelly jar out of the cupboard—the glass was thick and its shape squatty like an old-fashioned. He reached around to the hutch below where he kept his bourbon. He made himself a drink and retired to the living room, where I was expected to join him for "talk story"—the Hawaiian idiom for chewing the fat.

I was a teenager and, though I was bored listening to stories I'd heard often enough before at holiday dinners, I was dutiful. I took my spot on the couch next to Kubota and heard him out. Usually, he'd tell me about his schooling in Japan, where he learned judo along with mathematics and literature. He'd learned the *soroban* there—the abacus which was the original pocket calculator of the Far East—and that, along with his strong, judo-trained back, got him his first job in Hawai'i. This was the moral. "Study *ha-ahd*," he'd say with pidgin emphasis. "Learn read good. Learn speak da kine *good* English." The message is the familiar one taught to any children of immigrants—succeed through education. And imitation. But this time, Kubota reached down into his past and told me a different story. I was thirteen by then, and I suppose he thought me ready for it. He told me about Pearl Harbor, how the planes flew in, wing after wing, in formations over his old house in La'ie in Hawai'i, and how, the next day, after Roosevelt had made his famous "Day of Infamy" speech about the treachery of the Japanese, the FBI agents had come to his door and taken him in, hauled him off to Honolulu for questioning, and held him without charges. I thought he was lying. I thought he was making up a kind of horror story to shock me and give his moral that much more starch. But it was true. I asked around. I brought it up during history class in junior high school, and my teacher, a Jew, after silencing me and stepping me off to the back of the room, told me that it was indeed so. I asked my mother and she said it was true. I asked my schoolmates, who laughed and ridiculed me for being so ignorant. We lived in a Japanese American community and the parents of most of my classmates were the Nisei who had been interned as teenagers all through the war. But there was a strange silence around all of this. There was a hush, as if one were invoking the ill powers of the dead when one brought it up. No one cared to speak about the evacuation and relocation for very long. It wasn't in our history books, though we were studying World War II at the time. It wasn't in the family albums of the people I knew and whom I'd visit, staying over weekends with friends. And it wasn't anything that the family talked about or allowed me to keep bringing up either. I was given the facts, told sternly and pointedly that "it was war" and that "nothing could be done." *Shikata ga nai* is the phrase in Japanese, a kind of resolute and determinist pronouncement on how to deal with inexplicable tragedy. I was to know it but not to dwell on it. Japanese Americans were busy trying to forget it ever happened and were having a hard enough time building their new lives after "camp." It was as if we had no history for four years and the relocation was something unspeakable.

But Kubota would not let it go. In session after session, for months it seemed, he pounded away at his story. He wanted to tell me the names of the FBI agents. He went over their questions and his responses again and again. He'd tell me how one would try to act friendly toward him, offering him cigarettes, while the other, who hounded him with accusations and threats, left the interrogation room. "Good cop/bad cop," I thought to myself, already superficially streetwise from stories black classmates told of the Watts riots and from myself having watched too many episodes of *Dragnet* and *The Mod Squad*. But Kubota was not interested in my experiences. I was not made yet and he was determined that his stories be part of my making. He spoke quietly at first, mildly, but once into his narrative and after his drink was down, his voice would rise and quaver with resentment and he'd make his accusations. He gave his testimony to me and I held it at first cautiously in my conscience like it was an heirloom too delicate to expose to strangers and anyone outside of the world Kubota made with his words. "I give you story now," he once said, "and you learn speak good, eh?" It was my job, as the disciple of his preaching I had then become, Ananda to his Buddha, to reassure him with a promise. "You learn speak good like the Dillingham," he'd say another time, referring to the wealthy scion of the grower family who had once run, unsuccessfully, for one of Hawai'i's first senatorial seats. Or he'd then invoke a magical name, the name of one of his heroes, a man he thought particularly exemplary and righteous. "Learn speak dah good Ing-rish like *Mistah Inouye*," Kubota shouted. "He *lick* dah Dillingham even in debate. I saw on *terre-bision* myself." He was remembering the debates before the first senatorial election just before Hawai'i was admitted to the Union as its fiftieth state. "You *tell* story," Kubota would end. And I had my injunction.

The town we settled in after the move from Hawai'i is called Gardena, the independently incorporated city south of Los Angeles and north of San Pedro harbor. At its northern limit, it borders on Watts and Compton—black towns. To the southwest are Torrance and Redondo Beach—white towns. To the rest of LA, Gardena is primarily famous for having legalized five-card draw poker after the war. On Vermont Boulevard, its eastern border, there is a dingy little Vegas-like strip of card clubs with huge parking lots and flickering neon signs that spell out "The Rainbow" and "The Horseshoe" in timed sequences of varicolored lights. The town is only secondarily famous as the largest community of Japanese Americans in the United States outside of Honolulu, Hawai'i. When I was in high school there, it seemed to me that every Sansei kid I knew wanted to be a doctor, an engineer, or a pharmacist. Our fathers were gardeners or electricians or nurserymen or ran small businesses catering to other Japanese Americans. Our mothers worked in civil service for the city or as cashiers for Thrifty Drug. What the kids wanted was a good job, good pay, a fine home, and no troubles. No one wanted to mess with the law—from either side—and no one wanted to mess with language or art. They all talked about getting into the right clubs so that they could go to the right schools. There was a certain kind of sameness, an intensely enforced system of conformity. Style was all. Boys wore moccasin-sewn shoes from Flagg Brothers, black A-1 slacks, and Kensington shirts with high collars. Girls wore their hair up in stiff bouffants solidified in hair spray and knew all the latest dances from the Slauson to the Funky Chicken. We did well in chemistry and in math, no one who was Japanese but me spoke in English class or in history unless called upon, and no one talked about World War II. The day after Robert Kennedy was assassinated after winning the California Democratic primary, we worked on calculus and elected class coordinators for the prom, featuring the Fifth Dimension. We avoided grief. We avoided government. We avoided strong feelings and dangers of any kind. Once punished, we tried to maintain a concerted emotional and social discipline and would not willingly seek to fall out of the narrow margin of protective favor again.

But when I was thirteen, in junior high, I'd not understood why it was so difficult for my classmates, those who were themselves Japanese American, to talk about the relocation. They had cringed too when I tried to bring it up during our discussions of World War II. I was Hawaiian-born. They were mainland-born. Their parents had been in camp, had been the ones to suffer the complicated experience of having to distance themselves from their own history and all things Japanese in order to make their way back and into the American social and economic mainstream. It was out of this sense of shame and a fear of stigma, I was only beginning to understand, that the Nisei had silenced themselves. And for their children, among whom I grew up, they wanted no heritage, no culture, no contact with a defiled history. I recall the silence very well. The Japanese American children around me were burdened in a way I was not. Their injunction was silence. Mine was to speak.

Away at college, in another protected world in its own way as magical to me as the Hawai'i of my childhood, I dreamed about my grandfather. I would be tired from studying languages, practicing German conjugations or scripting an army's worth of Chinese ideograms on a single sheet of paper, and Kubota would come to me as I drifted off into sleep. Or I would have walked across the newly mown ball field in back of my dormitory, cutting through a street-side phalanx of ancient eucalyptus trees on my way to visit friends off campus, and I would think of him, his anger, and his sadness.

I don't know myself what makes someone feel that kind of need to have a story they've lived through be deposited somewhere, but I can guess. I think about the *Iliad*, the *Odyssey*, the *History of the Peloponnesian War* of Thucydides, and a myriad of the works of literature I've studied. A character, almost a *topoi* he occurs so often, is frequently the witness who gives personal testimony about an event the rest of his community cannot even imagine. The Sibyl is such a character. And Philomela, the maid whose tongue is cut out so that she will not tell that she has been raped by her own brother-in-law, king of Thebes. There are the dime novels, the epic blockbusters Hollywood makes into miniseries, and then there are the plain, relentless stories of witnesses who have suffered through horrors major and minor that have marked and changed their lives. I haven't myself talked to Holocaust victims. But I've read their survival stories and their stories of witness and been revolted and moved by them. My father-in-law tells me his war stories again and again and I listen. A Mennonite who set aside the strictures of his own church in order to serve, he was a Marine code-man in the Pacific during World War II, in the Signal Corps on Guadalcanal, Morotai, and Bougainville. He was part of the island-hopping maneuver MacArthur had devised to win the war in the Pacific. He saw friends die from bombs which exploded not ten yards away. When he was with the 298th Signal Corps attached to the Thirteenth Air Force, he saw plane after plane come in and crash just short of the runway, killing their crews, setting the jungle ablaze with oil and gas fires. Emergency wagons would scramble, bouncing over newly bulldozed land men used just the afternoon before for a football game. Every time we go fishing together, whether it's in a McKenzie boat drifting for salmon in Tillamook Bay or taking a lunch break from wading the riffles of a stream in the Cascades, my father-in-law tells me about what happened to him and the young men in his unit. One was a Jewish boy from Brooklyn. One was a foulmouthed kid from Kansas. They died. And he *has* to tell me. And I *have* to listen. It's a ritual payment the young owe their elders who have survived. The evacuation and relocation is something like that.

Kubota, my grandfather, had been ill with Alzheimer's disease for some time before he died. At the house he'd built on Kamehameha Highway in Hau'ula, a seacoast village just down the road from La'ie, where he had his store, he'd wander out from the garage or greenhouse where he'd set up a workbench, and trudge down to the beach or up toward the line of pines he'd planted while employed by the Works Progress Administration during the thirties. Kubota thought he was going fishing. Or he thought he was back at work for Roosevelt planting pines as a wind- or soilbreak on the windward flank of the Ko'olau Mountains, emerald monoliths rising out of sea and cane fields from Waialua to Kaneohe. When I visited, my grandmother would send me down to the beach to fetch him. Or I'd run down Kam Highway a quarter mile or so and find him hiding in the cane field by the roadside, counting stalks, measuring circumferences in the claw of his thumb and forefinger. The look on his face was confused or concentrated—I didn't know which. But I guessed he was going fishing again. I'd grab him and walk him back to his house on the highway. My grandmother would shut him in a room.

Within a few years, Kubota had a stroke and survived it; then he had another one and was completely debilitated. The family decided to put him in a nursing home in Kahuku, just set back from the highway, within a mile or so of Kahuku Point and the Tanaka Store where he had his first job as a stock boy. He lived there three years, and I visited him once with my aunt. He was like a potato that had been worn down by cooking. Everything on him—his eyes, his teeth, his legs and torso—seemed like it had been sloughed away. What he had been was mostly gone now and I was looking at the nub of a man. In a wheelchair, he grasped my hands and tugged on them—violently. His hands were still thick, and, I believed, strong enough to lift me out of my own seat into his lap. He murmured something in Japanese—he'd long ago ceased to speak any English. My aunt and I cried a little, and we left him.

I remember walking out on the black asphalt of the parking lot of the nursing home. It was heat-cracked and eroded already, and grass had veined itself into the interstices. There were coconut trees around, a cane field I could see across the street, and the ocean I knew was pitching a surf just beyond it. The green Ko'olaus came up behind us. Somewhere nearby, alongside the beach, there was an abandoned airfield in the middle of the canes. As a child, I'd come upon it playing one day, and my friends and I kept returning to it, day after day, playing war or sprinting games or coming to fly kites. I recognize it even now when I see it on TV—it's used as a site for action scenes in the detective shows Hollywood always sets in the Islands: a helicopter chasing the hero racing away in a Ferrari, or gun dealers making a clandestine rendezvous on the abandoned runway. It was the old airfield strafed by Japanese planes the day the major flight attacked Pearl Harbor. It was the airfield the FBI thought my grandfather had targeted in his night fishing and signaling with the long surf poles he'd stuck in the sandy bays near Kahuku Point.

Kubota died a short while after I visited him, but not, I thought, without giving me a final message. I was on the mainland, in California studying for Ph.D. exams, when my grandmother called me with the news. It was a relief. He'd suffered from his debilitation a long time and I was grateful he'd gone. I went home for the funeral and gave the eulogy. My grandmother and I took his ashes home in a small, heavy metal box wrapped in a black *furoshiki*—a large, silk scarf. She showed me the name the priest had given to him on his death, scripted with a calligraphy brush on a long, narrow strip of plain wood. Buddhist commoners, at death, are given priestly names, received symbolically into the clergy. The idea is that, in their next life, one of scholarship and leisure, they might meditate and attain the enlightenment the religion is aimed at. *"Shaku Shūchi"* the ideograms read. It was Kubota's Buddhist name, incorporating characters from his family and given names. It meant "Shining Wisdom of the Law." He died on Pearl Harbor Day, December 7, 1983.

After some years, after I'd finally come back to live in Volcano again, only once did I dream of Kubota, my grandfather. It was the same night I'd heard that HR 442, the redress bill for Japanese Americans, had been signed into law. In my dream that night Kubota was torching, and he sang a Japanese song, a querulous and wavery folk ballad, as he hung paper lanterns on bamboo poles stuck into the sand in the shallow water of the lagoon behind the reef near Kahuku Point. Then he was at a worktable, smoking a hand-rolled cigarette, letting it dangle from his lips Bogart-style, as he drew, daintily and skillfully, with a narrow trim brush, ideogram after ideogram on a score of paper lanterns he had hung in a dark shed to dry. He had painted a talismanic mantra onto each lantern, the ideogram for the word "red" in Japanese, a bit of art blended with some superstition, a piece of sympathetic magic appealing to the magenta coloring on the rough skins of the schooling, night-feeding fish he wanted to attract to his baited hooks. He strung them from pole to pole in the dream then, hiking up his khaki worker's pants so his white ankles showed and wading through the shimmering black waters of the sand flats and then the reef. "The moon is leaving, leaving," he sang in Japanese. "Take me deeper in the savage sea." He turned and crouched like an ice racer then, leaning forward so that his unshaven face almost touched the light film of water. I could see the light stubble of beard like a fine gray ash covering the lower half of his face. I could see his gold-rimmed spectacles. He held a small wooden boat in his cupped hands and placed it lightly on the sea and pushed it away. One of his lanterns was on it and, written in small neat rows like a sutra scroll, it had been decorated with the silvery names of all our dead.

JEANNE
WAKATSUKI
HOUSTON

COLORS

JEANNE WAKATSUKI HOUSTON *is the co-author of* Farewell to Manzanar, *a work based on her family's experience in a World War II Japanese American internment camp. For the teleplay script, which she also co-authored, she received a Humanitas Prize and a 1976 Emmy Award nomination. Born in Inglewood, California, in 1934, she has spent most of her life on the Pacific Coast. She holds a BA in sociology from*

San Jose State University and pursued graduate work at San Francisco State and at the Sorbonne in France. In 1984, she was one of fourteen American women over forty honored with the prestigious Wonder Woman Award for outstanding achievements in the pursuit of truth and positive social change. She received a Bellagio Fellowship for 1995.

COLORS! SEEING THE STAGES OF MY LIFE AS colors. Where did I get such an idea? I trace it back to 1956, when I was twenty-one years old working as a group counselor in a Northern California juvenile detention hall. It was my first full-time job. I was supervising teenage girls brought in for violating probation, running away from home, and sometimes more serious crimes. But most often the offense was "incorrigibility."

Jessica T. (fictitious name) was a racial mix of Filipina, Samoan, and French. One of the "incorrigibles," she was brought to the hall for breaking probation, or more precisely, for getting into a fight. Jessica was well known to the staff at Hillcrest. She was sixteen and since the age of twelve, when she was booked for running away from a foster home, had been a frequent visitor to the hall.

When I came on shift one afternoon, the other supervisors were chatting in the lounge about Jessica, lamenting her fate, which they believed would be a sentence to CYA (California Youth Authority). I had never met her, but surmised from the tone of the talk that she was someone special, someone I would have to contend with in a serious way.

"Now, don't let her looks scare you," said one of my colleagues. "She can grimace like a gorilla, but she's really a teddy bear."

By the time I unlocked the door to the rec room where the girls enjoyed free time outside their otherwise locked cubicles, I was anxious about meeting Jessica. A blast of music greeted me. I looked around the lively room. She wasn't hard to miss. Almost six feet tall, wiry black hair frizzed out in a halo (unusual hairstyle in those pre-sixties days), she stood away from the group, tapping her feet and snapping her fingers to Elvis Presley and "Blue Suede Shoes."

I introduced myself. "I'm Miss Waka. You must be Jessica."

Jessica glared. "How come you're *Miss* Waka?" She emphasized "Miss." Her voice was melodic and didn't match the piercing hostile eyes.

I waited for her to grimace, trying to remain calm and in control of the situation. All the supervisors shortened their names. Mrs. Finlof was Finney; Mrs. Sullivan was Sully; Mrs. Coulter was Coulty, etc. Since I was so young, only a few years older than some of the girls, the staff thought it would be more appropriate that I be called *Miss* Waka, instead of a nickname. I thought fast. "Well, can you think of a good name to call me?"

Her eyes flickered, met mine, and looked away. Then she broke into laughter, a light tinkling sound, incongruous with her bulky body.

"I sure can." Her eyes now were friendly. "I know you must really be crazy to work in a place like this . . . really crazy. So you should be called Wacky."

From that day on, I was known at Hillcrest as Wacky. There was some talk among the staff that the nickname could be construed as disrespectful, but since I was not offended, the question was dropped. The truth of the matter was that I liked being seen as "fun" and "unserious," which the nickname implied. It was very sober business trying to maintain a "homelike" atmosphere in an institution with locked doors, high cement walls, and regimented routines. I wanted to seem frivolous, to lighten the responsibility and authority so loudly announced by the ring of keys jangling from my belt.

Jessica and I became friends. The court date when she would learn her fate was late in being set, which meant she remained at the hall for an unusually long time. I was then part-time, but worked some day shifts, allowing closer contact with the girls once they were out of school (held at the hall). I discovered Jessica had unusual artistic talent. I encouraged her to spend her spare time drawing and painting, which she plunged into with great enthusiasm. Even though I knew very little about art, artistic subjects became our mode of communication.

She would say, "Wacky, today is a green day, so I'm painting landscapes . . . you know, like Picasso or whatever his name . . . even though I'm feeling blue." Then she'd laugh, her big full-lipped mouth open, exposing white gapped teeth.

I'd say, "Well, Jessica, make good use of your blue period." And I'd drop some artists' names I really knew nothing about ". . . like Rembrandt and Monet. They used blue."

When she was upset and angry, usually after a visit with her probation officer, she would stomp down the hall muttering, slamming a fist rhythmically into her open palm. Her face would be dark and ferocious, and she'd pass me saying, "Don't come near me, Wacky, I'm really muddy." Even though I was sure she would never turn that wrath on me, I heeded her words, warned by the tattooed letters L O V E on the fist smashing into her open palm.

I brought her paints and paper and books on art. In a way, I was educating myself as well. Soon, the rec hall and her room's walls were covered with paintings, splashes of vivid colors—rainbows, flowers, butterflies, jungle animals. The pictures were not what one expected to see from a person who looked like Jessica. With her wild hair, powerful size, and often tough vocabulary, she kept the other girls at a distance. But with the staff, particularly me, she was gentle and humorous.

One day I was called into the front office and mildly reprimanded by an uncomfortable administrator. It appeared I might be practicing favoritism, he said. Perhaps I was identifying with Jessica. Since I was at least a foot shorter and sixty pounds lighter, I was nonplussed by the remark. "What do you mean 'identifying' with her?" I asked innocently.

He cleared his throat. "You're both Asians, you know. You don't want the other kids to think you're favoring her because of race."

I was astounded. This hadn't entered my head. Speechless, and also too unconscious then about my own identity as an Asian American to respond indignantly, I only nodded my head and left his office.

I was the only Asian group supervisor working at the hall during the day. (A Japanese American male worked the graveyard shift.) Asian delinquents were rare. "Orientals," as we were called then, were the model minority, hiding in the closet of "respectability," hoping to become invisible in a society still reeling from the Second World War and Korea.

Angry at this accusation, but still too young and inexperienced to fight back, I decided to deal with the situation by withdrawing from Jessica. I tried to do it subtly by working the graveyard or mornings, or if I was on shift during the afternoon, I would become involved in other activities. This didn't affect her.

"Hey, Wacky," she'd say, friendly as ever, "when are we going to paint a mural together? Let's do Chicano . . . like Diego Rivera!" It was as if she knew my plight, understanding institutions and group behavior better than I.

. . .

Then the day arrived when she was sentenced to the California Youth Authority, the last stop on the road that had begun in a foster home, spiraled down to
a convent and then a juvenile hall. Her probation officer came to see me. "I'd
like to ask a very unorthodox favor of you," she said. "Jessica will be transported to Sacramento next week and we're afraid she's going to bolt. We hate
to handcuff her in the car . . . and she said she wouldn't run if you could
accompany her."

Miss Brown was a tough PO but also had a heart. No one wanted any juvie
to attempt an escape while being transported to CYA. The consequences could
be formidable. I agreed to go.

We left San Mateo at midmorning, timing it so we could stop for lunch at a
popular restaurant outside of Davis. Somewhat like the final supper for con-
victs in death row, lunch at the fine restaurant was a last meal on the "outs"
before the kids were locked up by the state. They could order anything they
wanted—which was usually a hamburger, fries, and a Coke. Jessica ordered a
shrimp salad.

"I'm really scared, Wacky," she said with a trembling voice. Tears rolled
down her cheeks. The driver of the car, another PO returning to Sacramento,
dabbed her own cheeks with a handkerchief. She was crying as much as Jessica. I later learned this was not uncommon among officers having to transport
delinquents to CYA. To them, as far as rehabilitation was concerned, it might
as well be death row.

I didn't cry, remembering the warning not to identify. Then Jessica said,
"You know, Wacky, I understand. You used to be such bright colors. You
were red and orange and purple and turquoise. And now you're fading. You're
like a color that's fading away."

By the time we dropped Jessica off in Sacramento, I was drained. After
leaving the restaurant, she had wept the whole time, her large body shaking as
if she were riding a motorcycle. My final words to her were "Don't be afraid,
Jessica. Van Gogh was crazy and Gauguin had leprosy. Look how famous they
are!" The absurdity of my statement made her laugh. She relaxed and was
actually smiling when she walked haughtily toward the building with the PO.
Before entering she waved and yelled, "Bye, Wacky. Stay colorful."

RED

The color red pervades my earliest memories of childhood. Primary and powerful, its hues are vibrant, lighting up a time that was grounded in family.

The youngest of ten children, I was born in Inglewood, California, on September 26, 1934. At the time, my father was farming what was then the outskirts of Los Angeles. Today, huge airliners streak across asphalt runways which cover the rich soil where he raised strawberries, green beans, and lettuce.

I have no concrete memories of that time, only stories told within the family, of life on the farm. My older brothers and sisters talk about how I used to get lost in the bean patch, wandering for hours amidst tall poles of green beans, a barefoot waif wailing in the succulent forest while the rest of the family searched. I don't remember this, and in a way, I am glad. My family refers to the thirties as the dust bowl period of *our* history, dull and gray instead of the bright red I remember.

"You're so lucky, Jeanie," they say as I cringe with guilt. "We had to eat cabbage sandwiches and line our shoes with cardboard to cover the holes in the soles."

So I was born during the Great Depression. But when I was two my father turned to commercial fishing, and we moved to Ocean Park, a small coastal community whose main attraction was its amusement pier. Ocean Park Pier, now long gone, was our "playground." It was a magical place. With sweet vanilla perfume from cotton candy, candied apples and saltwater taffy wafting around the noisy shooting galleries and thrill rides, and neon lights and freak shows bombarding my senses, it is no wonder my memories remain so vivid. The pier was my nursery school, the amusement attendants my sitters. The neighborhood kids and I spent most of our days there.

The roller coaster, shoot-the-chutes, and Ferris wheel were forbidden territories, which was all right with me, since I saw too many dazed revelers screaming with terror and throwing up after rides. It amazed me anyone wanted to be thrilled like that. The freak shows and tunnel of horror were more my speed. Although I wasn't supposed to go, I would sneak in, wrapping my arms around someone's legs while I stared at the bearded lady and Siamese twins. I see a sharp picture of the pinhead dressed in a Japanese kimono, nervously twisting a sequined purse with thin blue-veined hands. He especially intrigued me because he was small, not much taller than me, and wore heavy makeup, bright lipstick and face powder which failed to cover the purple five o'clock shadow of his lower face. His hair was swept up into a small bun from which dangled Japanese ornaments.

One day, as I gazed at him—more awed than curious—he looked me straight in the eyes. I remember being shocked, feeling a pang of pity, feeling badly and not understanding why. I know now those beady black eyes had drawn from my childish heart its first feeling of compassion. I never went back, even when the rest of the gang came ranting home one day, excitedly describing the "geek" who bit off chicken heads. I had no interest, and as it turned out—so the story goes—my sister Lillian got too close to the wild man and he tore out a clump of her hair.

The merry-go-round was my favorite. Giant roan stallions with flowing manes and jeweled saddles: I watched them gallop past, forelegs bent gracefully in the air, rising and falling in time with the nickelodeon music. I fell in love with the marbled stallions, never missing a chance to ride them, which was often, since the attendant let the gang ride free. I can still feel the smooth cold porcelain of muscled flanks, which I stroked and petted after a day's hard ride. I was faithful to my inert friends for many months until a new concession opened at the end of the pier. It was a live pony. A little white horse tethered to a stake posted in the middle of a circle. After riding around the circle, children could then be photographed, posing in cowboy hats and chaps or fur hats and muffs. I was enthralled. A real live horse that could respond to my passionate devotion!

But it was expensive. I nagged and whined at Mama to let me ride the pony. Finally she gave in, but only after deciding a picture in my new red coat she bought for my older sister's wedding would be worth it.

As "karma" would have it, my infidelity had its consequences. After riding around in circles, proudly displaying my new coat, we stopped for the photo.

For some reason, the pony bucked. I flew off the saddle onto the ground. Screaming, I rolled in the manure-laden dirt, more terrified by the shouting adults and Mama's cries than by the fall. But it was traumatic. The smell of horse manure can still accelerate my heartbeat. I have never ridden a horse since, except at fairs and amusement parks where those shiny porcelain horses beckon like long-lost lovers.

YELLOW

The Second World War is a swirl of yellow. Yellow for the hot, dusty desert where I spent three and a half years in an internment camp for Americans of Japanese ancestry. Yellow for stinging whirlwinds and fierce dust storms that pricked the skin like needles and coated everything, including our lips and eyelashes, with thick ocher powder.

When Japan bombed Pearl Harbor on December 7, 1941, I was seven years old. The FBI came to our house and arrested my father on false charges that he was supplying enemy Japanese submarines with oil from his fishing boat. He was incarcerated in a federal prison in Bismarck, North Dakota. We didn't see him again for a year.

In April 1942, my mother, nine brothers and sisters (some married), and I arrived at Manzanar, located off Highway 395 in eastern California between Death Valley and Independence. The book *Farewell to Manzanar*, authored by myself and my husband, James D. Houston, relates in detail my remembrances of camp life.

But the book was written twenty years ago, the writing of it releasing and thus healing the deepest wounds of that experience. Since then, other memories have risen to the surface. Only after that project was completed did I recall that my first experience with books occurred in Manzanar.

Before going there, I remember having a fleeting acquaintance in kindergarten and first grade with readers and children's pictorials. In our home at Ocean Park there were few books. Thus, it was with incredulous astonishment that I viewed a huge pile of hardbound books mounded in the center of a firebreak near our barracks.

In the first months at Manzanar, there were no schools or libraries. And so, it seems, some charitable organizations, apprised of this, had sent truckloads of books to stock a library. Unfortunately, there were no available buildings to shelter them, so they were dumped in the middle of the spaces between barrack blocks—bleak, sandy acres left open in case of fire.

The pile was a jagged mountain range as huge as a two-story building. I had never seen anything like it and scrambled up the peak with other kids, sliding over slick pages, jamming legs between crevices. We played mountain climbing and war, throwing books at each other and hiding in foxholes dug into the sides. It didn't occur to us to read the material which provided us with such a wondrous playground. But after a week or so of diligent mountaineering, a few thunderstorms and dust storms dampened our enthusiasm. The book heap, now worn down to a hill, was abandoned.

One sunny afternoon, as I walked across the firebreak, a glint caught my eye. The book graveyard was still except for pages fluttering in the wind like earthbound kites. I soon discovered the source of light: framed in a shiny gold gilt, a scene of Rapunzel letting down her long hair from a tower's window shone from a book of fairy tales. I was entranced. Who was this beautiful lady with long yellow hair? I leafed through the book and found I could read the print. That afternoon I sat down amidst the torn and water-stained wreckage and read every story in *Hans Christian Andersen's Fairy Tales*.

Until the books were removed to the empty barrack which became our library, I explored the mountain again and again, no longer adventuring, but searching and scavenging for more stories of fairies, and princes, wicked step-mothers, and gem-studded kingdoms. Like a prospector seeking a second strike, I jealously guarded my stake, rummaging and examining until I found dozens of fairy tale books and took them home to our barracks.

This was my initiation into the imaginary world of written words. From fairy tales I advanced to mysteries—Nancy Drew became my idol. I read about Katrina, the Russian ballerina who rose from a starving peasant background to the Czar's palace. I read some classics—*The Scotsman, The Deerslayer, The Pathfinder*—and even attempted *Wuthering Heights*. At ages nine and ten, the mind is resilient. It is open and inquisitive. It is also bent on survival. Books became my major form of recreation, my channel to worlds outside the confined and monotonous routine of camp life.

ORANGE

I look into the kaleidoscope and see the period after Manzanar as essentially the color orange—intense, concentrated, and rich—rich with memories of awakenings, of social interaction outside the family. Puberty and hormones. Adolescence and social initiations.

When the Second World War ended with the bombing of Hiroshima and Nagasaki, we were relocated to a defense housing project in Long Beach, California. Ironically, it was only a few miles from Terminal Island, the Japanese fishing community where my father last fished before he was picked up by the FBI. For many years Terminal Island had been a unique ghetto populated by Japanese fishermen and their families. Today it is part of the port of Long Beach and a base for the Navy.

Cabrillo Homes was a large cluster of brown square buildings, some two-storied with eight apartments and the others long, low bungalows of four. They were federally built for defense plant workers and families who swarmed to California during the war, drawn by work in the shipyards. When the war ended, some returned to their homes in the South, Midwest, and East, but many remained, still living in the housing project.

What a different world! From a racially homogeneous one-mile-square community, I entered a multiracial and multicultural matrix, a ghetto where our only common denominator was poverty. It was my first experience living among African Americans and Latinos. In Ocean Park, we had lived in a Caucasian neighborhood, mostly Jewish and Italian. At Cabrillo Homes, I met, for the first time, Americans of Polish, Cuban, and Mexican descent. I heard, for the first time, the twangs and drawls of the language of Oklahoma, Texas, Missouri, Georgia—even the clipped whine of Boston.

Ah! Cabrillo Homes! Crossroads for America's hopefuls—halfway house for America's economic and political refugees. We were an early experiment in cross-cultural living. At Manzanar, Glenn Miller and the rising young swooner Frank Sinatra were our musical idols. In the housing project, country-and-western music and Mexican *rancheras* blared from open windows. I became a fan of Roy Acuff, Red Foley, and Bob Wills and the Texas Playboys. I learned to sing in Spanish, delighting my Mexican friends with renditions of "Tú Solo Tú" and "Ella," popular *rancheras* sung by Jorge Negrete and Pedro Infante. At age eleven, I was thrust into this varied environment—a new stucco landscape, strange and somewhat fearsome, but alight with bright orange.

My first boyfriend lived across the street from me. Green-eyed, blond, and freckled, Billy Fortner was the archetypal "boy next door." He was an only child whose parents had come to California from North Carolina to work for the Navy. When his mother called from their upstairs apartment, "Bil-leee, Bil-leee," in her soft southern drawl, I envied him and wished my mother would call for me with such tenderness and gentility. But my mother, of course, would never dream of calling for any of us publicly; she never even raised her voice in the home.

I learned to play post office and spin the bottle with Billy, Doris Jean, and several other adolescents in the neighborhood. I mention Doris Jean because she was the spunky ringleader of our clandestine games. She lived in the apartment underneath Billy's, part of a large compound of buildings from which I felt excluded. Our apartment was in a long, low bungalow. Where the kids across the street played seemed out of bounds for me, a private club whose membership mandated living in that complex. The main reason, though, was that the families who lived there were all Caucasian and from the South.

But one day Doris Jean knocked on my door and after introducing herself asked if I wanted to work with her and some other kids for her father. Flattered by the invitation, I enthusiastically accepted without even asking what the job would be. It turned out Doris Jean's stepfather operated cigarette vending machines which he placed in restaurants and bars around town. In those days, a pack of cigarettes cost about twenty-two cents. The machines took quarters, which meant the customer's change should be three cents. Because the machines did not make change, our job was cutting a slit in the side of the cellophane wrapping around the pack and sliding three pennies down its side. He paid us ten cents a carton.

Doris Jean's parents usually were absent on Saturdays. When they were gone we worked fast so we could play the games wily Doris Jean had learned in Texas and magnanimously taught us. Although Billy was part of the gang, he didn't stuff pennies, since he was a few years older and had a paper route.

But he joined our after-work soirees, which thrilled the girls, who all had a crush on him.

I experienced my first kiss playing spin the bottle. It was Billy's spin and the bottle stopped, pointing at me! I remember apprehension, excitement, curiosity, and fear churning within as we entered the bathroom and closed the door.

"I don't know how to kiss," I whispered.

"Don't be scared," he said. "Just close your eyes."

Shaking, I squinted my eyes tight and waited for what seemed like hours for the touch on my lips that was supposed to change my life forever. It was disappointing. His lips could easily have been the back of my own hand.

But I liked the game, mostly because of its secretiveness. Even though Billy's kiss never sent me into ecstasy, I loved him wholeheartedly. He was always kind, and since I didn't have a bike like most of the other kids, he would take me for rides and even offered to teach me how to maneuver one.

I was shocked a few months later when Vernon Hicks came to our apartment with a message.

"Billy's leaving this afternoon, goin' back to North Carolina," he whispered conspiratorily, "and wants to kiss you goodbye."

I ran across the street thinking there was going to be one last game of spin the bottle at Doris Jean's house. But Billy was standing by the stairs, dressed in new going-away clothes. He beckoned for me to come behind the building. It was clear there wasn't going to be any game. At first I hesitated, terrified by the thought of being kissed by choice rather than by chance. But love for cavalier Billy overcame my timidity and I joined him. Neither of us said a word. I closed my eyes and with pursed lips waited for the usual brush, the sweet but impersonal touch. This time it was different. Gently he cupped my face with his hands and kissed my lips . . . not once but three times . . . softly and slowly. I remember thinking this was the way they kissed in movies. Then his mother's soprano voice called, "Bil-leee . . . Bil-leee . . . we're going."

"Goodbye," Billy said, squeezing my hand.

He hesitated, waiting for me to say something. But I couldn't respond. I was frozen. I finally uttered, "Goodbye, Billy." That's all I said. To this day I have regretted never saying what I wanted to . . . like "Write me" or "Where are you going?" or "I love you and thanks for being such a great first-kisser."

Billy disappeared from my life in a suitcase-laden taxi—his father seated in front with the driver and he with his mother in the back seat, waving to me even as the orange-and-black cab rounded the corner a block away.

Whenever I hear a soft southern drawl or anyone mentions North Carolina, I wonder about Billy, my blond and freckled samurai. I wonder where he went, what he became—and if he ever remembered me.

I was still living in Cabrillo Homes when the idea of becoming a writer germinated. I was in the seventh grade. Our junior high was new and didn't have a journalism class from which a newspaper could be written and published. A search for writing talent began by having students write an essay about a memorable event in their lives. The winners would form the journalism class—if they wanted—and publish the school paper and annual.

I wrote about hunting grunion in Ocean Park with my family before the war. On full-moon nights when the tides were high, the grunion would "run." Small, silvery fish about the size of anchovies, they would fill the waves, fluttering and flipping, glinting in the moonlight as my family scooped them up with buckets. We cooked and ate them there on the beach, the bright moon and bonfire turning night into twilight, while a balmy Southern California breeze cooled the summer air.

On the strength of that essay I was asked to join the journalism project. Until that moment I had no idea what the word "journalism" meant. But I was intrigued and enthusiastically plunged into the new class. I soon became editor-in-chief of the school paper, which we called the *Chatterbox*.

The step from reading fairy tales to editing a newspaper was a big one, and, I see now, this experience in junior high school was one of the crucial events in my life. That I could write was clearly programmed in my mind by a wise teacher who knew about validating youngsters, about directing them to higher goals—even when circumstances did not seem to support it. In the late forties, with the Second World War barely over, who would encourage a young Japanese American girl living in a ghetto to work toward becoming a writer? Only an idealistic, fair-minded person. I was lucky to have met such a person in junior high school, my English teacher.

She planted the seed, but it didn't really sprout for many years. Although I continued to write for my high school newspaper in Long Beach and majored in journalism for the first two years at San Jose State University, I had no tangible goal. In those days, Brenda Starr was a comic book character who was a glamorous newspaper reporter. In a childish way, she was my idol. Somehow I was going to be a newspaper journalist like her! This was fantasy, of course. In my second year of college, reality set in.

One day I went to see the Journalism Department head for advice about my major. I didn't know him very well, having taken only one class from him, "Press and the Public." I used to see him rushing around campus, in his navy-blue suit and tie, looking like he had just scooped the story of the year. I heard he had been a rather famous newspaper correspondent before he came to San Jose State.

I sat down in his office, a messy room with yellowed newspaper clippings on the wall and scattered over his desk. A small Persian rug, gray with lint, covered part of the floor.

"Now, Jeanne, just what do you intend to do with a journalism degree?" he asked.

"I really don't know," I answered. "That's why I've come to see you. I guess I would like to be a reporter."

He peered at me with steady blue eyes. "I'm going to be honest with you, my dear. Newspaper writing jobs are hard to come by for men. For women, it's almost impossible."

I was crushed. I had known it was a tough field for females since only a few of us were majors, but I wanted to believe becoming an Asian Brenda Starr was possible.

"You might think of switching over to advertising." He continued when I didn't respond, "It's still in the Journalism Department."

My heart sinking, I said, "Oh, I don't think I'd like advertising."

He scratched his curly brown hair, gray at the temples. Without looking at me, he said, "I can only tell you that you would have a very hard row to hoe trying to land a job with a newspaper. Believe me." He hesitated. "You're a woman . . . and you're Oriental. That's double tough."

At first I didn't know how to take his words. Was he racially prejudiced himself? Or was he being kind, trying to help prevent a more disastrous disappointment later on?

Gently, he said, "Maybe you should think about changing your major. You're only a junior now, so it won't be a problem."

Fighting back tears, I thanked him and left the office. After a few days, I realized he spoke the truth. All the Asians on campus were majoring in "invisible" fields—lab techs, engineering, nursing, occupational therapy, secretarial —fields open to Asians for jobs. I decided to change my major to sociology and social welfare.

GREEN

Three years before I had that conversation, my family had moved from Cabrillo Homes up north to San Jose, where my father tried for the last time to find a future in farming. San Jose in 1952 was the center of a lush agricultural region. Prune, apricot, and cherry orchards crisscrossed the Santa Clara Valley, carpeting it with fragrant blossoms in the spring. Compared to the tough streets and bare landscape of Cabrillo Homes, San Jose was gentle and quiet, a midsize farming community enjoying its organic wealth.

My father raised strawberries—in the beginning as a sharecropper with Driscoll, Inc., and later on his own. At the housing project, my friendship with two Mexican sisters and with members of a car "gang" called the King's Men had given me some training to communicate with my father's farm workers. They were *braceros* from Mexico and spoke no English. I could speak some Spanish, mostly street argot.

When we first moved up north, I was devastated. I liked the fast street life and found farming dull and "unsophisticated." I missed my friends. When the Mexican *braceros* arrived to pick berries, I found comfort in speaking with them and singing the Mexican songs I had learned at Cabrillo Homes.

Looking at the green memory fragment, I think of Calistro. Jovial, good-humored Calistro! Middle-aged and married, he had left his family in Chihuahua to earn money in El Norte. He had four children, whose picture he proudly showed to everyone he met, and he was a good musician, strumming an old cracked guitar during lunch hour to entertain the other workers.

One day I noticed him sitting barefoot by the irrigating flume. I thought he was cooling his feet in the water flowing through the open wooden trough. As I approached him, I saw he was lining his shoes with cardboard to cover large holes in the soles. I remembered my older sisters' and brothers' stories of the Depression, how they too had resoled their worn shoes with cardboard. I had always felt guilty for not suffering the deprivations they had to endure. When I saw Calistro reenacting that potent family story, I decided to atone. I bought him a new pair of boots.

Needless to say, he became a devoted friend. When I revealed I could sing in Spanish too, our friendship was sealed. As we picked strawberries under the relentless California sun, we sang to alleviate the hardship of stoop labor and heat. He taught me a cheerful song called "Mi Cafetal," which I still can sing today.

Aunque la gente vive criticando
Me paso la vida sin pensar en nada
Pero no sabiendo que yo soy el hombre
Que tenga una hermosa y linda cafetal . . .

"Although people live criticizing the life I lead so idly, they do not know I am the man who has a beautiful coffee plantation. . . ." He loved bologna sandwiches, and I liked the hot burritos the *braceros* were served for their noon meal. We traded lunches. I always added a thick onion slice to the bologna sandwich, which he greatly appreciated.

By befriending the workers, I eased through the first summer away from Long Beach. When autumn arrived and the *braceros* began leaving, I had grown to like the pastoral pace, the clean green world of Northern California. But I hated saying goodbye to Calistro.

The day he left he brought me a gift. Wrapped in newspaper, it was a matchbox with a tiny worn crucifix tucked inside. The figure of Christ was silver, delicate and smooth, and the cross was fashioned out of dark wood. I knew it was probably Calistro's most valuable possession. I still have the crucifix, safely stored with other good-luck fetishes I have collected over the past years.

BLUE

Marriage. Blue diamonds, sapphires, sparkling turquoise light. The colors radiate from deep pools and surging surf, mountainous coastal valleys, lush rain forests—the jeweled landscape of the Hawaiian Islands.

At San Jose State I met Jim Houston. We were both journalism majors with Spanish minors and thus had all the same classes. We began dating. After graduating from college, Jim went to Hawai'i, and I remained on the mainland, working at Hillcrest Juvenile Hall.

After six months in the Islands, Jim sent me a Valentine. It was an unusual card, a long slender ti leaf with BE MY VALENTINE inked on one side and WILL YOU MARRY ME? on the other. I later learned the ti leaf was used in Hawai'i for ceremonial purposes, the belief being that it had powers to bless and consecrate. In those days mail from Hawai'i took at least two weeks. By the time the Valentine arrived, the usually lush green leaf was a brownish husk. But the message printed on it had not lost one bit of its luster.

Within a month, after a thirteen-hour flight from San Francisco, I arrived at Honolulu at seven in the morning. We were married that evening during a spectacular sunset at Kaiser Lagoon, now part of the Hilton Hawaiian Village complex in Waikiki. Jim and his friends had made all the arrangements weeks before; so our only task was to buy a ring, which we hurriedly did that morning.

We were married on the beach, where the only person wearing shoes was Reverend Sam Saffrey, who was fully attired in black robe, tie, and suit. Bible in hand, the sunset glinting off his glasses, he officiated the "traditional" part of the wedding.

For the Hawaiian part, Winona Beamer and Ed Kenny, professional singers and dancers whom Jim had befriended in Kona, performed a ritual of chants, drumming, and symbolic rites. Both Ed and Winona are steeped in their Hawaiian heritage and have worked at reviving Hawaiian culture for many years.

When we married in 1957, respect and acknowledgment of indigenous cultures was not as prevalent in the public consciousness as it is today. In fact, Winona recently revealed ours was the first wedding ceremony she had chanted for.

It was hauntingly beautiful. They blew conch shells—to the east, west, north, and south. They rattled gourds and planted a ti leaf in the sand. A burnished brown calabash held kukui nuts, rocks, and shells which Winona gracefully retrieved, each one symbolizing a quality bestowed on our marriage —kukui nut for strength, shells for protection, lava rock for union. The final rite was the draping of a long maile lei over both our shoulders. Maile is a vine that grows in high rain forests, mostly in the Big Island and Kaua'i, and is prized by Hawaiians for its fragrance. Like the ti leaf, it is often used to bless ceremonies. We have been married now for thirty-four years. Perhaps their "mana," or spiritual power, flowed through that maile lei, binding us together in a strong and unusual way.

After the discouraging conference with my journalism teacher at San Jose State, I gave up hope of becoming a writer. I plunged into psychology and sociology and wanted to become a field probation officer, those POs who worked in the community supervising delinquents on probation. Ironically, the same argument by my journalism professor to dissuade me from a writing career was also used by the head of the juvenile hall when I asked to apply for a job in the field.

"This county is not ready for an Oriental PO, especially female," I was told by an honest administrator. "You're better off as a group supervisor back in the unit."

Jim's intention, as long as I had known him, was to be a writer. By the time his request for marriage came, I was ready to hand over all my ambition to him and vicariously to experience his writing career as a "support" person. Besides, I was a "female of the fifties" and an American with a Japanese cultural background. It was not odd to "live in the country of his shadow"—a phrase I remembered from a Japanese poem.

The seed to become a writer, planted by my English teacher in junior high, nurtured through high school and for two years in college became dormant. It remained dormant for many years as my priority shifted from career for myself to wife and mother. It was not until 1971, fourteen years after our marriage on the beach, that the thought of writing resurfaced.

With Jim's encouragement and help, the long-buried seed came to life. *Farewell to Manzanar,* our collaboration, was my reentry into the world of writing other than as Jim's most avid fan. Later in this essay I relate in detail how and why this change came about.

GRAY AND LAVENDER

Jim held an ROTC commission from San Jose State. Our honeymoon in Paradise ended when he received orders from Texas to report for training at Lackland Air Force Base, after which he would be sent to England. That fall, I took a train across the states to New York, where I boarded a Dutch liner for a five-day crossing of the Atlantic and my first visit to Europe.

After the tranquil blue of Hawai'i, England was sharp, provocative, and heady. Elegant silver, delicate lavender lace. In many ways I found England to be almost overwhelmingly strange. Weather was a big factor. Except for the three harsh winters in Manzanar, I had never experienced such damp cold that penetrated through layers of wool straight to the bone.

It was the East Anglian fog—thick mist rising from bogs and marshes, shrouding the countryside, sometimes never lifting for weeks at a time. I was used to sandals and tennis shoes, cotton shorts and T-shirts and spending most of the day outdoors. I had to buy a new wardrobe, with unaccustomed accessories such as scarves, gloves, woolen underwear, and fleece-lined boots. There were days when I never ventured outside, loath to leave the warm hearth of the kitchen fireplace.

Our first home in England was a ten-room, four-hundred-year-old town house called "The Roost." Its rooms were small, some the size of large closets. Jim had to duck to pass through doorways. It was my first acquaintance with coal fires, musty Oriental rugs, and antique furniture. The crooked, creaking floors and dark hallways reminded me of scenes from *Great Expectations,* and I fully expected to see Lady Havisham sitting in one of the bedrooms—or the ghost, perhaps, of Mrs. Hawker, the lady of The Roost who had died there two years before.

When we moved into our home we had agreed with the rental agent to continue allowing a photographer the use of a small hut in the backyard as a darkroom. For several months we never laid eyes on our phantom neighbor. Then one rare warm and sunny day, I sat outside in the yard. A very tiny woman emerged from the shedlike building and, seeing me, approached shyly. She had short graying hair, thick and curly, and a smooth olive complexion. Even from a distance I was drawn to her smiling eyes, twinkling hazel eyes that looked both mischievous and curious.

As she walked toward me, I noticed she limped. Her back was deformed, causing her to appear stooped. "I must take your picture!" She almost shouted. It was as if lightning struck! Before I could answer or even say "hello," she had whirled around and in a flash had reentered the darkroom. When she emerged again, she carried a square box camera a little smaller than a shoebox. Dancing around me like a drunken elf, she snapped pictures, all the while chattering in heavily accented English.

"So you are the Americans," she said, looking at me through the camera lens. "But you are different, yes? You don't drive those giant cars, so much they look like tanks. And where are you from? China? Japan? Shangri-La? Oh, what a lovely picture this will be!"

Occasionally she would look up from her lens, not at me, but at the sky. I later learned she was famous for the soft natural quality of her work. She never used artificial lighting, depending fully on the light from the sun.

"It's nice, too, that you shop at the greengrocer's and Mr. Kincaide's butcher store. Most Americans shop at your base, and really, they keep their homes much too warm. It's not healthy. By the way, dear child, my name is Bertl . . . Bertl Gaye."

I was delightfully dumbfounded by this sprightly woman. When I recovered enough to tell her my name, she said, "But what a strange name you have . . . you don't look like a 'Hooston.' " She prolonged the "oo's." "Are you not a Chinese princess or a samurai warrior?"

I laughed and told her my father was actually from a samurai family in Japan. "Then I shall call you 'Sami,' " she said. "It suits you better."

We had no previous idea who our resident photographer was, nor had we made any inquiries. Yet Bertl seemed to know about us, about Americans. After we became friends, I learned the air base was not very popular among the villagers—especially when Americans brought huge cars, Buicks and Hudsons, that hogged their narrow roads, oversized refrigerators that blew out wiring. And, of course, there was the terrifying possibility the shrill jets streaking overhead, sometimes breaking their centuries-old windows, could be carrying nuclear bombs!

Bertl lived across the street, alone except for holidays and summer, when her son Adrian, then fourteen, came home from boarding school. I spent many afternoons and evenings in her spare but tasteful house. I helped garden, sipped afternoon tea, and enjoyed many delicious meals with her. She introduced me to classical music . . . Bach, Schubert, Dvořák, Brahms. During many bitterly cold evenings Jim and I huddled with Bertl in her small living room, playing Scrabble while Mozart's "Eine Kleine Nachtmusik" warmed our spirits.

Near the end of Jim's tour in England, she moved to Cambridge, where she leased a large flat with rooms she could rent to students. That summer she decided purposefully to board two German students attending English-language classes. I happened to be staying with her while Jim was traveling on the Continent.

"This is a lesson, Sami. Watch what happens," she said. "They will wonder if I am a Jew, but I will not tell them unless they ask. Then we can have a talk." She said this without malice. I knew that Bertl had fled Austria in the thirties and that her family had died in the death camps of Germany. She never talked much about her past. But sometimes she would reminisce about her youth in Berlin, mentioning acquaintance with Oppenheimer, Teller, Planck, and Szilard. At the time I didn't recognize the importance of these physicists, and Bertl never dwelt on their fame. But I knew she was a pacifist and strongly opposed to nuclear development.

Bertl cooked the two German students tasty meals. She assisted with their English-language studies. She took them to concerts and picnics. I could see they were growing fond of her, enjoying her wit and wisdom as I did. But the charged question never came up.

Then the last week of school arrived. Bertl said, "They will ask me tomorrow, Sami."

They did. At breakfast Mara, the dark-haired one, hesitantly asked Bertl if she was a Jew. When Bertl confirmed she was, both girls began to weep.

"Why do you cry?" she said gently. "It is not your crime. But you must go home and tell your parents you have spent your summer with a Jew, a Jew who didn't spit at you and treated you well. Then, they can cry, not you."

They embraced Bertl. "How you can show respect for me is to fight against nuclear bombs. No bombs! Go back to Germany and protest this madness!"

Years later I heard from Bertl that Mara had become a peace activist. I now see my time with Bertl taught me to be an activist of another kind. I, too, believe in peace and abhor nuclear weaponry. But Bertl's greatest lesson for me was about forgiveness, about understanding and about "passing it on." Today, I try to express these values in my writing. In my life, I try to live them.

Bertl Gaye, my Austrian Bodhisattva, will always remain a shining silver light in my memories of England.

VIOLET

In 1961 we returned from Europe after three years in England and nine months in Paris, France. Our eldest child, Corinne, was born and six years later the twins, Joshua and Gabrielle. When Cori was eighteen months old, we moved from Palo Alto, where Jim was attending graduate school at Stanford, to Santa Cruz, where we still live today.

One day my nephew, who was going to UC Berkeley, came over to visit. It was 1971. He was taking a sociology course and for the first time in his life, outside of talk in the family, had heard about Manzanar.

"Aunty," he said, "you know I was born in Manzanar, and I don't know anything about the place. Can you tell me about it?"

"Sure," I said, "but why don't you ask your folks?" I felt no hesitancy in talking about the internment camp and wondered why he couldn't get information from them.

"I have, Aunty, but they seem reluctant to talk about it. Like I shouldn't be asking or there's some skeleton in the closet." That's strange, I thought. I then began telling him about life in camp—about the schools, the outdoor movie theater, the baseball games, the judo pavilion, dances, and the beautiful rock gardens. Whenever my family got together and we happened to talk about camp, we would joke about the lousy food, the dust storms or the communal showers, or we talked lightheartedly about recreational activities. I reiterated the same stories to my nephew in the same superficial way.

He looked at me intently, as if never seeing me before. "Aunty, you're telling me all these bizarre things. I mean, how did you *feel* about being locked up like that?"

For a moment I was stunned. He asked me a question no one had ever asked before, a question I had never dared to ask myself. Feel? How did I feel? For the first time I dropped the protective cover of humor and nonchalance. I allowed myself to "feel." I began to cry. I couldn't stop crying.

He was shocked. What had he done to send me into hysterics? I was embarrassed, and when I gained control of myself, I told him I would talk to him some other time. But now I understood his parents' reluctance to discuss too deeply the matter of the internment.

At the time, I was "Aunty" to thirty-six nieces and nephews. Seven had been born in camp. I realized none knew about their birthplace, Manzanar. Since it seemed too painful to talk about it, perhaps I could write a memoir, a history—just for the family.

I had not written for years. I tried to begin. But I found myself in tears, unable to concentrate. Was I having a nervous breakdown? It was apparent my nephew's innocent question, a question he had a right to ask, had opened a wound I had long denied ever existed.

I turned to Jim. "I'm having trouble writing this memoir."

"What memoir is this?" I hadn't told him about my project. "What seems to be the problem?"

Embarrassed, I explained, "I can't stop crying whenever I try to write about Manzanar. I think I'm going crazy."

"Let's talk about it," he said, now intrigued.

Through tears I told him what I could. I was emotionally honest for the first time. I remembered feelings—of loss, of shame and humiliation, of rage, of sorrow. He sat quietly, listening. Then he said, "I have known you for almost twenty years, have been married to you for fourteen . . . and I never had any idea you carried all this around. This is not something to write just for your family. It's a story everyone in America should read."

Thus began our collaboration on *Farewell to Manzanar* and my return to writing. We spent a year working together; I talked for hours into a tape recorder; we interviewed family and other internees; we researched the libraries.

When the book was published in 1973, my life changed. The year spent delving into those three years of my childhood and its aftermath was as powerfully therapeutic as years with a psychiatrist. I reclaimed pride in my heritage. I rediscovered my ability to write. I realized I could no longer hide "in the country of my husband's shadow." With Jim's encouragement and support, I left the comfortable safety zone of domesticity and ventured out into the open field. I began to write again.

Violet. Ah! Violet. My favorite color. A mix of red and blue. How fitting that the red of my happiest childhood memories and the blue of Hawai'i and marriage should fuse to produce the "violet" period of my life! Red for groundedness, strength, yin power. Blue for expression, communication, yang power. Violet for spirit, the fusion of yin and yang.

I don't know whatever happened to Jessica, my friend from Hillcrest Juvenile Hall. I hope she is an accomplished artist someplace. Wherever she is, I wish her a "colorful" life and thank her for the friendship which inspired this memoir.

WHERE ARE YOU FROM?

GEETA KOTHARI *was born and raised in New York City. Her work has appeared in various journals and, most recently, in the anthology* Her Mother's Ashes and Other Stories by South Asian Women *(TSAR Publications, 1994). She is the editor of* "Did My Mama Like to Dance?" and Other Stories About Mothers and Daughters *(Avon, 1994) and lives in Pittsburgh, Pennsylvania.*

"WHERE ARE YOU FROM?"

The bartender asks this as I get up from my table. It's quiet at the Bloomfield Bridge Tavern, home of the best pirogies in Pittsburgh. I have just finished eating, just finished telling my boyfriend how much I love this place because it's cheap and simple, not crowded in the early evening, and has good food.

"New York."

He stares at me, but before he can ask another question, I'm down the stairs, in the ladies' room, washing my hot face. When I come up again, I glare at him.

"I hate this place," I say to my boyfriend. "That man asked me where I'm from."

The man has no reason to ask me that question. We are not having a conversation. I am not his friend. Out of the blue, having said no other words to me, he feels that it is okay for him, a white man, to ask me where I am from. The only context for this question is my skin color and his need to classify me. I am sure he doesn't expect me to say New York. I look different, therefore it's assumed that I must be from somewhere, somewhere that isn't here, America. It would never occur to him to ask my boyfriend, who is white —and Canadian—where he's from.

For years, I practiced saying "New York," in answer to that question. When I was younger, I complained to my parents about people asking where I was "really" from. My dad insisted on an answer something like "I am an American citizen, born and raised," which sound like the words of an immigrant, believing that if she says them often enough, she will become one.

My parents came to the United States ten years apart; they met here, married, and after my sister and I were born, talked about going back to India. (My mother never "immigrated"; she came to work for the United Nations and remains, today, an Indian citizen.) Throughout our childhood, peppered with "home leave" visits to India—the United Nations jargon for the trips its international staff took to their countries of origin—India was known as "home." Not any particular place there, just the whole country: home. We were always on the brink of returning there permanently.

I have not been to India in ten years, something which shocks most of my Indian friends, and even surprises my parents, though together we have watched the years go by, each one marked by vague talk of going to India. I no longer call it home. I hear the word as a slip of my tongue; I hear grad students and understand that they don't mean Atwood Street in Oakland. I am not from there, this place they call home, and even though I have emotional and cultural ties to it, these become more and more tenuous as the years go, as I struggle to keep them alive with an internal snarl to all those who want to do it for me, with their questions and the implication that I don't belong here. For if I don't belong here, where do I belong? I gave up the romantic notion that Mother India is waiting for my return, with open arms, welcoming and accepting. When this happened, I'm not sure; at some point I unpacked my bags, a slow and difficult thing to do, made worse by the assumptions behind a simple question. For what the question implies is: when am I going back to where I really come from?

I stand by the racks of evening wear, idly looking through $3,000 dresses covered in plastic. Beads and sequins are in this year, at Kleinfeld's & Son, a wedding emporium in Brooklyn. We are in the evening-wear section of the store, where my friend Jenny has tried on three shiny satin dresses. She emerges from the dressing room behind me.

"Find anything?" she says, a little too brightly.

I show her a very short tank dress, heavy with glittery brown and golden yellow beads. It has a low, revealing back, and a modest front. The weight of the beads makes it swing slightly, with a life of its own. At $2,800, it can be neither washed nor dry-cleaned. This is not my kind of dress—too revealing, too expensive, too useless. Still, I am intrigued by it. It is well cut, carefully stitched together, heavy like chain mail. It's a power dress; most men wouldn't know what to do with a woman who had the guts and the money to wear this dress.

Suddenly, Ada, our personal salesclerk, takes the dress from me and shoves it back on the rack.

"No, no, no. What do you want with a dress like that? You see this back—anyone can stick his hand down your tush. No, sweetheart, if you want a nice evening dress, let me show you what I'd get for you."

She pulls out a dark pink shiny dress, shirred up the front and cinched at the waist with a low neck and puffed short sleeves. The material feels as if a stray cigarette ash would be enough to send it up in flames. It's slightly innocent and very accessible in its appeal, revealing a little bit of cleavage and collarbones, chastely covering the rest of the body.

"Here, this would be perfect for you. Some sheer black hose, a pair of black heels, some nice long earrings—you'll be set. You'd have to fix your hair a little, maybe curl it and let these"—and she flicks my overgrown bangs—"fall over your forehead. A little bit of makeup, and I guarantee, you'll have the right man asking you out."

She looks at Jenny, who nods weakly. After all, that is the point, to have the right man ask me out. "Don't you think she has a beautiful face? She's wasting it, just wasting it. Look at you," she says gravely, scanning my black jeans, green turtleneck, and gray vest, half covered by a man's down coat. She searches my face, waves a finger at me. "I don't know, you just look so—so European."

Not European, but "different" from the average Kleinfeld's customer. Not only are we different in our unwillingness to spend $1,500 on a wedding dress, which is why we ended up in the evening-wear section, where we can find dresses for $400, but we look different too. Jenny's freckled face is vaguely foreign—her mother is Japanese—while my brown skin is often mistaken for anything from Italian to Iraqi.

A blond woman in gray sweats pushes past us and starts sifting through the sequined dresses. Ada ignores her, still concerned with my husband-catching outfit. The blond pulls my dress out and holds it against her.

"I just wanted to fit in." Jenny sounds gloomy, in our cab heading back to Manhattan. "I really wanted to find a dress there."

I try to make her—and myself—feel better.

"You couldn't have found a dress there. Look at the hideous stuff they had. You need to shop downtown, at Barneys or at some SoHo boutique. Kleinfeld's is not for you."

Well, at least Ada didn't ask me "Where are you from?" But it's implicit; she can't nail me down, so she's not going to ask. If Robert, Jenny's fiancé, had been there, would Ada have taken charge of us the way she had? No doubt she meant well; but she merely showed us, once again, that there is a club in this country, and we don't belong. In this club, Americans are blond and white and can wear whatever they want; the rest of us can't and don't. We know our place. I don't fit into Ada's idea of who I am by assuming that I too can wear a backless, sequined dress.

If Robert had been there—a white man representing power—Ada would have seen that at least Jenny was marrying the "right" man. Ada knows that women have traditionally found their place in society through marriage. Judging by the brisk business at Kleinfeld's—reflecting an industry that thrives in the midst of a recession—and Ada's concern that I meet the "right man," women are still expected to and do marry for economic stability and identity. This means not being questioned about our right to be here, not being patronized: "But where are you really from?" It means not having to explain ourselves: "Well, my parents are from India, but I was born in New York." Jenny's fiancé, Robert, with his extended WASP family and network of friends, has those well-established roots. No one questions his right to be here, and once she marries him, I imagine, no one will question Jenny's either.

I know, of course, that that's not true. I'm looking for an easy way out, a way to avoid that confrontation. I find it confusing because my cultural identity is grounded in India. Even though I was born and raised in New York, I have a psychological connection to India fostered by my parents. When a person operating under some misguided, unexamined ethnographic curiosity asks, "Where are you from?" I say, "India." It's a defensive answer to a question that is implicitly degrading. When I say, "India," I am telling that man in the bar: "My culture is as important as yours. Why should I have to explain when you don't have to explain yours?"

Asked again, by a different person, a person not so intent on pointing out my difference, and I'll say, "New York." I associate my identity, my sense of who I am, with the place I have lived in the longest. The need to categorize people is offensive only in the ignorance with which it's done, with the assumption: "I'm normal, therefore you don't need to know where I'm from. I'm American, and I look it. You don't." When I say, "I'm from New York," I'm saying, "I'm American too. I'm not in a different category."

I did not go to an all-girls school for anything if not good manners and a sense of owing the world an explanation. When someone asks that dread question, what I really want to say is what my father often says: "None of your business." But in addition to looking different, I am also a well-bred, polite female product of Western, WASP culture, so instead I secretly ponder the advantages of marrying white.

I marry white—the Canadian boyfriend, who insists that identity is not static and that I am looking for a foothold where there is none. And since I do not adopt his WASP name, do not change anything about my own name or the way I look, few things change. On the phone, trying to order vitamins from New York, I am asked, "Are you from India?"

Instantly, I understand why this man's accent seems vaguely familiar; however, I do not ask him where he was from.

"My parents are."

I curse myself for explaining, then justify it—I need these vitamins, his good graces. But there is more.

"Where in India are they from?"

And now I cannot remember what I said, but I know I did not answer the question. For when an Indian person asks, "Where are you from?" whatever answer I give is full of connotations and meanings to that person that I, since I am not in the thick of Indian popular culture, or even Indian-American culture, barely understand. When I say, "My mother is Punjabi and my father's Gujerati," I am identified in terms that I don't understand. When a white person calls me a Paki, I understand that. It's something I can chew, it's definable, and only a blind fool would see it as a misunderstanding on my part. This has happened.

However, when an Indian woman (and though she tells me where she's from, it has no meaning, so I instantly forget), the wife of the department chair, probes my origins, the effect is more subtle. When I explain to her that my mother is Punjabi, she nods with satisfaction. "Yes, I was wondering how you could look this way and have a *guju* name." She is condescending, a difficult thing to prove, and her tone insulting. In fact, I have to call my parents to find out if I've been insulted. They are equally vague. "Yes, *guju*, derogatory, just ignore it. Where is she from anyway? Don't know? What's her name? Oh yes, that's a so-and-so name. . . ."

In a word, endless things are revealed. Someone asks me if my first name is common in India. It is more than that. It is a religious name—people are so pleased when they guess *Bhagavad-Gita*—and it may say more about me than there actually is. Or maybe not. Such a name, one with strong religious and devotional connotations, is unlikely to be used by a Muslim family. Unlikely, but not definitely. I try to pin my mother down on this one, but she won't allow me. "Well, it is unlikely, but if people—Muslims and Hindus—are close friends with a family, they may adopt names from that family. And my friend, who is Christian, used Hindu names for all her daughters."

She waffles less on other questions. My mother tells me that "Where are you from?" is typical *desi* behavior. Not only do people understand that the Punjab and the Gujerat are two separate states, with their own languages, cultures, and regional differences. This question is more than that. On the plane going to my father's hometown, newly married, my mother sat next to a man who asked her where she was from. "And the questions don't end there," she says now. "It's where's your father from, your father's father, what community do you belong to." In Gujerati, the question translates to "What is your place of origin?" All so that the inquisitor can place you, either below him or side by side, to make himself feel better. Presumably, if he places you above him, the questions will end, and you will sit in stony silence for the rest of the trip.

In the United States, I have little idea what it means to answer an Indian with "My mother's Punjabi, my father's Gujerati." I don't have much to say about my grandfathers on either side, and even if I did, I'm not sure my information would be satisfying. It is slightly ridiculous that I have to ask my parents if I've been insulted; on the other hand, my ignorance surely must deny the inquisitor some satisfaction.

I don't think about my name in daily life. I know that often I have to spell it out (my father's voice: "K as in Kenneth, O as in Oscar . . .) over the telephone, where I'm most likely to be asked, "Where's your name from?" or "That's a pretty name. Where is it from?" Is it because they can't see me that this more polite, yet equally nosy question comes out? Would the inquisitor understand if I said, "It's Gujerati"? Would he or she even care? I'd like to try this—use specificity to cut the questioning short. When another Indian asks me, the trick is to avoid specificity; when the guy in the bar asks, I want to get as specific as possible.

I am nineteen. It's June, and I am in summer school in Boston. Geoff has invited me to spend some time at his stepbrother's house on the shore, outside of Boston. Like me, he is from New York, and when I first meet him, he seems familiar. He knows the things I know. He has traveled. I don't have to explain myself to him. Lately, however, our relationship is not progressing; delighted to be included in his family activities, I eagerly accept his invitation.

I remember few details of the day. From the porch of this big old house, we can see John Quincy Adams's house across the bay. The rocky beach is about half a mile long, the water pure and clear. Geoff and assorted male cousins and friends spend most of the day in the water. I remain on the porch with Geoff's elderly father and various older people, occasionally offering to help the two other women there. Ruthie is the stepbrother's wife. The other is also a wife; she and her husband have brought along their one-and-a-half-year-old daughter.

The boys splash and shout in the glittering water. The adults on the porch discuss law and stocks. Ruthie flits in and out of the kitchen, an efficient hostess, resting on the arm of her husband's chair every few minutes. I sit on the porch, eating watermelon and politely spitting the seeds into my hand. The day is perfect, clear and sunny, making the whole beach shimmer like a dream. I am bored.

Everyone is dressed in khaki shorts and polo shirts, both the men and the women. There are the usual questions about me: how I know Geoff, where my parents are from, what they do, where I go to school. ("Smith College? Really?") Ruthie's blond sun-streaked hair is held back with a headband. Her dry, tanned hands betray some age and her fingernails are unpolished and cut short. She wears a simple gold chain around her neck, and her ears are unpierced. She says she's never had the courage.

Right now, I have no courage either. I try to ignore the lump growing in my throat and tears forming behind my eyes. I feel sorry for myself, awkward, unable to talk to these older people around me, unable to play with the boys. I am wearing a white-and-red flowered sundress. I don't look like anyone else there.

The whole day—the clear sky, the smiling, tanned people with gleaming white teeth, the old well-kept house with the porch overlooking the sea—is perfect. This is what Americans, real Americans, look like, and this is how they play: extended families by the shore, picture-perfect in matching Ralph Lauren outfits. I believe this, and so I blame myself for not knowing better, for showing up dressed like an Island Mama.

Geoff's father wears a suit and tie. We are the only people not in uniform. He doesn't seem to mind. Of course not. This is his land, his place. No one has ever said to him, "But where are your parents from?" I feel excluded, from the water and on the shore.

Later, Geoff blames me. Somehow, I should have known to bring a bathing suit. I simmer and call him a few names, telling him I am not an orphan from the city who needed him to take me to the shore to enjoy a nice day. I feel released from a cage when we finally stop seeing each other.

Even if I had them, words could not explain it to him, someone who has never experienced being alone like that, who never will experience it, except by choice, if he travels, or by accident, if he gets lost in the wrong neighborhood. In both situations, he is a tourist, only temporarily there. It was up to me to fit into his world, not him into mine. I know everything about his life, his background; the most interest he can muster about mine is his thrill with the exotic. More than ten years later, I'm still angry, only this time not at myself.

■ ■ ■

If the way I look makes people uncomfortable, so does my voice. In the English boarding school I spent my teens in, I am ignored for my first year. Yet when I speak, girls at the front of the room turn around to look at me. My face gets hot; I stutter. Seeing the Indian body that houses this loud American accent, they are incredulous. During break, they command me to speak, like a talking doll, but no one listens at any other time.

When we sing hymns in the morning, I can no longer control my alto voice and end up singing out of key. Girls stare, smirk, whisper; someone jabs me with her elbow. Pretty soon, I stop singing. I whisper the Lord's Prayer. The following year, I read out loud from the Bible to the entire assembly, but I never sing again.

My English friends could not understand how one could be Indian and American, how I could look one way, and sound another. My letters home, when I was depressed about homework or the weather, hide my anger, my loneliness, my confusion. I didn't feel normal, didn't feel flattered when one of my friends said, "I don't consider you Indian at all." Yet in an argument about racism in South Africa (how, I wanted to know, could she stand to visit a country where people were segregated according to skin color?), the same friend said, "Well, you would like it there. Indians are treated very well."

When it was convenient, I was Indian; when it wasn't, I was American. If I asked questions, argued, said anything that sounded "different," I was Indian. As an American, I ran with the "in" crowd, was elected to student government, and played the Angel Gabriel in our Christmas tableau.

While I am happy for Jenny, I am a little bit envious and a more than little afraid of watching her get swallowed up. I remember Geoff's initial fascination, which eroded into a cold expectation for me to fit in or shut up. When Jenny tells me all she wants is to fit in, I understand, and I worry. I worry because Jenny and I haven't talked about this, not really, and I don't know if she will want to once she's married. These days, she buys more of her clothes at the Gap and is learning how to ski. I scrutinize Robert for signs of Geoff. What is he willing to give up? How much will she give up? Do women like Jenny and me, teased and ignored, called names and made invisible—either a

Paki or not seen at all—really find what we want in our relationships with white men? Is it such a safe haven from the isolation of childhood?

Although I'm irritated by the unasked, the dread "Where are you from?" I am a little flattered that Ada the salesclerk thought I was "too European." Unlike Jenny, I was secretly glad to be set apart from the Kleinfeld's crowd, to be different and difficult to classify, a barely recognizable Indian, a disputable American.

And yet, if I enjoy looking different, difficult, how is it that I cannot imagine wearing that little chain-mail dress? How is it that after seven years in Pittsburgh, I am a walking ad for the Gap? I didn't replace that bright sundress, now outgrown. My favorite colors are dark, muted; for a while it was black before I understood that a tall thin black-haired woman in black attracted as much attention, was as exotic, as if she were wearing a traditional tunic and baggy pants.

When one of my students pierces her nose, a raw red wound that festers before it heals, I am surprised by my reaction. She's white, and this is a fun thing for her to do, a way to distinguish herself in the crowd. No one will ask her when she's leaving; no one will ask about the cultural significance of her pierced nose. People will categorize her, no doubt, but meanly I think: she has asked for it. I am both envious and scornful of her, aware that these emotions are two sides of the same coin. I want that choice, to pierce my nose as Indian women have done for centuries, and I don't have it. I stick out already; this is all I can handle.

Who I am is a difficult question. If identity is formed in reaction to societal institutions, to community, then my identity is in flux. I'd like to fit in, to be the same as other Americans, but the people asking me where I'm from don't let me. They're pointing out my difference, making sure that I know I'm not one of them. I see myself as American, but not the American they're looking for, and I am forced to identify with another group whether I want to or not.

Assuming, of course, that this other group wants me. As children, my sister and I were raised in an international community, in the shadow of the United Nations, among children who were taught, right from age five, that "it's a small world after all." Our closest friends were from Tanzania, Zaire, and

Nepal. I remember cocktail parties for the adults, while all the kids ran around cramped three-bedroom apartments in the same building complex. My very best friend was a girl whose father was an American Jew and mother Japanese. Our time together was spent reading: I went through all her Nancy Drew, Hardy Boys, and Bobbsey Twins books; she read my Indian comics, graphic retellings of old Hindu and Sikh stories.

By the time we were ten, cultural differences—the way our parents raised us out of mainstream America—had started to show. For though my parents did not actively participate in an Indian community of either the Punjabi or the Gujerati kind, they were still very much concerned with raising their children Indian, with resisting assimilation, even as their own actions contradicted this.

When did I notice that we had no Indian friends, that the few we knew had disappeared, moved to Parkway Village, which might as well have been another country? My parents thought we could have it both ways, the best of America while holding on to some essential Indianness. What was it to be Indian? There were things that Indians didn't do: they didn't have boyfriends or girlfriends; they didn't smoke (though my father had for several years), party, or have fun; they worked hard at school. "Read," my father would say, every time I talked about a party I wanted to go to or some other such frivolity. Americans were interested only in fun, instant gratification, fulfilling their desires with no concern for community and family. The rules were different for them, especially for white girls.

I once read that sex and sexual morality are most often the areas where issues of cultural identity are played out. When, as an economically independent adult, I moved in with my boyfriend, my parents didn't disown me, as I'd been led to believe they would. Instead, they worried about what they would tell "the family." My mother thought it would make her family anxious, that they wouldn't understand. As for my father's family, with whom we had little contact, it was hinted darkly that my disgrace would be their pleasure, at his expense.

Each visit to my parents ended up with my mother or me in tears, and my returning to Pittsburgh filled with the dread of "the community." Every time I met an Indian, I worried that it would get back to the family what I was doing, whom I was living with. What community this was exactly I wasn't sure, but I feared its censure and worried about exposure for the two years I lived with this man.

Mercifully, the relationship ended. And after years of waiting for "the community" to descend on me, tear me apart, brand me "P" for promiscuous, I finally began to look for it, instead of simply accepting my parents' word that it was there.

If identity is formed in relation to certain institutions, in reaction to other people, then who or what had formed my identity? What was I pushing up against or allowing to mold me? Where was the tension, if there was no Indian community in my life? I was supposed to be Indian, but I hadn't the slightest idea of what that was. Getting more specific was even less help—I could articulate less about Punjabis and Gujeratis than I could about Indians.

My parents, I suppose, had thought we would pick it up from them. But two people are not enough of an example—at least not of the kind they wanted to be. We needed the pressure of friends and other family members to mold us. We had this, but it came from friends, most of whom were not Indian. After my parents, the most influential adults in my life have been my mother's women friends, none of them Indian. At my sister's wedding lunch, of the twenty-five people present, only six were Indian, and that included me, my sister, and my parents. The other two Indians were friends of the family; one half Gujerati, the other Bengali. At my father's right hand sat the woman who introduced him and my mother; she is Jewish.

Without other Gujerati or Punjabi kids to play with, or other Indian adults to learn from, my sister and I were molded by non-Indians. Years later, my parents are trying to understand this, to answer my questions, my accusations. My father blames his family and my mother's family for not providing the support they needed. Family support is a crucial part of traditional Indian cultures. My mother tells me how hard it was for her, as an Indian woman at the United Nations, to get any support from her fellow Indian workers; she had not come up through the civil service and she was not a man. When their wives entertained, she knew that she had neither the time nor the inclination to match them dish for dish. "That's how it was," she says, "if someone had us over and made seven dishes, then the next week I'd have to reciprocate with nine dishes."

Superficial reasons, but grounded in more fundamental differences that compelled first my mother and then my father out of India. When I talk about not fitting in here, I am surprised that my mother understands and matches me with stories of her childhood, the bright, even brilliant eldest daughter of a father who valued boys so much he cried when his youngest granddaughter was born and asked the doctor if he was sure it was a girl. As for my father, he left a city where too many people knew him and a prominent position at the hospital to get away from a joint family governed by customs that gave him no voice and little control over his life. They were odd pegs back home. No wonder we never returned.

This is the family we worry so much about offending. This is the community to which we never belonged. My inheritance is my parents' ambivalence about all they left behind and all they held on to, their inconsistency and inability to pin down an identity for me, to give me the scaffolding of what it is to be Indian.

Following the destruction of the Babri Masjid in Ayodhya, I join a group of graduate students on the campus I teach at in weekly discussions on communal violence in India. I am the only Indian American at these meetings. The subtext of most of the conversations is lost on me; I hang on to familiar signs —the side-to-side nodding of the head, difficult to translate, but something all Indians seem to do when we get together; certain words—*theek, desi, achha, array*—small words that bridge the gap between me and these foreigners.

Full of questions and few answers, I am drawn to the meetings by an emotional need, a connection to India that is less defined than theirs. I am tentative in my comments, defensive in my questions ("I know this is a stupid question but . . ."), initially cowed by their superior knowledge of India and things Indian.

Later I understand that belying their politics and strong opinions is the denial of their desire to stay in this country. Dissertations are prolonged while visits to India are made over long, hot summers; people move from one temporary appointment to another, extending their work visas. No one talks about green cards, at least not in my presence. A return to India for one couple is rescinded at the last minute and everyone rejoices—he found a job, she found a job, they're staying.

There are few opportunities back home, though few will openly admit this. Few honestly talk about the future, until I press the issue, argue that to talk about India and religious fundamentalism is fine, but that our discussions draw no support from Indian Americans, mostly undergraduates, the children of other graduate students perhaps, who settled here twenty years ago. "Yes, we need to figure out how to reach these ABCDs," they say. "They know nothing."

ABCD—American-Born Confused Desi (Desi as in a person from *desh*, from India. It takes on many connotations depending on who's using it; in this case, it refers to someone lacking in affinity to their origins). The equivalent pejorative acronym is FOB, Fresh Off the Boat, something none of them would like to be labeled. Yet they have no problem talking about ABCDs as a lesser species, as if I am not in the room or have transcended my confusion through my involvement with the group.

I understand different things than perhaps they'd want me to. Although my parents wanted me to associate with Indians, although they talked about community, they never thought to explain that calling myself Indian (or Punjabi or Gujerati) didn't automatically guarantee acceptance or identification. They knew this from their own experience, yet I wanted to believe that to be in a crowd of Indians guaranteed fitting in. My evidence came from visits home, where all I needed to do was change my clothes, and that would be it—I was in. An illusion, brokered by cousins who accepted us and treated us equally, as neither less nor more than them because we lived in America. And the moment I opened my mouth—the American-accented English, the lack of Punjabi or Gujerati or Hindi—I was out again, identified as different.

In the third grade, my parents discovered that after several years of after-school tutoring, I couldn't/wouldn't speak Hindi. I couldn't say a word in public, made shy by what I heard as a French accent in my Hindi and my father's correcting my speech. I spoke French fluently, having spent every day since kindergarten in a bilingual class. But I couldn't speak Hindi. I had failed as an Indian.

Thus began the silence that would follow me into adulthood. At the base of it was a deep mistrust of my understanding of who I was and my connection to a group I didn't even share a language with. That this silence found its way into my writing is not surprising. I worried that I didn't know enough to write about myself, about being Indian in the United States. I knew nothing. And if I couldn't be a perfect Indian, a Punjabi or a Gujerati or both, then I wasn't going to try. I couldn't risk anyone finding me out; so long as I kept quiet, no one would.

I kept silent at the graduate student meetings, hiding my ignorance, which made me less than everyone else in the room. Finally, unable to bear the implicit slurs against American-born Indians, my exclusion from the conversation, I spoke. First I argued, aggressive in my desire to hear my voice; as I relaxed into my voice, heard it after such a long silence, I began to trust it.

My voice, my voice, my voice. When I return to the States, after five years in England, people still use my voice, reading me in ways I don't understand. When Ada says I look European, I am not surprised; people have wasted a lot of their time trying to place me. At college parties, well-bred Ivy League boys would ask, "Where are you from?" "New York," I'd say, and they'd take it as an opening, but it would never lead quite where they wanted it to. "You don't sound like you're from New York," or "What kind of New York accent is that?" Now I wonder if they were waiting for the accent of television or movies—at best Woody Allen, at worst Amy Fisher. According to one man, I sound like I have a mouth full of potatoes. To another, I sound like I am from Connecticut. When I ask him what this means, he amends his comment, saying I sound like I came from a snotty private school on the Upper West Side.

I am not surrounded by people who are underprivileged; Smith College is private, as are several other colleges in the area. When I explain that I'd gone to school in England (apologetically, of course), that my parents do not speak with a funny Peter Sellers accent, that I've traveled (apology for my mother's job), conversation stops. Women in my house avoid me, feel sorry for my German roommate because she can't live with a white American; men stay away mostly (except for the drummer from UMass, still a friend nearly fifteen years later), and I am easy prey for the kind of losers who either ignore my background altogether or need an exotic accessory to make their lives more interesting.

Classifying others in a so-called classless society is one of our greatest hypocrisies. What right had I to go to private school, to travel, to speak

French fluently? What right had I to be at Smith College, talking with an accent, but not one anyone expected from me? People wanted to know how I'd ended up in England, as if I'd taken a place away from them, but no one wanted to listen to the history of the British Empire and how it affected my parents. How it never occurred to them, when I was having trouble in school, to look for a school in the States. Our Tanzanian friends were in boarding school by this time, and I ended up in the same school as another friend. My parents did what their community did for prepubescent girls on the edge of making life really difficult. They sent me to England because that is what they knew, both in India and in the States. An alternative did not exist.

How to explain this bubble I grew up in? Why explain it? Why did it bother people so much that I didn't meet their expectations as an Indian or as the American product of Indian immigrants? That I could go to Smith, but still wear bright, primary-colored clothes, hand-stitched by a tailor in Delhi? As Geoff found out, I was civilized, but not civilized enough. All the education in the world would not get me a place in that Ralph Lauren ad.

As much as the *desi* wants to equalize or subordinate me with his nosy questions, so did these preppy kids I met in my first year back in the States. If they felt threatened, white women and men, sensing that the world would not be their oyster only, my reaching into their culture and taking what I wanted made things worse.

I can hear a voice in my head telling me I'm making too much of idle party talk. I am defensive, angry, and it scares the voice. I hear Geoff's voice, without his face, maybe the face of the man I lived with several years ago. I was listening to this voice when I moved to Pittsburgh. Between this and my fear of the "community," I wrote very little, not even my journal.

If I am angry about anything it is about the years I lost in this uncertainty, in this going back and forth between two cultures, accepting myself in neither. I am angry about the way people labeled me and the number of times I've let them, simply because it was easier than fighting, easier than explaining something I myself couldn't articulate.

In the grad students I meet, I see a strong sense of identity, both as Indians and with their regions. Even as they extend their deadlines, settle for jobs in the far-flung reaches of Nebraska and South Dakota, distant names on a map, even to me, the idea of going back to India, "home," provides them with security. It is easy for them to scoff at us ABCDs, running around in search of an identity. It is easy for them to mock the eighteen- and nineteen-year-old undergraduates who worry about dating and hide boyfriends from their parents. When I suggest that it is with these issues that one begins, that we can use such personal and seemingly trivial issues to begin a dialogue, I am ignored. After all, I have crossed over. I am with a white man. What do I know?

I am speculating again, wondering how much my relationships with white men have compromised my identity within the Indian community. I have asked to be put on the mailing list for the Indian Students Association a number of times, but I continue to not exist as an Indian faculty member, as a member of the mainstream of Indian campus life. My marriage to a white man, I'm sure, excludes me further. The nominations for the third annual Pride of India Awards (advertised in the *India Tribune*, an Indian-American newspaper), in which the awardee "will become Symbol of dedication, commitment and inspiration to Asian Indian Youth from various parts of North America," must, among other things, provide a photograph and "sketch of Family and Community involvement (Including origin of parents & spouse if married)."

I know, without needing to be told, that I am not the role model these organizers are looking for, even without my husband and lack of sanctioned community involvement. I ask too many questions, and my parents made it impossible, a long time ago, for me to accept the kind of scrutiny that membership in the Indian community (whatever it is) entails. I am my father's daughter, and the voice that says, "None of your business," gets louder and louder each day.

I didn't think I would marry the Canadian. In the beginning of our relationship, we fight a lot. I am angry at him for not being Indian, for not understanding immediately what I'm talking about, for insisting on a relationship when I've told myself that I will only marry an Indian, if I marry at all. I wanted something solid for my identity. I'd failed to find it with white men, who had expectations based on my changing and becoming white or maintaining the exotic, like a jungle orchid, a prize to show off or challenge their family with.

In the car, as he drops me off at the gym, I say, "I wish you were Indian." Everything else about him is okay, but if only he were Indian, if only I didn't have to explain certain things to him, if only he could accept the superstitions I was raised with, rather than asking "why" all the time. I cannot stand explaining myself anymore. He doesn't understand my unwillingness to view this life as anything other than temporary; I tell him I don't buy things because it would mean too much to worry about when I go away to India. I want someone who will accept this, who will understand without my speaking, who can tell me something about being Indian. I curse myself for continuing to sell out, for compromising myself.

At times, I think it would be easier if I had just come here, a new Indian, a Punjabi like my mother. She lived here ten years, alone—and lonely, at times —before mutual friends introduced her to my father. What kept her from going out with white men? What kept them away? I feel weak compared to her, like I've given in, like I don't care about India, about our roots, our family, home.

I imagine that whatever questions my mother had, her identity as a Punjabi, and an Indian, was not in question. Her understanding of it as something solid and strong, even after forty years in the States, confuses me. How does she know?

I fear that I will be asked to give up an identity I'm not even sure I have. When the boyfriend in the car asks, "What do you mean, you're Indian?" I hear the frustration in his voice. It mirrors mine. How to explain an emotion? How to make him understand what I myself have barely begun to articulate?

In traditional Indian cultures, the family makes an effort to find a groom or bride for the unmarried children. Apparently, such efforts were made at various times by my mother's relatives, on my behalf. My father put them off—I had to finish my education, which was true. Overall, though, my parents failed to meet this responsibility. The mechanisms for this failure had been set in place early on; without contacts in the community, Punjabi or Gujerati, here or in India, how could they miraculously produce a suitable son-in-law on demand? And how could they reconcile their abhorrence of a humiliating process that treated women like cattle with their desire to see their daughters settled and married to the best of men? "We couldn't bear to let you girls parade in front of strange men like meat for sale," my mother says.

We make a last-ditch effort. While I am dating my husband-to-be, my mother responds to an ad in the paper. The boy (as men are called in the matrimonial-ad context) is the son of a Punjabi mother and a Gujerati father. He's just like me. Even though we've been told these ads are bogus, it's worth a shot. I agree to let her write.

The mother never responds. Is it because I am a writer? Or because the man is looking for an Indian wife, not an ABCD? Or does my mother not provide enough details? She is not desperate enough. She doesn't send a photo, and probably fails to discuss our place of origin in any great detail. Does she mention her work at the United Nations? Had they gotten word, through the mysterious community grapevine, of my live-in relationship with a man?

I can't say that I'm disappointed. I'm getting used to my boyfriend, to his questions, which are irritating mostly because they mirror mine, and I can't answer them. He doesn't make a big deal about my being Indian nor does he ignore it. We have a common language, and if there's a subtext to our conversation, it is one we both understand.

And, gradually, I begin to feel more comfortable in my own skin, less worried about not being enough of one thing or another. Through the graduate students I meet, I understand myself more, accept that we are not the same, that I've been looking for something that perhaps doesn't exist for the way I've chosen to live my life. For although my parents' actions and choices decided much of my life, I am the one who finally chooses to accept myself and the life I'm leading.

We imagine communities based on nationality, race, ethnicity, religion that give us an instant and easy identity, as long as we don't question them. While a solidified "community" gives a secure sense of belonging, a framework with which to look at the world, it can also deaden us. To belong to a community defined along the rigid lines of categories which are subjective at best but treated as all-encompassing truths is important but also divisive. We see people in terms of who belongs and who doesn't. And those who belong must conform to the ways of the community, censoring their actions and words, either consciously or unconsciously.

My mother once said that the moment she started reading, she knew she couldn't stay in her community. "Once you've been exposed to ideas, you ask questions. I was always getting into trouble with my mouth." Yet I know it was hard for her to leave. She and my father both paid a price as immigrants in this country; they gave up security and opted for a community born out of other connections—professional, recreational, intellectual. Yet, until recently, our group of close family friends seemed second best—not blood relatives, not Indians—as though we were making do until the "real thing" came along.

I got married because one day I realized that I was tired of not being in the mainstream—of America, of India, of Indian American life. Marriage, no matter whom I married, is one aspect in which I am like the majority of people in this country. I wish that I could have simply lived with my boyfriend, but I have at last agreed with my parents: white women can do things, go places, wear clothes that I can't. And, as my sister says, most people understand marriage; it crosses cultural barriers and gives women a weight in a patriarchal society that they wouldn't otherwise have.

Depressing as this is, I am fighting on so many fronts, this one I decided to concede. When people ask where I'm from, what I don't need are more questions about my connection to the man I'm with. I don't need people speculating on the nature of our relationship or what my parents think (always an issue for Indians). The wedding band I deliberately wear says it all.

My struggle with "Where are you from?" continues. Some of my friends are hurt by what they read as an accusation (although all my inquisitors are relative strangers); my husband wants to know if there's a way to revise the question so that "it signals inclusion, a desire to give/accept voice." I don't know what that question would be, but it seems to me that first of all we need to begin with an awareness that a seemingly innocent question usually masks a combination of fear and desire. This is a shared burden; a revision of the question begins when people take responsibility for their motives instead of denying them. For people who come from and live in tightly knit communities, this is hard to imagine. This may be the only question they know how to ask. It may be the only question they ask.

For, as my mother knows, as my father knows, the price we pay for asking questions of ourselves and those around us is high. My husband, one of a few people in his working-class community to go to college, knows this too. He is uncomfortable when he goes home. Yet my parents argue, in their old age, that people long for that old community they came from. What they really want is the harmony, simplicity, and security of a community that they have fictionalized over the years. That this community only exists at the expense of their experience of the last forty years has not struck them, yet I do not see them packing up our apartment in New York and returning "home."

Like it or not, home is here: the United States, New York, Pittsburgh. So when the bartender wants to know where I'm from, I give him the short answer. I resist the urge to explain, to apologize, to feel guilty for putting him on the spot. I have not been back to the Bloomfield Bridge Tavern in nearly two years, but perhaps it is time to go back, to show him, and myself, that I'm not passing through. Where I'm from, in the end, is none of his business. He only needs to know that I'm here.

GERALDINE
KUDAKA

BAD
BLOOD

GERALDINE KUDAKA *is a poet, writer, and filmmaker. She has been published in* New Letters, Califia, Breaking Silence, The Third Woman, Time to Greez!, *and* An Ear to the Ground. *Her first book of poetry,* Numerous Avalanches at the Point of Intersection, *was released by Greenfield Review in 1979. She has edited* Third World Women, Beyond Rice: A Broadside Series, *and most recently* On a Bed of Rice *(Anchor, 1995). She has worked as a poet, curator of the Sargeant Johnson Gallery, and San Jose Museum of Art's film program director. She lives in Los Angeles, where she is*

EUGENE AHN

story editor for Lumiere Films and is completing her film Random Selections: A Question of Beauty.

I AM THE THIRD DAUGHTER OF FIVE CHILDREN. MY OLDEST sister, Sada, is four years older than I. My youngest sister, a year and seven months younger. My brothers, identical twins, are one year seven months older. It is no wonder they are separated from me by exactly one year seven months. One year seven months is enough time to wean an infant before the next pregnancy, the next birthing.

My mother met my father because her brother had served with him in the 442nd. I can picture two Army buddies sitting in the barracks, one saying to the other, "Eh, you wanna meet my sistah?" In a drawer full of family photos, my father's relationship to other men is verified. Hat askew, he swills beer in front of ice-packed barracks, arm draped around another uniformed *kanaka*. Not my uncle. There is no photo of my father and uncle together. I do not need the grainy dots of a photograph to verify what my father has said. I can picture my father and uncle each holding up a bottle of beer, toasting to their future. While these two *kanakas* were getting drunk, across the world, in Honolulu, my mother and her girlfriends called themselves the Chickencoop Girls.

The Chickencoop Girls were all waitresses. In their photograph, the Girls have round, hopeful faces. This was when my mother was engaged to a *haole* soldier stationed in Hawai'i. When his parents found out their young white son wanted to marry an illiterate Japanese waitress, they threatened to disinherit him. He told my mother he had made a mistake, and left. I don't know how long after that my mother married my father.

If my father were alive, he would mutter something about karma. But my father is dead, and my mother only speaks of the past in bitter recriminations. Thus, I am forced to construct a history made up from bits of information. Through nuances and glances, small offhand phrases that, pieced together, make up inaccurate memories. My mother would look at the way I have linked these fragments together to create history. She would shake her head and mutter something about bad blood. My linking is wrong. My brain doesn't work right. My brain leaps, and an image remains. An image which proves bad blood.

I am several months old. My mother has her hands full with my brothers, who are two years old and sick. Two baby boys, heirs to the family name, sick. My older sister stands next to my crib holding my bottle. Sada's four-year-old attention wanders, and my bottle drops, slipping out of my mouth. I cried, frustrated and angry. I am hungry. Sada's four-year-old hands do not know how to hold a bottle to feed me. My mother is sick, pregnant with my younger sister. My mother does not hear me crying.

Twenty-odd years later, as an adult, I am aware of primordial hunger. My childhood memories have failed me. I am bothered by shadowy figures. I discover the fragments which have made me what I am. I discover hidden truths. Buried inside my body, there is the insatiable mouth of an infant searching for its mother's perfect breast. I delve deeper. I start to meditate and images continue tumbling. While one part of me is fully present, another part slides to a time when my mother is pregnant with me. Going through my father's coat pockets, she finds a letter from a woman who is the mother of his child. Angered, betrayed, my mother wants nothing to do with my father. She does not want his child bloating her belly, making her piss. Damned by my father's betrayal, she wants to cut out that part of him growing inside her body. She wants to cut me out of her body. I am not wanted . . . Breathe, I am told. This is the only way to let go of the pain. Breathe, and one day it shall pass . . .

That was how my mother found out about Rie's existence, and the existence of my half sister, Kimie. My mother kept breathing, and forgave the father of her children. A year later, my younger sister was conceived. My two sisters, my brothers, and I grow up completely unaware of this other child of my father, Kimie. Years later, my half sister tells me bitterly, "I knew when your birthdays were. I was told about you, everything. Your names. Your ages. What you did in school. I even knew you won gymnasium meets." Kimie is bitter because she imagines having two parents is far better than one. She thinks legitimacy means happiness. She does not realize that her name was never mentioned, and we could never have imagined it was possible for our parents to have been anything other than what they were. I let that thought go and follow another memory.

I was crawling on the floor, moving on all fours through the door, into the kitchen. My mother was cooking. Her hair was up, and she had an apron tied around her waist. She was using a pair of long chopsticks to stir a large pot. There was a high chair next to the stove. I crawled toward the chair, and explored the space between its crossbars. Using my tiny arms, I wedged my fat body through the crossbars. The bars grabbed, trapping me between their wooden jaws. I let out a wail. My mother shouted. Throwing her chopsticks down, she rushed over and pulled me from the chair. Her efforts wedged me tighter. My arms thrashed about, and my mother pushed and screamed. I wailed with all my might, more frightened of my mother's terror than my wooden prison. I was terrified of being trapped in a chair. Frightened of my mother's anger directed at me because I had gotten stuck. To my mother, terror was the same as anger. I had caused her terror. I made her angry. Later, when I asked my mother about this unbidden image, she said, "Yes, your father heard you screaming. He came running into the room. He hit me. Then he took an ax and broke apart that chair. This is how he treated me."

My sister says, "You were always the brave one. Don't you remember? There was that old pig in the corral, and you used to ride it like a bronco." And I laugh, remembering that mean old sow. I was a scrawny five-year-old. Clambering onto the rails of the corral, I would jump on the pig's back. Angered, the old sow would shift her weight. Heaving from one side to the other, she got up squealing and bucking. She would run around the corral fence, trying to dislodge me by rubbing against the wooden rails. The trick was staying on the longest, and if you were bucked off, getting out of the corral before the sow attacked. A squealing pig makes a lot of noise, and if my mother heard us, she would come running out of the house, ready to slap us on our heads. When we butchered that pig, I had to help my father use the Skil saw to cut its legs off. My father made me stand there while the blade sliced through the pig's thick skin, chopping through the spine, cutting the animal in two. I was crying, but my father made me stay there. Pigs, he said, weren't pets. They were food. He handed me a hunk of meat. I leaned over and threw up, carefully aiming at the wall. I knew better than to ruin food.

That night, my mother set a plate in front of me. I looked at it. It was pork. "Eat," she said, and I shook my head, refusing. She slapped me, and repeated, "Eat." I shook my head. My father joined in, "If you know what's good for you, you'll eat." I picked up a forkful, put it in my mouth, and began to gag. A glance toward my father was sufficient to make me force back the gagging. As I slowly chewed, he looked at me and said, "If you want to cry, I'll give you something to cry about." I swallowed, then took another forkful. After a few bites my throat tightened up and I opened my mouth, spewing over the table. My mother leaned over the table and slapped me. My father pointed toward the kitchen and ordered me to clean up the mess. As I wiped the vomit up, my brothers and sisters silently cried and chewed. Then I washed the cleaning rags and my mother placed a plate of rice and vegetables in front of me. For a long time after that, I refused to eat meat.

It's curious because in spite of all these sad things, I remember that the light in Hawai'i was softer. Running over the rocks and looking for fish as the tides ebbed out, and the mist from the Blow Hole spraying our faces. Or the old woman next door with skeleton bones tattooed on her hands. Garden in the yard, a fat calico cat, and the blue-and-white uniforms we wore to our one-room Catholic schoolhouse. The whites turned red because of the iron ore in the soil, much to the dismay of stern nuns who believed that the purity of our uniforms reflected the state of our souls. I seem to remember having an extended family, and my sister tells me, years later, that an old, stooped-over man would come and give her candy. My grandmother Uta tried to shoo this man away, but he came and gave my sister candy. Sada thinks he was somehow related to us, but cannot remember how. She remembers he was nice to her, that he would spoil her.

She remembers him spoiling her because after we moved to the mainland, my mother and father worked two jobs. My sister became our surrogate mother. It was her job to make sure her four brothers and sisters ate, did their homework, and had clean clothes. We were all expected to pitch in, but chores were delegated by age and sex and Sada was responsible for whether we performed our chores. She was the eldest. The firstborn. She made dinner and had to pick up our clothes, papers, books, and toys before my parents came home. Sada helped my mother feed clothes through the old-fashioned wringer. Emily and I rinsed in the backyard. Even in winter, we rinsed in a huge aluminum tub using cold water from the garden faucet. We rinsed, squeezed, and hung the weekly laundry. Sada was responsible for whether Emily and I did a good job. She also made sure we did our homework. Emily was the baby.

Of the daughters, she did the least amount of work. My brothers' only job was watering the garden in our huge backyard. In the evenings, my father would come home from his factory job at the Ford Motor Company. If he took a nap on the couch, my mother would get angry and send him out to work in the garden. My mother ran the house, and in her stead, my sister. Which is why Sada always remembered that bent-over old man who, I learned much later, was our great-grandfather Gongoro Higa. He was the only one who let Sada feel like she was a child.

We moved to California in the late fifties. I was so shy that when Mrs. Smith asked me to come to the front of the class and talk about myself, I froze in my seat, convinced she was talking to someone else. "Gwendolyn. That is your name, isn't it? No, it's Geraldine. That's a very nice name. Very nice." She repeated my name, and I looked around, hoping against hope that it was someone else. No, it was me. She told me to come to the front of the class-room. I was taught that teachers were like gods. They had to be obeyed. So I dragged my body out of its seat and reluctantly stepped forward. "Yes, come to the front of the class," she said, "and introduce yourself. We're so happy to have a new student. Isn't that right, class?" As she droned on, I stepped forward. With rigid legs, I turned and faced the class. I looked at the thirty or forty faces. A stream of warm liquid ran down my leg. My face squinted and I burst into tears. Mrs. Smith was gracious. She excused the class for an early recess and sent me home.

After that first day, school became my refuge. It was my escape from the grayness of my family's house. It was easy because in my family books were more sacrosanct than God. Studying and homework was an excuse we could use for anything. My father had finished the ninth grade, then went to trade school. My mother had never gone beyond the third grade. Third-generation Hawaiian plantation families, they had both been forced to end their education and work to help support their family. Then they had their own family, which circumvented any future plans for themselves. Their hopes and dreams lay in us kids.

In an effort to maintain discipline, my parents constantly reminded us how hard their lives had been. My mother was particularly bitter about her child-hood. When we complained about our own lives, my mother would laugh and say, "Oh, you think we treat you bad? Humph, if you could only see the way *my* mother treated me . . . You kids don't know how good you have it." She would show us burn marks on her arms and legs, and tell us about *yaito*. About her mother leaning over and placing the tip of her burning cigarette against her flesh. Burning her. Scarring her forever.

My father would remain silent. Years later, when I became an adult and got to know my father, I was quite surprised. My childish impression was of a silent, taciturn man who wanted to read books and do crossword puzzles. My father told me there were other things he wanted to do with his life, but because he had children, he had to work. That all he could do was work to feed the many mouths around his table. His dreams were overwhelmed by hungry responsibilities. He said this now, but when I was a child he said nothing.

Consumed by day-to-day struggles, my parents were incapable of understanding the emotional needs of their American offspring. Theirs was the old-country way, *"Shikata ga nai* . . . It can't be helped." Just do what has to be done, and survive. They were the Depression generation. They didn't take survival for granted, and the luxury of emotional angst was beyond them. Getting by and surviving was all that mattered.

Watching *Donna Reed* and *Father Knows Best,* we had a different sense of America. When we tried to talk to my mother about this Hollywood vision of family life, she laughed and said white people could not be trusted. That for all their talk of love, our neighbors' barbecues showed what they were really like. The parents ate steaks, and fed their children hot dogs. This, my mother said, showed what America really was. Not *Donna Reed.* Not *Father Knows Best.* Unlike our family. When my mother set a plate of fried chicken on the table, my father picked first. Then came the children. My mother ate last, choosing the worst parts for herself. Necks and backs, she said, were the tastiest part of a chicken.

My mother was always worrying about getting ahead. About money. She wanted to make sure we had everything she didn't have in her own childhood. The practical, material things were important. When I asked her about love, she said, "What do you mean? We fed you, didn't we?" That was proof of love. And then she would show me her *yaito* scars. "Look," she would say, "if we didn't love you we would do this to you. We would scar you and burn you." This comparison was irrelevant to me. It was like describing the taste of

Coca-Cola to someone who has never drunk soda. It was beyond comprehension.

When I complained about the preferential treatment given my brothers because they were boys, my mother laughed and said, "In the old country, they threw baby girls out to the wolves." I was lucky. I lived. She would patiently explain that my brothers would grow up and marry. They would become heads of households with children to support. This is why education was more important for my brothers than it was for me. Because they would marry and their children would continue the Kudaka family name. When I swore I would never marry and take on another family name, she laughed. She said I didn't understand life. I would see things differently when I grew up. I would one day understand that it was woman's place to suffer. That women bore the brunt of life's burden because of what we had between our legs. Men could screw around, but it was women who paid the price. Women were destined to suffer because that's the way life was, and there was no point in fighting destiny—which was the same as biology.

The irony was that our own lives were so different from what she was trying to teach us. She worked. She worked constantly, and was always tired. Yet she wanted me to believe that if I learned the skills of being a woman— which meant cooking and cleaning—I would find a man to take care of me. Her dreams for me included college, but college was not a preparation for a career. I was being raised to go to college as a prelude to marriage. College was the place to meet and find the right kind of doctor or lawyer.

By junior high, I was allowed certain freedoms even my older sister, four years senior, was refused. My accelerated scholastic program offered excuses for absences from the home. Its mere existence provided my parents with a modicum of proof that I didn't need supervision. I could always say I had to go to the library. Sada was the eldest and had to set an example. She could not do anything. I wore lipstick and eyeliner. I had to sneak out of the house and apply my lipstick walking to the bus stop, but I did it. I went out on a date before my sister.

In her junior year, Sada met her best friend Leilani's ex-boyfriend, Harlan. Harlan had dropped out of school and was "poor white trash." He slouched like James Dean. He smoked in the corridors and was a belligerent truant. He was in and out of Juvenile Hall. Harlan liked Sada. Sada was so flattered by his attention that she started secretly meeting him at the library. This ended her friendship with Leilani. Convinced that she was being seen as something other than a plain, unloved drone, a light exploded. She started to take risks. Contriving excuses to leave the house, she snuck out to meet him. Lying to my parents, she covered up her absences. But her behavior changed, and one day my father discovered her secret. She came home late one evening, and he was waiting, belt in hand.

My father beat her so badly that Sada could barely walk, all the while accusing her of being a whore. Of being cheap. We children huddled in our room, listening to screams and shouts. The slash of the belt whipping air. Slashing flesh. Later that night, Sada and Harlan ran away. They were gone for several days. When they finally returned, my mother made them get married. There was no other choice. My seventeen-year-old sister was no longer a virgin.

My mind has blocked out the details of what followed. The major events remain, standing out like twisted beams after a holocaust. The anxiety of my mother twisting her hands, her head bent over her arms. The silence of the house. My father has disappeared from these memories. I know that he was there, but I do not remember him. He fades, and in his place my mother looms, bitterly accusing us all of bad blood. My sister was guilty of bad blood. We all were. We were tainted. We had bad blood in us. This was the only litany which broke the silence. This, and her anger at my father.

I do not link my sister's running away as the cause of what happened next. She was not the cause of my running away, nor my parents' divorce. With her departure, the family disintegrated.

I was ironing clothes when the phone rang. My mother answered the phone. The call was for me. I don't remember if it was a boy or girl. I was thirteen, entering my boy-crazy phase. I was humiliated by a pimple or the smell of my armpits. I spent hours worrying about hairy legs, blackheads, and excess weight. My head was filled with girlish dreams of living in Parisian garrets or dancing in New York. With my girlfriends, I worried about boys and homework. What so-and-so was really like. Whether so-and-so liked us. My awakening sexuality made my mother nervous.

My mother screamed at me to get off the phone. I continued talking. Angered, she walked up behind me and slammed the receiver down. I snapped,

"What did you do that for?" She grabbed the handset and hung it up. She screamed, ordering me back to the kitchen to continue ironing my brothers' starched jeans. I got angry. My mother was screaming at me because I had left on the iron and was wasting electricity. I did not understand why I had to wash, starch, and iron my brothers' clothes. My family's rules infuriated me. I didn't understand why I had to work so hard when the only contribution my brothers made was watering the vegetable gardens. Furious, my mother struck me. Then she struck me again, and again. She hit the ironing board. The iron fell off and burned my thigh. I screamed, so my mother hit me again because *I* had burned my thigh—*I had caused myself* to get burned. I started running away from her blows. She chased me around the table, trying to hit me with her fists.

After several rounds, I threw down chairs to block her path, but that did not stop her. She jumped over and continued to chase me. Then I picked up a broom and turned around. Facing her, I said, "If you ever hit me again, I will hit you back. I swear." She struck me, and I hit her with the broom. My mother became hysterical. She screamed I was no good. Howling, she said I beat her just like my father beat her. Shrieking. After all she had done, I turned out like this. Bad blood.

I dropped the broom and walked out of the house. My brother Kenneth tried to talk me out of leaving, but I opened the screen door. I stepped out into the porch, then started walking down the street. As I crossed the street, I felt this incredible wave of exhilaration. I knew then that I would never return to my parents' home. That I was finally free to find someplace where I could be happy. I looked up, and the skies were blue. My life lay ahead, ready to be made.

It was the tail end of the Haight-Ashbury. The Grateful Dead and Janis Joplin still played in Golden Gate Park for free. I was sixteen, and Kalani, who was Sada's old friend, Leilani's younger sister, helped enroll me in San Jose State's experimental New College.

Our curriculum consisted of two courses, "Man and Man" and "Man and Society." In "Man and Man," we studied human relationships. Our textbooks included *The Kinsey Report* and Masters and Johnson's *Human Sexuality*. Margaret Mead and other noted anthropologists, sociologists, and philosophers taught "Man and Society." When antiwar demonstrations and student protests mushroomed across the country, New College joined the picket lines en masse. We were next door to Berkeley, where the Free Speech Movement started, to Oakland, home of the Black Panthers, and to San Francisco State's Third World Strike. We marched against the war, and as a result, I lost my financial aid and could no longer afford to remain in college.

Moving to San Francisco, I gravitated toward Chinatown. Kearny Street was a hotbed of activity. The Red Guards started up patterned after the Black Panthers. I hung out listening to slick Chinatown guys talking about the takeover of the lumpen proletariat. I saw Asians waving the Red Book and studying Mao. I heard my peers shout, "Through constant struggle—vigilant battles fought on all fronts—we can overthrow the white ruling class and its lackeys. We can make a better world." And I truly believed that we could end oppression and make a better world.

Back then, whenever anyone said "movement," it was with a capital M. The Movement was an entity, a living being. It was a world encompassing Brothers and Sisters united by blood. It was a family. It was the smell of a jasmine-enclosed courtyard filled with my large extended family. I had been looking for family and this, I thought, was finally a place called home. There was a bond. We were Asians. We were creating history.

But families are never what they appear to be. Even families you make and pick for yourself. I discovered in the Movement, as in any other family or social structure, justice came from power. Who had the most authority and influence wielded the most power. The Women's Movement existed, but that was for white people. Within the Asian Movement, we were family. We didn't need to talk about women's issues, because the Revolution came first. After the Revolution, we would deal with women's issues. But the fissures were there, and when they erupted, I was caught in the living fire. I began to believe the Movement had failed because people were the same in the Left and the Right. Nice people. Bullies. Egotists. Men who preyed on young girls. Women who hated other women. Rhetoric did not change people's needs. My own included. What I had wanted from my "family" I was not getting.

I did not belong in Chinatown. Though I look Chinese, and even wore jade, which further identified me as Chinese, I would always answer truthfully,

"No, I'm not Chinese." Next would come the questions, "What are you?" Okinawan. What's that? The Ryûkû Islands are part of Japan. Oh, Japanese. Dead silence. In the minds of the old-timers, memories of wartime brutality and the Massacre of Nanking surfaced. I was guilty of Japanese crimes. I was guilty of coming from elsewhere, and for many whose boundaries were tied to the ghetto, those who came from outside were always suspect. If nothing else, we outsiders had the option to leave. And that option, in and of itself, made us suspect. Why were we there? We must want something, because, given the chance, everyone wanted out of the ghetto.

I moved to Los Angeles to work with the Japanese American community. Hiro, the chairman of an Asian American group aligned with the Brown Berets, Black Panther Party, Red Guards, and other "revolutionary lumpen proletariat" groups, moved in on me. One day I woke up and realized this man had moved into my basement apartment. He had driven me around, fed me dinner, helped me rent an apartment, then spent one night and never left. I was seventeen and didn't know how relationships developed. He was a nice enough man. Well liked by the whole Japanese community. He was also old enough to be my father. In his late thirties, Hiro had spent most of his adult life in San Quentin prison. Hiro justified our age difference by saying that the years in prison did not count. He was really just a few years older than I. My mother had given up hope, but Hiro redeemed her faith in my continuing the blood. Hiro was Nihonjin. I was Nihonjin. Once the blood is broken, you are no longer "of the people." I was redeemed by Hiro's Japanese blood. His blood made it possible for my mother and me to speak.

There were periods when my mother and I were able to talk, but mostly, my past is alienated from hers. Of spending birthdays, Christmas, Thanksgiving, and New Year's Day at friends' homes. Of feeling an ache inside my chest when the conversation would inevitably turn to my family. Why wasn't I there, with my own family? I had no answers. I couldn't say "orphan," and the word "dysfunctional" hadn't yet entered our vocabulary. Standing by Hiro, those questions were not asked. His presence eliminated them. It was automatically assumed I had taken that step from ancestral home toward a new family unit. I was barely eighteen, and couldn't think in terms of permanence. My energies were focused on other areas, and, as I said, Hiro was a nice enough man. Then I went to Cuba.

Boarding the boat in Nova Scotia, I spotted Gato Henriques through the crowds. Olive skin, piercing black eyes, and an aquiline nose. Our eyes locked, and that was that. A friend who had traveled with me saw the way our eyes connected. She shook her head, tsk-tsking, then reminded me of Hiro waiting in Los Angeles. It was too late. Out of about a boatload of several hundred Americans, we had found each other. Gato Henriques, my first love. My father later said Gato and I met because we were destined for one another. It was fate. It was karma.

Whatever it was, it changed our lives. When we left Cuba, I returned to Los Angeles and Gato stayed in New York. We agreed to wait for one another. I knew I had unfinished business in Los Angeles, but I was not prepared for the repercussions. Hiro was devastated, and his moping rendered him ineffective. In our radical Asian American circles, I was actually brought up on "counterrevolutionary" charges. I had betrayed the Asian Movement by falling in love with a Latino. Hiro's ineffectiveness was the direct result of my "counterrevolutionary actions," and therefore my responsibility. (Picture the village adulteress dragged through town and stoned.) The reaction of my radical Marxist comrades was similar to my family's. When I took Gato to meet my mother, she chased us out, screaming. Calling him a wetback. Spic. To her, working in the canneries, Mexicans were the lowest of the low. She would have rather I stayed with a Japanese felon old enough to be my father than be with a wetback.

I withdrew from the Movement and submerged myself in film school. With four others, I moved into a dilapidated house located in a black ghetto. Three of my roommates were involved in the Angela Davis' Defense Committee. Two of us had been to Cuba. Police helicopters constantly circled the house, beaming their lights into the rooms. Bright blocks of white light circling the walls, back and forth, as the tup-tupping noise boomed through the shabby walls. The FBI had interrogated my family and relatives, even questioning next-door neighbors in Hawai'i about my trip to Cuba. I buried myself in school, taking 18 units a quarter, and pined for Gato. Sitting in a darkened room, watching films like *Battle of Algiers, Harp of Burma,* and *Memories of Underdevelopment,* I dreamed of creating works which could create a revolution. And I waited for Gato.

I loved Gato, and was incapable of loving him. It has taken me years to realize this. To realize that love is a skill which is learned. We are born with the desire to love and be loved, but loving is not an inherent skill we carry out of the womb. True loving is an acquired skill.

And it is something we take for granted.

Gato and I loved each other with such an intensity we nearly killed each other. There's no other way to explain it. The passion we felt for one another caused us to change our lives, to sell our blood, to know when to make that precise phone call which would make all the difference in the world when you're thousands of miles apart. Between applications of paint on a Young Lords mural, he would call from New York. Moving from one temporary couch to another bed, he would check in at that very moment when I needed to hear his voice. Standing in the snow, he comforted me long-distance. On pay telephones, his love was doled out in quarters and dimes. Finally, the calls weren't enough.

He came to Los Angeles. One night, there was a wail of sirens, and a helicopter tup-tupping overhead, its lights swirling through the room. Minutes later, the FBI came pounding on our door. Gato was a Sandinista supporter and a draft evader. There was a White FBI Agent and an Asian FBI Agent. The White Guy played the heavy. He shoved his burly shoulders into the door and pushed. The flimsy door wobbled. The White Heavy shouted, ordering me to open the door. I screamed back, "Where's your warrant? Let me see a warrant."

"Hey, wait a minute," the Asian Guy calmed the White Guy. "Don't break the door down."

"Damn right!" I shouted. I slid down the door, my heart beating rapidly and hyperventilating with fear.

"Listen," the Asian Agent said in his coolest tone, "we just want to talk. That's all." He told me that there was a warrant out for Gato's arrest, and they knew I knew where he was. He tried to persuade me to open the door but I already figured out the scene we were playing. White Guy plays the Heavy. Asian Guy, the Good Guy. A scene straight out of cop films, with a twisted casting. I'm Asian, he's Asian. This is supposed to create a camaraderie. Sure, I'm suppose to believe him because we're of the blood.

Good Guy offered to slip me the warrant to give to Gato the next time I saw him, but the envelope was too thick to slide under the door. All I had to do was open the door. Leave the chain latch on, and he'd pass the envelope. White Heavy butted in, saying if I didn't open the door, the TAC Squad would break it down. Gato kissed me. *"Mujer,"* he said, "I don't want anything to happen to you." He told me to keep them occupied while he tried to escape. I tried to stop him, but he bounded up the stairs, to the second-floor fire escape overlooking the alley. I talked to Nice Guy, buying time, then opened the chain-latched door an inch. Heavy used this gap to bust the door down, ripping the latch off the jamb. Nice Guy sauntered into the room, looked me up and down, scanned the dumpy room, then seriously asked me, "What's a nice girl like you doing in a place like this?" I burst out laughing.

No arrest, just another harassment. After they left, the tup-tupping ended. Night returned to its ghetto quietness, a silence broken by the shrill sirens blaring in the distance. Night returned, and Gato came back, for the night. It wasn't safe for him to be in Los Angeles. I held him, and cried when he left for San Francisco. A year later, I moved to San Francisco to be with him. We lived in the Mission District.

"Oye como va," Santana sang, *la música* blaring from windows, cars, and shops. We lived on 22nd and Treat streets, in the heart of the Mission. Around us were the rhythms, smells, and sounds of Central Americans, Mexicans, and Puerto Ricans. Surrounded by a few whites, blacks, and a hell of a lot of Latinos, I felt slightly out of place. I was Asian, and I longed for the smells of my own people. It was two bus rides to Kearny Street, the heart of Chinatown. Or the 16 Mission bus to the 22 Fillmore to Japantown. Either way, my home was with Gato. Gato worked to make the Mission my home, always introducing me and making sure his friends were my friends. My Spanish improved, and I made my own connections in the Mission. But there was always an underlying question of identity. How much of my identity was I willing to change for a man?

I inherited video equipment from another Asian American filmmaker, and decided to organize a group of Asian women to make a film. A still photographer, a UN translator, a grad student, and three executive secretaries made up the Asian Women's Film Team. Within a space of a few months, Eve, one of the secretaries, had taken over the group. Eve was gregarious, fun-loving, and highly talkative. I was taciturn. I never felt comfortable in groups of people. Whereas Eve loved to gossip. She would call up other women and worry over what was happening. She talked about weight and insecurities. She easily made bonds.

Eve and I became best of friends. Eve believed she was free of traditional Japanese thinking, yet would argue for the superiority of male children. I believed bodies were simply temples to the mind, and that children had to be valued regardless of sex. I argued in favor of intellectual, personal, and spiritual freedom. Eve believed that, as Japanese, we had to first be proud of our ancestry. That race determined soul.

"Eve," I would say, "I'm not Japanese. I'm Okinawan."

Okinawa was once an independent kingdom. An unarmed, pacifist, animistic country which Japan invaded in the sixteenth century and took over by force in order to gain access to the China trade. We had our own culture and language, which Japan tried to destroy by outlawing it in the early nineteenth century. The result of Japanese military suppression was a mass exodus of a populace whose language and religion, like the Native Americans', was intrinsically tied to the land. There are more Okinawans living outside of Okinawa today than on Okinawa itself. The largest population of "Japanese" outside of Japan is the Okinawan community of São Paulo, Brazil. During World War II, Japan marched 120,000 young students off the cliffs of Okinawa to "stop the Americans from winning the war." Japan sacrificed Okinawa to save itself, but looked down on Okinawans as *jiboro-ken*, or "pig people."

"Please," I said, "don't try and make me proud of something I am not."

"But you are," she said. "Okinawa belongs to Japan."

"Okay, I'm Japanese," I conceded, "and you, you're American. If I have to call myself Japanese, then you can't say you're not American. You were born here. Your father is in the CIA. You're about as American as they get."

We would go around and around, and beneath all of this back-and-forth banter, our love grew. Eve conceded that Japan's militaristic imperialism had harmed Asia, and that it was quite possible males were not inherently superior, but drew the line when I declared we humans were not biologically heterosexual. She refused to accept that, as a species, sexuality was culturally determined. She thought that, as an intellectual, I lived too much in my head, that my ideas were too radical, but at the same time believed in my vision. Eve said, "You want to build empires, which is okay, because the world you want to create is better than the world we live in."

Eve decided to learn sound so we could make films together. I would shoot, and she would record sound. When I organized an apprenticeship program to get more women and Third World people into films, Eve worked with me, making calls. Sending out mailings. Organizing meetings. She was the female complement to the world I had created with Gato. At one pole, there was Gato. There was the masculine artist, the poet, the linguist, the essence of the Mission, who was studying Nahuatl, the ancient Mayan tongue. On the other side was Eve, the primordial female. The small, round Japanese woman with waist-length hair and a round moon face who worshipped Japanese femininity. Eve, who was my ally as I entered films.

I had left one narrow enclave, that of the Asian Movement, and got into Third World filmmaking, which was another enclave. Then the Mission. These three were facets of the same reality, that of the Third World artist. Of a fluid world where the language of musicians, writers, painters, dancers, and filmmakers merged into the same words, into the same struggle. And as Third World artists, our lives were a struggle. On my birthday, Gato went down to the plasma center and sold a pint of blood to make me a special dinner of *gallina en mole con arroz y vino*. He gave me the key of words when we could barely pay rent, much less buy film. We lived in a world of poets praising Bob Marley, of bodies swaying to Jah, of painters paying tribute to Che Guevara, Lumumba, and Ho Chi Minh. We lived amidst people struggling to survive.

This was a very different world from films. Filmmakers were white, mostly males from the middle or upper classes. Men who talked about the value of investment tax credits, who were connected to Francis (Coppola), who had martinis before dinner. Who had washing machines and mortgages. These men were different from the Third World artists Gato and I knew, but they were aligned to the Third World Struggle. They belonged in a separate enclave, that of the liberal white world. They were the same as socialites who contributed to the Black Panther Party. They wanted to change the world, to give people like me access to their world. I was both a mascot and a political ideal. I represented the new breed that they took under their wing.

When I told a tall anemic man with failing kidneys that I wanted to shoot, he sat me down and taught me how to strip down a camera. He said, "You can pay your rent by learning how to take apart a complicated piece of machinery." I got over my traditional upbringing. I realized that if my car broke down, I didn't have to lift up the hood and wait for a man to stop and help me. I could learn how to fix it myself. I was raised in a family where anything outside the house belonged to men, where technology belonged to men, and I, as the little woman, kept my place in the kitchen. And entering this door liberated me financially.

Gato said he was glad that this was helping me get jobs, yet at the same time, tension started developing between us. I was becoming the breadwinner. I said words and heard an echo of my mother shrieking at my father, demanding he get up off the couch and weed the garden. I couldn't stop the echo. Each success made him feel less a man.

He admitted one day that I was better known in the Mission than he. That he was jealous of my success as a writer and as a filmmaker. It humiliated him that Latinos thought I was Latina, that people he didn't know thought I was part of *la comunidad,* that as an artist, a writer, I was more known than he— and I wasn't even Latina. I was shocked. I felt inconsequential. I couldn't make films. I felt I didn't belong. "No," Gato said, "you walked that walk, talked that talk, and strutted through the streets like you belonged." For a Latino, belonging is attitude. Latinos had always embraced others. *Negritos, indios, y blancos* are all part of La Raza.

We wrote up agreements and contracts, promising peace. Swearing that the struggle lay outside the home, our arguments and reconciliations continued to peak higher and higher. Each time we'd have a fight, one of us would leave. But it never surprised me when I would find myself walking down Folsom Street when Gato would suddenly materialize. It was that way even when we got into a fight on the street and walked off in opposite directions. We would end up drawn to the same bus, the same corner, never able to escape what Gato called "our lasting long terrible affair."

Our terrible intimacy and my other worlds drove me crazy. I ended it badly. We had shared a house with another couple. We were all moving out. I saw a studio apartment, a small one-room overlooking the shipyards and the 101 freeway. I stood in front of the sixteen-foot bay windows, and the tears and words we used against each other came back to me. The deadly accuracy which comes out of intimacy used to wound. Words which only lovers could use to slice each other apart with razor efficiency. We did this to each other in spite of our love. Staring at the ships, at the cars driving below on the freeway, I decided to leave him.

I spent the next month in front of that huge bay window watching the cars on the freeway below. The accidents, the time it took for the Highway Patrol, the nonstop traffic. Even at night, passersby slowed down for a better look at accident victims. I watched the traffic and mourned the loss of our affair.

Eve understood. Eve listened to me mourn and reminded me I left Gato because I could not be in films and be with him. Because my worlds tore me apart. Gato hated that I worked and survived. I ran from film sets, each night driving back to my world with him. I ran from a world of white men in Pendleton shirts back to San Francisco, where Gato glared at me because each success made him feel less and less, and I didn't know how to make him feel better. Eve said it wasn't my fault I couldn't find words to appease his ego. It should have been enough that I was bringing home money. She attacked his macho limitations which proved his male pride was more important than love. Eve reassured. I wasn't crazy. She had witnessed it all. She listened to me cry. She realized I would have never been with him if he wasn't the man of my dreams.

Gato read a poem he had written before we had ever met, which everyone believed was about me: "Your images have floated back to me / blurred and sharp . . . indeed at times a whore . . . a witch . . . you're young and don't know what lies beyond these bedroom walls . . . in the days when you were the queen and I the jester / those were the best times my love / following you behind mirrors of false society and down the lanes of white amerika . . . now you stand with your bags packed / ready to leave the streets that gave you birth and go wandering among the hands that have no pity and words that tell no truths. But one day . . . one day *mujer, mujer* you're going to come back wearing their clothes, speaking their words, doing their things and I'm going to lead you down the alleys we fought and the streets where we played and the rooms where we made love . . . you're going to see your people whom you abandoned and deserted *y mujer vas a llorar.*" Woman, woman will you cry?

I watched the sun rise up over the bay, silhouetting the Erector Set lifts of working cargo ships. I regretted leaving him, but nothing I could do could change what had happened. Gato finally closed the door on me and said no more. *Mujer,* I can't handle it anymore. I had left him, and that leaving had irrevocably changed what lay between us. Gato was cool. He wanted to avoid repetition. Packing a few belongings with a book of Baudelaire's poems and tapes of Augustin Lara, he took a Greyhound bus to Tijuana. Gato walked across the border, then got on a train and continued south. South, past Guadalajara, Yucatán, and to Guatemala, where he listened to the parrots. Hitchhiking, traveling on buses and by foot, until he finally crossed into Nicaragua, where he joined the Sandinistas.

I realized I had always needed him, but didn't know how to need. That I wanted love, but was incapable of loving. I was frantic. I was bleeding from self-inflicted wounds. I needed him. I had walked away and Eve watched me crawl back. Eve saw Gato turn his head, and the way I wept. Everywhere I was, Eve was, sharing my hopes and pains.

I put on my fedora, skirt, heels, and painted my lips a bright red. I danced the night away in a Lycra bodysuit. After the discos closed, there were after-hours clubs. Eve and I went with an entourage of Asians who lived in the Mission. Mostly Chinese, from Hong Kong. Once, we had just walked into a disco when a big husky man asked me to dance. I hadn't even ordered a drink. I said, "No, thanks," then followed Eve to our group of friends. After our drinks arrived, I got up from our table to go to the bathroom. He followed me, maneuvering his burly torso through the crowd and blocked my path, demanding, "What's the matter with you bitches?" He demanded to know why hot Asian bitches always turned him down. Did we think we were too good for him? The scene got uglier, and when he pushed me against the wall, I screamed. The bouncer threw him out. It was like that when we went out to straight clubs. Men who had come there trying to score saw a group of pale-skinned, black-haired China dolls too stuck-up to dance or talk. We made their bile rise, and they had to prove that they were men enough for us. All we wanted to do was dance. We didn't go to clubs to pick up men. We liked to dance and listen to music. Straight discos became such a hassle that we stopped going to them and went to gay clubs. There, we could twirl and laugh, smile and clap our hands without anyone batting an eye.

Back then, we didn't "date." We went out and hung out. We were in the artistic, post-college scene too hip to "date." We went to each other's houses, had coffee, wine, and late-night conversations. We didn't do this by prearranged calls, asking for a Friday evening "date." We went out in a group and units would form. Couples. Couples whose configurations were constantly fluctuating.

Peter made me dinner and waited until I would show up at his apartment, always late. Peter played his saxophone and treated me sweetly. But Peter was not Gato. Dwight was a nice Japanese American community activist who had a girlfriend. Dwight came over and painted my studio walls six times because he knew I believed in the purity of white. Dwight was willing to leave his girlfriend for me. When I said no, Dwight whispered, "Bitch. I was willing to give it all up for you." There were others, and there were those of Eve's. Gary was a pale-skinned Chinese American poet who listened to jazz. One night Eve got up from his futon. She put her clothes on and muttered, "Gary, your poetry's okay." Her hand waved in the air as she delivered the killing blow, "Yeah, it's okay, but Geraldine is a far better writer than you'll ever be. She's smarter, prettier, and has more natural talent in her little finger than you'll ever have."

The next day, when I ran into Gary, his eyes drifted. I couldn't figure it out until Eve relayed what had happened. Thereafter, when his eyes refused to meet mine, I would look at Eve wryly and say, "Eve, just leave me out of your affairs. If you want to dump a guy, dump him. But don't use me as an excuse." Eve shrugged her shoulders, countering, "But you *are* a far better writer. Gary's just a lamebrain guy who thinks with his dick."

"And whose fault is that?" I asked.

Eve laughed. "Not mine. He was that way when I found him."

I sighed. Unable to come up with a more convincing argument which could stop Eve from being Eve, I accepted her.

After my sister Sada and I had left home, my mother threw my father out. My parents had two homes, the first a small two-unit property we had first moved into when we came here from Hawai'i and the second, three blocks away, was a three-bedroom, two-bath affair we called the Big House. My mother lived in the Big House with my brothers and Emily. My father moved into the studio apartment behind the Little House. When my younger sister Emily said she was getting married, my father quit work. He spent his days reading, going to the racetrack, and babysitting Sada's son, Ulysses.

Though I myself can spend days on end reading, without talking to a soul, my father's reclusiveness bothered me. I insisted he get out, and gave him a key to my apartment. He drove up to San Francisco, to my apartment overlooking the freeway, and parked behind Eve's Volkswagen. He had a key, which he didn't feel like using. He rang the bell. I buzzed him in.

He pointed toward the street, "Whose Volkswagen parked outside?"

"The beige one?" Eve answered, "That's mine."

My father told her she had been rear-ended. As a Volkswagen's engine was in the back, she should check the engine block if she hadn't done so already. Eve ran out, my father following. A few minutes later they returned. Eve was shaking her finger, clearly accused him of senility. There was no dent. My father looked at his feet and shuffled sheepishly. But the next day, exactly where my father had pointed, there was a dent. I was as shocked as Eve.

Living with my father, I had discovered he was another man than the one who shared my childhood home. My father believed in karma. He said the sins of a parent descended on their children. He looked at my brothers, my sisters, and me with a sense of regret and failure. He regretted beating Sada. He now felt responsible for her dropping out of school and marrying Harlan, who had abandoned her while she was pregnant. He was responsible for my running away and the breakdown of the family. To make up, he had become Sada's babysitter and Ulysses's surrogate father. He drove back to San Jose whenever Sada needed him to babysit. He made me dinner, listened to my friends and me talk. He believed in what we were doing, but worried. When was I going to settle down? Get a real job? I was a poet for the Neighborhood Arts Program, but this was not a job. A job was something unpleasant. I worked in films, but the money I made was highway robbery. We took him to clubs and parties, but he didn't like the music and crowds. He worried if I would ever get married.

I met Ly Ba at a meeting in Chinatown. Tall, fine-boned, elegantly handsome, Ly Ba reeked of sensitivity. I averted my eyes, glancing at the floor. Eve poked me in the ribs. "Hey," she said. I looked up, a grin on my face. She curled her lips. "Okay, what's going on?" I shook my head—"Nothing"—then cast a quick glance at Ly Ba. After the meeting, Eve rolled her eyes. "Don't tell me that's the kind you like," she muttered.

Offended, I asked, "What kind?"

"You can't fool me."

"Who's trying to fool you?"

"You are. Don't try to pretend. I saw you ogling him."

I admitted being interested in Ly Ba. But that was all. I doubted if I would ever meet him again. "Why not?" Eve demanded. "What kind of a feminist are you? Why can't you go after the man you want? Are you the kind of woman who just sits there and lets the man pick? Maybe that's the problem. And you know what they say. Scum rises to the top. You get what you deserve."

"You're right," I conceded. "I'm a coward."

Eve laughed, and later that night, I called Ly Ba. He was asleep. His roommate woke him up. We got together later that week, had a bite, and talked. He liked running and its endorphin highs. That's why he was so thin. That, and his delicate appetite, which I got to know over the next year.

When my father met Ly Ba, he said, "Watch out for him." I asked him, "Why?" He mumbled, "That guy is no good." Irritated, I demanded to know why. Was he being jealous? Protective? Fatherly? My father said, "Those Hong Kong guys are dog-eat-dog. That one only thinks of himself." Impossible, I said to myself. Ly Ba was the Americanized version of the perfect Chinese scholar. Born and raised in Hong Kong, Ly Ba had spent his years in a Jesuit school before he came to California to study art. He was brilliant, sensitive, and the first man I looked at twice since Gato.

Ly Ba was also impotent.

Getting up out of bed, I walked out into the hallway and found my father drinking coffee in the kitchen. His drink was instant coffee. He didn't like espresso, *caffè latte*, or cappuccino. Just Taster's Choice. He looked at me, his cup between his palms, and nodded. A slight lift of his head and nod was his expression of concern. I answered by shrugging my shoulders and raising my eyebrows into a caret. No words. I did not elaborate. My father knew Ly Ba was in my bedroom. We had all had dinner earlier that night. I did not tell him

Ly Ba had said this is the way it was with him. That his impotence was why his wife left him. My father did not need to know.

But I didn't believe Ly Ba when he said it wasn't my fault. I believed there was something wrong with me. Maybe it was, as my mother had said, bad blood. That was why this refined Chinese scholar spent hours walking and talking with me, why he proclaimed I was the one who understood him, yet was unable to consummate our relationship. I read every book on the subject, trying to discover why. I did not want to believe it was simply bad blood. There had to be a cause, and a cure. Eve laughed and said it was because he was a wimp. I had picked the wrong man. My father didn't say anything but it was clear Ly Ba was not right for me.

While this was happening, my film school colleagues were releasing their first feature. Their ability to raise money and direct made me question my life. I believed in outcome, and lacking the financial power to direct, I concluded I had made a mistake. I thought my Marxist politics had betrayed art. I had gotten sidetracked into labor issues. Into suing the CBS network and the union for discrimination. Into trying to change the face of the film industry by changing the makeup of its labor pool. I decided that I would either make a film or get out of the industry. But I couldn't create for pure personal pleasure. A film of mine had to have a political context. I chose the International Hotel. I decided to make a straight-ahead documentary. A newsreel cameraman helped me gain access to reels of unprocessed film. These documented the beginning of the hotel struggle and included a meeting between the Tenants Association and Mayor Alioto. They also showed the formation of the first picket lines and manongs talking in Tony's barbershop. I had to process the footage, which resulted in a $10,000 lab bill. Back then, there were no grants for political filmmaking. I didn't have a trust fund or a monied family. I had to make money working on features, commercials, and news to pay off the lab.

Behind the glamour, film work is hard and grueling. Overtime does not start until after ten, twelve, or fourteen hours of work. With the exception of a few rare women doing hair, makeup, wardrobe, or script, I was surrounded by men. Wall-to-wall men, all white. Big, burly guys. I saw news crews celebrating the igniting of a Symbionese Liberation Army house, cheering as its human occupants were burned to cinders. I knew of studio engineers faking a technical failure to prevent Bobby Seale's speech from being televised. These men were part of an industry which started to change only after the Supreme Court and the Justice Department intervened. One of these men came up to me at the start of a union show and said, "I've heard about you, and I hate your guts." I coolly replied, "The feeling is mutual." Throughout the show, he and his men heckled me with catcalls of "Yokohama Mama," whistling and cupping their crotches. They refused to provide me assistance. After we had wrapped, he asked me to have a cup of coffee with him. He said, "You know, for a Jap, you're all right." I quickly retorted, "For a racist, you're all right." "Let's get one thing straight," he shouted, "I'm not a racist. I'm a bigot. Got that? A bigot. B-i-g-o-t." He pounded on the table to emphasize, "I'm *not* a racist."

That was the end of the show. During the next two shows, I hated being in motels with these guys so much that I would drive back to San Francisco and return to location for the next day's call. I had to be with friends. It wasn't a choice. I had to eat rice, be among faces of color. Working location hours is exhausting, but my drives back to San Francisco made my days even longer. I didn't have a choice. I couldn't stand being on location. I ended up sleeping less and less. My health was deteriorating, and I was in emotional chaos.

Ly Ba said, "You know, there are a lot of people in the community who don't like you. They think you're too hard. You're not Asian enough. They don't know you like I do, but it bothers me. I can't talk about you. You have this awful reputation of being a difficult woman. I don't know what to do. I don't know how to explain my friendship with you." There was a long silence as his words took root. I said, "I don't know how to be different." I tried not to cry, but I couldn't stop small tears. Ly Ba took my hand and we continued walking.

Eve was the one who defended me. When anyone said anything negative, she snapped back. Her protectiveness created problems, but I accepted them. Eve believed in me. She also understood there was a part of me infinitely lost. She saw I tried to find myself in other lovers, but was haunted by Gato's ghost. I wept at inopportune moments. I was so entwined in my own personal drama that I did not really understand when Eve said she loved me. I didn't realize how seductive my suffering was. Nor see Eve's friendship as the emotional salve of my life. I did not comprehend the obsessiveness with which she loved me.

Eve and I went to a New Year's party with our trendy Hong Kong friends. Noted drag queen performer Sylvester performed live. I wore a long white velvet dress with a feathered hat. We danced, drank, and partied. I drank too much. Eve drove me home in my car. I was too drunk to safely drive home from her apartment. Eve made me coffee, but the only cure was sleeping it off. We were in the habit of spending the night at one another's apartments. I thought this time was no different, but in the middle of the night I woke with Eve's hands over my body. Exploring, demanding, possessing. I was too drunk to protest.

The next day, as we were crossing Army Street, Eve grabbed my arm. On the other side of the underpass, the light turned green. "Be careful," Eve said as she grabbed my arm. "You could get hit by a car."

I turned away, "You're turning into an overprotective mother." Eve grabbed for my arm, missed and ran to keep up with my faster pace.

"Because I worry about you," Eve protested. "Don't be mad at me because I love you."

The more I tried to run from Eve, the tighter she held on. Eve's fingers on my arm made me picture macho men wistfully seeking demure women. I laughed, realizing men who wanted a soft little woman holding on to them deserved the stranglehold of clinging vines. Blind to the bond between master and slave, the macho does not realize Eve makes them the master.

"Well," she said one day, "I've been sleeping with your father."

I looked at her. Was this supposed to make me mad?

"But I wasn't attracted to him. That's why I stopped sleeping with him. I was never interested in him." She took a deep sigh, then looked down at the ground. "The only reason I seduced him was because I'm still in love with you. I know it was wrong, using him like that. I don't know what I was thinking. Somehow, because he was your father, that made him appealing." She looked up and continued, "I felt that by making love to him, I could still make love to you. Don't be mad. I did it because I love you."

Like Eve, I had used love. I let Gato fly. My love immortalized him above the realm of the ordinary. I look back and ask, "Was it Gato or the act of loving which obsessed me?" Is it me or the symbol of me which Eve loves? I am tall, thin, androgynous. Plump moon-faced Eve holds on with a tight grip.

Our friends look at us and wonder what has happened. I, who advocated bisexuality, am probably homophobic. I rejected Eve. I am confused. For Eve, who has been so much a part of me, I cannot feel anything but betrayal. But how can love be a betrayal? I have encounters with women and discover it is not homophobia. It is Eve. I cannot love Eve any other way than as my friend. The woman closest to my heart, who has shared my life, cannot take the place of a lover.

My father moved out of my apartment, back to his one-room studio, where he lived on peanut butter sandwiches and instant coffee. I had felt guilty. I drove him away. Now I was relieved and confused. My best friend seduced him, but it was my fault. She wanted me. Whatever was important to me became important to Eve. She wanted everything I touched. Eve became the goddess Kali who devoured the world in order to re-create. She ate everything around me to possess me. And I loved Eve. I loved Eve and gave her permission to possess. It was my fault. I grieved for my father. I realized my opening my life to him had made him feel pain. It was like watching a party going on through a window, of wanting to be part of it while knowing what you glimpsed would never be your world. He did not belong. He was older, less educated, and worn by years of working. He was of another generation. He belonged in a world of instant coffee and peanut butter sandwiches.

I have a recurring dream of flying. Standing on a windswept plateau, I hold out my arms and, with a few steps, lift off. My arms catch in the wind, and I move. Always, my dreams end with me flying over the blue seas. I look at my life, and wonder about the choices I have made. My health is a disaster. I have burned bridges. I thought freedom could be bought, but each success left me empty. There was always something else which could be done. My frantic activities, so reminiscent of my mother, have brought me the same measure of reward. I look around and ask, "What is the point of all this?" I hear in my voice an echo of my mother.

I dream of the colors of my childhood. I dream of trekking through the underbellies of jungles, of riding the Orient Express from the tip of Penang, through Southeast Asia, and into Turkey. I dream of the Sahara, of camels and lions. I decide to pack it all in. Shelving the International Hotel documentary, my manuscripts, I announce I am leaving for Asia.

Before I leave the United States, I ask my mother if there was anything she would like me to do while I was in Asia. She asked me to visit her sister, Aunt Tsuyuko, in Los Angeles, and her mother, Uta, in Maui.

I meet my mother's younger sister, Aunt Tsuyuko, in an overly air-conditioned coffee shop with orange flocked wallpaper. She says, "Do you know?" I look at her. Aunt Tsuyuko was unmarried, had been involved with a married man for years, and in therapy for even longer. As far as my mother was concerned, Tsuyuko had made a mess of her life. Wasting money all those years on a therapist. Being involved with married men. Now a spinster who lived beyond her means, Tsuyuko asked me if I knew. Was it the married man? The therapy? So I shook my head. She then tells me the story of my mother's family.

At the turn of the century, her grandfather, my great-grandfather Gongoro, left his village in Okinawa saying, "If I fail, I will die before I return." Migrating to Hawai'i, Gongoro worked cutting cane on the sugar plantations. When he was promoted to *happaiko* (carrying loads of sugarcane), he sent for his wife, my great-grandmother Tsuru.

My aunt fidgets with her purse. "You know, your great-grandmother was a beautiful woman." She nervously pulls out an envelope and hands me a faded photograph of Tsuru. "This is your great-grandmother."

I see a strong face, beautiful in its stark simplicity, but it is her eyes which are surprising. She has hypnotic, piercing eyes which, combined with the downward tilt of her lips, immediately draw attention. I comment, "She looks mean."

"Mean?" My aunt laughs. "No—unhappy. She had a hard life."

She explains that my great-grandmother Tsuru's family were weavers. Tsuru herself had the family weaving patterns tattooed up the length of her fingers, all the way to the wrist. Recalling the bonelike patterns I had seen on old women's hands, I ask, "Is that why they tattooed the hands? Because of the weaving?"

"Not just that. In the old days they did that to stop the Naichis from kidnapping Okinawan women and taking them to Japan. But it's dying out, that habit. No one does it anymore. You know, nowadays being Okinawan is not such a big deal. But back then, in your great-grandmother's time, only a few people spoke Japanese. Your great-grandfather Gongoro could. And his children, your grandfather Taro and his brother, they could read and write Japanese."

I hand my aunt back her photo of my great-grandmother. "My mother doesn't look anything like her."

"They say your mother looks like your great-grandfather Gongoro. See" —she points to Tsuru's face—"the high forehead and narrow face are nothing like your mother's. But you have her eyes. Even your eyebrows, the way they arch, are like your great-grandmother's."

"Mine?" My hand goes up to feel my brow, "This arches up because of a scar I got as a kid. There's no hair here. That's why it slants up."

"I thought it was because of her."

"My mother says I take after my father's mother."

"Good thing," my aunt says. Then continues her story.

Great-grandmother Tsuru had two children, one of whom became her father, my grandfather Taro. A plantation woman, she worked beside her husband in the field. Setting her children down at the edge of the fields, she followed the machete-wielding men, picking the burnt stalks up, stacking them into piles, then rushing back to breast-feed her young children. When they got older, she continued checking up on them to make sure they were all right or were doing their homework. At the end of the day, she gathered them up and rushed home to get Gongoro's bath ready. In addition to working in the fields and raising their children, she prepared food, cleaned up, did the laundry, and raised food. All of this entailed heavy labor—drawing water from the well, lighting wood fires, and scrubbing the laundry by hand.

After working in the fields, Gongoro would go out with his friends for *sake no sakana*, to eat and drink. A common practice in Okinawa, *sake no sakana* was a right immigrant men exercised as often as they could on the Hawaiian plantations. Tsuru would get angry because after they had worked so hard, Gongoro squandered what little money they had on *sake no sakana*. When she complained, Gongoro became angry. He believed a man must beat a woman to turn her into a wife. Tsuru defended his behavior with *"Wataru sekan ni oni wa inai,*" an old saying which meant "There are no devils in the world—people are people everywhere." Gongoro was no different than any other man. He was the same, no better or worse. This she understood.

Tsuru's moderate temper and kind heart made her very popular with the many unmarried men working on the plantation. They would jump up to volunteer for *ímáru,* the traditional labor-sharing practice of men banding together to help each other accomplish a single task. She listened to their troubles and did small favors. Patching holes, hemming pants, or giving out Mason jars of homemade pickles. Great-grandfather was jealous. He beat her when other men paid her too much attention. But he was also proud that she was an aristocratic weaver. When she worked by his side in the fields, Tsuru wore a cotton bonnet made out of bleached rice bags to keep her skin pale and soft.

As their children grew, the family prospered. Their two sons were fluent in Okinawan, Japanese, and English. Being able to communicate trilingually, Taro and his brother worked as *luna,* or overseers, on the plantation. They were informal "lawyers" who helped immigrants translate documents, file papers, or apply for visas. The eldest, Taro would inherit the family name and property. When it came time for Taro to marry, they turned toward Okinawa.

Using a matchmaker, they looked around for suitable prospects. When a likely candidate was located, the astrologers did a forecast, matching charts and personal histories. Were the families from similar class backgrounds? Did the *noro,* the priestess shamans, predict an auspicious match? Gongoro's emissaries looked in their home village and neighboring villages to find Uta.

Rankled that her younger sister was the most popular village belle who already had several suitors, Uta was lucky that astrologers had forecast her match with Taro. Her belief that she could do better than her younger sister was finally justified. In this firstborn son, trilingual and a *luna,* Uta had finally found a suitor who outranked all of her sister's suitors put together. She readily accepted the go-between's proposal. At sixteen years of age, Uta went to her husband, whom she had never seen, as a mail-order bride.

Crossing the Pacific, she looked forward to Hawai'i. Hawai'i meant new hope. An escape from economic and political repression. One of her fellow passengers stood at the rail sadly singing *Sanyamá,* the heartrending farewell song of an Okinawan king exiled in Satsuma territory, but in Uta's heart, the fast-paced, merry *kacháshí* played. She had no use for sad songs of exile. The quick-tempoed merry dance music of the common folk matched her departure from the land of her birth. But Uta's dreams were short-lived. After giving birth to six children, tragedy struck.

Gongoro and his friends had worked the whole week. It was the end of the week, and the men went out for *sake no sakana*. Brown and hardened by the hot sun, the men drank to celebrate. Or to forget. Life had not turned out the way they had expected. Long ago, many of them had sworn they would return to Okinawa rich men. Gongoro now knew this would never happen. Not for him. *Sake no sakana* made it bearable. In hard distilled liquor, he could forget. In the bottle he could find pleasure. Someone pulled out a samisen and sang. In the wee hours of the morning, he staggered home.

It's unclear whether it happened in their bedroom or if Tsuru was waiting in the living room. Was she sewing pieces of a quilt, her feet tucked beneath her hips, when he staggered into their house? Or did he kick the bedding off her? Waking her to his bitterness? Or was she sitting there waiting, her mouth frozen in a tight-knit frown? The details leading up to the event are unclear, but its aftermath is irrefutable.

Gongoro beat Tsuru. This had happened many times throughout their marriage, but this time Gongoro went too far. Gongoro struck a blow which caught her under the jaw and threw her against the wall. She dropped to the floor, her neck broken. Gongoro killed Tsuru. Though accidental and unpremeditated, it still came down to the same thing—my great-grandfather murdered my great-grandmother.

I am shocked. I cannot breathe.

My aunt Tsuyuko's voice shakes as she tells me of the family becoming *etta*, of turning "untouchable." Of the superstitious traditions which speak of crimes in the family running through bloodlines. Of blood link. Of the desperate poverty that descended on the family, and of Grandmother Uta turning from her empty cupboards to face six hungry children. Of her heart turning cold, of hate jelling. Tsuyuko looks down at the coffee cup, then stares up at the ceiling. She talks in a haze, bitterly describing the family's ostracization by the community and their move to the barren countryside.

"This is why we turned out this way. The ground was like a black hole.

Everything we poured into it was lost. Water, fertilizer, nothing made it produce. The soil was no good. It was used up. We moved from our house in town to a barren desert of volcanic rock. We had to grow food to sell, but there was never enough. And what did grow, what could be sold, went to market. All the good stuff. We kept the rejects. The twisted vegetables too deformed to sell, the string beans too old and tough that nobody wanted. Those we kept and ate. I used to think that it was because of the twisted eggplants. The deformed Japanese eggplants shriveled up inside of us, growing like worms. Making us as black and bitter as the food we ate. I look back and think to myself: God, how lucky you are. How lucky you were able to survive. But we didn't come out unscathed. We turned out just like the stuff we ate. Your mother, she had it the worst. She was the firstborn. I still can see her at nine years old. Turning around, looking back, and my mother, Uta, shooing her away. Sending her off to work at Dr. Jerome's house. Every month Hana came back with her paycheck. That Hana! How she used to fight with the old lady! The two of them fought like cats and dogs. Oh, I know Hana's difficult, but don't blame your mother. Your grandmother was the one who made her that way."

I am stunned. Everything Tsuyuko says falls into place. At nine, my mother being sent to work as a domestic in the plantation doctor's house. Her small hands bringing home her paycheck so Uta could feed her other five children. Uta, who burned her children with smoldering tips of cigarettes, who reveled in her husband before he became outcast. Pariah. Who hated her fall from grace. Who hated her children. Related by marriage, it was in the blood. Bad blood.

My aunt Tsuyuko and I are both crying. She takes out my great-grandmother's photo and says, "This is for you. You keep it."

A week later, I get on a plane to fly to Hawai'i. It has been over ten years since I have last been home. My grandmother Uta and her friend, Nakasone-san, pick me up at the airport. I am driven to the local tourist spots. Uta and Nakasone-san do not get out of the car. They drive to places they would not normally visit because I am there. After the three-hour tour, she takes me to her home. It is the house we lived in when I was a child. The old woman next door remembers me. She laughs, talks about my cat. The calico cat I left behind when we moved away from Hawai'i. I had not remembered the old woman but recall the tears I shed as a little girl for my cat.

My grandmother opens the door of her light green house and we enter a screened porch filled with orchids. In the next room a koto and a samisen are propped against the wall, next to a *butsudan* (altar). Lugging my bags, I stop to examine the photos on the mantel, but Nakasone-san says, "Later. There will be time later." He leads me into a room which once belonged to my uncle Maasaki, who died in the 442nd. He tells me he and my grandmother Uta are tired. They are old. They don't go out anymore. The drive into town and my tour wore them out. *Gomen nasai*. After a nap, they will prepare the bath and dinner. Put your things away, take a rest. We will see you later. He shows me an empty dresser drawer my grandmother prepared, then leaves.

I open the dresser drawers. The smell of mothballs wafts out. In the closet, rows of Hawaiian shirts wait for their long-dead owner to return. Standing there, I think to myself that ghost stories are merely another way of viewing history. To me, the granddaughter raised on the mainland, my grandmother's favorite son's room has become a memorial to the dead. Everything is the way it was when he was still alive. He is not a part of history. His clothes are waiting for him to return, ready to slip over his ghost. Even his khaki uniform hangs erect, next to his girlfriend's picture. Still living. Waiting.

Looking in the mirror, I wonder about other ghosts. I go into the living room and examine the row of photos on the mantel. I find a picture of myself from the fourth grade, a rat's nest of curls surrounding a gap-toothed smile, and pictures of my aunts, uncles, and cousins. But even in the *butsudan*, I cannot find a picture of my great-grandmother Tsuru. It is like the family started from the birth of Uta's children. No trace of Gongoro or Tsuru.

The effort of unpacking is too much. I pull out toiletries, then lie on the bed, trying to reconcile stories of the woman who burned her children with my grandmother today. I think of the round waddling figure waiting for me at the airport gate, and cannot recognize her. The smiling face of an old woman who laughs too much. Whom, if I didn't know better, I would think of as kind. But I know my mother, aunt, and uncles do not lie. Terrorized by Uta, my mother and her siblings ran away as far and as fast as they could. My mother told me

Uta is now old and lonely. She has no one. No one, that is, except Nakasone-san, who some say has been my grandmother's lover for nearly fifty years.

I fall asleep and wake to Nakasone-san's knocking. The bath is ready, he says. He and *babang*, my grandmother, have already bathed. I should come and bathe while the water is still hot. I grab a robe and follow him. He leads me to a small hut in the backyard. Uta comes out from behind the hut. Worried that I was still sleeping, she has just added a log to the wood-burning water heater. Warning me that the log could make the *ofuro* too hot, she shows me how to turn on the garden faucet to cool the bath. They leave. Beams of light stream through cracks, illuminating the dank wooden walls and slatted floor.

Scrubbed clean, I go into the kitchen and watch her carefully peel off slivers of meat from a chicken for *okazu*. She warns against waste. Everything, she says, has a use. Nakasone-san sits at the table, tapping the Formica pattern with his nails. I ask if I can help. She directs me to a cupboard where I find a *katsuo kezuri-ki*, a grater used to shave dried fish, then digs out a dried mackerel. Holding the mackerel, she shows me how to grate the fish to make paper-thin bonito flakes for the *miso shiro*'s soup base. Taking the fish from her, I look at it. I have never seen a whole, dried mackerel. The bonito I use for stock comes pre-flaked in individually wrapped packets or in powdered granules. She tells me this was sent to her by one of my uncles. Holding it up, I notice a small wriggling form disappearing into a hole. "Oh my God," I say, "the fish is riddled with worms."

"*Na ne?*" she asks. I point out the holes lining the body. Nakasone-san finds a pair of glasses. He examines the mackerel, then hands both to Uta. She puts on his glasses, examines the fish, then laughs. She tells me not to worry. Turning the oven on to high, she bakes the fish to kill the worms. She says worms are protein. Worms, fish, it's all the same.

She entertains me with her stock of dried mushrooms, gourds, and seaweed while Nakasone-san takes over my job of shaving thin slivers off the dried fish for soup. Opening the freezer, she reveals a Tupperware container of chicken innards. With Nakasone-san's help, she gives me her recipe for gizzards, ginger, and *miso*. Shares her secret of saving odd pieces of chicken skin, which fried in its own fat is like cracklings, or cooked with *shoyu* and red pepper spices up rice. I decide to fill her in on recent discoveries.

I tell her I had lunch with Tsuyuko and ask about her husband, Taro, my grandfather. She laughs and says, "Taro? Hmmm, long time go bambye. No remember. *Shita nai.*"

Thinking that perhaps she does not want to talk about Taro in front of Nakasone-san, I switch tacks and ask her if I look like my mother. No, she says, I take after my father's side of the family.

Getting up, I return with my great-grandmother Tsuru's photo. I hand it to her, asking where Great-grandfather Gongoro and Great-grandmother Tsuru are buried. She looks at the picture, then hands it to Nakasone-san, who stares at it mutely. Uta says she doesn't know who the woman is.

"Isn't this your mother-in-law, my great-grandmother Tsuru?" I ask.

Uta switches between pidgin English, Japanese, and Okinawan. She claims she is confused and does not understand what I am asking. She bustles around the table, setting out bowls of food.

But I need to know. I cannot forget my mother. As she spoons out three bowls of *miso shiro*, I persist trying to show her the photo. I ask her about *yaito*. I want to know why she used *yaito*. She brushes it off, saying she can't remember. Nakasone-san stands up and moves between me and my grandmother. He uses his body as a barricade. He tells me she is an old woman. "She has suffered a lot. She has heart trouble now. Don't make trouble. It's all past. Better to forget."

"Come," she says, "sit down." My grandmother places a bowl of rice next to my *miso shiro* in front of me. I pick up my chopsticks and pick out a green wing of seaweed. Cupping the bowl between my hands, I drink the thick rich broth. *"Oishi,"* I say, "it is good." I lift my finger to my eyebrow and stroke the fine hairs, then reach for a steaming bowl of rice.

THE FAINTEST ECHO OF OUR LANGUAGE

CHANG-RAE LEE *was born in Se-oul, Korea, in 1965, and came to the United States with his family when he was three. A graduate of Yale College, he is an assistant professor in the University of Oregon Creative Writing Program, where he was also a Jacob K. Javits Fellow while he earned his MFA. His first novel,* Native Speaker, *was recently published by Riverhead Books/Putnam.*

MICHELLE BRANCA-LEE

MY MOTHER DIED ON A BARE JANUARY MORNING in our family room, the room all of us favored. She died upon the floor-bed I had made up for her, on the old twin mattress from the basement that I slept on during my childhood. She died with her husband kneeling like a penitent boy at her ear, her daughter tightly grasping the soles of her feet, and her son vacantly kissing the narrow, brittle fingers of her hand. She died with her best friend weeping quietly above her, and with her doctor unmoving and silent. She died with no accompaniment of music or poetry or prayer. She died with her eyes and mouth open. She died blind and speechless. She died, as I knew she would, hearing the faintest echo of our language at the last moment of her mind.

That, I think, must be the most ardent of moments.

I keep considering it, her almost-ending time, ruminating the nameless, impossible mood of its ground, toiling over it like some desperate topographer whose final charge is to survey only the very earth beneath his own shifting feet. It is an improbable task. But I am continually traveling through that terrible province, into its dark region where I see again and again the strangely vast scene of her demise.

I see.

Here before me (as I now enter my narrative moment), the dying-room, our family room. It has changed all of a sudden—it is as if there has been a shift in its proportion, the scale horribly off. The room seems to open up too fast, as though the walls were shrinking back and giving way to the wood flooring that seems to unfurl before us like runaway carpet. And there, perched on this crest somehow high above us, her body so flat and quiet in the bed, so resident, so immovable, caught beneath the somber light of these unwinking lamps, deep among the rolls of thick blankets, her furniture pushed to the walls without scheme, crowded in by the medicines, syringes, clear tubing, machines, shot through with the full false hopes of the living and the fearsome calls of the dead, my mother resides at an unfathomable center where the time of my family will commence once again.

No one is speaking. Except for the babble of her machines the will of silence reigns in this house. There is no sound, no word or noise, that we might offer up to fill this place. She sleeps for a period, then reveals her live eyes. For twelve or eighteen hours we have watched her like this, our legs and feet deadened from our squatting, going numb with tired blood. We sometimes move fitfully about, sighing and breathing low, but no one strays too far. The living room seems too far, the upstairs impossible. There is nothing, nothing at all outside of the house. I think perhaps it is snowing but it is already night and there is nothing left but this room and its light and its life.

People are here earlier (when?), a group from the church, the minister and some others. I leave her only then, going through the hallway to the kitchen. They say prayers and sing hymns. I do not know the high Korean words (I do not know many at all), and the music of their songs does not comfort me. Their one broad voice seems to be calling, beckoning something, bared in some kind of sad invitation. It is an acknowledgment. These people, some of them complete strangers, have come in from the outside to sing and pray over my mother, their overcoats still bearing the chill of the world.

I am glad when they are finished. They seem to sing too loud; I think they are hurting her ears—at least, disturbing her fragile state. I keep thinking, as if in her mind: *I'm finally going to get my sleep, my sleep after all this raw and painful waking, but I'm not meant to have it. But sing, sing.*

When the singers finally leave the room and quickly put on their coats I see that the minister's wife has tears in her eyes: so it is that clear. She looks at me; she wants to say something to me but I can see from her stunted expression that the words will not come. Though I wanted them earlier to cease I know already how quiet and empty it will feel when they are gone. But we are all close together now in the foyer, touching hands and hugging each other, our faces flushed, not talking but assenting to what we know, moving our lips in a silent, communal speech. For what we know, at least individually, is still unutterable, dwelling peacefully in the next room as the unnameable, lying there and waiting beside her, and yet the feeling among us is somehow so formidable and full of hope, and I think if I could hear our thoughts going round the room they would speak like the distant report of ten thousand monks droning the song of the long life of the earth.

Long, long life. Sure life. It had always seemed that way with us, with our square family of four, our destiny clear to me and my sister when we would sometimes speak of ourselves, not unlucky like those friends of ours whose families were wracked with ruinous divorce or drinking or disease—we were untouched, maybe untouchable, we'd been safe so far in our isolation in this country, in the country of our own house smelling so thickly of crushed garlic and seaweed and red chili pepper, as if that piquant wreath of scent from our mother's kitchen protected us and our house, kept at bay the persistent ghosts of the land who seemed to visit everyone else.

Of course, we weren't perfectly happy or healthy. Eunei and I were some-times trouble to my parents, we were a little lazy and spoiled (myself more than my sister), we didn't study hard enough in school (though we always received the highest marks), we chose questionable friends, some from broken families, and my father, who worked fourteen hours a day as a young psychia-trist, already suffered from mild hypertension and high cholesterol.

If something happened to him, my mother would warn me, if he were to die, we'd lose everything and have to move back to Korea, where the living was hard and crowded and where all young men spent long years in the military. Besides, our family in Korea—the whole rest of it still there (for we were the lone émigrés)—so longed for us, missed us terribly, and the one day each year when we phoned, they would plead for our return. What we could do, my mother said, to aid our father and his struggle in this country, was to relieve his worry over us, release him from that awful burden through our own hard work which would give him ease of mind and help him not to die.

My mother's given name was Inja, although I never once called her that, nor ever heard my sister or even my father address her so. I knew from a young age that her name was Japanese in style and origin, from the time of Japan's military occupation of Korea, and I've wondered since why she chose never to change it to an authentic Korean name, why her mother or father didn't change the names of all their daughters after the liberation. My mother often showed open enmity for the Japanese, her face seeming to ash over when she spoke of her memories, that picture of the platoon of lean-faced soldiers burning books and scrolls in the center of her village still aglow in my head (but from her or where else I don't know), and how they tried to erase what was Korean by criminalizing the home language and history by shipping slave labor, draftees, and young Korean women back to Japan and its other Pacific colonies. How they taught her to speak in Japanese. And as she would speak of her childhood, of the pretty, stern-lipped girl (that I only now see in tattered rust-edged photos) who could only whisper to her sisters in the midnight safety of their house the Korean words folding inside her all day like mortal secrets, I felt the same burning, troubling lode of utter pride and utter shame still jabbing at the sweet belly of her life, that awful gem, about who she was and where her mother tongue and her land had gone.

She worried all the time that I was losing my Korean. When I was in my teens, she'd get attacks of despair and urgency and say she was going to send me back to Korea for the next few summers to learn the language again. What she didn't know was that it had been whole years since I had lost the language, had left it somewhere for good, perhaps from the time I won a prize in the first grade for reading the most books in my class. I must have read fifty books. She had helped me then, pushed me to read and then read more to exhaustion until I fell asleep, because she warned me that if I didn't learn English I wouldn't be anybody and couldn't really live here like a true American. *Look at me,* she'd say, offering herself as a sad example, *look how hard it is for me to shop for food or speak to your teachers, look how shameful I am, how embarrassing.*

Her words frightened me. But I was so proud of myself and my prolific reading, particularly since the whole year before in kindergarten I could barely speak a word of English. I simply listened. We played mostly anyway, or drew pictures. When the class sang songs I'd hum along with the melody and silently mouth the strange and difficult words. My best friend was another boy in the class who also knew no English, a boy named Tommy. He was Japanese. Of course, we couldn't speak to each other but it didn't matter; somehow we found a way to communicate through gestures and funny faces and laughter, and we became friends. I think we both sensed we were the smartest kids in the class. We'd sit off by ourselves with this one American girl who liked us best and play house around a wooden toy oven. I've forgotten her name. She'd hug us when we "came home from work," her two mute husbands, and she would sit us down at the little table and work a pan at the stove and bring it over and feed us. We pretended to eat her food until we were full and then she'd pull the two of us sheepish and cackling over to the shaggy remnants of carpet that she'd laid down, and we'd all go to sleep, the girl nestled snuggly between Tommy and me, hotly whispering in our ears the tones of a night music she must have heard echoing through her own house.

Later that year, after a parents' visiting day at school, my mother told me that Tommy and his family were moving away. I didn't know how she'd found that out, but we went to his house one day, and Tommy and his mother greeted us at the door. They had already begun packing, and there were neatly stacked boxes and piles of newspapers pushed to a corner of their living room. Tommy immediately led me outside to his swing set and we horsed about for an hour before coming back in, and I looked at my mother and Tommy's mother sitting upright and formally in the living room, a tea set and plate of rice cookies between them on the coffee table. The two of them weren't really talking, more smiling and waiting for us. And then from Tommy's room full of toys, I began to hear a conversation, half of it in profoundly broken English, the other half in what must have been Japanese, at once breathy and staccato, my mother's version of it in such shreds and remnants that the odd sounds she made seemed to hurt her throat as they were called up. After we said goodbye and drove away in the car, I thought she seemed quiet and sad for me, and so I felt sadder still, though now I think that it was she who was moved and saddened by the visit, perhaps by her own act. For the momentary sake of her only son and his departing friend, she was willing to endure those two tongues of her shame, one present, one past. Language, sacrifice, the story never ends.

Inside our house (wherever it was, for we moved several times when I was young) she was strong and decisive and proud; even my father deferred to her in most matters, and when he didn't it seemed that she'd arranged it that way. Her commandments were stiff, direct. When I didn't listen to her, I understood that the disagreement was my burden, my problem. But outside, in the land of always-talking strangers and other Americans, my mother would lower her steadfast eyes, she'd grow mute, even her supremely solemn and sometimes severe face would dwindle with uncertainty; I would have to speak to a mechanic for her, I had to call the school myself when I was sick, I would write out notes to neighbors, the postman, the paper carrier. Do the work of voice. Negotiate *us*, with this here, now. I remember often fuming because of it, this one of the recurring pangs of my adolescence, feeling frustrated with her inabilities, her misplacement, and when she asked me one morning to call up the bank for her I told her I wouldn't do it and suggested that she needed "to practice" the language anyway.

Gracious God. I wished right then for her to slap me. She didn't. Couldn't. She wanted to scream something, I could tell, but bit down on her lip as she did and hurried upstairs to her bedroom, where I knew she found none of this trouble with her words. There she could not fail, nor could I. In that land, her words sang for her, they did good work, they pleaded for my life, shouted entreaties, ecstasies, they could draw blood if they wanted, and they could offer grace, and they could kiss.

But now—and I think, *right now* (I am discovering several present tenses)— she is barely conscious, silent.

Her eyes are very small and black. They are only half opened. I cannot call up their former kind shade of brown. Not because I am forgetting, but because it is impossible to remember. I think I cannot remember the first thing about her. I am not amnesiac, because despite all this *I know everything about her*. But the memories are like words I cannot call up, the hidden vocabularies of our life together. I cannot remember, as I will in a later narrative time, her bright red woolen dress with the looming black buttons that rub knobbly and rough against my infant face; I cannot remember, as I will soon dream it, the way her dark clean hair falls on me like a cloak when she lifts me from the ground; I cannot remember—if I could ever truly forget—the look of those soft Korean words as they play on her face when she speaks to me of honor and respect and devotion.

This is a maddening state, maybe even horrifying, mostly because I think I must do anything but reside in this very place and time and moment, that to be able to remember her now—something of her, anything—would be to forget the present collection of memories, this inexorable gathering of future remembrances. I want to disband this accumulation, break it apart before its bonds become forever certain.

She wears only a striped pajama top. Her catheter tube snakes out from between the top buttons. We know she is slipping away, going fast now, so someone, not me, disconnects the line to her food and water. The tube is in her way. These last moments will not depend on it. Her line to the morphine, though, is kept open and clear and running.

This comforts me. I have always feared her pain and I will to the end. Before she received the automatic pump that gives her a regular dosage of the drug, I would shoot her with a needle at least five times a day.

For some reason I wish I could do it now:

I will have turned her over gently. She will moan. Every movement except the one mimicking death is painful. I fit the narrow white syringe with a small needle, twisting it on tight. I then pull off the needle's protective plastic sheath. (Once, I will accidentally jab myself deep in the ring finger and while I hold gauze to the bloody wound she begins to cry. I am more careful after that.) Now I fill the syringe to the prescribed line, and then I go several lines past it; I always give her a little more than what the doctors tell us, and she knows of this transgression, my little gift to her, to myself. I say I am ready and then she lifts her hips so I can pull down her underwear to reveal her buttocks.

I know her body. The cancer in her stomach is draining her, hungrily sucking the life out of her, but the liquid food she gets through the tube has so many calories that it bloats her, giving her figure the appearance of a young girl who likes sweets too well. Her rump is full, fleshy, almost healthy-looking except for the hundreds of needle marks. There is almost no space left. I do not think it strange anymore that I see her naked like this. Even the sight of her pubic hair, darkly coursing out from under her, is now, if anything, of a certain more universal reminiscence, a kind of metonymic reminder that not long before she was truly in the world, one of its own, a woman, fully alive, historical, a mother, a bearer of life.

I feel around for unseeable bruises until I find a spot we can both agree on.

"Are you ready?" I say. "I'm going to poke."

"*Gu-rhaeh,*" she answers, which, in this context, means some cross between "That's right" and "Go ahead, damn it."

I jab and she sucks in air between her teeth, wincing.

"*Ay, ah-po.*" It hurts.

"A lot?" I ask, pulling the needle out as straight as I can, to avoid bruising her. We have the same exchange each time; but each time there arises a renewed urgency, and then I know I know nothing of her pains.

I never dreamed of them. Imagined them. I remember writing short stories in high school with narrators or chief characters of unidentified race and ethnicity. Of course this meant they were white, everything in my stories was some kind of white, though I always avoided physical descriptions of them or passages on their lineage and they always had cryptic first names like Garlo or Kram.

Mostly, though, they were figures who (I thought) could appear in an *authentic* short story, *belong* to one, that no reader would notice anything amiss in them, as if they'd inhabited forever those visionary landscapes of tales and telling, where a snow still falls faintly and faintly falls over all of Joyce's Ireland, that great muting descent, all over Hemingway's Spain, and Cheever's Suburbia, and Bellow's City of Big Shoulders.

I was to breach that various land, become its finest citizen and furiously speak its dialects. And it was only with one story that I wrote back then, in which the character is still unidentified but his *mother* is Asian (maybe even Korean), that a cleaving happened. That the land broke open at my feet. At the end of the story, the protagonist returns to his parents' home after a long journey; he is ill, feverish, and his mother tends to him, offers him cool drink, compresses, and she doesn't care where he's been in the strange wide country. They do not speak; she simply knows that he is home.

Now I dab the pinpoint of blood. I'm trying to be careful.

"*Gaen-cha-na,*" she says. *It is fine.*

"Do you need anything?"

"*Ggah,*" she says, flitting her hand, "*kul suh.*" *Go, go and write.*

"What do you want? Anything, anything."

"*In-jeh na jal-leh.*" *Now I want to sleep.*

"Okay, sleep. Rest. What?"

"*Boep-bo.*" *Kiss.*

"Kiss."

Kiss.

This will be our language always. To me she speaks in a child's Korean, and for her I speak that same child's English. We use only the simplest words. I think it strange that throughout this dire period we necessarily speak like this. Neither of us has ever grown up or out of this language; by virtue of speech I am forever her perfect little boy, she my eternal righteous guide. We are locked in a time. I love her, and I cannot grow up. And if all mothers and sons converse this way I think the communication must remain for the most part unconscious; for us, however, this speaking is everything we possess. And although I wonder if our union is handicapped by it I see also the minute discoveries in the mining of the words. I will say to her as naturally as I can— as I could speak only years before as a child—*I love you, Mother,* and then this thing will happen, the diction will take us back, bridge this moment with the others, remake this time so full and real. And in our life together, our strange language is the bridge and all that surrounds it; language is the brook streaming through it; it is the mossy stones, the bank, the blooming canopy above, the ceaseless sound, the sky. It is the last earthly thing we have.

My mother, no longer connected to her machine, lies on the bed on the floor. Over the last few hours she suffers brief fits and spasms as if she is chilled. She stirs when we try to cover her with the blanket. She kicks her legs to get it off. Something in her desires to be liberated. Finally we take it away. Let her be, we think. And now, too, you can begin to hear the indelicate sound of her breathing; it is audible, strangely demonstrative. Her breath resonates in this house, begins its final cadence. She sounds as though she were inhaling and exhaling for the very first time. Her body shudders with that breath. My sister tries to comfort her by stroking her arms. My mother groans something unintelligible, though strangely I say to myself for her, *Leave me alone, all of you. I am dying. At last I am dying.* But then I stroke her, too. She keeps shuddering, but it is right.

What am I thinking? Yes. It is that clear. The closer she slips away, down into the core of her being, what I think of as an origin, a once-starting point, the more her body begins to protest the happening, to try to hold down, as I am, the burgeoning, blooming truth of the moment.

For we think we know how this moment will be. Each of us in this room has been elaborating upon it from the very moment we gained knowledge of her illness. This is the way it comes to me, but I think we have written, each of us, the somber epic novel of her death. It has taken two and one-half years and we are all nearly done. I do not exactly know of the others' endings. Eunei, my sister (if I may take this liberty), perhaps envisioning her mother gently falling asleep, never really leaving us, simply dreams of us and her life for the rest of ever. I like that one.

My father, a physician, may write that he finally saves her, that he spreads his hands on her belly where the cancer is mighty and lifts it out from her with one ultimate, sovereign effort. Sometimes (and this ought not be attributed to him) I think that his entire life has come down to this struggle against the palpable fear growing inside of his wife. And after she dies, he will cry out in a register I have never heard from his throat as he pounds his hand on the hardwood above her colorless head, *"Eeh-guh-moy-yah? Eeh-guh-moy-yah?" What is this? What is this?* It—the cancer, the fear—spites him, mocks him, this doctor who is afraid of blood. It—this cancer, this happening, this time— is the shape of our tragedy, the cruel sculpture of our life and family.

In the ending to my own story, my mother and I are alone. We are always alone. And one thing is certain; she needs to say something only to me. That is why I am there. Then she speaks to me, secretly. What she says exactly is unclear; it is enough, somehow, that she and I are together, alone, apart from everything else, while we share this as yet unborn and momentary speech. The words are neither in Korean nor in English, languages which in the end we cannot understand. I hear her anyway. But now we can smile and weep and laugh. We can say goodbye to each other. We can kiss, unflinching, on our mouths.

Then she asks if I might carry her to the window that she might see the new blossoms of our cherry tree. I lift her. She is amazingly light, barely there, barely physical, and while I hold her up she reaches around my neck and leans her head against my shoulder. I walk with her to the window and then turn so that she faces the tree. I gaze longingly at it myself, marveling at the gaudy flowers, and then I turn back upon her face, where the light is shining, and I can see that her eyes have now shut, and she is gone.

But here in this room we are not alone. I think she is probably glad for this, as am I. Her breathing, the doctor says, is becoming labored. He kneels and listens to her heart. "I think we should be ready," he says. "Your mother is close." He steps back. He is a good doctor, a good friend. I think he can see the whole picture of the time. And I think about what he is saying: *Your mother is close.* Yes. Close to us, close to life, close to death. She is close to everything, I think; she is attaining an irrevocable nearness of being, a proximity to everything that has been spoken or written or thought, in every land and language on earth. How did we get to this place? Why are we here in this room, assembled as we are, as if arrayed in some ancient haunted painting whose grave semblance must be known in every mind and heart of man?

I count a full five between her breaths. The color is leaving her face. The mask is forming. Her hand in mine is cold, already dead. I think it is now that I must speak to her. I understand that I am not here to listen; that must be for another narrative. I am not here to bear her in my arms toward bright windows. I am not here to be strong. I am not here to exchange goodbyes. I am not here to recount old stories. I am not here to acknowledge the dead.

I am here to speak. Say the words. Her nearness has delivered me to this moment, an ever-lengthening moment between her breaths, that I might finally speak the words turning inward, for the first time, in my own beginning and lonely language: Do not be afraid. It is all right, so do not be afraid. You are not really alone. You may die, but you will have been heard. Keep speaking— it is real. You have a voice.

THE
WINGED
SEED

LI-YOUNG LEE *was born in 1957 in Jakarta, Indonesia, of Chinese parents. In 1959, his father, after spending a year as a political prisoner in President Sukarno's jails, fled Indonesia with his family. Between 1959 and 1964 they traveled in Hong Kong, Macao, and Japan, before arriving in America. In 1990, Li-Young Lee traveled in China and Indonesia. His several honors include a fellowship from the Guggenheim Foundation in 1989, a Writer's Award from the Whiting Foundation in 1988, and the Delmore Schwartz Memorial Poetry Award for*

ARTHUR FURST

his first book of poems, Rose *(BOA Editions, Ltd.), in 1987. Li-Young Lee's second collection of poems,* The City in Which I Love You, *won the 1990 Lamont Poetry Selection of the Academy of American Poets. In 1995, he was awarded the I. B. Lauan Award from the Academy of American Poets. He resides in Chicago, Illinois, with his wife, Donna, and their children. This essay was excerpted from his memoir of the same name, which was published in the spring of 1995.*

IN MY DREAM MY FATHER CAME BACK, DRESSED IN THE clothes we'd buried him in, carrying a jar of blood in one hand, his suit pockets lined with black seeds.

His gray wool suit seemed hardly worn, except for the shoulders and elbows, which were buffed smooth, I guessed, from rubbing against his narrow coffin. And then I saw his shoes. They were completely wrecked; their leather cracked, nicked, creased, cross-creased; their puckered seams, where the stitching came unraveled, betrayed his naked feet. Sockless, his ankles were frightening, and only the thinnest soles kept him from walking on bare feet.

I began to cry, realizing: *He walked the whole way*. I thought of him climbing alone the hundreds of identical stairs up from his grave in Pennsylvania, and then, obeying some instinct, walking west to Chicago, toward his wife, children, and grandchildren. When did he begin his journey? I wondered. In the dream, I felt ashamed, disturbed by the thought that while he looked for me, for us, his family, we were quite unaware of his arrival, which might have taken him years for all I knew, since no one ever told him where to find us. It hurt to think of him walking for years along the blind shoulders of highways, through fields, along rivers, down sidewalks of North American cities and villages; walking day and night; talking to no one; walking; a dead Chinese man separated from the family he brought to this country in 1964; a stranger to most when he was alive; an Asian come to a country at war with Asia; now a stranger in death. I kept looking at his shoes.

The family began to gather for a photo to commemorate his return, during which commotion he seemed distracted; he had an appointment to keep. While everyone stayed busy seating and reseating before the camera, crowding to fit into the view, I saw he sat, not in his accustomed place, at the center, but, instead, at the end of the front row, where he seemed not only comfortable but uninterested. I thought to myself: *I hope his shoes don't show up in the photo. That would shame him, such shoes, and the raw anklebone.* And then I was certain he'd soon ask me a question and I wouldn't know the answer.

Immediately after the photo was taken, he stood up and walked over to me, who, come to think of it, had been sitting in the dead man's accustomed place. He told me to say goodbye. We had to go. I would be going with him. His words were a blow. I didn't move. Noticing, he asked if I wanted to come with him after all. I answered: *Of course.* I lied.

He said: *Very well. I'll wait for you by the locks.* Then he went out the door.

I looked at the thirteen people I call my family, and felt suddenly excluded. But then I felt, like miles of water rising in me, a feeling that I could never leave them.

But my father's shoes. How wrecked they were, how old and battered. I said out loud: *He's so poor. His shoes, poor Father, his shoes.* I felt I should go with him, and began to think over the many names and faces of people I'd have to say goodbye to, concluding that going with my father was what I *must* do. But when I walked over to say goodbye to you, Donna, I could not touch your face.

If it meant leaving, I could not bring myself to touch you. I began to tremble; trembling, I needed to touch you. Yet I could not, no matter what if . . . yet it meant . . . as it is . . .

Love, what is night? Is a man thinking in the night the night? Is fruit ripening in the night the night?

Night is the night carried, death by the rectangular, black-lacquered trunk my father hauled on his back until he got tired, and then my brothers and I took turns shouldering it. It sits now under the living-room window of my mother's apartment, its lid inlaid with jade and mother-of-pearl, depicting a scene from a Chinese opera. I'm dying of the white bedsheet my mother uses to cover it, and the potted white begonia that sits on the sheet, dropping its flowers that lie like lopped ears pressed to a story. Inside the trunk, between many layers of blankets, wrapped in cloth and old newspapers, are the cool jades and brittle porcelains my parents carried over the sea, and a box that used to hold a pair of women's boots. In that box are hundreds of black-and-white photographs of people I've never met, pictures like the one that sits in a gilded frame on the cabinet of my mother's big-screen TV. It is a picture of my mother's family, a complicated arrangement of aunts and uncles, first and second cousins, concubines and slaves, and each member sits or stands in strict accordance with their relation to my mother's grandfather, the Old President,

Yuan Shih Kai. It is a feudal hierarchy impossible for me to understand completely, but which my mother grasps at a glance, remembering exactly if it was the Old Man's sixth son, Supreme Virtue, by the fourth wife, Rich Pearl, or the second daughter, Jade something, of the ninth concubine, Have Courage, who killed with a slingshot all the goldfish in the ponds that decorated the twenty acres of formal gardens my great-grandfather owned. And she knows exactly which wan face belongs to the uncle who, forbidden to marry his thirteen-year-old niece, in grief gave up his inheritance, left for Mongolia to live in a hut, let his hair grow to his knees, and wrote page after page of poems and songs about the one called Exquisite Law, who, in the photograph, is carried in the arms of a servant whose face has been blacked out, as all the servants in the photograph have been blacked out, so that the babies they hold (not their own, but the children of the masters) look like they're floating.

Is night my ancestors' gloomy customs, then? Will I ever be free of their tortoiseshell combs and smoking punk, hand-tooled jambs that stalled and amazed me at temple thresholds in a provincial capital? Will I be free of my great-grandfather's three thousand descendants? Soon, there will be so little of me I may actually arrive. Soon, I'll be born. Soon, I'll know how to live. Soon, my teeth may stop hurting me. Soon, I'll be able to sleep. At the moment, something I never read in a book keeps me awake, something the night isn't saying, the wind is accomplice to, and the rain in the eaves keeps to itself, an unassailable nacre my woman encloses, a volatile seed dormant in my man, something I didn't see on the television, something not painted on billboards along the highways, not printed in the magazines at the supermarket checkouts, something I didn't hear on the radio, something my father forgot to tell me, something my mother couldn't foresee owns an unbroken waist and several ankles, a stem proclaiming an indivisible flower, a lamp sowing a path ahead of every possible arrival.

I remember, as long as I knew him, my father carried at all times in his right suit pocket a scarce handful of seeds. *Remembrance,* was his sole answer when I asked him why. He was pithy. He slept with his head on a stone wrapped in a piece of white linen I washed once a week. Up until I was nine years old, I napped with him, making myself as small as possible so as not to wake him. I remember how, when he turned over in bed, I made room, wedging myself against the wall, my left arm under my head for a pillow, my legs numb. I lay very quietly while he snored. I lay wide awake against his flesh while he slept with his head on the stone wrapped in the cloth which smelled of his hair, a rich oil. When he died, the stone kept a faintest impression that fit the shape of his head. My mother carried it out, and left it under one of the thirty-six pines that enclosed two sides of the property on which our house stood, the third side the fence where the morning glory climbed. Some days the depression in my father's pillow must fill with rain, just enough to give a cardinal a drink. Or maybe somebody has found it by now, has used it as part of a wall, where it fits to another stone shaped like a man's skull. We burned almost everything else before selling the house and moving. Out of the heap of his papers, notebooks, manuscripts, photographs, and letters, my sister Fey, almost obligingly, chose one scrapbook of newspaper clippings to keep, which none of us ever looked at after we left Pennsylvania. Everything else we fed to a roaring fire we'd made in the backyard between two apple trees. While we all stood about the fire, which we kept alive two days and two nights without sleeping, one hot mote shot out and creased my youngest brother's thigh, burning through the cloth of his pants and several layers of skin. His leg owns the scar to this day.

I never asked my father in remembrance of what he kept those seeds. I knew better than to press him when I was a boy. Now I'm a man, and he is dead, and I feel a strange shame that I don't know what happened to those seeds. Did we bury them with him? Is morning glory breaking his pewter casket's tight lip this second? Is morning glory blooming on a cemetery hill in Pennsylvania? Didn't I one day kneel in the mud and snow, halfway up a hillside, halfway to my father's grave, and hold my wrist to an icy cataract, and see the shriveled vine and the gold seed pods?

Is that my father in his undershirt, bent at a table, studying a sentence, darkening the lamp? Is that my father cutting out pieces of colored paper to make lancet-shaped windows, the lamp and the scissors-bird winking and seeming to fly?

His one hand holds the scissors and slowly squeezes it closed, while feeding into its blades with his other hand the folded tissue papers colored red, yellow, green, and blue. Turning the little stack of them along the faintly penciled lines, he lets fall a little shower of tiny bright leaves. These he glues to the pieces of one-eighth-inch-thick cardboard he's painted gold, and into which he has already cut the window openings. Three identical walls and together they made the sides and the rear of the temple.

What it took a great king seven months to accomplish with stone and 300,000 slaves, it took my father nearly four years to complete out of cardboard and paper, a feat of love, or someone serving a sentence. *And there it is unto this day*. The speaker of the sentence is referring to Solomon's Temple. The sentence follows a long and detailed description of that fabulous house of the covenant. And *where* is it this day? One must not ask. Where is that magnificent temple? For it lives only in the sentences of its description, and only inside the imagination of the reader of those sentences.

He'd begun the project as a gift for my sister when she turned eleven on the ship to Macao. That winter, Ba was being transferred from the prison in Jakarta to another in Macao. We would not get there, and Ba would not finish the gift in time for his daughter's birthday. Instead, due to a series of oversights and accidents on the part of the Indonesian War Administration, as well as a friend's timely arrival in a secret boat, we would end up in Hong Kong for Christmas, where construction on my father's temple continued; and then Japan, where building went on; then Singapore; and on, and on, each place new, while one thing remained the same: on a ship or in a tiny apartment room, a table was cleared where my father bent alone over his Bibles and dictionaries, translating his books of Genesis and Exodus; or else his wife and children sat by him while he resumed work on his temple.

There was no rest. Mumbling in Hebrew, Greek, English, and Chinese, Ba was moving us from one place to another. And he was building as we moved. What began as a toy for his daughter became the sole activity around which the family gathered, no matter where we lighted for a week or a month. And the real genius of the thing was not only its true-to-life, full-scale construction, nor its swinging doors complete with bolted locks, nor even the tenderness in the details of the faces of the seraphim, but its portability. For each piece could be gently dismantled, unfolded, spread flat, and put into a box to be carried across borders, barriers, into provinces, jungles, over seas and lands as language to language, landscape to landscape, we carried Ba's Temple of Solomon.

And Ba was dying. Something terrible must have happened to him during his time in prison, for he left that place damaged. Something about him persuaded us he was in the last of his wholeness. And the close air we shared in holds of ships and trains and little tenement rooms dogged us, his woman and children. Our clothes smelled musty, our shoes grew tight even as they disintegrated, the pages of his dictionaries grew yellow and water-stained, our bodies smelled like . . . dying. How can I explain this? How could anyone ever understand who has never gone through it? We slept the sleep of the dying. We ate the food of the dying. We saw sores begin to erupt all over Ba's body. We feared, at one point, it might be a form of leprosy. We heard him complain about severe aching in his joints. Yes, Ba was dying. And we were dying to arrive, to put behind us the dying on the islands, the rounding up and dying en masse. So we made our escape. Out of forgeries we made our flight. Out of accidents and silences, out of the steps of the fleeing who went before us. And though our course seemed aimless, decided by nothing but fear, Ba assured us it was momentous, even predetermined. Our seemingly incoherent and stray rovings across the horizontal plane of seemings and doings were, in fact, he convinced us, a continuous unfolding of vertical and ultimate meaning. And since the nature of moving is collecting, naturally we collected: curly sea foam, scaly archipelagoes and leafy rain, lunatic moths, jeweled eyes of snakes, curled tails of monkeys, and the fangs of the monkey king, two snakes coiled on the back of a turtle, a cream-colored gecko uttering a concrete cipher, dawns the color of evening gongs, temple bronzes that owned the look of things having been too near the sun, black zones of one or two seas, *thank-you*'s and *please*'s in different tongues. On Ba's scuffed, cracked leather accordion case, we collected colorful stickers of steamships and airplanes, and emblems of airlines and train lines and shipping lines, our whole wandering pieced together by such lines, the only continuity our bodies in time, and Ba's relentless work on his temple. We saved and collected anything at all that might be of use, from thin colored tissue papers to the foil from cigarette packs or the beautifully colored envelopes of Christmas cards. And Ba built it. While Ba and Mu collected lines on their faces, he built it. While Fey, Go, Be, and I accumulated body weight and size, he built it. According to the instructions God gave to Solomon, Ba made it, his own splendid temple.

The front wall bore a wide, double-door entrance on either side of which was a tight grouping of four windows. And around every window of all four walls, my father cut with a razor a beveled edge to make a frame, exposing the gray cardboard beneath the gold paint. Then, around each frame, in fine lines of black ink, he decorated the windows with minute curlicues, leaves, vines, scrolls, waves, human and animal figures, no two sets of windows bearing the same motif, no two leaves of a single window alike.

The lintel and jambs of the doorway, as well, were embellished with profuse and singular details, indicating the obsessive and aching hand of a maker whose playfulness was surpassed only by his determination. The surface of the cardboard double doors was scored and cut to look like thick planks of wood, while the studs and horizontal bands of metal lashing the planks together were made from colored construction paper. These were the walls of the outer sanctuary, which was further surrounded by colonnades. The columns were made by scoring with a razor blade a series of close vertical lines on a piece of cardboard, which was then folded along the lines to make a fluted shaft. Because the entire project was designed to be dismantled easily, the shaft was attached to a simple base and capital by a system of tabs and slots. Fourteen such columns supported a pitched roof whose gables were adorned with detailed renderings of scenes from the Old Testament up to the time of Solomon; mainly depictions of trials and slaughter. The roof itself could be lifted off to reveal the colonnade of the inner court, at the center of which stood the pillars Jachim and Boaz, guarding the cella, the final and innermost room in which knelt the two six-winged seraphim brooding over the Ark of the Covenant. The entire project sat on a cardboard stage ascended to from any direction by six such stages of succeeding size.

But where is it now? Gone. Like everything else. And even while we were moving, I was moving to eventual awareness that all was not right, that all we ended up amassing was ephemera: songs in languages we didn't know, memories of fragrances of indeterminate flowers, loose chants and charms, silhouettes of huts and minarets; while Ba was reenvisioning Genesis and Exodus. We carried our clothes in bundles, our books and shoes were rotten. We were sleeping standing, eating squatting, putting the bowl to our lips, while Ba meticulously scissored, folded, tucked, and layered into existence his house of worship, while his little indomitable gold watch tolled the relentless hours. And naturally we were casting off as we looked ahead. We were jettisoning luggage, names, and bodies. There was Ty, my brother. Then there wasn't. There was Chung, another brother, then there wasn't. Brothers swallowed up in some murk we called, conveniently, The Past, as though it were a place we could return to, as though we weren't leaving them behind with the passports we left behind, the jewelry and the books come finally undone. As though making the faces of the seraphim in the exact likenesses of Ty and Chung were a suitable memorial. And we were waxing tired, waxing bewildered, for we were departing in order to leave, leaving in order to leave some more, some more tired, some more old.

And by the time we got to America, my feet were tired. My father put down our suitcase, untied my shoes, and rubbed my feet, one at a time and with such deep turns of his wrist I heard the water in him through my soles. Since then I have listened for him in my steps. And have not found him. Since then I hear with my naked feet, those lilies, fine-boned swans crossed at the necks, those ears. My father's feet were ulcerous, as was his body, diseased. And water denied him days at a time, administered in a prison cell in Indonesia, ruined his kidneys, and changed the way he lay or sat or knelt or got up to walk the whole way down the stairs.

What did my father mean when he said: *Remembrance?* I remember I was born in the City of Victory on a street called Jilan Industri, where each morning the man selling sticky rice cakes goes by pushing his cart, his little steamer whistling, and by noon the lychee man passes, his head in a rag, bundles of the fruit strung on the pole slung on his neck, while at his waist, at the end of a string, a little brass bell shivers into a fine and steady seizure. I remember I was named twice, once at my birth, and once again after my father, in his prison cell, dreamed each night the same dream, in which the sun appeared to him as a blazing house, wherein dwelt a seed, black, new, dimly human. And so one morning, at a white metal table in the visiting yard, he and my mother decided my name, which, said one way, indicates the builded light of the pearl, and said another, the sun.

It was 1959, the year of the pig, eighteen months after I was born, that my father was arrested by the military police working under President Achmed Sukarno, because of things he'd been saying to a handful of men and women who came down every evening to the banks of the Solo River to wash their rice, or beat their clothes clean on the stones, or shit behind the makeshift rattan screens. He'd been warned several times before his arrest that what he talked about those evenings, sitting beside the Solo, might be considered seditious. When he didn't stop, the Indonesian War Administration accused him of being a spy and threw him in prison for nineteen months. But what could a person say about night and seeds, for it was night and seeds my father talked about, that might so offend a military regime? What is a seed? My son's fourth-grade textbook says something about monocots and dicots. Is it monocot or dicot seeds dictators fear? What was so dangerous about the letters he wrote to my mother and had smuggled out of jail that she had to burn them immediately after she read them? What does a seed enclose that might be considered dangerous to anyone? What was it my father said, standing at evening by the Solo?

Did he say seed planted deep at one sill declares a new house at a further turn of the sun.

Did he say seed is good news, our waiting done.

Did he say seed is told, kept cold, scored with a pocketknife, and then left out to die, in order to come into a further seed, speaking the father seed, leading to seed, if seed can be said to lead, a road we sow ahead of our arrival.

What did he say? Think.

I remember my father's sermon on the seed, which he told by candlelight, in the church basement in Pennsylvania. It was during the blizzard of 1975. The Women's Auxiliary sat in a circle around him, sewing blankets. He leaned across a table and said that the hour had come for us to put an ear to the seed, to hear the lightning scratched there, late news of our human spring. Or was that his sermon on the spring? From my father's sermon on the trees, I remember only the sound of trees. From things he said on the falling leaves, I recall a rake left lying in the apple orchard. From what he told about the seven boats, all I have are ten broken stairs darkening to the sea. What was it he said about the seed? Only the seed that hoarded winter to its heart . . . ? Only the water broken into by winter could . . . No. That was his sermon on winter. On that topic he had a lot to say; so much, in fact, that he devoted a month of Sundays to it, though I remember only his notion that there were not many winters in a life, but only one, a fathering winter, a paternal January and eternal season. That, he claimed, is the winter we have to outwinter, crucial season of death. In the face of death's winter, it's best to keep a wintering heart, detached to its depths, the wider scope of indifference. That was his January message, told with alarm in his otherwise even voice, like a warning I keep in my head these days when I am the exact age he was when I was born. His symbol for attachment was the proverbial house built on sand. Disengagement turns the ground solid, was what he tried to tell me. I regarded his words as the natural claim of a man who'd been forced to disengage over and over, having at eight years old lost a sister to rabies, at twelve the nanny who helped birth him and even fed him her milk, at sixteen a mother to murder, at twenty-five a first son to China, and at thirty a second to meningitis. So if he thought he was warning me, or anyone else, I think he was talking to himself those afternoons. Those afternoons in winter all become one winter afternoon, a room of light scarcely furnished with a ladder-backed chair; a cold, bright, enclosed porch where dry, brittle ivy hung like small bells from stone pots and my father stood talking, while I wrote down what he said. For I was my father's secretary from the time my writing was legible to him, around the age of fourteen. I wrote what my father thought out loud each Friday after school, helped him memorize it all day Saturday, and knew if he spoke or misspoke Sunday morning, when he opened his mouth for the sermon.

He began reciting on Saturdays when the sun was slightly past its zenith, yet bright in the highest ice-tipped branches of all four black trees outside the manse windows. The tree trunks were cast into shade, as half the house was by afternoon, from which depths a child's voice, my brother's, could be heard. He was reading out loud the stories from that great book our father made us read each day and my brother read all day Saturday. I could hear my brother's bored monotone coming from his shut room, while I listened to my father recite and I read along in silence the typed draft of his previous day's thinking, I wished I could be reading the book my brother was reading.

There were a lot of books in that house. But there was ever only one book: the one my father used to teach me to read. Called by him The World, it was bound by unseen thread and glue, and covered in black leather; the book which, I believed, had no author other than a three-bodied God, a monster in my eyes. The words of the book formed two black columns on white leaves thin as tracing paper. But it was the pictures I thought most about as my father spoke and I waited to correct him.

The pictures in the book were as strange as the stories they illustrated. The beautiful pictures, richly colored, filled my head as I followed my father from room to room, from the study to the screened-in porch, helping him commit his words to his memory, and, inevitably, to mine, even if all I was thinking about were those pictures. Of bodies, naked or barely draped in blue robes and red robes, the brown and yellow breasts of old men and young men, the golden shoulders and thighs of thick-limbed women and girls, the fleshy waist of God, his white beard and huge hands, and the pale neck of a virgin mother. But also the other bodies, the shamed attitudes of two naked ones, a murdered brother falling under a red sky, a sacrificial son bound on an alter, a decapitated giant, a blind beggar, a stranger knocking, a crucified thief. There were many pictures. But together they made one picture: my father.

Without fail, like a train on time, each Saturday night, with my father's words ringing in my head, I dreamed of him. Sometimes he said things I felt I had to write down, but I couldn't find pencil or paper. Sometimes I followed him as, in his black coat, he climbed up and down a narrow ladder, saying things I forgot upon waking. Sometimes he sowed a handful of sparrows and seeds across my mother's kitchen table, scattering them, tiny and many, impossible to gather. In a recurring dream, I walk, late and in a hurry, toward my father's church, which shrinks as I approach, becoming soon the size of a dollhouse, and growing smaller and smaller the nearer I come. By the time I reach its red double doors, the church is the size of a walnut, and I have to crawl on my hands and knees to enter. He meets me inside. Sitting with his back against the chancel and his legs hugged to his chest, he smiles, welcoming me. I crimp and hump, twist and tuck my limbs this way and that in order to sit across from him, while he, to make room for me, closes like a fist, pulls himself into a tight fetus until, finally, we are sitting face to face, bony knee to bony knee, burning forehead to wrinkled forehead, sucking the used air. Light from the stained-glass windows, broken up and translated into a various spectrum, falls sallow on our faces. And in this dream, as it was when he was alive, I look down, veering from his black eyes. I was never allowed to look my father straight in his eyes. Only one time did I do that. It was an accident. It was during church service, and I don't know how long he had been staring at me, but by the time I saw him, it was too late, because by then I was looking directly into his eyes. And then there was no turning away. His gaze forbade it. And I wanted nothing more than to look away, to avoid his penetration. Yet I wanted nothing more than to look. I wanted nothing more than for *him* to look away. *I* would penetrate *him*, I thought. So I looked. And looked. What did I see? A formidable head, black eyes, black brows, black mustache. Full, almost sensuous lips. It was the head I'd seen on posters and flyers all over Hong Kong when we lived there and he preached to thousands each week.

My father was not among us, for he'd been arrested months ago by the military police, and was now in prison awaiting trial. High on a wall was the poster of the man who'd had him arrested: Achmed Sukarno, President of the Republic of Indonesia. His huge head set on a thick neck, he seemed to gaze over the commotion of the market, over the roofs of stalls and the heads of shoppers, the tables of meats, and fruits, and cloths, and vegetables, and assorted musical instruments and Muslim paraphernalia, over the traffic of the daily, over the trees, over the river Solo, over the tumult of the present into some other clarity. For he had a look about him of someone whose attention was wholly trained upon a great immanence. The artist of the poster must have been looking up at him when the portrait was made, for the contour of the head with a fez on it, and the massive, medal-bedecked shoulders, resembled nothing so much as an image hewn from a cliff.

While his face was everywhere, our father, on the other hand, was hidden from us, a prisoner in the ruler's palace, so we believed. The palace was surrounded by armored cars, jeeps, and khaki-uniformed, belt-strapped men, wearing buttons and medals and guns. And then, just as suddenly, Fey gasped: *It's Ba! Where?* our mother asked, startled. *It's Ba!* Fey said again, pointing to the poster. And when our mother saw that Fey was pointing at the picture of Sukarno, she broke into tears. We pleaded: *Don't cry, Mu, it's Ba*, while she shook her head, explaining that no, it wasn't our father. *Have you forgotten what your father looks like?* she asked.

The fact is, by that time, our father seemed a virtual stranger to us, and the hours we spent waiting for him seemed endless. And while our mother's absence from us as she spent all her days at the prison became an emptiness around which our activities circled, it only punctuated that greater absence we called Ba, our father. Though our mother was often absent, Ba was The Absent One. He grew immense as our mother's days and thoughts revolved around his not being there. And though we daily hoped for his release, his absence had begun to feel like a permanence we simply lived with, never doubting it, reliable as gravity, or True North. It became our very world, and as a world, he became less keenly felt, more and more assumed, as though we'd always lived without him, as though he hadn't been taken from us only six months ago, but ages ago. Ba's absence receded from our daily thoughts into abstraction, even while we became its most intimate inhabitants. And this even though we prayed in front of his picture each night.

Each night, our mother repeated for us the story of our father: he was a prisoner, she would try to get him out, we had to pray. By that time, though, our praying had changed. Without our realizing it, the subject of our prayers, Ba, had gradually become the object of our prayers as well, so that we were praying *to* him as well as *for* him. Each night, standing before his photograph, my brother Go and I on either side of our sister Fey, we prayed, ending: *Dear Ba. Help Ba. We love Ba. Amen.* Judging by the way we prayed, it was up to Ba to get himself out of his absence and restore himself to us.

In those days, we were often visited by groups of three or four soldiers looking for money or sellable goods. So it wasn't a surprise when, one morning, while we were eating breakfast, they came to our door. But refusing to be bought off by cigarettes or money this time, and acting insulted by the bribes they'd often enough accepted, the officer in charge extended a few official apologies, and then gave prompt orders to his underlings to search the house thoroughly. By the time they left, all of Ba's papers, letters, and manuscripts were collected, boxed, and removed. Also taken away were any pictures we had of him, including the photograph on the little black table we prayed to each night. During the ransack, Sheeti and Lammi, our nannies, cried: *Give us Dwan's pictures! Let the children have their father's images!* while our mother stood wooden, silent, all trace of feeling seemingly erased from her.

Yet we continued to perform our nightly ritual in front of the empty table that had previously held his photo. Our mother instructed us to fix in our minds a clear image of Ba's face before we began to pray. Standing before the table and the absent photograph, we all three closed our eyes to see his face, and then uttered our supplications for the man called Ba, to the power called Ba. But the image was no longer vivid. We were beginning to lose the subject of our prayers. With it, we were losing the object. Our endeavor grew vaguer and vaguer.

Years after that incident, though, I was looking into my father's eyes. And I knew what his look meant. It meant: *I see you clean through.* And I could not look away. So there we were that day, me standing in blue among the choir, listening to a woman perform her solo before the rest of us joined in refrain, and my father, seated behind the pulpit, stilled, robed, looking like a fluted black monument. And I knew that the body he covered from neck to midcalf was scaly and rough, practically sloughing off when he scratched and scraped it, itchy, with a silver kitchen knife. And I knew that pinned to him beneath his robe and black mantle was the red rosebud I'd given him that morning, wilting, shot through by the needle, pressed between a heavy weave and my father's wild heart.

While the soloist urged: *Come to the mercy seat* and *Come to the seat of love* to the congregation, men, women, children, sleepers, believers, rich, poor, every hair of every head numbered, I stared straight into my father's eyes, and within seconds was no longer looking, only stubbornly locked, gaze and gaze with him, my black irises to my father's.

I would lose. I had to. I could not sustain it. Against my every will and command, my eyes, betrayers that they are, deserters that they are, looked down, my face burning with . . . what? Shame? Anger? Fear? Could he see what was burning my cheek? Was my rose staining his lapel?

I was seventeen, and I had seen that look on my father's face numerous times. There was sternness in it, but it was more than sternness. There was even something predatory about it, though it went beyond anything merely animal. It was my father possessed. But in my dream of the little church, he cups his hands as though he's gathered something to show me. I lean forward and look down into his hands. Two trees. He shows me two bonsai trees. It is some sort of miracle, and I am moved to the beginnings of terror by the intensity, the reality, of what I'm seeing: a miniature tree growing out of each of his palms, and encircling the base of each trunk is a slim ring of blood. The branches of the trees are tangled, the gnarled thorny limbs of the left-hand tree braided with the black, flower-laden branches of the right-hand tree. *It is so real,* I say, and suddenly have the sensation that something has been revealed to me, that what he shows me explains everything between us. He speaks, or I hear the words out of nowhere: *According to how you sow, for thorn or flower . . .* then the voice falters, and I wake, but not before I notice we are wearing the same shoes.

When my father preached between 1963 and 1964, on the island of Hong Kong, he drew crowds in such numbers that rows of folding chairs had to be set up in the very lobbies of the theaters where his revival meetings took place, while loudspeakers were set up outside, where throngs of sweating believers stood for hours in the sun, listening to him speak and pray.

Once, while my sister and I were buying sugarcane from our favorite street vendor, the afternoon suddenly filled with red-and-blue leaflets dropped from an airplane. My sister snatched one out of the air and the two of us looked at a picture of our father, under which was printed, in Chinese and English, the words *Your Friend,* and then the time and place of the next meeting of the Ling Liang Assembly and Ambassadors for Christ. I recognized the photograph as the same one my mother had taken of our father a little over a year ago on the boat from Indonesia to Hong Kong. His profile, taken by the camera from a lower angle, was backed by the sky and mast, perfect for the image of a helmsman or captain of souls. Only his family knew that when the photo was taken, we were on the way to a detention center. My father and his family were being shipped from one prison in Jakarta to another on some remote island, where, so we were told, we would be given a house and yard which we would not be permitted to leave. But on the way there, a former student of his from Gamaliel University pulled up alongside the ship with a smaller boat, so my parents assembled us in the night, and one stood above the other and handed to the one below, by hoisting over a railing, one by one, each of their five children. The two boats, big and small, rocked unevenly, the gap between them closing and widening, yet less dangerous than a guard asleep somewhere, or else awake but turned away to earn my father's bribe. By the next morning we were in the home of a congregation member of the Ling Liang Assembly. It was during one of the evening revival meetings, when members from the congregation gave personal testimonies of the working hand of God, that my father, convinced we had escaped harm due to some miracle and for some higher purpose, recounted the horrors of the last three years fleeing Sukarno and our rescue. Within a year of that testimony, he was performing mass baptisms in the ocean at night. Hundreds gathered once a month on the beach to watch my father take off his silk suit jacket, his narrow leather shoes and silk socks, roll up his sleeves, and wade out into the dark water, from where we could here him beckoning: *Come! Come to me, come further, don't be afraid.* And one by one he embraced them and plunged them backward into the surf.

Many years later in the United States, and nearly five years after my father had died, I was eating with my family in a Chinese restaurant on the South Side of Chicago when we discovered through a friendly conversation with the proprietor that he and his wife had been great fans of my father, and had left the Ambassadors for Christ after my father left Hong Kong. The man recollected our father's first testimony and remembered sermons he found particularly memorable. He recounted to us our own story as though it were someone else's: the narrow escape, the faked names, the path to freedom and God. I was filled with a mixture of sadness and disgust, even shame. He sat with us and drank cup after cup of green tea, he and my mother weeping and weeping.

Why did I feel disgust? The facts were plain enough, and my father told them plainly, and the man remembered them accurately, to the astonishment of all of us. And it didn't bother me much that my father or this man attributed so much to a divine hand. I too believe that we are, all of us, for the most part, carried by something beyond us. And though I'd argue emphatically about this or that aspect of God with my father, that wasn't what bothered me when I heard that man in the restaurant talk, good man that he was, kind that he was, a fellow immigrant, as lost in America as we were. Part of me felt such confusion and anger I was almost ready to disavow everything. Why? What makes a person want to disavow his own life? What did I feel so uneasy about? What was it I felt I needed to tell that man? What little detail did I need to give him, to explain he'd got it all wrong? What irked me? Why don't my shoes fit?

WINTERBLOSSOM GARDEN

DAVID LOW *was born in Ridge-wood, New York, in 1952. He lives in the East Village in New York City and works as a book editor and writer. He has received a Wallace Stegner Writing Fellowship, a New York State Arts Council Grant, and a National Endowment for the Arts Fellowship for his fiction writing. He has been a fellow at the MacDowell Colony and Yaddo. His short stories have appeared in literary magazines*

BARBARA WOIKE

and anthologies, including Ploughshares, Mississippi Review, *and*
Kansas Quarterly.

I HAVE NO PHOTOGRAPHS OF MY FATHER. ONE HOT
Saturday in June, my camera slung over my shoulder, I take the subway
from Greenwich Village to Chinatown. I switch to the M local, which becomes
an elevated train after it crosses the Williamsburg Bridge. I am going to
Ridgewood, Queens, where I spent my childhood. I sit in a car that is almost
empty; I feel the loud rumble of the whole train through the hard seat. Some-
day, I think, wiping the sweat from my face, they'll tear this el down, as
they've torn down the others.

I get off at Fresh Pond Road and walk the five blocks from the station to
my parents' restaurant. At the back of the store in the kitchen, I find my father
packing an order: white cartons of food fit neatly into a brown paper bag. As
the workers chatter in Cantonese, I smell the food cooking: spareribs, chicken
lo mein, sweet and pungent pork, won ton soup. My father, who has just
turned seventy-three, wears a wrinkled white short-sleeve shirt and a cheap
maroon tie, even in this weather. He dabs his face with a handkerchief.

"Do you need money?" he asks in Chinese as he takes the order to the
front of the store. I notice that he walks slower than usual. Not that his walk is
ever very fast; he usually walks with quiet assurance, a man who knows who
he is and where he is going. Other people will just have to wait until he gets
there.

"Not this time," I answer in English. I laugh. I haven't borrowed money
from him in years but he still asks. My father and I have almost always spoken
different languages.

"I want to take your picture, Dad."

"Not now, too busy." He hands the customer the order and rings the cash
register.

"It will only take a minute."

He stands reluctantly beneath the green awning in front of the store, next
to the gold-painted letters on the window:

WINTERBLOSSOM GARDEN

CHINESE-AMERICAN RESTAURANT
WE SERVE THE FINEST FOOD

I look through the camera viewfinder.

"Smile," I say.

Instead my father holds his left hand with the crooked pinky on his stomach. I have often wondered about that pinky; is it a souvenir of some street fight in his youth? He wears a jade ring on his index finger. His hair, streaked with gray, is greased down as usual; his face looks a little pale. Most of the day, he remains at the restaurant. I snap the shutter.

"Go see your mother," he says slowly in English.

According to my mother, in 1929 my father entered this country illegally by jumping off the boat as it neared Ellis Island and swimming to Hoboken, New Jersey; there he managed to board a train to New York, even though he knew no English and had not one American cent in his pockets. Whether or not the story is true, I like to imagine my father hiding in the washroom on the train, dripping wet with fatigue and feeling triumphant. Now he was in America, where anything could happen. He found a job scooping ice cream at a dance hall in Chinatown. My mother claims that before he married her, he liked to gamble his nights away and drink with scandalous women. After two years in this country, he opened his restaurant with money he had borrowed from friends in Chinatown who already ran their own businesses. My father chose Ridgewood for the store's location because he mistook the community's name for "Richwood." In such a lucky place, he told my mother, his restaurant was sure to succeed.

When I was growing up, my parents spent most of their days in Winter-blossom Garden. Before going home after school, I would stop at the restaurant. The walls then were a hideous pale green with red numbers painted in Chinese characters and Roman numerals above the side booths. In days of warm weather huge fans whirred from the ceiling. My mother would sit at a table in the back where she would make egg rolls. She began by placing generous handfuls of meat-and-cabbage filling on squares of thin white dough. Then she delicately folded up each piece of dough, checking to make sure the filling was totally sealed inside, like a mummy wrapped in bandages. Finally, with a small brush she spread beaten egg on the outside of each white roll. As I watched her steadily produce a tray of these uncooked creations, she never asked me about school; she was more concerned that my shirt was sticking out of my pants or that my hair was disheveled.

"Are you hungry?" my mother would ask in English. Although my parents had agreed to speak only Chinese in my presence, she often broke this rule when my father wasn't in the same room. Whether I wanted to eat or not, I was sent into the kitchen, where my father would repeat my mother's question. Then without waiting for an answer, he would prepare for me a bowl of beef with snow peas or a small portion of steamed fish. My parents assumed that as long as I ate well, everything in my life would be fine. If I said "Hello" or "Thank you" in Chinese, I was allowed to choose whatever dish I liked; often I ordered a hot turkey sandwich. I liked the taste of burnt rice soaked in tea.

I would wait an hour or so for my mother to walk home with me. During that time, I would go to the front of the store, put a dime in the jukebox and press the buttons for a currently popular song. It might be D3: "Bye Bye, Love." Then I would lean on the back of the bench where customers waited for takeouts; I would stare out the large window that faced the street. The world outside seemed vast, hostile and often sad.

Across the way, I could see Rosa's Italian Bakery, the Western Union office and Von Ronn's soda fountain. Why didn't we live in Chinatown? I wondered. Or San Francisco? In a neighborhood that was predominantly German, I had no Chinese friends. No matter how many bottles of Coca-Cola I drank, I would still be different from the others. They were fond of calling me "Skinny Chink" when I won games of stoop ball. I wanted to have blond curly hair and blue eyes; I didn't understand why my father didn't have a ranch like the rugged cowboys on television.

Now Winterblossom Garden has wood paneling on the walls, Formica tables and aluminum Roman numerals over the mock-leather booths. Several years ago, when the ceiling was lowered, the whirring fans were removed; a huge air-conditioning unit was installed. The jukebox has been replaced by Muzak. My mother no longer makes the egg rolls; my father hires enough help to do that.

Some things remain the same. My father has made few changes in the menu, except for the prices; the steady customers know they can always have the combination plates. In a glass case near the cash register, cardboard boxes overflow with bags of fortune cookies and almond candies that my father gives away free to children. The first dollar bill my parents ever made hangs framed on the wall above the register. Next to that dollar, a picture of my parents taken twenty years ago recalls a time when they were raising four children at once, paying mortgages and putting in the bank every cent that didn't go toward bills. Although it was a hard time for them, my mother's face is radiant, as if she has just won the top prize at a beauty pageant; she wears a flower-print dress with a large white collar. My father has on a suit with wide lapels that was tailored in Chinatown; he is smiling a rare smile.

My parents have a small brick house set apart from the other buildings on the block. Most of their neighbors have lived in Ridgewood all their lives. As I ring the bell and wait for my mother to answer, I notice that the maple tree in front of the house has died. All that is left is a gray ghost; bare branches lie in the gutter. If I took a picture of this tree, I think, the printed image would resemble a negative.

"The gas man killed it when they tore up the street," my mother says. She watches television as she lies back on the gold sofa like a queen, her head resting against a pillow. A documentary about wildlife in Africa is on the screen; gazelles dance across a dusty plain. My mother likes soap operas but they aren't shown on weekends. In the evenings she will watch almost anything except news specials and police melodramas.

"Why don't you get a new tree planted?"

"We would have to get a permit," she answers. "The sidewalk belongs to the city. Then we would have to pay for the tree."

"It would be worth it," I say. "Doesn't it bother you, seeing a dead tree every day? You should find someone to cut it down."

My mother does not answer. She has fallen asleep. These days she can doze off almost as soon as her head touches the pillow. Six years ago she had a nervous breakdown. When she came home from the hospital she needed to take naps in the afternoon. Soon the naps became a permanent refuge, a way to forget her loneliness for an hour or two. She no longer needed to work in the store. Three of her children were married. I was away at art school and planned to live on my own when I graduated.

"I have never felt at home in America," my mother once told me.

Now as she lies there, I wonder if she is dreaming. I would like her to tell me her darkest dream. Although we speak the same language, there has always been an ocean between us. She does not wish to know what I think alone at night, what I see of the world with my camera.

My mother pours two cups of tea from the porcelain teapot that has always been in its wicker basket on the kitchen table. On the sides of the teapot, a maiden dressed in a jade-green gown visits a bearded emperor at his palace near the sky. The maiden waves a vermilion fan.

"I bet you still don't know how to cook," my mother says. She places a plate of steamed roast pork buns before me.

"Mom, I'm not hungry."

"If you don't eat more, you will get sick."

I take a bun from the plate, but it is too hot. My mother hands me a napkin so I can put the bun down. Then she peels a banana in front of me.

"I'm not obsessed with food like you," I say.

"What's wrong with eating?"

She looks at me as she takes a big bite of the banana.

"I'm going to have a photography show at the end of the summer."

"Are you still taking pictures of old buildings falling down? How ugly! Why don't you take happier pictures?"

"I thought you would want to come," I answer. "It's not easy to get a gallery."

"If you were married," she says, her voice becoming unusually soft, "you would take better pictures. You would be happy."

"I don't know what you mean. Why do you think getting married will make me happy?"

My mother looks at me as if I have spoken in Serbo-Croatian. She always gives me this look when I say something she does not want to hear. She finishes the banana; then she puts the plate of food away. Soon she stands at the sink, turns on the hot water and washes dishes. My mother learned long ago that silence has a power of its own.

She takes out a blue cookie tin from the dining-room cabinet. Inside this tin, my mother keeps her favorite photographs. Whenever I am ready to leave, my mother brings it to the living room and opens it on the coffee table. She knows I cannot resist looking at these pictures again; I will sit down next to her on the sofa for at least another hour. Besides the portraits of the family, my mother has images of people I have never met: her father, who owned a poultry store on Pell Street and didn't get a chance to return to China before he died; my father's younger sister, who still runs a pharmacy in Rio de Janeiro (she sends the family an annual supply of cough drops); my mother's cousin Kay, who died at thirty, a year after she came to New York from Hong Kong. Although my mother has a story to tell for each photograph, she refuses to speak about Kay, as if the mere mention of her name will bring back her ghost to haunt us all.

My mother always manages to find a picture I have not seen before; suddenly I discover I have a relative who is a mortician in Vancouver. I pick up a portrait of Uncle Lao-Hu, a silver-haired man with a goatee who owned a curio shop on Mott Street until he retired last year and moved to Hawaii. In a color print, he stands in the doorway of his store, holding a bamboo Moon Man in front of him, as if it were a bowling trophy. The statue, which is actually two feet tall, has a staff in its left hand, while its right palm balances a peach, a sign of long life. The top of the Moon Man's head protrudes in the shape of an eggplant; my mother believes that such a head contains an endless wealth of wisdom.

"Your Uncle Lao-Hu is a wise man, too," my mother says, "except when he's in love. When he still owned the store, he fell in love with his women customers all the time. He was always losing money because he gave away his merchandise to any woman who smiled at him."

I see my uncle's generous arms full of gifts: a silver Buddha, an ivory dragon, a pair of emerald chopsticks.

"These women confused him," she adds. "That's what happens when a Chinese man doesn't get married."

My mother shakes her head and sighs.

"In his last letter, Lao-Hu invited me to visit him in Honolulu. Your father refuses to leave the store."

"Why don't you go anyway?"

"I can't leave your father alone." She stares at the pictures scattered on the coffee table.

"Mom, why don't you do something for yourself? I thought you were going to start taking English lessons."

"Your father thinks it would be a waste of time."

While my mother puts the cookie tin away, I stand up to stretch my legs. I gaze at a photograph that hangs on the wall above the sofa: my parents' wedding picture. My mother was matched to my father; she claims that if her own father had been able to repay the money that Dad spent to bring her to America, she might never have married him at all. In the wedding picture she wears a stunned expression. She is dressed in a luminous gown of ruffles and lace; the train spirals at her feet. As she clutches a bouquet tightly against her stomach, she might be asking, "What am I doing? Who is this man?" My father's face is thinner than it is now. His tuxedo is too small for him; the flower in his lapel droops. He hides his hand with the crooked pinky behind his back.

I have never been sure if my parents really love each other. I have only seen them kiss at their children's weddings. They never touch each other in public. When I was little, I often thought they went to sleep in the clothes they wore to work.

Before I leave, my mother asks me to take her picture. Unlike my father, she likes to pose for photographs as much as possible. When her children still lived at home, she would leave snapshots of herself all around the house; we could not forget her, no matter how hard we tried.

She changes her blouse, combs her hair and redoes her eyebrows. Then I follow her out the back door into the garden, where she kneels down next to the rose bush. She touches one of the yellow roses.

"Why don't you sit on the front steps?" I ask as I peer through the viewfinder. "It will be more natural."

"No," she says firmly. "Take the picture now."

She smiles without opening her mouth. I see for the first time that she has put on a pair of dangling gold earrings. Her face has grown round as the moon with the years. She has developed wrinkles under the eyes, but like my father, she hardly shows her age. For the past ten years, she has been fifty-one. Everyone needs a fantasy to help them stay alive: my mother believes she is perpetually beautiful, even if my father has not complimented her in years.

After I snap the shutter, she plucks a rose.

As we enter the kitchen through the back door, I can hear my father's voice from the next room.

"Who's he talking to?" I ask.

"He's talking to the goldfish," she answers. "I have to live with this man."

My father walks in, carrying a tiny can of fish food.

"You want a girlfriend?" he asks, out of nowhere. "My friend has a nice daughter. She knows how to cook Chinese food."

"Dad, she sounds perfect for you."

"She likes to stay home," my mother adds. "She went to college and reads books like you."

"I'll see you next year," I say.

That evening in the darkroom at my apartment, I develop and print my parents' portraits. I hang the pictures side by side to dry on a clothesline in the bathroom. As I feel my parents' eyes staring at me, I turn away. Their faces look unfamiliar in the fluorescent light.

II

At the beginning of July my mother calls me at work.

"Do you think you can take off next Monday morning?" she asks.

"Why?"

"Your father has to go to the hospital for some tests. He looks awful."

. . .

We sit in the back of a taxi on the way to a hospital in Forest Hills. I am sandwiched between my mother and father. The skin of my father's face is pale yellow. During the past few weeks he has lost fifteen pounds; his wrinkled suit is baggy around the waist. My mother sleeps with her head tilted to one side until the taxi hits a bump on the road. She wakes up startled, as if afraid she has missed a stop on the train.

"Don't worry," my father says weakly. He squints as he turns his head toward the window. "The doctors will give me pills. Everything will be fine."

"Don't say anything," my mother says. "Too much talk will bring bad luck."

My father takes two crumpled dollar bills from his jacket and places them in my hand.

"For the movies," he says. I smile, without mentioning it costs more to go to a film these days.

My mother opens her handbag and takes out a compact. She has forgotten to put on her lipstick.

The hospital waiting room has beige walls. My mother and I follow my father as he makes his way slowly to a row of seats near an open window.

"Fresh air is important," he used to remind me on a sunny day when I would read a book in bed. Now after we sit down, he keeps quiet. I hear the sound of plates clattering from the coffee shop in the next room.

"Does anyone want some breakfast?" I ask.

"Your father can't eat anything before the tests," my mother warns.

"What about you?"

"I'm not hungry," she says.

My father reaches over to take my hand in his. He considers my palm.

"Very, very lucky," he says. "You will have lots of money."

I laugh. "You've been saying that ever since I was born."

He puts on his glasses crookedly and touches a curved line near the top of my palm.

"Be patient," he says.

My mother rises suddenly.

"Why are they making us wait so long? Do you think they forgot us?"

While she walks over to speak to a nurse at the reception desk, my father leans toward me.

"Remember to take care of your mother."

The doctors discover that my father has stomach cancer. They decide to operate immediately. According to them, my father has already lost so much blood that it is a miracle he is still alive.

The week of my father's operation, I sleep at my parents' house. My mother has kept my bedroom on the second floor the way it was before I moved out. A square room, it gets the afternoon light. Dust covers the top of my old bookcase. The first night I stay over I find a pinhole camera on a shelf in the closet; I made it when I was twelve from a cylindrical Quaker Oats box. When I lie back on the yellow comforter that covers my bed, I see the crack in the ceiling that I once called the Yangtze River, the highway for tea merchants and vagabonds.

At night I help my mother close the restaurant. I do what she and my father have done together for the past forty-three years. At ten o'clock I turn off the illuminated white sign above the front entrance. After all the customers leave and the last waiter says goodbye, I lock the front door and flip over the sign that says "Closed." Then I shut off the radio and the back lights. While I refill the glass case with bottles of duck sauce and packs of cigarettes, my mother empties the cash register. She puts all the money in white cartons and packs them in brown paper bags. My father thought up that idea long ago.

In the past when they have walked the three blocks home, they have given the appearance of carrying bags of food. The one time my father was attacked by three teenagers, my mother was sick in bed. My father scared the kids off by pretending he knew kung fu. When he got home, he showed me his swollen left hand and smiled.

"Don't tell your mother."

On the second night we walk home together, my mother says, "I could never run the restaurant alone. I would have to sell it. I have four children and no one wants it."

I say nothing, unwilling to start an argument.

Later my mother and I eat Jell-O in the kitchen. A cool breeze blows through the window.

"Maybe I will sleep tonight," my mother says. She walks out to the back porch to sit on one of the two folding chairs. My bedroom is right above the porch; as a child I used to hear my parents talking late into the night, their paper fans rustling.

After reading a while in the living room, I go upstairs to take a shower. When I am finished, I hear my mother calling my name from downstairs.

I find her dressed in her bathrobe, opening the dining-room cabinet.

"Someone has stolen the money," she says. She walks nervously into the living room and looks under the lamp table.

"What are you talking about?" I ask.

"Maybe we should call the police," she suggests. "I can't find the money we brought home tonight."

She starts to pick up the phone.

"Wait. Have you checked everywhere? Where do you usually put it?"

"I thought I locked it in your father's closet but it isn't there."

"I'll look around," I say. "Why don't you go back to sleep?"

She lies back on the sofa.

"How can I sleep?" she asks. "I told your father a long time ago to sell the restaurant but he wouldn't listen."

I search the first floor. I look in the shoe closet, behind the television, underneath the dining-room table, in the clothes hamper. Finally after examining all the kitchen cupboards without any luck, I open the refrigerator to take out something to drink. The three cartons of money are on the second shelf, next to the mayonnaise and the strawberry jam.

When I bring the cartons to the living room, my mother sits up on the sofa, amazed.

"Well," she says, "how did they ever get *there?*"

She opens one of them. The crisp dollar bills inside are cold as ice.

. . .

The next day I talk on the telephone to my father's physician. He informs me that the doctors have succeeded in removing the malignancy before it has spread. My father will remain in intensive care for at least a week.

In the kitchen my mother irons a tablecloth.

"The doctors are impressed by Dad's willpower, considering his age," I tell her.

"A fortune teller on East Broadway told him that he will live to be a hundred," she says.

That night I dream that I am standing at the entrance to Winterblossom Garden. A taxi stops in front of the store. My father jumps out, dressed in a bathrobe and slippers.

"I'm almost all better," he tells me. "I want to see how the business is doing without me."

In a month my father is ready to come home. My sister Elizabeth, the oldest child, picks him up at the hospital. At the house the whole family waits for him.

When Elizabeth's car arrives my mother and I are already standing on the front steps. My sister walks around the car to open my father's door. He cannot get out by himself. My sister offers him a hand but as he reaches out to grab it, he misses and falls back in his seat.

Finally my sister helps him stand up, his back a little stooped. While my mother remains on the steps, I run to give a hand.

My father does not fight our help. His skin is dry and pale but no longer yellow. As he walks forward, staring at his feet, I feel his whole body shaking against mine. Only now, as he leans his weight on my arm, do I begin to understand how easily my father might have died. He seems light as a sparrow.

When we reach the front steps, my father raises his head to look at my mother. She stares at him a minute, then turns away to open the door. Soon my sister and I are leading him to the living-room sofa, where we help him lie back. My mother has a pillow and a blanket ready. She sits down on the coffee table in front of him. I watch them hold each other's hands.

III

At the beginning of September my photography exhibit opens at a cooperative gallery on West Thirteenth Street. I have chosen to hang only a dozen pictures, not much to show for ten years of work. About sixty people come to the opening, more than I expected; I watch them from a corner of the room, now and then overhearing a conversation I would like to ignore.

After an hour I decide I have stayed too long. As I walk around the gallery, hunting for a telephone, I see my parents across the room. My father calls out my name in Chinese; he has gained back all his weight and appears to be in better shape than many of the people around him. As I make my way toward my parents, I hear him talking loudly in bad English to a short young woman who stares at one of my portraits.

"That's my wife," he says. "If you like it, you should buy it."

"Maybe I will," the young woman says. She points to another photograph. "Isn't that you?"

My father laughs. "No, that's my brother."

My mother hands me a brown paper bag.

"Left over from dinner," she tells me. "You didn't tell me you were going to show my picture. It's the best one in the show."

I take my parents for a personal tour.

"Who is that?" my father asks. He stops at a photograph of a naked woman covered from the waist down by a pile of leaves as she sits in the middle of a forest.

"She's a professional model," I lie.

"She needs to gain some weight," my mother says.

A few weeks after my show has closed, I have lunch with my parents at the restaurant. After we finish our meal, my father walks into the kitchen to scoop ice cream for dessert. My mother opens her handbag. She takes out a worn manila envelope and hands it to me across the table.

"I found this in a box while I was cleaning the house," she says. "I want you to have it."

Inside the envelope, I find a portrait of my father, taken when he was still a young man. He does not smile, but his eyes shine like wet black marbles. He wears a polka-dot tie; a plaid handkerchief hangs out of the front pocket of his suit jacket. My father has never cared about his clothes matching. Even when he was young, he liked to grease down his hair with brilliantine.

"Your father's cousin was a doctor in Hong Kong," my mother tells me. "After my eighteenth birthday, he came to my parents' house and showed them this picture. He said your father would make the perfect husband because he was handsome and very smart. Grandma gave me the picture before I got on the boat to America."

"I'll have it framed right away."

My father returns with three dishes of chocolate ice cream balanced on a silver tray.

"You want to work here?" he asks me.

"Your father wants to sell the business next year," my mother says. "He feels too old to run a restaurant."

"I'd just lose money," I say. "Besides, Dad, you're not old."

He does not join us for dessert. Instead, he dips his napkin in a glass of water and starts to wipe the table. I watch his dish of ice cream melt.

When I am ready to leave, my parents walk me to the door.

"Next time, I'll take you uptown to see a movie," I say as we step outside.

"Radio City?" my father asks.

"They don't show movies there now," my mother reminds him.

"I'll cook dinner for you at my apartment."

My father laughs.

"We'll eat out," my mother suggests.

My parents wait in front of Winterblossom Garden until I reach the end of the block. I turn and wave. With her heels on, my mother is the same height as my father. She waves back for both of them. I would like to take their picture, but I forgot to bring my camera.

DAVID MURA

THE INTERNMENT
OF DESIRE

DAVID MURA *is the author of*
Turning Japanese: Memoirs of a
Sansei *(Anchor/Doubleday), which
won a 1991 Josephine Miles Book
Award from the Oakland PEN. His
works of poetry are* After We Lost
Our Way, *which won the 1989 National Poetry Series Contest, and* The
Colors of Desire *(1995, Anchor/
Doubleday). He has also written* A
Male Grief: Notes on Pornography
& Addiction *(Milkweed Editions).
His memoir on race and sexuality*

from a Japanese American perspective will be published by Anchor/Doubleday in 1996. Mura has received many honors, including two NEA Literature Fellowships, a Discovery/The Nation Award and a Lila Wallace—Reader's Digest Writers Award. He lives in Minneapolis with his wife, Susan Sencer, a pediatric oncologist, and their two children, Samantha and Nikko.

CHICAGO IN THE FIFTIES. THE GREAT YEARS OF Ernie Banks, pounding line-drive home runs or soaring wallops into Waveland Avenue, his lean, whiplike arms and ever-ready smile. Years of the brief ascent of the White Sox, who get to the World Series, win the first game, which I see with my father, and then lose four straight to the Dodgers of Larry Sherry and his untouchable sinker. Years of Mayor Daley, when the city was still "safe" and, as in Mussolini's Italy, "things worked." Still the city of the broad shoulders and clean winds off the fresh, clear surf-flecked waters of Lake Michigan, city of the stockyards and the el and the Magnificent Mile, of quiet ethnic neighborhoods where people know their place and the garbage is cleared away like clockwork. Picnics at Wilson Beach or Foster Beach, when we didn't notice the ethnics and the "white trash" (because we were ethnic too or because the different classes mingled more then?). School trips to the Museum of Science and Industry or Natural History with their mysterious, basemented mummies, sealed from air and natural light. Trips to the great lions that guarded the museum of art, confrontations with Seurat, the abstractions of modernism; trips to the planetarium, where the planets and stars reeled above us and I whispered to my maiden aunt so many names of planets and constellations she marveled at my memory. The train ride at the Lincoln Park zoo and the great cages of gorillas and tigers. Corned-beef hash and brownies at the cafeteria of Marshall Field's. Just a few years before the suburbs drained the city's whites and wealth (and our family, too).

Their small diaspora of the war and the internment camps long over, my family lived in an apartment on Broadway, about a mile from Wrigley Field, one block off Lake Shore Drive, with its luxury high-rises. Whether they were actually luxury high-rises I don't know, but that's the way we thought of them as we rode our bikes back and forth between the Addison and Belmont. They loomed above the traffic with views of the lake we could only imagine. In their lobbies gleamed gold chandeliers, an occasional doorman. The traffic streamed by, glinting in sunlight.

The building we lived in was a three-story ugly brown-brick corner structure. At the bottom of the landing out back was a dirt courtyard and an alley entryway of shadows and cinder. The building was owned by my uncle Lou's family, the Hirakawas; his wife, Aunt Ruby, was my father's sister. We were all Nihonjin with the exception of the Tenants, who were Jewish. The Hirakawas, the Ogatas, who owned the camera shop where my father worked his second job, the Fukayamas, the Uyemuras.

Uyemura was our family name until I was seven, when my father shortened it. "For better bylines," he said. He worked at INS, the International News Service. Everyone was always mispronouncing the "Uye." "You-ee stir-ee bowl-ee up," Michael Ogata used to say. He was the oldest among us, the best athlete, rivaled only by Jimmy Paris, who was Chinese and whose parents ran Paris's Hand Laundry just down Broadway. "Ooey, ooey"—rhyming with "gooey"—the others would chant. Hakujin would sometimes pronounce it "Oi-yea," which always reminded me of the phrase "Hear ye, hear ye . . ." called out by clerks of the court on television.

Everyone spoke English except for a few choice phrases and the names of food. Among themselves, the Nisei spoke English. Those who spoke Japanese spoke it to their parents, the Issei, and there weren't many Issei around. My mother's mother had died shortly after the war; my father's mother died when I was four or five. Later, both my grandfathers returned to Japan and remarried. Usually, it was the older Nisei, the eldest children, who spoke the best Japanese and so neither of my parents was as skilled in Japanese as Aunt Ruth or Auntie Sachi. Would my parents have spoken Japanese to us if they were fluent? Probably not. What purpose would it serve? And of course, those Japanese Americans who settled in the Midwest probably had less of a desire to return to the past or their cultural roots than those who went back to the West Coast after the internment camps.

Surrounded by relatives and other Japanese Americans, going to the Japanese American Congregationalist Church, a bugler in the Nisei Drum and Bugle Corps, which practiced at the Uptown Buddhist Church, I lived in our little ethnic enclave cozily unconscious of any issues of identity. Whenever the name of a new person came up in conversations, one of my relatives would always ask, "Nihonjin or hakujin," "Japanese or white person," though even this simplified bifurcation of the world slipped hazily by me, because of my lack of Japanese. I mean I sensed what these words meant, but I was never quite sure. Perhaps I just simply wasn't attentive enough. Years later, I would be embarrassed when, in my first book of poems, I wrote the word for Japanese pickle as "utskemono" rather than "tsukemono" and some critic took this as a mark of my ignorance and distance from my ethnic background. Which, of course, it was.

I am standing in the sunken courtyard that leads to the basement lockers and washing machine and furnace of our apartment building. It is late afternoon. I am five years old. There is no one about. In the dark under the porch are the rusted garbage cans, large industrial canisters, where Jimmy Hirakawa once saw a rat scurrying. I'm wearing corduroy pants, a T-shirt, a cowboy hat, and Keds. I look at the windows above me. Is anyone looking? I don't know. Slowly, deliberately, I begin to pull down my pants, exposing myself, hoping for what, frightened of what, thrilled with what, who knows, but the feeling that returns now in memory and engulfs me seems so familiar, echoed often in other experiences as I grow older. No one leans out the window and shouts, no one sees me, the crime, the secret goes undetected, if not unremembered.

Two years later, I'm in the bushes, near the berry tree, in the empty lot. Michael Ogata is shooing out the younger kids; only he and Jimmy Paris and an older girl are allowed to look. Flies buzz in the heat, a cabbage white flutters by. I feel their gaze behind me, I'm riveted, confused by their attention, by what I've agreed to do, and again, this time under the watchful gaze of others, I pull down my pants and expose my buttocks. Why are they watching like this? Why am I doing this? I feel flush with excitement, shame, attention, regret. It is over in a few seconds. And I walk out of the bushes, no different than when I entered.

In grade school, especially after we moved from the city to the Chicago suburb of Morton Grove, I was always a member of the elite in class. I got good grades, but more importantly, I was the third-best athlete, behind Greg Jacubik and Gary Hansen. As third-best athlete, I was the one who tipped the scales. When we played softball or football, whichever side I was on generally won. And in basketball, Gary and I vied for the top slot, this despite the fact that he had been set back a grade earlier and was actually a year older than me. Back in the neighborhood around my house, I was one of the Little League All-Stars, the quarterback whenever we played football.

But when junior high rolled around and sexuality reared up, I suddenly felt out of it. Some barrier suddenly appeared between myself and the white, mainly Jewish, students around me, but I didn't know what that barrier was. I knew I was Japanese American, that I looked different from almost all the other students, but I never talked with anyone about this. I had no language for it, and this ensured a zone of silence around the topic. Perhaps it was merely religion—we were going to an all-white Episcopalian church by then (in contrast to the Japanese American Congregationalist Church we'd gone to in the city). Or perhaps it was merely my personality, some defect of character. Or perhaps I shouldn't have been so concerned about making it with the in crowd, perhaps I was simply a snob in hiding.

At any rate, I can mark the event where things changed. I was in eighth grade, and captain of the intramural basketball champions. Every year, the champion team played a team of all-stars from the other teams. The odds were generally in favor of the all-stars. The night before the big game I sat outside the school with Steve Fine, the forward on our team, waiting for the bus. Steve said he hoped he played well in the game, because on Saturday everyone was going to be talking about the game at the boy-girl party at Marla Friedman's house. I nodded; I felt the same way.

The game was close throughout. But Rick Gordon, who was guarding me, constantly overplayed his hand, and I was able to drive past him for several layups. At a certain point, Greg Jacubik, who was guarding the baseline, gave up a couple baskets. As captain, I made a substitution. As the clock wound down to the last seconds, the game was tied, and the All-Stars had the ball. I saw Allan Rosenbloom glance at Rick Gordon and I pounced into the passing lane, intercepted the pass, and before they knew it, I was making the winning layup. I had scored over half of my team's points.

I dressed for the party on Saturday night carefully, with the proper Levi's and paisley shirt and brown penny loafers, the style of dress that the kids from Skokie called "collegiate." Its opposite was "greaser," and if you were in neither of these categories, you were simply unworthy of mention. I spent several minutes before the mirror, patiently grooming my pompadour. I walked the three blocks to Marla Friedman's house, still warmed by the memory of my last-second basket, immune to the brisk November wind that buffeted about me. I recalled how Laura Bennett seemed startled at how good I was, better than Allan Rosenbloom or Rick Gordon or any of the other guys from Skokie, the ones she'd gone to grade school with. Laura Bennett, the prettiest girl in the class, whom I had a secret crush on and who, through the luck of the draw, was my science partner.

But when I got to the party, no one talked about the game. The male centers of attraction were Rick Gordon and Jeff Lappins, even though Jeff Lappins hadn't even played in the game. No, he was the hero of another game —spin the bottle. As the Searchers sang "Needles and Pins" on the stereo, when it was my turn to spin the bottle, something happened. I began kissing Andi Levine and I couldn't stop; I just held my lips to hers for the longest time. And everyone laughed. So I did the same thing on the next spin. And the next. At one point the bottle I had spun pointed to Laura Bennett. I turned to look at her dark face, her long dark hair, her almost Italian-looking eyes, her full mouth, all vaguely reminiscent of Sophia Loren, of someone several years older. But what I saw in her eyes was a mixture of mock horror and a real, though slight, repulsion, as she made a show of backing up and putting her hands up before her face, fluttering them there as if waving away a stream of gnats. She ran to the other side of the room and refused to kiss me. Everyone laughed.

The next Monday at school I was labeled "Lover Lips." I tried to wear this moniker as a mark of distinction, though I knew that wasn't quite the case. All I knew was, the rules had changed. A line had appeared, I'd been singled out, but it was too threatening to tie my body, the way I looked, directly to what I felt—a burgeoning sense of shame.

Cut to Minneapolis, May 1978. I'm at a disco. As the glittering ball twirls dots of light across the room, I turn to see a woman staring at me. She looks vaguely like Ann-Margret in *Carnal Knowledge*. Uncertain at first, then flattered, I soon detect something odd in her gaze, as if what she was staring at is not really me. It is a gaze which forms its own field of vision, its own world. But I ignore that. It is enough that she is looking at me. I ask her to dance.

She is even drunker than I am, though I can barely tell that (I've also smoked a couple of joints). Almost immediately she invites me back to her apartment. Her eyes are steel gray. Her hair smells of perfume and smoke. She wears a black dress, very tight, high heels. Her hair is full, brushed and sprayed high off her forehead. I like that.

She tells me I remind her of someone she knew in Paris. She starts speaking in French. I try to respond, but can't remember anything from my college courses. She switches back to English, but keeps on lapsing into French phrases, in a way that would seem affected if she and I were not so drunk. But in our separate, inebriated states, the effect is surreal, as if switching back and forth between a dialogue in the original language and then a dubbed version. She asks me if I know the martial arts, if I've ever lived in Paris. I've never been out of the country, I tell her.

I follow her to her apartment. Her car weaves back and forth on the highway, barely making it off the exit. We're in a section of town I've never seen before, a rim of apartment buildings along the highway. She runs a stoplight, then another. I start laughing, half expecting her to wreck her car. I'm worried about losing her and I keep close, running the stoplights like her, twenty miles over the speed limit. A mild adrenaline rush. Part of the chase.

Her apartment is small, one bedroom, nondescript. There's a photograph of a nine-year-old boy on the table at the end of the couch. A dim light in the kitchen. She doesn't bother to turn on anything else. She pours herself a bourbon, offers me a drink.

She talks of her boyfriend in Paris, a Japanese Japanese. He drove a Jaguar, owned a clothing store, was a black belt in judo. He'd take her to Monte Carlo to play baccarat, on drives through the wine country of Burgundy. They'd stay at little châteaus, eat in four-star restaurants at roadside inns, in small out-of-the-way towns. The vineyards sped by, arbor after arbor; then fields of wheat, rippling like the sea. The speedometer over a hundred. Inside the riders feel nothing, only the roar of the engine, its terrible power.

She was in love with him, though she never states this directly. She talks instead of his glamour, how he was unlike anyone she had ever known. His dark skin, his wealth, his sophistication. He did not want children, never talked about her boy, who was only four then.

Her stories are jumbled, the slurred speech of a drunk. She keeps looking at me, as if by staring, by drinking more, I would become this Japanese, this man she could never forget. She says I look like him, that I am beautiful too.

In the bedroom, for a long time, all she lets me do is kiss her. After a while I get up to leave. She pulls me back. I get up to leave again. She pulls me back. She's wearing a black slip, which she never takes off. Something about the way her body changed after her child.

When we make love, she begins to make guttural noises and starts spouting curses in English and French, shouting at me to shoot her with my jism, to fill her pussy. It startles me, this talk so like what I've dreamed of. I feel soiled, alive. I order her to tell me how she loves my cock, she sputters back her response. When I don't come right away, she asks what's wrong. Nothing's wrong, I say. She worries that she's too large, she has had a child. Nothing's wrong, I repeat.

She does not seem interested in finishing her pleasure, and this bothers me, I who have prided myself on that. She seems in a frenzy of her own making, a fit of epitaphs in her own solitary battle. I come slowly, and for a long time.

Immediately afterward, I want to leave. She's worried again, and talks about her boy. A half hour later, the curtains are pale and translucent. I sit at the edge of the bed, pulling on my underwear. She stubs out a cigarette on the nightstand, and lies back down on the pillow, staring at the ceiling. We do not talk about whether I'll call her again.

I did go back, once or twice. Each time, she talked more about the Japanese in Paris. It was for me the first time my race had been the main force of attraction, what compelled it to happen. It made me feel odd, as if I were not really there. I wished it would happen more often. I knew it would not. There was something oddly demented about this woman, as if she were not really present, as if she were some mysterious machine with the shell of a consciousness, a face like those sets in Hollywood where this is only the illusion of depth and, behind the surface structure, there's nothing but a few beams propping up the charade. It disturbed me. And yet, I was thrilled by the sex, how she was so conscious of my color, my otherness. How my race had, with this woman, become a source of power.

. . .

"Did you hear what Sam Stauber did?" asks Jerry Scheider. "He and Bob Tortelli pulled Cindy Federbusch down on the playground after school and beat her box."

"Sharon Warshawski's sister got pregnant and had to be sent away."

"Do you know what John Matz and Bobby Hooks do after school? They put their penises under a faucet and run the water on them. And then they get the sensation."

"I wish I could get the sensation."

"Lyle and Gary get dressed up in his sister's underwear."

"Did you see the *Playboy*s in Terry's basement? His father has a whole stack of them."

"She kept on going, 'Please, Terry, please,' and I said, 'Police? I don't hear the police.' "

"Cindy Federbusch wears falsies."

"No way."

"How do you know?"

"I know."

"What base did you get to?"

"Jane Hansen gives hand jobs."

"The girls from Fairfield are real sluts."

"Susie Fukovitch? Her name is Susie Fukovitch?"

Fifth, sixth, seventh grade, all this talk I eagerly listen to and don't quite understand, don't quite believe. The terrible, enraged power of young boys, the savagery of their sex.

By high school, long before I lost my virginity, Herbie Bartlett and Terry Hoffberg were both screwing their girlfriends, and Herbie had several girls on the side, some who would screw, some who would only let him finger them.

I never heard any talk like this from Bob or Doug Hoshizaki, though obviously this sample is too small to draw any conclusions.

It was in eighth grade, sometime in the fall, a gray day, in late October, when I discovered my sexuality. This time period was the last I was ever to get in trouble at school for conduct. Through my grade school years, I was constantly being reprimanded for talking in school. Although I did well scholastically I always seemed to be mouthing off, making wisecracks. Given my more quiet nature as an adult, it's hard for me to convince friends now how absolutely obnoxious I could get then.

Were my actions in school a result of the strictness of my home life? My father had a second-generation immigrant's fierceness, and he still kept to some of the strictness of Japanese culture and schooling. I was not to be frivolous or to misbehave like other kids; I was constantly being admonished to "buckle down," and on my report cards my father would constantly write—in a second-generation sense of the formalities of English—"I have talked to David and he has assured me his deportment will improve." In essence, what he meant was: "I have spanked, I have beaten David, and have told him that more of the same will be coming if he doesn't shape up." Somehow, as evidenced by the F in deportment I was to get in science class that fall, these beatings never helped. But all this was about to change.

I am lying in bed. My room, on the second floor of our bi-level, is dark. My mother has gone to the store. I cross the hall to my parents' room, which looks so much like the bedrooms of my friends' parents. There's a dresser in Swedish modern, two mirrors at each end; a nightstand on both sides of the bed. A green quilted bedspread. Everything is neat, uncluttered, though not as neat and uncluttered as my parents' bedroom in later years (my mother's sense of aesthetic seemed gradually through the years to become more upper-class, cleaner, sparer, a yoking of her economic aspirations and her Japanese heritage).

I don't remember if I looked in the nightstands, though I know I did later. Instead, I slide open their closet. (It is a scene I've described often before, in poems, letters for my therapist, prose jottings.) The hangers all face one way, as do the shoes, lined precisely in a row. There's a gold quilted garment bag, about two feet wide. I slip my hands inside and—I don't know even now how I knew it was there, though my therapist, years later, remarked that news travels unconsciously in families, does not need the directness of speech—I pull it out. A *Playboy*. June 1964.

On the cover is a woman in white tights, curled inside a moon. Quickly, I open to the foldout. I have seen *Playboy*s before, in my friend Terry Hoffberg's basement, in the locker room once at school. Each time I felt fascinated by them, drawn to them, at the same time, of course, feeling their forbidden nature, the sense of trespassing on something I can't name. But this is the first time I have seen one alone. The woman inside, Donna, is a blond, a UCLA coed; her breasts seem enormous. Though only eighteen, she seems frightfully older. Overwhelming, imposing in her beauty. (Years later, discovering her picture while in an X-rated secondhand bookstore, I feel disappointed; her body seems a bit bloated, chubby, her hairstyle crude, carrying the cardboard pompadoured chignons of an out-of-fashion era: the economy and fashion of desire.)

I sit down on my parents' bed. My penis is hard. I keep staring. I pull down my pants and look at my penis, fascinated by how big it is. I look at the glossy picture. How she leans on the edge of a red folding screen, over which a red blanket is draped, so that her body seems to be emerging from the act of undressing. She doesn't stare at the camera, it is me she's staring at. The curves of her breast, the dark brown of the nipples, float off the page, both attached to her body and detached, constituting a vision, a realm of their own. I make a game of pulling my foreskin tighter, trying to make my penis grow bigger. It too seems somehow detached, to take on a force of its own.

I look at the blue vein on the back of the shaft, the way it rises, can be seen through the skin. I feel this pleasure shooting through my body, a trembling I cannot control. A wave washes over me, another, a rending of my body from my consciousness, my consciousness from my surroundings, this instant from the continuum of time.

The moment I ejaculate I'm startled, overcome, staring at what shoots out of me, seeing, sensing that this is what explains the morning sheets, wet, sticky, cold. At the same time I feel I've done something wrong, something which should be kept secret; though I don't think I had any sense of invading my father's privacy, I know somehow I'm trespassing. But whatever frightened or guilty feelings arise, there also arises an urge to feel this pleasure again, to look at the pictures again, to experience this explosion inside. I bend down and wipe up the milk-white pool on the floor. I repeat the ritual. My secret life has begun.

Adolescence is when we learn the power of secrets and lies, when we learn to create a life apart from our parents. Through this act I had marked out an existence, a world of my own. But with this creation I felt no sense of power, because I had not created that existence, that world. It seemed to erupt from me or, in another sense, it created me. Certainly, it seems now impossible to talk of my life, of who I am, without the story of my sexual desires.

My discovery of sexuality was, I suppose, no different from that of many American adolescents. But the fervor with which I subsequently went back to this discovery, the endless, compulsive repetition of that act, marked me as different, though at the time I had no way of knowing this. I simply put the magazine back in my parents' closet, and again and again, waited for a chance to steal back, to take another look. In between I contented myself with the darkness under my covers, each morning when I woke up, each night when I went to bed. Two, four, six times a day. In a way my father's *Playboy* was like a stash of alcohol an adolescent alcoholic has discovered, only I didn't need that stash. All I needed was to be alone, behind a closed door.

Only now does it occur to me to think of how my father perceived these *Playboy*s, why he bought them or what my mother thought. Did he too masturbate over them? Did my mother object to them and, if she did, did she voice this objection? How did he reconcile these pictures with his increasing participation during those years in our Episcopalian church?

All of these seem the expected questions an American son might ask in such a situation. But there is an added element here. My father was a Japanese American in a generation where Japanese Americans almost always married inside their race. I remember reading a journal my father kept when he was twenty-four and living in Chicago, working at a country club. In the clubhouse kitchen one night, he and a few of the other Nisei boys are talking about women. The line that sticks out in my memory went like this: "Mas has gone out with white girls, and he says it wasn't that bad." I'm surprised at this remark that dating white girls wasn't significantly different, and at the same time, I wonder if he could have expressed what those differences were. His awareness of the color line was not the same as mine. From adolescence on, I felt that my inability to attract girls had something to do with my race. And yet I was only attracted to white girls and was sure I would eventually end up with one.

I try to imagine my father staring at the foldout of Miss June, the UCLA coed, try to imagine what are the connections through which he yokes his sexuality to hers. He is sitting on the toilet, in a washroom of blue walls and blue tile and blue porcelain. I can see him there, a magazine on his lap, but when I try to imagine him staring at that image I feel pained, that unbearable pain when we see the pain of a parent, yearning for what he or she cannot have. He puts down the magazine. She, the girl, the woman, is too far away. Beyond his world. Perhaps this explains why, in a few years, I find no more of these magazines in his closet.

It is I who keep the images from *Playboy,* in my briefcase, my closet, in my head. The images there, the beautiful white bodies, are not too far away for me to dream of, though they seem beyond my touching. In this, their presence in my life as images seems appropriate: the images are there before me, but what they portray is not. Somehow, in my coming back to them again and again, I am completing a path into America that my father started, but I am going beyond my father, into the pull and frustrations of desires he never quite permitted himself, though, for a brief period, these images, these *Playboy*s, were part of his life too.

On several afternoons, when I am fifteen, sixteen, seventeen, I see myself hunched over my desk, the harsh white fluorescent light shooting up through the page in the newspaper, the page of notebook paper, over which I trace the lines of bodies modeling dresses from Saks, lingerie from Marshall Field's. Or, in the sad farce of desire, the images are from comic books, Betty and Veronica from the *Archie* comic books. I brush in the sexual details, feel my body rushing to the moment when the picture is complete, when I will stare at these lines—how impossible, how strange, these are merely lines—and find a pleasure, a solace, a compulsion, I will keep with me all my life. Whenever I am alone. I should be studying, I know, but this, this must come first. Then I will study some more. Then I will do this again. I cannot take time to play, I must study. Only these breaks I cannot help, I cannot hold back.

Or perhaps it is a book, the passage where a man is tied to a chair, held prisoner by thugs. He begins talking to the woman who is to watch him, the talk sexual and slow, filled with the clichés of pornography that are not clichés because I want to believe them, because I am sixteen and have no knowledge of the world to compare to this text. The man discovers the woman is getting aroused, that her compulsion is to hear a man talk about sex, and as she unties one arm to let him touch her, he knows he will be able not only to escape but also to have her, again and again. I hear someone, my father, coming up the stairs. My body tenses. The door is locked, but I push the book back in my desk. I stare again at the algebra. My father goes back downstairs. I take out the book. I stare again at the cover, the stripper barely covered by a boa, her heavy black eye shadow and bouffant blond hair. She is standing in front of a blue curtain—thirty years later I can still see the cover. It's embedded in my memory deeper than any garden or tree, any member of my family, any conversation, any friend. A companion for my loneliness. Which I do not see.

Over and over through night after night, all through adolescence, I will repeat these actions. I will try to hide the wads of Kleenex by stuffing them deep in my garbage, by sneaking quickly across the hall and flushing them down the toilet. At the end of the night I will say to myself I have studied all night. And will almost manage to believe that lie. I will stroke myself to sleep and, clutching a wad of Kleenex, finally doze off. When I wake in the morning, I will begin again.

"I don't want you to burn yourself out," said my father. To be consumed with desire, to die. Desire is a death wish, is death, and so must be denied. He could not accept what I was, what I had become: a sexual creature, someone out of control. And my mother, my mother lowered her eyes.

At a certain age, at the age I discovered my sexuality, I stopped acting out in school, stopped misbehaving. And each night, in my sheets, each morning, in my sheets, I spilled some part of my desire, some part of my outrage. And no one knew. And everyone thought I had become good, had "buckled down," had "improved my deportment." I became, in the eyes of my parents, the model son and student they wanted, the son my father could not believe was ever depressed in high school, the son whose depression was seen by his mother, forcing her to be silent, to lower her eyes.

This story needs to be told in layers, each one darker, more disturbing than the next. It's a painful process, one I would rather avoid. This next layer is the most difficult yet. It starts somewhere near the end of graduate school. Or perhaps earlier. The beginnings are murky, it's never quite clear where I took the first steps.

There were bars in the city where the dresses glittered and the women's eyes were darkened by shadow, their hair smelling of smoke and Ralph Lauren. Young owners of restaurants or hair salons, students from Tehran or Saudi Arabia, football players, salesmen from fashionable shops. In other bars boots scuffed the sticky, beer-painted floor, jeans and long, straight hair. Bikers, high school dropouts or runaways, students out for a wild night. "Don't roll your bloodshot eyes at me," shouted the lead singer. There were the massage parlors on Lake Street, in storefronts without windows, a plain-looking woman on a stool behind a counter, a dark-paneled room with plastic chairs. There were the lobbies of porno movie houses with even plainer and older women in the ticket booths. Or the high-volume disco and lights of a runway in the strip joints in east St. Paul or on Hennipen, the young women from Fargo or Farmington, Brooklyn Center, who spring down to their haunches, balanced on high heels, a look of defiance. To these places came all types of men, as in a random sampling of demographics. Some smiled, at ease, sipping beers. Others were nervous, furtive, plying themselves with drinks. I was more like the latter.

I was in all those places, at different times. I was a quick drunk, I'd get stoned beforehand, with a bong or with brownies laced with marijuana. It was easier to talk to women that way. Or to stare at them, unabashedly. It was easier then to cross line after line, moving into forbidden zones with a boldness that almost astonished me, an increasing frequency that was fueled by a fury, a rage I was unable to articulate but could only enact, expressing elsewhere some unconscious knowledge, what I could not speak.

There was a ritual to my preparations, a set. A bath, a shave. Silk black pants or jeans, depending on the place. A silk or denim shirt and jacket. After sifting the seeds and branches from the marijuana leaves, I patted them down in the small wooden bowl of the bong, watched the flakes there glow, like red throbbing coals, burning brighter with each breath, transformed through toke after toke into a city of fire. Slowly, the buildings animate into dancing figures, shadows outlined against a basin of flames.

There is a knowledge that destroys. Each time I felt I had to go further, to lose myself. The minutes passed, I did not notice. I'd look up as if from a dream, take a sip of beer or vodka, then go back down. And all the while I was imagining women, white women, of course, preferably blond, though those I slept with were seldom so. I thought of this as a curse, born of my skin. I wished my face were leaner, tauter. Staring in the mirror, I sucked in my cheeks, imagining how I'd look a few pounds thinner, with a more prominent facial structure.

There was something out there, some woman, some image, that would transform me, let me enter that dream I was creating out of dope and booze and the magazines piled in my closet, their glossy pages of copulation and flesh, their world where there is no other reality but sex. *Playboy, Hustler, Swedish Erotica*. Or there were the movies in darkened theaters, the damp, acrid smell that wafted up around me as I sat amid a dozen other anonymous men.

The plots of the movies were improbable, at times ludicrous, at times tinged with a strange sense of morality, of sin and damnation. A young woman commits suicide; she has remained a virgin all her life, and now, in the after-life, she begs to go back for what she has missed. She is granted her wish, coupling with men and women, engaging in twosomes, threesomes, orgies, her desires are indefatigable, her eyes shut tight upon her pleasure, her lip quiver-ing. She sucks in breath through flared nostrils, urges her partner on. At the end of the film, she enters a circle in hell and is placed in a room with a middle-aged bearded man who talks on endlessly of the meaninglessness of existence and will not fuck her and has no interest in sex. This is her punish-ment, her eternity.

I watched this parable of damnation, believing and disbelieving. It was a construct, a fiction. I didn't care.

The film I remember best from that time is *Behind the Green Door*. In the opening scenes, a young white woman is kidnapped, grappled in through an alley door to a dressing room, stripped, bathed with oil by four handmaidens, who stroke her thighs, her stomach, her nipples, who kiss her lips. One kneels before her, the young woman closes her eyes. She is the same one on the Ivory Snow soap box, smiling her pure, white All-American smile, a baby cooing at her shoulder. And then she is laid upon a table by the attending women on a stage. The audience is in tuxedos and gowns and sits upon couches. The maître d' is a former pro football player. There are midgets, an enormously rotund woman. The atmosphere is of a carnival in a horror film. And now, to a quavering guitar and a strong bass beat, a black man emerges from behind a lighted door at the back of the stage. His face and chest are painted by streaks of white paint, a necklace of claws encircles his neck. He is naked except for white stretch pants with a large circle cut out at the crotch. He kneels before the young blond woman, and puts his tongue to her. She begins to writhe. The fat woman in the audience begins to touch herself, the dwarves begin to mount her. The black man pulls back, is serviced by one of the handmaidens, then guides himself in. They make love for a long time, you can feel her excitement mounting. From time to time, she opens her eyes and pulls his face down and kisses him. At the end, her head is shaking back and forth violently, as in a seizure. He is riding above her, propped on his arms. She screams again and again, slowly falling into whimpers, as the black man lifts himself off her quivering body and retreats from the stage in the same slow and deliberate motion as he entered. The film cuts to the young blond woman astraddle another black man, while three other men, two white, one black, are suspended before her on gymnastic rings.

This is one of the first porno films I watch with Susie, who has been living with me since college. The whole experience feels like a blur, a dream that eludes a sense of time or place, that seems a long, perpetual drifting in and out of consciousness, the images flickering on and off the screen above us. Like me, she too is drunk, stoned. I whisper to her, then long moments of silence. In the darkened theater we touch. The man in the row before us peers back. I notice him, I forget he is there. It is as if time is suspended. We take a taxi home, each of us too out of it to drive.

Later I will barely remember what we did that night, though the film images will be burned permanently on my psyche, like a talisman. I know the movie has something to do with miscegenation, with what we represent together. I know this has something to do with the other I am not, the black man, representative of the primitive, of Africa, striding across the screen, larger than life. Other myths, other taboos.

Nothing in my life has prepared me for this, but the images arrive with a knowledge and an answer that is almost automatic in its acceptance, in being fused into my brain. I hear echoes of literary passages, of the glossy pages in my closet, of cheap paperbacks with their rumors of black prowess. I know there is something missing, that I will never find my body, my Asian body, up there on the screen, and this rage erases all other considerations, consumes me. In the twisted logic coagulating in my brain, I know the world is evil, that innocence is a lie. I am determined to prove it, to create my own damnation.

And so I will find myself in that theater again and again, in the dark video booths of the porno store, the black plywood boxes with a single stool inside and image after image of copulation flowing before me, and the reek of stale urine and come wafting up from the floor. I am as alone in this box as I will ever be; at that moment it is the image of what my life must become, how it will end. I hold myself back, waiting to prolong what I think of as pleasure, the sensation that will spur me on through the night, through booth after booth, quarter after quarter, until my money is exhausted, though not my will to go on.

I return to our apartment unsatisfied. I have found no one at the bars. They have all rejected me. I do not know why. It is not just my ugliness, my lack of smoothness or confidence or money, my inability to carry on bar banter. In every face I see there, mainly white, a few black men, there is never one of my own, and if there is, she will be with some rich white boy, she will not notice me. She will look at me the way I might look at her if I did not desire her, as some remnant she must shed, a reminder of a world, a people, she wants no part of, she is better than that.

I think I have known evil. Have seen it in myself. But perhaps what arose inside me was merely a flimsy imitation. Showing again how little I knew of the world, how little I know.

I know I hated inside Susie whatever resisted me. I know I hated what it was I wanted, what I longed to see. And I knew I could not stop. That was the way I defined pleasure, what would set me at ease, in the same way jiggers of scotch will bring to some men, in time, the desired oblivion.

"To want a woman like a fix." That's one way of putting it. But at times a real woman, even one I had picked up or bought, was too dangerous, too threatening. There was a certain safety in images, photos or film, in watching others. A detachment born out of control, maintaining control, buying control.

The self that watched could not be violated. I could watch and watch and no one would know, no one would see. It was as if those on-screen were to live the actuality of sex, some in their own private hells, yes, but living nonetheless, while I was removed from life, set apart. The haze of hash helped, liquor, poppers. To get fucked up. To obliterate consciousness.

Certainly I felt rage. At women, at the men who had the women. At Susie. At myself. At my parents. At whites. At blacks. At yellows, the women for abandoning me, the men for being like me, something to be abandoned, invisible, to be laughed at like Hop Sing cooks and messengers, servants groveling before the white mistress and master.

What fuels the world of pornography is a desire for control, to see the entire world as sexual in a way that conforms to one's desires and fantasies, where the accidental should never occur and where the realm outside of sexuality should never intrude and take center stage. The various 900 telephone sex lines attempt to fulfill these dictates; these phone lines have in turn become a common trope for pornographic movies. Contrary to the arguments of those who defend pornography, there is nothing "natural" about these tropes. They are highly artificial, fictional constructions. They are attempts to limit human sexuality and human emotions, to deny our complexity, the multifarious nature of our needs. This is not to say that those tropes which enthrall a person do not tell us a great deal about that person.

There was a point in our relationship when I wanted Susie to tell me such stories, to repeat certain tropes I wanted to hear. I know she protested. And I don't remember exactly what it was that she wrote.

Still, I remember the tropes, the ones that compelled me. It is what I can't forget.

It is nearly fifteen years. I have gone past the movies, the affairs. I have entered therapy, a twelve-step group, have gone through recovery. I have given over to some higher power what I could not control, that image, that urge, that sense of damnation. I have confessed before others, not just my therapist, but men with their own stories to tell, stories of boyhoods far more gruesome than mine, stories filled with images of saunas, bookstores, movie houses, trysts in cars, hotels, a series of acts shuddering forward, past line after line we thought we'd never cross and did. And they listened to mine not merely with sympathy but with the empathy of one who knows what it's like to be there, in that world apart, the haven we sought.

Telling is a form of healing; the Catholics with their confession, Freud with his couch, both acknowledge this. To be shriven, to be understood, to be purged. To find the buried, the necessary emotion, and release it.

And so I have stopped. I do not go there anymore, though the wish remains, the images. And if I choose to write about it, it is in part because those images still come to me, still need to be described accurately, showing the truth they hide. There are days I'd rather let this process go, hide it in some file cabinet, to be pulled out decades from now, when it doesn't matter, when I don't fear exposure or exposing anyone I love or even anyone I know. When it will take on the shimmer of someone else's life, someone I no longer know.

In many ways I was lucky. One ironic piece of luck is that I went through my period of recovery before I began to question my identity, before tensions and differences began to arise between my white friends and me, before I started to renounce my honorary whiteness. It was a time when I felt a trust toward whites, and so could enter into the process of individual and group therapy without certain reservations that I now feel in my encounters with them. Today it would be more difficult for me to open myself to them and that process in the same way.

Over and over I have tried to write about my sexuality, the descent of those years. At first, I wrote about it in a neutral voice, essays on male sexuality and pornography that made no reference to race, that pretended race did not exist. It was easier to write about things that way, clearer. The writing came at first in short, hard bursts, epigrams of a new consciousness. I was reading feminist texts at the time, like Susan Griffin's *Pornography and Silence*, Adrienne Rich's *On Lies, Secrets and Silence*. I was reading twelve-step and therapy books, pushing myself past the crudeness of the prose, my hypercritical literary tics. I felt I needed to start all over again, to write, if obliquely, something that related more directly to the life I had been living, what I was trying to escape. I was trying to find more accurate ways of describing my life.

Perhaps even more than most Americans, Japanese Americans do not make a habit of talking about their sex lives. I've heard from certain Japanese American readers, particularly male, that the passages about sexuality in my memoir, *Turning Japanese,* made them uneasy. They seemed unnecessary, unseemly. Voyeuristic. Perhaps, as in any community that feels itself to be marginalized, there's a reluctance to reveal ourselves, our inner thoughts and feelings. It makes us feel naked, as if our lives were exposed to those with power over us, the white mainstream society.

Is this repression of sexuality connected with the repression of the internment camp experience? Many Sansei have complained that their parents never talked about the camps. Only lately do I feel like I've come to understand with more empathy why our parents kept this silence, how little support they found in the greater society to talk about what they had been through. After the war, the people the Japanese Americans met did not want to dwell on the camps; some were not even aware of their existence. Everyone wanted to get on with their lives. The Japanese Americans of my parents' generation could hardly be blamed if they did not want to point out to others, particularly whites, that they had been prisoners of the United States government during the war.

Such factors do not, though, completely explain why the Nisei did not talk of their experiences to their children. To understand this reluctance, I think we have to consider the great shame many Nisei felt about that experience, its gross humiliations and frustrations, its terrible sense of loss—of dignity, time, money, property, and a certain faith in America. Time, money, and property were gone forever; dignity might be recovered. But if they lost faith in America, they would end up like those who repatriated back to Japan or many of the No-No Boys in their community, confused and bitter. No, better to put the past in the past, to go on with life. *"Shō ga nai"*—can't be helped.

But if you repress one memory, other things get repressed too. Because memories reside not simply in the mind or spirit but also in the body. And prejudice and racism reside not simply in racial slurs or job discrimination but also in the ways all Americans feel about our bodies, the skin which surrounds us. It is not, of course, that the intrinsic value of that skin is any different for any human being. But social practice teaches us otherwise. We learn to read our bodies and the bodies of others. Upon such reading our survival often depends.

A classic example of this was the photo in *Life* during World War II purporting to show the difference between Chinese and Japanese. Up until this point most non-Asian Americans had not thought much about differentiating between these two ethnic groups, but suddenly the Chinese were allies and the Japanese the enemy. Of course, there were Chinese who looked like the Japanese photo and vice versa, and the marks of the distinction pointed out in the text beside the photos had little or no scientific basis. But the point was that such distinctions needed to be made; the bodies in the photos were, in one sense, blank screens upon which a societally created reading was imposed. The madness of such distinctions seems absurd in retrospect; at the time *Life* was absolutely serious. Certainly, for the Chinese Americans who wished to separate themselves from the Japanese Americans the *Life* diagrams were indeed necessary; some chose also to wear buttons which proclaimed, "I Am Chinese."

Such racial distinctions eventually create an internalized racism in the victims of this racism. In their assault against segregation, the NAACP lawyers used the evidence of a black sociologist which showed that black children, when presented with a white doll and a black doll, found the white doll more attractive and "better" than the black doll. And yet the children generally associated the black doll with themselves. The sociologist argued that this reflected the black children's damaged self-image, and he attributed that damage to the messages the children received under the system of segregation: the whole apparatus of segregation instructed black children to see themselves as inferior. (Of course, this instruction did not end with segregation.) One implication of the experiment is this: in the way the children saw the dolls and perceived value in the color of a person's skin lay an untold series of incidents, a history of social discourse, which instructed them in the values of segregation; the way they saw their bodies reflected a significant story of their lives.

All this is by now fairly familiar ground in the history of race in this country. What is not so familiar is how the socially created meanings of race affect the formation of sexual desire. The subjective predilections of each individual in our society, no matter what color, are related to the systematic configurations and hierarchies of race. The meanings and valuings of our sexual desires are not just subjective, they are societally created. Of course, to argue this goes against certain public notions of individual liberty which maintain that whom I desire is a private matter, while whom I hire is not. There is a separation, as it were, between the bedroom and the boardroom. You don't want the government or its laws meddling in your private life, what you do behind closed doors is your own personal matter, etc. But, of course, this does not mean that there isn't a relationship between whom I desire and whom I hire, or between whom I want my children to desire and whom I hire. And I suspect that America's squeamishness in examining this fact comes in part from a realization that the lines of race run deeper than we want to acknowledge and occupy a more intractable area of psyche than we're able, at this point in time, to deal with. I can change whom I hire more easily and more quickly than whom I desire.

Would a society without racism be one in which sexual desire is not configured along racial lines? I don't know. Is it desirable that all sexual desire ignore racial features? That seems an impossibility. What I do know is that an examination of sexual desire in relationship to race tells us a lot about each subject and who we are.

For almost all Japanese Americans of my parents' generation, you as a Japanese American married another Japanese American. Not a white person. Certainly not a black person. Not even a Chinese American. No, you married another Nisei, and there was no question about it. In contrast, over 50 percent of the third-generation Japanese Americans marry out, mainly with whites. Japanese Americans will often note this difference, but I've had very few discussions with them about what this change signifies, other than the seemingly natural process of assimilation. No one asks, for instance, why Japanese Americans don't marry other people of color more often. No one really inquires very deeply about how the Sansei view other Sansei in sexual terms. There are only the occasional remarks like "Sansei men are boring" or that some of the women have "daikon"—radish—legs, or the jokes about how certain Caucasian men always seem to be on the lookout for "Oriental girls." The questions about how our desires are formed or where they came from are somehow too troubling. They bring up too many questions about the "natural" process of assimilation.

Other than his remark about a friend dating a white girl in his diary, and perhaps through the *Playboy* in his closet and of course through his choice of my mother, my father has never said anything to me about how race factored into his sexual desires. Even more than sex itself, this subject was a real taboo.

Is this one of the reasons sex and race have become one of the driving themes informing my work? As a writer I constantly find myself working against the grain, trying to articulate what has not been said, experiences that have not been named, feelings forested by silence. In one of Rilke's poems, he talks about the father getting up from a table and leaving his children to ask the questions he has not asked. At the same time, I grew up in a world where the question of interracial sexual relationships was being asked. I've had to face certain issues neither my father nor his father ever had to face, and for which, understandably, they would have no answers.

In Bill Hosokawa's *Nisei: The Quiet Americans*, there's a revealing passage about the complexities of race in America:

> The evacuees who were sent to Arkansas had been astonished to find they were regarded as white by the whites and colored by the blacks. The whites insisted the Japanese Americans sit in the front of the bus, drink from the white man's fountain and use the white man's rest rooms even though suspecting their loyalty to the nation. And the blacks embarrassed many a Nisei when they urged: "Us colored folks has got to stick together."
>
> If there was no middle ground in the South's polarized society of black and white, in the rest of the country after the war, a Nisei could live as a yellow-skinned American without upsetting too many people, and he also discovered it was not particularly difficult to be accepted into the white man's world.

In many ways, most Japanese Americans of my father's generation decided to sit in the front of the bus. And many were guilty of the same racist attitudes toward blacks as white Americans. But putting aside their attitudes toward blacks for the moment, Japanese Americans made an understandable choice when confronted with the segregated buses: Sit where the power is. Don't associate yourself with those who are more oppressed than you; don't become partners with the powerless if you can avoid it. But what this means, paradoxically, is that Japanese Americans are no less connected to blacks than to whites, despite Hosokawa's fervent wish to be rid of the "racially polarized South." The racial identity of Japanese Americans was formed not just by the internment camps or by their dealings with whites but also against the backdrop of race relations involving blacks and other people of color. There was an unspoken message all about them in the camps, especially in the South: Things are bad now, but they could be worse. We aren't lynching your kind. Yet.

Do I overdramatize? A threat doesn't have to be carried out to be effective. The lynchings which were commonplace in the South where my father was interned were most often prompted by the charge that a black man had raped, or had sex with, a white woman; sometimes it was simply that he had "recklessly eyeballed" her. Behind this grotesque violence lay the fear of the black man's sexuality and the white woman's sexuality and the white man's own sexuality and the black woman's sexuality, which the white man had taken many times in the past and proof of which lay in the many mulattoes whom he saw as his inferior. The body tells us we are human, one species. We can copulate and procreate across color lines. This is a horrible, unspeakable truth in a society where the segregation of the races is still the norm. It brings up the suspicion that we all may be, after all, only human. That some are not destined by God or nature to be inferior, to have less of society's power and bounty.

Amidst this immense desire by whites to suppress black people, to project and deny their sexuality, the Japanese Americans did not call up the same vehement fears, though during the war those fears were certainly exacerbated. Did my father think of such issues when he looked across the floor at a Nisei dance in 1949, and saw my mother and said to his friend, "That's the girl I'm going to marry"? I don't think so. It would have seemed natural as rain to my father that he would marry another Nisei.

As Frantz Fanon has pointed out, it is a great temptation for a member of an oppressed minority to hide neuroses resulting from one's family system and one's own character by overemphasizing the very real political and social injustices one has experienced. According to Fanon, health can only come to such an individual when he or she separates the personal from the racial, the individual from the group. In his *Black Skin, White Masks,* he examines a black neurotic, Jean Veneuse, who uses his blackness as the sole explanation for his psychic condition, who explains his lack of concrete contact with others through "externalizing his neurosis" rather than confronting his own "infantile fantasies." Such an individual is not interested in health or psychological equilibrium, and if the social differences between blacks and whites did not exist, "he would have manufactured it out of nothing" in order to remain entrenched in his own self-hatred.

Trapped in his feelings of inferiority, Veneuse cannot escape the sense that the color of his skin is a flaw and he accepts the separation imposed on him by the color line. Fanon links this acceptance with a concomitant urge "to elevate himself to the white man's level," and sees Veneuse's sexual "quest for white flesh" as part of that attempt. Fanon argues that Veneuse's acceptance of the color line dooms him and keeps him from seeing that the world must be restructured and with it Veneuse's psyche.

Reading Fanon's description of Jean Veneuse, I feel both entrapped and penetrated; I see in his words my lifelong perception of myself as a "loser," an outsider unable to make "concrete contact with his fellow man." And I recognize in Veneuse's wish to blame each flaw and defeat on the color of his skin my own explanations of my sexual insecurity: I was a Japanese in a white world. Viewing sexuality in this way, growing up in a white community, I felt that every girl who rejected me somehow reaffirmed both my sense of a color line and my sense of inferiority. And yet, even now, rejecting this easy explanation, I still cannot answer a basic question: What effect did my color have on how the girls perceived me? Time and again, I would ask girls out, and even have one or two dates with them, until their parents inevitably discovered I was not Jewish. I could not even, as some of the goyim did, pretend I was Jewish. My color gave me away. Yet thinking of those rejections now, it could have been that the girls were not really interested in me, that they sensed the inevitable weakness, shame, and self-hatred I know I felt then. But was that sense of shame merely personal? Was it attributed to my family system? Or were there larger forces around all of us, forces none of us had the language to acknowledge?

. . .

Recently, I attended a panel which explored the internment in relationship to the experiences of Native Americans, African Americans, and, more recently, Arab Americans. During the panel I was struck by what a Lebanese American friend said about the Gulf War and its effect on her community. My friend began her talk listing the insults and attacks, the calls by the FBI in the middle of the day or the middle of the night, the rumors about plans to round up and detain Arab Americans. But then she focused on what she called "the veil." Rather than the scarf worn by Arab women, or the scarves worn by protesters of the Intafada, this veil was what came between Arab Americans during the Gulf War. This veil said, "Let us not talk about what is happening to us, about the threats and dangers, about the powers around us that control our lives and over which we have no say. Let us not speak of the racism, the humiliations we encounter, the pain of the stereotypes and taunts. Let us try to conduct our lives as if all were normal (whatever that means)." My friend talked of sitting in a kitchen with a friend and how they began to talk about the rise in hate crimes against Arab Americans. But then, suddenly, they shifted to another subject; the veil could be lifted for only a moment.

As I listened to my friend, I felt I understood the reaction of my parents' generation to the internment camps in a new way. I knew the veil she was describing had existed among Japanese Americans during and after World War II, and that this veil was one of silence and shame. It took away a certain easiness and intimacy within the community, and demarcated a zone of experience and knowledge and feelings that they could not express. I realized how much fear was in this veil, how great a sense of powerlessness, a lack of control. I saw that this veil comes up often when people are oppressed, where trauma occurs, and what a great effort it takes then for those people to lift this veil, to begin to look each other in the eyes and speak. I felt in a new way how the longer you live with this veil, the heavier it becomes.

I know now that my parents' sense of inferiority, their refusal to acknowledge the pain of the camps or recount the past, rose out of a very different racial situation than the one I grew up with. I am not here just speaking of the inevitable racial insults that must have been more prevalent in their youth than in mine, but of the more obvious trauma of the camps. My parents were imprisoned in the camps merely because of their color and race, not for anything they had done. In suffering this experience, they did not feel guilt, which comes from a sense of responsibility for one's actions. Instead they felt shame. Rather than focusing on actions, shame says that the very core of one's being, one's whole self is wrong, inferior, tainted. Of course, my parents did not speak of this shame; the nature of shame is silence. Besides, they were still partially Japanese by culture and shared with their parents strong impulses toward leaving things unspoken. At the end of the war, my parents left the camps wanting to prove to America that they were "true" Americans, whiter than the whites. Any mention of color would have spoiled that illusion, challenged their sense of acceptance.

If what my parents felt was racial shame, and if the only outward showing of this shame took place in my father's desire to leap into the middle class and then the upper middle class (and to have his son do the same), then perhaps there lay within the psychic network of my family an unspoken assumption about our color and race. This assumption was communicated silently and unconsciously, as is so much of what is communicated in families: "White is better, we are inferior. There's a color line in America—don't speak of it and perhaps it will vanish."

In what ways, then, did this message manifest itself? Since it could never be articulated openly, it came to the surface unconsciously, indirectly. Perhaps it first appeared when, as an infant with eczema, I tried to scratch away my skin, the painful covering that could not be undone. I know that for a certain period this nightly scratching cut away such patches in my arms that I had to be bandaged and then, at night, my parents had to bind my wrists to the sides of my crib. Or perhaps it erupted when, as an adolescent, I found my sexuality in a nightly ritual where visions of All-American foldouts came to me and shamed me with their unavailability, with a whiteness of skin that served as a marker for both my desire and inferiority.

At a certain stage the rage latent in any shame breaks the surface and speaks more forcefully if still obliquely. In this stage the sources of the rage are not known, and the person directs the rage at any number of objects in intimate relationships, in chance encounters on the street, in daily life. The destruction such unexamined rage can wreak is enormous. I believe this is what happened in my early relationships with women and sexuality, the part of my past that is so difficult still for me to accept.

At any rate, I do not think my parents could admit their rage: it had been stamped down in the camps, in the Japanese concept of *gaman*—endure; in their belief that by fitting in, by forgetting their cultural past, by becoming the model minority they could somehow attain whiteness. Their rage would have destroyed this belief, this front. Beyond defeat, their silence spoke of a need to put that defeat in the past.

And yet, I know the rage was there, shaping their life, the world of my childhood. I need only look to my father's rage to succeed, his need to keep me so tightly under his reins, his quick punishment of any errant move on my part. For years I looked at his rage as a question mark, a focus of dysfunction, part of a family system somehow linked to his parents, a history I knew little of. I failed to consider the public history, to ask how deeply the events of the internment or the forces that pushed assimilation shaped him. Mirroring his own conscious desires, I looked at him and my mother as deracinated subjects, outside the forces of race. This too was part of my sickness.

A couple of years ago, Gordon Hirabayashi, one of the four Japanese Americans to take the case of the internment to the Supreme Court, came to speak at St. Olaf, the small liberal arts school at which I was teaching. At lunch, on the day of his speech, I peppered him with questions about his case and the internment. How, for instance, had the Japanese American Citizens League (JACL) reacted to his suit? They were against it, he replied; the JACL didn't want to upset the authorities and were worried about the reaction of the white public to such suits. Hirabayashi said his protest probably came out of his Quaker background and his mother, who was very forthright in standing up for her beliefs and encouraged Gordon in his suit. He talked of walking all night in Seattle and breaking the curfew and finally walking into the police station and demanding that they arrest him. He told a story of how, when he was finally sent to the camps, it was long after all the other Japanese Americans had been transported, and he had to hitchhike to the camp where he was assigned. The irony of this still amused him.

Hirabayashi is slightly older than my father. He's a small, solidly built man, with salt-and-pepper hair and gold-rimmed glasses like my father, and his manner is relatively unassuming. The one exception is the passion he brings to stating the injustice of the internment camps and the treatment of the Japanese Americans during World War II. This anger still seemed to fuel his mission to continue speaking of this constitutional injustice and his defiance not only of the law or the War Relocation Authority but also of the members of his own community.

Listening to Hirabayashi, I realized I had never heard a Nisei adult talk so openly about the camps; I had never heard a Nisei declare so forthrightly that the camps were a blatant injustice, a trampling of the Constitution. Instead, my father and the members of my family had always talked of the camps as something to be forgotten, a mild discomfiting interlude, or even as something positive, a way out of the provinciality of the West Coast Japanese American community.

As this man of my father's generation propounded so eloquently against the camps, I felt this sudden shudder of recognition: If Gordon Hirabayashi had been my father, if my father had talked like this, I would not only know more about the camps or history, I would not only have grown up with different political beliefs. I would have felt differently about my sexuality, about my body, I would not have seen them as a source of wounding and shame. My identity, the most intimate of feelings about my own body, were directly tied to what had happened nearly fifty years ago—the signing of Executive Order No. 9066 and the internment of the Japanese American community.

In that instant of recognition I felt a gap between my own personal history, particularly my sexuality, and the history of Japanese Americans suddenly close. The private and the public, the individual and the group—it was all connected, captured in my body.

The internment camps rid the West Coast of the bodies that white Americans saw as evidence of an invasion, a foreign threat. The desire was to make those bodies of Japanese Americans invisible, silent. The camps were proof that the government and the white majority could accomplish such banishment, how deeply the private lives of the Japanese Americans could be invaded. In the camps, with their communal toilets and showers and barracks, there was little privacy; the fulfilling of sexual urges entered into a zone of muffling and public display, in an effort to work around the dictates of the facilities. Did this engender a further silencing around sexuality? At any rate, what did definitely come forth was an unease with the fact of internment and how easily their bodies could be imprisoned, manipulated, controlled. For the Nisei, to speak of their bodies was to bring up the specter of their powerlessness and their shame over that powerlessness. To speak of any sense of community put them in a double bind: both the way they looked and their Japanese cultural heritage, what bound them together, was what marked them as criminal.

The JACL tactic was to deny, as vehemently as possible, any ties to Japan. Instead, they constantly tried to seek similarities between them and the acceptable white citizens, and so they spoke of an abstract quality like patriotism which would know no color and erase difference. Such an approach seemed to some a logical way out of their dilemma. Let the rest be silent, the silence of their difference, of the body that they could not hide.

Like the JACL, Hirabayashi did not dwell on his difference. In certain ways, he also spoke to higher abstract principles which did not recognize the categories of race. But the JACL did not support Gordon Hirabayashi. This was because Hirabayashi, in arguing against the government, gave vent to an anger and a sense of outrage that others felt but kept silenced. Such anger and protest were seen as unpatriotic, as confirming that the Japanese Americans were not good Americans, that they were indeed alien, different. Hirabayashi saw his anger as part of his fight for principle, and it is his acknowledgment of his emotions which I think struck me. Such emotions reside within the body, are freed up through the body; they must break through barriers of shame in order to be released. And this perhaps is why I felt had he been my father my sexuality would have been quite different.

Still, the internal politics of the Japanese American community was more complicated than a binary opposition between Hirabayashi and the JACL. Hirabayashi's "No" was echoed by the No-No Boys, but because of the legal status of his protest and because his case did not represent a direct defiance of the draft and his patriotic duty, he did not seem to suffer the ostracism from the Japanese American community and the JACL that many of the No-No

Boys underwent after the war. For after the war it was those who sided with the government, those who said "Yes-Yes," who became the emblems of the community, its heroes. Also, perhaps because of the nature of his case, and his Quaker background and his own strength of character, Hirabayashi's anger did not slip into bitterness or despair like some of the No-No Boys, who felt betrayed both by America and by other members of their community. And then there were those Nisei who repatriated to Japan, some of whom were Kibei who had studied in Japan and felt a strong affinity with its culture and people, and some of whom were Nisei whose disillusionment and disaffection with America had grown too great.

From my position as a Sansei, I feel all these voices within me. And all of these voices, in turn, speak to me in the story of my own sexuality, in the sentences of my desires. Growing up, I took, along with my parents, the JACL version of history and assimilation and my vision of my sexuality tried, for a time, to make sense of this path. In Hirabayashi, I see someone who points me to a path beyond silence into the body my parents and history have bequeathed me, a zone of healing which recognizes the connection between politics and desire. In the No-No Boys I find an alienation, a veering past anger into bitterness and rage and despair, that often finds me as I look deeper and deeper into the issues of race. Certainly, the rage that fueled my sexuality from my late teens till my late twenties carries a similar emotional cast. In those who went back to Japan, I find a parallel in those moments during my trip to Japan when I felt I might, I could, become Japanese, a feeling that balanced between an attraction to Japan and a sense of alienation from America. And perhaps in both those moments when I felt a growing attraction to Japanese women and a resultant ease of my own sexual anxieties, some part of the Nisei who went back to Japan also speaks to me.

When I visit my parents, it's often in the summer. I walk in, I'm greeted by modest hugs, and we go to the living room, which is immaculately white—white walls, white carpet, white furniture, a blanched Andrew Wyeth on one wall, a Japanese ink-brush horse on the other. We begin talk—about my brother's newest girlfriend, his search to get a film script produced; my sister's poor-paying job at the public relations firm, her new boyfriend; my other sister's search for another new job—no talk of boyfriends for her, she's never had one. Rarely does the conversation float to my work, a void which is both comfortable and discomforting. I look out the back window at the immaculate lawn, and beyond to the golf course, where men in plaid pants, yellow shirts, and blue hats stalk off into the early-evening sun, the irons flashing in their hands, the bags pulled behind them, a world made more silent and peaceful by the pneumatic seal of the glass. I listen to the air conditioner's hum and long for the hot and sticky summer air, the air of the city from which my parents escaped years ago.

And if I search in that image for a story? There seems to be none. Their calm suburban world is timeless. Or perhaps, more accurately, time is refused admittance at the entrance to this subdivision; nothing happens here.

I know that somewhere, further back, something did happen, and in the connections between what happened then and this image now, there is a story, the shape of two lives, the lives of a family. I know also that I feel as distant from this story as my parents, perhaps even more so. Perhaps I too believe the past does not exist. Or if it existed, it existed on some plane so eccentric it has nothing to do with the present; it will involve fictional creatures who have nothing to do with my mother or father. I am left, then, with the split: there is the sense of some almost legendary past, where real events happened, where people argued, lost homes, had accidents, lost lives, and my parents' present suburban life, inhabited by golf courses and tennis games, watching the Masters or Wimbledon on CBS, the latest video from Blockbuster.

Where would I start investigating the past? Beyond the simple chronology of events, I have so many questions. I've come to see, for instance, that my father's feelings about sexuality, his body, were less problematic than mine. But what exactly does that mean? What was it like for my father after he got out of the camps and made his way back into American society? How did he carry out his high school teacher's admonition in the camps to be 200 percent American or her belief that he would find more good people than bad? He speaks so little about those years. How can I compare my experiences as a young man with his?

Like a bricoleur, I must make do with the tools at hand—a few anecdotes from my aunts, some stray remarks from my parents, history books, a few works of literature by Japanese Americans, and my own guesses and intuitions.

In the end I can't vouch for the truth of my version of the past. But I know it is truly my version, and therefore reflects the reality of Japanese Americans of my generation, of my time.

A Japanese American writer I know says that those of us who come from marginalized cultures are often bequeathed fragments, brief bits of the past, and nothing more. There are no unbroken threads, no fully developed tales or histories. There are too many secrets and occlusions, there are too many reasons to forget the past. And there are forces which do not want us to remember, do not want us to take those fragments and complete them, to restore them to some fuller life.

When my friend said this, I realized that I had always thought my situation personal, to be a result of my parents' silence and my own paltry imagination. I lacked the powers of storytelling, the ability to enter and re-create the past. I let myself be defeated even before I started writing. And in that way, our story would disappear.

I did not think about how strongly the culture may not want it to reappear. Imagination is intervention, an act of defiance. It alters belief.

NGUYỄN
QÚI - ĐUC

A TASTE
OF HOME

NGUYỄN QÚI-ĐUC *was born in Vietnam in 1958 and left his homeland in 1975. He has worked for the British Broadcasting Corporation in London and KALW-FM in San Francisco. He has written for* The New York Times, The Asian Wall Street Journal Weekly, *the* San Francisco Examiner, Zyzzyva, *and other publications. He received the Overseas Press Club of America's Award of Excellence for his reports from Viet-*

nam for National Public Radio in 1989. He is the author of Where the Ashes: The Odyssey of a Vietnamese Family.

STRANGE HOW THE FROZEN HEART OF AN EXILE IS instantly thawed in the 95-degree heat of Sài Gòn. Seven A.M. and it feels like high noon.

In America I can't even stand the smell of food this early, but here I suddenly want to go out and eat a whole bowl of fish ball noodle soup. And I want a tall glass of iced coffee. *Càfé sũa đá,* with sweetened, condensed milk, which they only use for baking in America.

I get ready to go out. The shirt I'm putting on makes me feel unprotected. I never wear a short-sleeve shirt in San Francisco. I pull on my trousers, then I remember that I can't leave my hotel room. I don't have a visa.

Việt Nam is the homeland, my homeland, and I needed a visa to come home. I should not have trusted the travel agent, who was sure a visa would be waiting for me at the Sài Gòn airport. Last night Viêtnamese custom officials seized my passport and sent me to this hotel.

It feels like I'm under house arrest. For a fleeting while, I relish the moment: there is something faintly romantic about being singled out and sequestered. I am a martyr; I feel important. But reality returns, and now I fear that I may indeed be truly arrested, and jailed.

Being holed up on the sixth floor of a government hotel is not my idea of being home. The ancient air conditioner hums loudly, but it only blows out warm air. I am thankful that the ceiling fan is still on the ceiling. It must be at least twenty-five or thirty years old, but it makes breathing in the room almost possible. All night I had kept it spinning as fast as it would go. This room is luxurious according to Sài Gòn's standards, and it costs more than most places. The authorities have sent me here so they can make money off me. The Viêtnamese have plenty of jails, but hotels like this one are more helpful to a country in need of foreign cash.

I'm hot, and I can't leave. I take off my shirt and walk out onto the balcony. The plastic sandals the hotel provides to its guests cut into my feet, and the heat feels like overactive and frustrated lust on my skin.

I've been up for an hour now and I have not had any coffee, but I feel awake, breathing in gulps of coarse and heavy air. After a few moments, my eyes are no longer blinded by the harsh sunlight, and I notice two construction workers on the roof of the hotel across the street. Their overalls are faded, and I can see that the back of their pants is almost white. The two men are leaning over a cement wall. I look down to the street and see two young girls pedaling around the corner. Construction workers are the same everywhere. Always on break, always shouting or whistling at women.

I go back inside and kick off the sandals. I want to unpack. I am compulsive about that. Whenever I travel, I unpack as soon as I get to a hotel room. When I go home, I am even more compulsive. I want to get things organized: what gifts to whom, which book I'll be reading first, as a means to later remember my first night home. But how can I unpack now? I don't even know how long I'll be here.

I call Cesais Tours, the representative of my travel agent in San Francisco, and I let the phone ring and ring. I'll try again at 7:30, I say to myself, and turn to organizing my cassette tapes. I've brought along several tapes of Middle Eastern music, I am obsessed by it. I even have an inexplicable attachment to the mullahs' passionate chanting of passages from the Koran. I've come to think of the Middle East as a spiritual home, even though I have never traveled there. It is the music of the region that has long seduced me: I hear in it the struggle of a people, and people who struggle move me. So now I have brought these tapes to Việt Nam, as if I wanted to merge the two homes. I arrange the tapes on the nightstand, and remember that all the artists are in exile: a Turkish musician in Connecticut, a Syrian and a Tunisian in Paris, and an Iranian violinist in Los Angeles. I assume nostalgia is what adds to the way these artists play their instruments or sing their songs. I put on the tape of the Turkish singer Omar Faruk Tekbilek, and hear again how haunting his voice is. I can't tell what he is singing about, but the songs are mournful, and I imagine they are all about the sorrow of exile.

I want to get out of this hotel. I want to explore my home, even in the heat. I want to walk up and down the streets, smell the tropical fruits, hear the chatter of women going to the morning market. I imagine myself in all kinds of places, and I get all jittery. I call downstairs to order a cup of coffee. I think coffee will calm my nerves.

The receptionist answers in stiff but passable English: "May I help you?"

"*Anh ơi, cho tôi xin một ly cà phê được không anh?*"

"What room, sir?"

"Three-oh-two," I say. Then in Việtnamese: "*Ba lẻ hai. Tôi là người Việt mà anh.*" But I am Việtnamese, brother. I try to put a smile in my words, but I fear I sound angry all the same.

"*Dạ, dạ,*" says the receptionist. Then he says, "*Xin lỗi anh, tại vì . . . em tưởng anh người Hồng Kông . . .*"

I interrupt him. I don't need his apologies, I don't want to hear what else he thinks about me, polite as he sounds. "*Cà fế sữa đá nghe anh, cám ơn anh,*" I say. "Iced coffee, brother, thank you, brother."

I put down the phone. Why does he think I am from Hong Kong? But how does he know who I am, what I look like? Did he see me checking in last night? Then why did he ask for my room number? What else does he know? Is he just nosy, or does he work for the secret police?

Holed up in this hotel room, I have no answers to any of my questions about the people who live in my homeland. The differences between us become more pronounced. They live here. I am only visiting.

I turn to my suitcase and, unable to unpack, I decide to repack it. It takes half an hour, during which time I take two breaks to call the tour operator. No answer. The coffee comes, I have no Việtnamese money to tip the waiter. He smiles graciously and glances at the portable cassette player, pausing to listen for a quick second to the Turkish music before walking out of my room.

I take my coffee out to the balcony. The construction workers have gone. I sweat and feel sticky. I go in, take another shower. When I come out, I stand under the ceiling fan without drying myself. I try to tie the towel around my waist but it is too small. I am too fat.

I had been fat as a young boy, but after I arrived in America the year I turned sixteen, I became more rotund. For years, American food had seeped into me, and I've grown and grown, and it seemed Việt Nam was slipping further and further away. But that homeland has stayed in the heart, and I have never stopped wanting to go home. I was allowed to go back once in 1989, and another time the next year. The third time I tried, I was denied a visa. I was in exile all over again, and it hurt.

I wasn't giving up on going home however. This time I left America with the blind belief that a visa would be available at the Sài Gòn airport. From the luggage area, I walked to the customs desk, noticing a photographer taking instant head shots of people. When the customs officer sent me to him, I was relieved. I paid two dollars for the photographs and thought I didn't look too bad, considering that I had just spent nineteen hours on a crammed aircraft flying home from America, with a four-hour interval at the busy but lifeless airport in Seoul.

After I handed in my passport and photos, I waited for forty minutes. I slipped the customs and immigration officer at the desk five dollars but he gave them back to me. The man had gold teeth and spoke with a Hà Nội accent. "I'll get you a cab to the hotel, you'll stay there tonight. Don't go anywhere. Call your travel agency; otherwise I'll come by tomorrow to straighten out your visa problem."

"Nó muốn kiếm chút tiền hối lộ rồi," someone whispered in my ears and disappeared. "He wants some bribe money."

"Can't you handle it for me right now? I'll pay whatever fees," I said to the customs and immigration officer.

"I don't want any money. Just go to the hotel."

He pulled me by the arm, and waved for a taxicab. Sài Gòn now has a fleet of airport taxis, and I no longer had to fight and negotiate with whoever was operating whatever means of transportation was available. I stood in amazement, staring at the white-and-blue taxi for a long moment. It was then that I caught a glimpse of a friend from high school. His hair had gone white in many parts, his cheeks hollow, and he was darker-skinned, but I recognized him instantly. I called out to him. "Trung, Trung!"

Trung turned around, but the officer was pushing me into the taxi. Only after I had settled inside and looked out the window did I realize my friend wore the uniform of an airport porter. I shifted in my seat. The taxi was pulling away.

On the way to the hotel, I regretted not attempting to stop the taxi, to get out and talk to Trung. Not that I was confident our conversation would go well. After the excitement of finding one another, we would have had to acknowledge the differences in our lives. Home is a place of no escape.

The taxi driver told me he could take me to my relatives' in Sài Gòn. In the morning, he would come back to pick me up to bring me to the hotel. "It'll cost you a lot of money to stay here tonight. I'll make sure you get here early tomorrow, before the officials arrive. They will take your money here and issue you a visa. There won't be any problems. Where do your relatives live?"

They're all in America, I almost said. I have no immediate family left in Việt Nam. "The hotel will be fine," I said to the driver. "I'll work things out tomorrow."

The cassette tape comes to the end, the Turkish music dies. I sit down on my bed to turn the machine off. I pull out the drawer of the bedside table, and I'm surprised by the colorful cover of a thick book, the Sài Gòn telephone directory—thick as the San Francisco one. Things seem normal somehow. This country has been isolated from the world for two decades, but a telephone book in the drawer of a hotel room makes things normal. And it helps take away my feelings of being locked up.

I take a long while, ten, fifteen minutes, to flip through the book. All the names are in Vietnamese, all the Nguyễns and Đoàns and Ngôs and Trầns and Hồs. I read the names with amazement: Sài Gòn is full of people with private telephones now. But I know none of them. I have no one I can call.

Except Cesais Tour. Someone answers this time, and she recognizes my name. "Yes, yes, we know about you. We'll get you a visa this afternoon. Forty-five dollars," she says.

"This afternoon?" I ask.

"Rest your heart, brother," she says. "*Anh cứ yên tâm.* We take care of a lot of visiting overseas Việtnamese."

I am an overseas Việtnamese, a *Việt Kìều.* I have been in exile in America for twenty years. I've waited for a long time to come home. Each of the times before when I had been able to go home, I've stayed for four or five weeks. Each time I have rediscovered more of the things that once were familiar. This time I hope to confirm that I can actually stay for a longer while. That I can shed the outer layers American life had placed on my skin, to readjust to Việtnamese life with the deeper parts of me, the parts I know have remained Việtnamese. I want to confirm that I can again live in my estranged homeland. So far I've only had a glimpse of it, and the names in the phone book, the construction workers, the girls on their bicycles, all still seem distant.

I say none of this to the woman from the tour company. "It's all right, sister," I say, and thank her before putting the phone down. I put in another tape, and with my suitcase packed and ready, I have nothing left to do but to sit back and begin to wait. The music is soothing, but after a while I can't sit still. I pace my room. I call Cesais Tour every hour. And then I dial a number outside the country. It is now possible to dial direct from Việt Nam to the United States. A communications link, cut off for twenty years after a war that has lasted just as long, has been reestablished between the former enemies. I dial the number to our apartment in San Francisco and lie to my wife. "I'm all right," I say. "It's great to be back."

In between hasty words of love, and mundane news about the weather, our landlord and our cat, she tells me there is a demonstration by the *Việt Kiều*s in San Francisco. Over a thousand people have converged outside a hotel in the city's financial district. They are refugees, boat people, former political prisoners who have made their home in America. On this day, they have come to the hotel to protest the presence of a delegation from Hồ Chí Minh City, which, like all of its residents, I still call Sài Gòn. The delegation is in San Francisco for a conference, sponsored by *The Wall Street Journal*, to discuss investment opportunities in Việt Nam. President Clinton had lifted the nineteen-year-old trade sanctions against Việt Nam, and business with a former enemy is the priority of the day. America is trying to catch up with Japan and Taiwan and Singapore and the European nations who have been signing all kinds of deals with Hà Nội.

For many of the *Việt Kiều*s, this is travesty. They oppose the communist government in Việt Nam, and they oppose all contacts with Việtnamese officials. Their banners contain harsh words about communism and human rights conditions in Việt Nam. Some of the *Việt Kiều*s become violent, some are always vocal, some more reasonable. Others speak loudly against trading with Việt Nam, but they quietly carry on with visits to their relatives or business trips to Việt Nam.

The more violent *Việt Kiều*s have driven some of us into silence. As they complain about the tyranny of a communist system, they create terror within the Việtnamese community in the United States: one can easily be labeled a communist sympathizer. Houses have been set afire, and people have been shot. But writers can't keep quiet. I write about all tyrannies, and so I have made enemies within the Việtnamese community in America. The Việt Nam

War ended in 1975, but for many Việtnamese who had been driven from their homes, the war continues.

In the late 1970s and early 1980s, I received complaints about the apolitical tone of my Việtnamese radio broadcasts. I moved away from San Jose, which has the second-largest concentration of Việtnamese population in the United States, and avoided large gatherings of Việtnamese. There had been times in those days when I feared the noises outside the door to my apartment, and I hesitated before picking up my ringing phone. I became an exile within a community of exiles.

For twelve years my father was jailed by the communists in Việt Nam. Still, there were those who considered what I wrote about Việt Nam in the late 1980s to be propaganda for the regime in Hà Nội. On the other hand, the Hà Nội authorities denied me a visa because I've helped expose the terrible conditions in communist Việt Nam. My inability to go home then enhanced my status with the Việtnamese in America, but all the same, I felt the humiliation and frustration of not being accepted by either side, of not belonging. The demonstrators in San Francisco would hate to find out I'm in Việt Nam now, and perhaps they would have a good laugh that I am put away in this hotel room.

"I wish these people wouldn't drag this war out anymore," I say to my wife.

"Just take care, and come home soon."

"I am home," I say.

Home. Twenty years in America has not been enough for me to call it home. I know I should appreciate the open doors I found when I first came to America at the end of the war, but I have trouble loving America: the images of American soldiers charging through Việtnamese villages are lodged too deeply in my mind. Political and historical considerations aside, I simply don't feel I belong in America. Underneath the initial mat of welcome America gave an exile, I keep finding things that bother me about life in the West. I function well enough in a culture that values individual achievements, and there is something admirable about the American spirit of moving on in search of wider horizons, of facing the challenges of a new world. But making yourself anew in America also means abandoning friends and family: I miss the sense of community, the traditional bonds that get thrown away in the pursuit of the American Dream.

I find the work-dominated life in America dehumanizing, I detest the racism hidden behind politically correct attitudes. I struggle with the moral corruption, the materialistic bent, and the pretense of offering freedom to the people. I am sad that many Việtnamese can't stop taking the advice of TV commercials and resist the urge to be a consumer. Like the majority of people in America, we go about our lives rushing from office to home, working from year to year only to go from one mortgage and credit card payment to the next. We are slaves, but pleased to have an income, and we continue to work at jobs we don't like. Sacrificing for the next generation is the Asian excuse we use for no longer dreaming about a different future, no longer pursuing hobbies and work that can bring satisfaction. When I think of a life in America, I think of a life locked inside a house or an office, without time and patience.

Ever since I was a child, going to school in the morning, as normal as any children in the world, but going to bed at night fearing rockets, I have been living in a world of contradictions. As a grown man, I have not become used to the black-and-white simplicity of Americans and their righteous ways. Ensconced in San Francisco, I hide from Southern California's conservatism, the East Coast's superiority complex, Washington's self-absorption, and the blind flag-waving patriotism in the rest of the country. Still, San Francisco is in America, and America doesn't question itself all that incisively. I think of America as an adolescent without a soul.

And so I keep trying to come home. To a place I call home. But Việt Nam is having trouble welcoming me back. In a Sài Gòn hotel room, I am forced to lie to my wife, to say that I feel safe. I am physically in Việt Nam. But I must wait for the approval from Customs and Immigration to get out of this hotel. Then I must wait for the people of Việt Nam to let me reach them and their souls.

"I thought you were Korean," the pedicab driver says to me.

I am in downtown Sài Gòn. My visa had finally been approved, no explanation had been offered for its delay. I have moved to one of the hundreds of mini-hotels that have surfaced all over the city: brand-new cinder-block buildings, with square rooms still smelling of cement and paint, cooled by air conditioners newly imported from Thailand and Taiwan. The buildings have simply gone up, charmless next to the French villas with faded façades and crumbling columns. They seem characterless even when compared to the ugly angular three-story structures inspired by the pragmatic architecture from the days of warfare.

It had taken over half an hour to fill out all the proper registration forms at my mini-hotel, and as soon as I unpacked and showered, I went out in the streets, with no particular destination. I simply wanted to be out.

I have a load of Việtnamese piasters in my money belt, and I wander from street to street, overwhelmed by the heat and the noises, at times self-conscious because some people stare at me, the giant Asian man with a crisp white shirt in their midst. After a while, I get used to smiling at those who stare at me, and I am happy that most people are too busy with their chores to pay attention to me.

My mini-hotel is five minutes from the business and tourist center of Sài Gòn. The late-afternoon breeze coming from the riverfront cools me and dries my sweat-drenched shirt. I approach the pedicab just behind the building that used to be the South Việtnamese House of Congress. Now it is the city's performance hall. It keeps changing colors every time I've visited, yet the coats of whitewash never look new. There is something in me that is attracted to what's old, however, and I find the bright streets and clean buildings of American cities sterile and without character in contrast.

The pedicab driver at first speaks to me in English. He keeps repeating that he thinks I am Korean. It takes a few moments for him to believe that I am a native speaker of Việtnamese. "But you're so fat," he says in the end.

I no longer look like people in Việt Nam. I am fatter than most people here, and my skin has turned pale after the years away from the tropical sun. My baggy khaki pants look awfully out of place in a city where most men wear tight-fitting dress slacks. I want to convince the pedicab driver and others that a Việtnamese soul has remained intact within me, but they only notice that I prefer shoes and socks rather than the plastic sandals everyone here wears. My hair is short, while the men here are still hanging on to the long-haired fashion of the 1970s. In its isolation since the end of the war, Việt Nam has remained unglued from 1975. At least this is true of the southern half of the country, even though the garish signs from war-related wealth of the 1970s have been replaced with the somber poverty of the years of communism.

I tell the pedicab the address of a friend's house. We circle the central boulevards, heading toward the main thoroughfare out of the city. This evening, a few lampposts and building fronts in the blocks around the performance hall are decorated with red banners. It's Hồ Chí Minh's birthday. I'd expected this to be a holiday with huge government-sponsored ceremonies, especially in this city that bears his name, but nothing has happened. Cars and motorcycles circle the kiosks, everyone rushes along the wide boulevards, coming, going, carrying on with their chores in a normal business day. I can't tell whether anyone is thinking of Hồ Chí Minh. In the North, more people remember Hồ Chí Minh as the leader who brought independence to Việt Nam. In Hồ Chí Minh City, he is often thought of as the traitor who brought communism to the country. But people don't even tell acerbic jokes about him anymore. All I hear now are the noises of the marketplace. There are no tributes to a revered leader or the interminable communist propaganda on a public-address system.

The pedicab driver leans over close to my head and laughs at his own earlier mistake. "You really look Korean," he says. "I hate driving the Koreans. They're real cheap. And they always look down on us. They say to me our people are stupid, and they're more advanced than us. But I bet without the wars and communism, we'd be far ahead of them," he says.

I can't think of anything to say to the driver. I keep thinking of Hồ Chí Minh, of how he spent his adult life fighting foreigners, leading the wars that took the lives of thousands of people. Independence has been regained, but along with independence came the unworkable policies of a communist system. Now that that system is all but bankrupt, the foreigners are all over Việt Nam, with arrogant and imperialistic attitudes barely disguised. Meanwhile, Hồ Chí Minh's former comrades-in-arms and devoted followers are marching away from his socialist dreams. They are all smiles and open arms with the foreigners with whom they fought bitter wars. Chinese, French, Japanese, all are welcome now. The foreigners do not attack the Việtnamese with guns and helicopters anymore. They are not forcing their way into Việt Nam to be lords of the land, or to secure a market. Today, they are welcomed back by the communists, who allow them limitless access to Việt Nam, turning the country into a consumer market and the people into cheap laborers. Like a moth flying toward a flame, I keep wanting to go home, believing that, along with Westerners, I can play a role in bringing about political openness. But a sadness overcomes me, for I realize it is much too easy to import the worst traits of capitalism. Democratic ideals are harder to achieve.

I shudder in the hot evening in thinking of the millions that have died in all those years to keep the foreigners out. I think of the destruction of the country by bombs and rockets and defoliants. My pedicab ride takes me past monstrous glass-and-steel and stucco structures springing up over the Sài Gòn skyline, and I feel angry. The anger gets worse when I see all around me now the destruction of the soft-mannered and gracious ways of the Việtnamese. Capitalism is the game now, at least in Sài Gòn, and it is ruthless.

"But aren't the Koreans and other foreigners creating lots of opportunities for the people here?" I ask my driver.

"Yeah, many of us are benefiting from them, but mainly in Sài Gòn," the driver says. "It's gonna take a long time before we can all breathe better."

I stop talking to the driver, but I carry on a debate with myself. A long time, but how many will breathe better? How many will die in construction accidents, how many will lose a home to make way for skyscrapers? How many will succumb to modern diseases, to pollution and environmental damages? And how many will have to sell their Việtnamese soul? I want to recognize that the prices for development, modernization, and prosperity are high. Capitalism is corrupting, and it shows signs that it can turn those fierce and dedicated communists in the Việtnamese leadership into greedy people. I even believe that out of this mess may come a degree of democracy. But how do I explain to a hungry pedicab driver any of this?

He pedals hard to move his pedicab with my weight in it. When he slows down to regain his breath, he asks about my stay in Việt Nam. "You should come back here," he advises me. "You can make a lot of money. Make sure you earn a foreigner's salary, though. And then you can buy anything you want, live like a king." He points to a vintage French car parked on the side of the street, a meticulously restored Citroën in burgundy and beige, with a glinting chrome grill. White linen covers the back seats. "See that car?" asks the pedicab driver. "You can buy that. All the foreigners are buying those cars now. When can a Việtnamese here afford one like that? Nobody here can buy them, but you can. Bring your dollars here, buy anything you want."

"That would be nice," I say. "But I don't think I can afford it."

"You live now in America. What's a few thousand dollars to you?"

My friend Vĩnh is more realistic about my financial powers. "Are you on assignment or did you pay your own way back here?"

"Doesn't matter. I'm just glad I can be back home. How are you?"

"Breathing in, breathing out, surviving."

Vĩnh had been a classmate from elementary school. I found him in my first return trip, a man who has retained his boyish looks but whose eyes wear the dull expression of a seasoned man. Vĩnh had been smuggling and selling all sorts of things on the black market to feed his parents and four siblings.

"Your eyes are looking worse," I say to him. "Why don't you stop drinking?"

"You'd be drinking too. In fact, do you want a beer? It's only to help me sleep."

I wonder how many Việtnamese need help sleeping. On the way to Vĩnh's, I have gone past countless beer halls packed with men sitting on stools barely off the ground. And I've noticed that in some restaurants, the waiters simply bring out cans of beer for you as soon as you sit down. Việt Nam has turned into a drinking nation, and Vĩnh is, I think, an alcoholic. His eyes are ocher where they should be white. Vĩnh pours me a beer, and I accept it. Refusing it would be an act too transparent: a feeble, judgmental, and improper demonstration that I am worried about him drinking so much. I needed the beer as a way to strengthen our friendship. I wanted a way to make me feel closer to my friend and his misery. I'll need help sleeping tonight in any case. In a couple of weeks, I'll leave, go back to America. Vĩnh's yellowed eyes might appear in my dreams then, but for now, I desperately need to break down the barriers between two former classmates with different adult lives.

Vĩnh says he no longer wants to leave the country. Years before, he had made three attempts to escape by boat. He had been unsuccessful and jailed.

Now he says he has too much work. "Services. This is a poor country, we haven't got anything to offer people. To make money, we can only offer our services. Labor services, hotel services, food, do it all for people."

Vĩnh is now helping a sister run an auto-repair shop. I keep thinking of the way the workers there used to switch the steering wheels in the cars—smuggled in from Thailand—from the right side to the left. The workers changed the floorboards, the pedals, the dashboard, the electrical wiring, etc., all that for seventy dollars. The garage has now expanded, and more services have been added. The last time I saw Vĩnh, he was talking about struggling to bring a meal to the table each day. Tonight, he is letting the beer flow, and he actually encourages me to come back. "Just make sure you're here to provide some type of service," Vĩnh says as he pours me another beer. "Otherwise, what are you going to do here?"

I ask Vĩnh about fitting back in, living and working in Việt Nam. "Write, but you can't get published here. That'll be like asking for a jail sentence. Besides, how much do you think words and meanings can earn for you here? Sell something else."

"Do you think I can live here, though?"

"Why not? But remember that black hair and yellow skin doesn't mean you're a local person. You're a foreigner. Can you afford the houses people rent out to foreigners?"

"How expensive is that?"

"If you can't afford it, you live like me. Out here in the outskirts of town, dusty and dark. People and rats and dogs and motorcycles packed on top of each other . . . And your wife . . ."

"Well . . ."

"And what about your parents in America? Can you leave them there by themselves? Who's going to take care of them? They won't come back here, will they?"

"No," I say, but give up on saying anything further. Vĩnh is full of questions, and he knows some of the answers. I hide from them, and I hide from Vĩnh, much as I want to confront everything about coming home and again living in Việt Nam.

. . .

I leave Vĩnh in a haze. As my pedicab turns into the downtown area, I feel the terror of my youth, when Việt Cộng soldiers threw hand grenades into the early-morning markets of our town, or tore up our nights with rockets from surrounding hills. For years after the Tết offensive of 1968, when Việt Cộng soldiers invaded our hometown, captured my father and marched him away to prison, these men in olive-green uniforms had haunted my sleep.

Tonight, I can recognize the same uniforms and pith helmets that had driven so much fear into my stomach. A dozen soldiers are running in formation just ahead of me. For a few moments, their mechanical footsteps pound my heart. Seeing them in numbers is to come face to face with the men that had once intruded on my sleep, turning my nighttime images into nightmares. The pedicab pulls to a stop. The soldiers run across our path, at arm's length from me. I sit still—as if waiting for them to surround me in the darkness. I become hostage to them for a second, and then I can see their faces. I recognize that these are boys who would not have been born in 1968. They could not have known much about the war that has been so much a part of my life. Gradually my fears disappear; the soldiers continue on with their formation, away from me.

"That'll be the parade for Uncle Hồ's birthday," the pedicab driver says. I laugh, unable to think of anything to say. The driver explains that he is serious. "They have to do something for the birthday. But they know nobody cares. So they take a midnight run, a parade for themselves, really." A parade without an audience, without a crowd.

I ask the driver to take me for another tour of Sài Gòn, promising him a sum of money that would barely buy me a meal in a run-down restaurant in San Francisco's Chinatown, but he accepts my proposal with gratitude, and with grace, considering how tired he seems from pedaling an overweight *Việt Kiều*. From my pedicab seat, I stare out into the darkness. Houses set behind walls and the overhanging trees blend themselves into a continuous shadow, punctuated by a few lightbulbs too infrequent to let me have a real look at Sài Gòn at rest. The insane activities of the day are gone. It is quiet now but I can't see clear enough to imagine myself in a room, a house in this city. I regret the alcohol in me that is preventing me from answering the questions in my head.

We ride around for half an hour, my mind clears a little, and I think of a room. A writer's place, late at night, with an old bench, a rustic table, open windows. A breeze, cricket calls, and petals from a dying chrysanthemum falling over a golden mango. A lone lightbulb casting just enough clarity over a page. For now, the page is still blank, but at least I can see the questions. I'll have to question my ability to leave my parents without a son to care for them, my obligations to friends in America. I'll question how I can live in a society still not free from communism, the return of the Westerners and the traders. I'll have to question again and again how I can leave the freedom I've discovered in America. But in the quietness of this Sài Gòn night, the questions don't seem so daunting anymore. I know that without them coming home is impossible. Time and patience have been rare all these years in America. In Việt Nam, I will have time, I will learn to be patient again. After that, the answers will come.

"I'll run into you again soon," I say to the pedicab driver outside my mini-hotel. He smiles and thanks me. I wave goodbye, not explaining that I suddenly feel sure that I will come home to live. And when I need a late-night ride to clear my mind and help with my writing, I am sure I will look for him again.

MOTHER TONGUE

AMY TAN *was born in Oakland, California, in 1952. Her first novel,* The Joy Luck Club, *was published by Putnam in 1989. A finalist for the National Book Award, the novel was translated into nineteen languages, including Chinese, and later became a film directed by Wayne Wang. She has also published a second novel,* The Kitchen God's Wife *(1991), and a children's book,* The Moon Lady *(1992). Her stories have appeared in* The Atlantic, Grand Street, Lear's, *and* Mc-Call's, *among other magazines.*

Her essay "Mother Tongue" first appeared in The Threepenny Review *and was included in* The Best American Essays 1991. *Tan is at work on a third novel,* The Year of No Flood. *She lives in San Francisco and her imagination.*

I AM NOT A SCHOLAR OF ENGLISH OR LITERATURE. I cannot give you much more than personal opinions on the English language and its variations in this country or others.

I am a writer. And by that definition, I am someone who has always loved language. I am fascinated by language in daily life. I spend a great deal of my time thinking about the power of language—the way it can evoke an emotion, a visual image, a complex idea, or a simple truth. Language is the tool of my trade. And I use them all—all the Englishes I grew up with.

Recently, I was made keenly aware of the different Englishes I do use. I was giving a talk to a large group of people, the same talk I had already given to half a dozen other groups. The nature of the talk was about my writing, my life, and my book *The Joy Luck Club*. The talk was going along well enough, until I remembered one major difference that made the whole talk sound wrong. My mother was in the room. And it was perhaps the first time she had heard me give a lengthy speech, using the kind of English I have never used with her. I was saying things like "The intersection of memory upon imagination" and "There is an aspect of my fiction that relates to thus-and-thus"—a speech filled with carefully wrought grammatical phrases, burdened, it suddenly seemed to me, with nominalized forms, past perfect tenses, conditional phrases, all the forms of standard English that I had learned in school and through books, the forms of English I did not use at home with my mother.

Just last week, I was walking down the street with my mother, and I again found myself conscious of the English I was using, the English I do use with her. We were talking about the price of new and used furniture and I heard myself saying this: "Not waste money that way." My husband was with us as well, and he didn't notice any switch in my English. And then I realized why. It's because over the twenty years we've been together I've often used that same kind of English with him, and sometimes he even uses it with me. It has become our language of intimacy, a different sort of English that relates to family talk, the language I grew up with.

So you'll have some idea of what this family talk I heard sounds like, I'll quote what my mother said during a recent conversation which I videotaped and then transcribed. During this conversation, my mother was talking about a political gangster in Shanghai who had the same last name as her family's, Du, and how the gangster in his early years wanted to be adopted by her family, which was rich by comparison. Later, the gangster became more powerful, far richer than my mother's family, and one day showed up at my mother's wedding to pay his respects. Here's what she said in part:

"Du Yusong having business like fruit stand. Like off the street kind. He is Du like Du Zong—but not Tsung-ming Island people. The local people call putong, the river east side, he belong to that side local people. That man want to ask Du Zong father take him in like become own family. Du Zong father wasn't look down on him, but didn't take seriously, until that man big like become a mafia. Now important person, very hard to inviting him. Chinese way, came only to show respect, don't stay for dinner. Respect for making big celebration, he shows up. Mean gives lots of respect. Chinese custom. Chinese social life that way. If too important won't have to stay too long. He come to my wedding. I didn't see, I heard it. I gone to boy's side, they have YMCA dinner. Chinese age I was nineteen."

You should know that my mother's expressive command of English belies how much she actually understands. She reads the *Forbes* report, listens to *Wall Street Week,* converses daily with her stockbroker, reads all of Shirley MacLaine's books with ease—all kinds of things I can't begin to understand. Yet some of my friends tell me they understand 50 percent of what my mother says. Some say they understand 80 to 90 percent. Some say they understand none of it, as if she were speaking pure Chinese. But to me, my mother's English is perfectly clear, perfectly natural. It's my mother tongue. Her language, as I hear it, is vivid, direct, full of observation and imagery. That was the language that helped shape the way I saw things, expressed things, made sense of the world.

Lately, I've been giving more thought to the kind of English my mother speaks. Like others, I have described it to people as "broken" or "fractured" English. But I wince when I say that. It has always bothered me that I can think of no way to describe it other than "broken," as if it were damaged and needed to be fixed, as if it lacked a certain wholeness and soundness. I've heard other terms used, "limited English," for example. But they seem just as bad, as if everything is limited, including people's perceptions of the limited English speaker.

I know this for a fact, because when I was growing up, my mother's "limited" English limited *my* perception of her. I was ashamed of her English. I believed that her English reflected the quality of what she had to say. That is, because she expressed them imperfectly her thoughts were imperfect. And I had plenty of empirical evidence to support me: the fact that people in department stores, at banks, and at restaurants did not take her seriously, did not give her good service, pretended not to understand her, or even acted as if they did not hear her.

My mother has long realized the limitations of her English as well. When I was fifteen, she used to have me call people on the phone to pretend I was she. In this guise, I was forced to ask for information or even to complain and yell at people who had been rude to her. One time it was a call to her stockbroker in New York. She had cashed out her small portfolio and it just so happened we were going to go to New York the next week, our very first trip outside California. I had to get on the phone and say in an adolescent voice that was not very convincing, "This is Mrs. Tan."

And my mother was standing in the back whispering loudly, "Why he don't send me check, already two weeks late. So mad he lie to me, losing me money."

And then I said in perfect English, "Yes, I'm getting rather concerned. You had agreed to send the check two weeks ago, but it hasn't arrived."

Then she began to talk more loudly. "What he want, I come to New York tell him front of his boss, you cheating me?" And I was trying to calm her down, make her be quiet, while telling the stockbroker, "I can't tolerate any more excuses. If I don't receive the check immediately, I am going to have to speak to your manager when I'm in New York next week." And sure enough, the following week there we were in front of this astonished stockbroker, and I was sitting there red-faced and quiet, and my mother, the real Mrs. Tan, was shouting at his boss in her impeccable broken English.

We used a similar routine just five days ago, for a situation that was far less humorous. My mother had gone to the hospital for an appointment, to find out about a benign brain tumor a CAT scan had revealed a month ago. She said she had spoken very good English, her best English, no mistakes. Still, she said, the hospital did not apologize when they said they had lost the CAT scan and she had come for nothing. She said they did not seem to have any sympathy when she told them she was anxious to know the exact diagnosis, since her husband and son had both died of brain tumors. She said they would not give her any more information until the next time and she would have to make another appointment for that. So she said she would not leave until the doctor called her daughter. She wouldn't budge. And when the doctor finally called her daughter, me, who spoke in perfect English—lo and behold—we had assurances the CAT scan would be found, promises that a conference call on Monday would be held, and apologies for any suffering my mother had gone through for a most regrettable mistake.

I think my mother's English almost had an effect on limiting my possibilities in life as well. Sociologists and linguists probably will tell you that a person's developing language skills are more influenced by peers. But I do think that the language spoken in the family, especially in immigrant families which are more insular, plays a large role in shaping the language of the child. And I believe that it affected my results on achievement tests, IQ tests, and the SAT. While my English skills were never judged as poor, compared to math, English could not be considered my strong suit. In grade school I did moderately well, getting perhaps B's, sometimes B-pluses, in English and scoring perhaps in the sixtieth or seventieth percentile on achievement tests. But those scores were not good enough to override the opinion that my true abilities lay in math and science, because in those areas I achieved A's and scored in the ninetieth percentile or higher.

This was understandable. Math is precise; there is only one correct answer. Whereas, for me at least, the answers on English tests were always a judgment call, a matter of opinion and personal experience. Those tests were constructed around items like fill-in-the-blank sentence completion, such as "Even though Tom was _____, Mary thought he was _____." And the correct answer always seemed to be the most bland combinations of thoughts, for example, "Even though Tom was shy, Mary thought he was charming," with the grammatical structure "even though" limiting the correct answer to some sort of semantic opposites, so you wouldn't get answers like "Even though Tom was foolish, Mary thought he was ridiculous." Well, according to my mother, there were very few limitations as to what Tom could have been and what Mary might have thought of him. So I never did well on tests like that.

The same was true with word analogies, pairs of words in which you were supposed to find some sort of logical, semantic relationship—for example, "*Sunset* is to *nightfall* as _____ is to _____." And here you would be presented with a list of four possible pairs, one of which showed the same kind of relationship: *red* is to *stoplight, bus* is to *arrival, chills* is to *fever, yawn* is to *boring.* Well, I could never think that way. I knew what the tests were asking, but I could not block out of my mind the images already created by the first pair, "*sunset* is to *nightfall*"—and I would see a burst of colors against a darkening sky, the moon rising, the lowering of a curtain of stars. And all the other pairs of words—*red, bus, stoplight, boring*—just threw up a mass of confusing images, making it impossible for me to sort out something as logical as saying: "A sunset precedes nightfall" is the same as "a chill precedes a fever." The only way I would have gotten that answer right would have been to imagine an associative situation, for example, my being disobedient and staying out past sunset, catching a chill at night, which turns into feverish pneumonia as punishment, which indeed did happen to me.

I have been thinking about all this lately, about my mother's English, about achievement tests. Because lately I've been asked, as a writer, why there are not more Asian Americans represented in American literature. Why are there few Asian Americans enrolled in creative writing programs? Why do so many Chinese students go into engineering? Well, these are broad sociological questions I can't begin to answer. But I have noticed in surveys—in fact, just last week—that Asian students, as a whole, always do significantly better on math achievement tests than in English. And this makes me think that there are other Asian American students whose English spoken in the home might also be described as "broken" or "limited." And perhaps they also have teachers who are steering them away from writing and into math and science, which is what happened to me.

Fortunately, I happen to be rebellious in nature and enjoy the challenge of disproving assumptions made about me. I became an English major my first year in college, after being enrolled as premed. I started writing nonfiction as a freelancer the week after I was told by my former boss that writing was my worst skill and I should hone my talents toward account management.

But it wasn't until 1985 that I finally began to write fiction. And at first I wrote using what I thought to be wittily crafted sentences, sentences that would finally prove I had mastery over the English language. Here's an example from the first draft of a story that later made its way into *The Joy Luck Club*, but without this line: "That was my mental quandary in its nascent state." A terrible line, which I can barely pronounce.

Fortunately, for reasons I won't get into today, I later decided I should envision a reader for the stories I would write. And the reader I decided upon was my mother, because these were stories about mothers. So with this reader in mind—and in fact she did read my early drafts—I began to write stories using all the Englishes I grew up with: the English I spoke to my mother, which for lack of a better term might be described as "simple"; the English she used with me, which for lack of a better term might be described as "broken"; my translation of her Chinese, which could certainly be described as "watered down"; and what I imagined to be her translation of her Chinese if she could speak in perfect English, her internal language, and for that I sought to preserve the essence, but neither an English nor a Chinese structure. I wanted to capture what language ability tests can never reveal: her intent, her passion, her imagery, the rhythms of her speech and the nature of her thoughts.

Apart from what any critic had to say about my writing, I knew I had succeeded where it counted when my mother finished reading my book and gave me her verdict: "So easy to read."

J O H N   Y A U

A   LITTLE
MEMENTO   FROM
THE   BOYS

JOHN YAU *was born in Lynn, Mas-*
sachusetts, in 1950. His books include
volumes of poetry, Radiant Silhouette:
New and Selected Writing *1974–1988*
(Black Sparrow Press, 1989) and
Edificio Sayonara *(Black Sparrow*
Press, 1992), criticism, In the Realm
of Appearances: The Art of Andy
Warhol *(Ecco Press, 1993), and fic-*
tion, Hawaiian Cowboys *(Black Spar-*
row Press, 1994). His current projects
include organizing the Ed Moses retro-
spective for the Museum of Contempo-
rary Art, Los Angeles, and finishing a
book on the film actress Anna May
Wong.

JENNY SCOBEL

THERE WERE THREE OF US: JOHNNY YAMAMOTO, VIRGO Van Dyke, and me. We all met each other a few months earlier in Mike's Last Dive, a bar in TriBeCa, which, before loft buildings became fashionable residences for dentists, movie stars, and other members of the upper echelons of the service industry, was where artists, would-be artists, and others, like me, lived, holed up like criminals. Most of us were at the bottom end of the service industry, the ones who plastered or plumbered by day and painted or wrote at night. This was a neighborhood where everyone presumed you lived a double life, but few understood why some of us had to live more than that.

Mike's Last Dive was a decaying, turn-of-the-century bar with sawdust on the floor. It had one pool table in the center of its square, high-ceilinged room, like a brightly lit, grass-covered traffic island at night, meandering lines of cars rushing by. There was a long, narrow bathroom that smelled as if grizzled whalers used to line up and piss there. A sweet, sickly smell of disinfectant, urine, cigarettes, and stale beer had soaked into the bathroom's tile walls, tin ceiling, and wooden floor. I always felt like I was pissing in a cold cave or a decrepit refrigerator.

Mike and his brother Ethan ran the place, and were somewhere between seventy-five and a hundred. They had fewer teeth than most infants, but only occasionally drank directly from a bottle, usually beer.

The only decoration in Mike's Last Dive was a frayed marlin someone had mounted on the wall above the bar, its dark wood shelves stocked with bottles. A string of red and green Christmas lights, tinsel, and silver and blue teardrop ornaments dangled from its comically ferocious grin. No one remembered who put the marlin up or why it had been wrapped in lights and Christmas decorations, and no one ever thought of changing it. The regulars called the marlin Uncle Bill for some reason or another. If no one knew who was batting champion in the American League in 1953, everyone chimed in: "Ask Uncle Bill."

Late one night, Johnny, Virgo, and I kept crossing each other's paths on the way to the toilet or, while standing and watching some of the regulars playing pool, we'd look up and see a face looking back, curious. We began checking each other out, circling each other, slowly, like animals in heat.

Why did we begin talking? Well, the obvious reason is that we immediately recognized that we were mongrels, confused children whose parents came from different worlds, which in our cases meant Asia and Europe. We were what was left after the collision; we were the things they had dropped on the floor.

Shortly after the fires that swept across the world died down, our parents emigrated from some smoky crater in Asia to America, Canada, and Costa Rica. At first, they were stalked by the ghosts of their past, and were afraid of the shadows lurking in the corners of their future. Eventually, they developed routines which helped them adjust, made them seem like they were part of the pattern. They became an accountant, a research scientist, and an engineer. They held jobs with no public visibility. They lived in a zone drained of light by the past, squeezed of money by the present, and stared at by the disapproving future. The men sat at tiny desks and wondered when history would leave them alone, while the women walked stoically through a world that whispered as they passed.

Their eldest children became loners by default. They can't seem to find a group that will take them in, that they can run with. They don't feel quite at home with anyone, even themselves. We're those children, the ones who smirk inwardly, but now we're in our twenties, drinking in different bars in downtown Manhattan, a few blocks from Wall Street and those who believe that home is wherever they can go and spend other people's money.

Each night, Johnny, Virgo, and I tell stories about what it is like to be regarded as a Martian by those who claim to be our friends. It's as if we have to tell all the stories lodged inside our chests so as to never have to tell them again, to each other or ourselves.

"My father's Japanese, my mother's German," Johnny states with a diplomat's flair. "The worst of both worlds. I grew up speaking Spanish."

"You want to know what it's like to have a Dutch name but slanted eyes?" Virgo asks. It is a question he has asked and answered in many different ways.

"You want to know what my fourth-grade teacher said to me on the first day of class? She asked me if I had been adopted," Virgo says softly, his voice bordering on a hiss.

"Oh yes," I tell her. "When I was born, Mrs. Pringle, my parents decided it would be better if they gave me away, but got some money in return. You see, my enlightened parents wanted to open a fancy Chinese restaurant in downtown Vancouver, that was their lifelong dream. When I was born, Mrs. Pringle, they saw their one and only chance at redemption and bundled me and took me into town. There, they sold me to a nice old Dutch guy who rolls cigars. His wife made me these wooden shoes." Heels click together in the din of voices, a hand rises in phony salute. "Yes, Mrs. Plingle, this is why I'm so well behaved."

We snicker and guffaw in agreement. Virgo's glad he finally has friends who will knowingly roll each morsel and crumb of his offerings around on their tongues, lick their lips, and hoot and howl for more. We are ravenous dogs who gather in this noisy room each night, and tell more tales. No meat is too tough for us to tear from the bone. We're coyotes who've wandered into a ghost town.

Sometimes Johnny would look at me and smile, and I knew what was coming. "You got English and Chinese parents, the best of both worlds. You got two fucking histories to live up to, while I got two to live down. Ha."

"Yeah, right. You a scrawny samurai and me a gimp coolie," I answer. And all three of us laugh.

Best, worst, up, and down. There is no middle ground, no safe place for us in the world, no belief that will take us in, soothe us. We live on the poison we secrete, and spend our nights characterizing ourselves in derogatory terms. It is the only defense we know. Our motto: Beat them to the punch before they beat you to a pulp.

Every night, we drink until we are standing on our heads and the world is melting like a candle, blue and red neon tears running down dirty walls, dusty windows, and dank warehouses full of a century of crud. Whalers' bones and broken phones. Dusty trunks and lumpy bunks.

After Mike or Ethan announces last call, we go and stand outside in the cool night air, pointing at the people trying to cling to the moon and broken streetlights, afraid now that gravity has gathered them up and delivered them to the deck of a storm-tossed ocean liner. A slippery world with no safe place to stand and nothing to grab on to. It is one of the only times we feel at home.

To us, the young Wall Street types are all the same. A bunch of well-groomed, faceless young men, who take off their suit jackets when they play pool and think they are entitled to talk to every woman who drifts in through the doors alone. They are sure that money gives them the power to be at home wherever they go, and fervently believe that they are on their way to heaven, not on their way out the door and down the chute.

The ups and the outs, that's how I saw the world. Those were the only two real places on the map, the rest was an illusion, the place where the earth finally becomes an edge and the little sailing ship falls forever.

Johnny, Virgo, and I learned to lower our anger to a slow but steady flame. Each night we sidled up to it with alcohol, saw how close we could come to it without having the bombs go off in our faces. That was our power, coming as close to the ticking heart as possible, and still being able to lift the drinks, one after another, with a cool, disinterested hand, a hand that could belong to someone else, someone who was dead, someone whose muscles only moved when the electric volts punched in their white-hot charge.

I don't know who came up with the idea first, probably Johnny, who hadn't had a job in nearly two months, but we all agreed it was a quick, sure way to make some money. Sand floors, paint walls, and plaster. We would help the people we hated move into TriBeCa, and then, if we were smart and lucky, we would move on. Go to San Francisco, Los Angeles, Paris, Rio, or Berlin. Somewhere, we told ourselves, there was a city and a bar where we could dream about the future, rather than picking through the bones of the past.

I doubt if any of us saved money that year. I doubt if we believed there was anywhere we could go. Paradise was a glitzy bar six blocks away, but we preferred Mike's Last Dive. It was our watering hole, our oasis. We could have found it blindfolded, that's how deep it was lodged in our souls.

We usually worked from eleven in the morning to around seven or eight o'clock at night, sometimes later. Then we headed off to our separate apartments, washed the dust off our bodies, squeezed the ache out of our muscles, changed, and met up around ten or midnight. Then life began.

Eating and drinking. Often just drinking. Scoring some dope, smoking it. Then eating and drinking. Taking pills, smoking dope, and drinking. Lots of loud music. Swallowing, snorting, smoking, and drinking. Washing the dust from our brains.

The next morning was always the same. I tried pulling my body off the bed and onto the floor. A poor specimen of human desire, I tried to maintain an erect position, tried not to crash into the table or wall. I wobbled like a gyroscope winding down, trying desperately to speed up and get my balance again. I washed, then dressed. It was all an act of memory. I went out, bought coffee, met the others, rented equipment, and went to the job. Began sanding or painting. Finished, I would stumble home, spend an hour washing my extremities, and then go out and wash the inside. An act of cleansing. All of us rode a merriless merry-go-round.

Sometimes I fell asleep on the floor, a prone body wearing a face mask, passed out in the corner of a big empty white room, sweat soaking through my shirt. I could feel the cool floor beneath me. It was almost erotic, lying there on the floor, clouds of sawdust rising all around you, the entire room vibrating to the steady hum of Johnny or Virgo pushing a sander up and down the floor. Magic fingers, I thought to myself before drifting off. Oh, warm magic fingers, take me away from this world.

Lila is one of the people who hired us after hearing about what we did from Lola, her downstairs neighbor and one of our earliest employers. She lived alone on the top floor of a bird-stained loft building in SoHo.

"I work in the record industry, I'm a sound mixer," she said the first night we met her. "I can make the trumpets turn into honey. I'm the reason you hear what you do."

Johnny, Virgo, and I were at her place to see what had to be done, as well as discuss money. Lila was wearing a red satin jacket, tight black stretch pants, and a shiny black silk blouse that clung to her like Saran Wrap. She had long black hair, which she tied into a knot above her head. Strands dangled down and framed her pale, oval face. She looked like a cross between Pebbles Flintstone and the girl everyone in high school used to whisper puts out, as if they had actually benefited from or been threatened by her generosity.

Lila was staring at us with disdain. We were looking at her as if she was a cute but full piggy bank, something to break open and rob. We wanted her paper and her coin, something negotiable, not her body, which, athletic and attractive as it was, Johnny, Virgo, and I had learned to live without.

Lila was either on her way out or just got in, and Johnny, Virgo, and I were standing there, telling her we'd be honored to sand her floors, paint her walls, move her furniture, such as it was, out of the way.

Yes, we'd gladly and lovingly get down on our knobby knees and lick your toes, kiss your shoes. Just give us two hundred and fifty dollars a day to divide among us, and we'll be out of here in a week. In return, your floors and walls will glisten like television teeth.

To our surprise, Lila agreed to it. She was going to be in LA for ten days on business and wanted everything done by the time she got back. We waited until we were out the door and charging down the stairs before we started grinning. It was the most money we had ever gotten from anyone.

It started out as an easy job and we finished a lot of the basic stuff in the first few days. Once the floors of both rooms were sanded, we started painting the walls.

I don't know why we didn't notice it right away, but we didn't. Anyway, the second time Johnny and Virgo moved Lila's bed, I, for some reason or another, probably pure nosiness, pulled back the bedspread, with its silk-screened images of Elvis's record covers.

"Holy shit, that's the biggest fucking vibrator I've ever seen." Johnny was the first to notice it.

It had been lying under her black satin pillow.

"You're right. I thought it was a flashlight or something," I say.

"That's no flashlight," Virgo exclaims. "Man, I've never seen one so big. A flashlight that big would be illegal. Why, it would be declared a dangerous weapon. Hell, man, it's big enough to be a dildo for lonely girl elephants."

"You've actually seen one of these things before?" I ask. I was a bit incredulous. Where had Virgo seen a vibrator before? I mean up close, not on the other side of a window in a store in the Village.

"Yeah, my little sister, Denise, has one," he says matter-of-factly. "I saw it the last time I visited her in Vancouver."

"Hmmmmmm," Johnny says, trying to sound like a motor.

At first, we stand there staring at it, as if it's the Christ child lying in the manger and we're the three Wise Men. Hey, look what we brought you, when actually it's the other way around and we know it. Lila is giving us more than money, she's giving us one of her secrets. But we're greedy and want more, because we're tired of our own secrets.

We begin laughing, nervous at first, then we grow silently curious about whether she has a diary or not, whether she may have written something revealing in its pages. We are thinking: Does her vibrator have a name and can we find out what it is? Ralph or Max, maybe? The Long and Mighty Dumbo and his electric nightstick? We're stuck in a kaleidoscope, but this time we believe it's Lila's, and not ours.

It didn't take long for us to begin going through her things, pulling open drawers, checking the closet, opening boxes. We found it on a shelf, tucked away behind some books. Her leather-bound diary.

We spend the rest of the afternoon taking turns reading it aloud. The other two guys holding long poles, and rolling the white paint up and down the walls, trying not to break stride. Little tears of milk slurping down the walls.

Lila likes to keep a running record of her sexual fantasies. Near as we can figure it, she uses the vibrator on an average of twice a day when she is working and up to four times a day on weekends. The diary is filled with descriptions, some carefully printed in purple ink, others hastily written in pencil. One scrawl in maroon lipstick is smudged and illegible.

There's the garage mechanic who fixed her car, a young blond lead guitarist, the quiet saxophonist who played backup on the third cut of a big hit album, the messenger who stopped and asked for directions, someone seen in the street, her best friend's boyfriend and his best friend at the same time, Clark Gable, Paul Newman, and Mick Jagger—she has had them all, more than once. Different combinations, contraptions, and situations.

"Lila's kind of like a Chinese menu," Virgo says after reading some more pages.

"Yeah," Johnny chimes in. "Choose one from column A and two from column B. A little duck sauce for my breasts, a little mustard for my thighs. And don't forget to bring me my big fortune cookie."

Johnny and I laugh and continue painting. The afternoon swirls away. Blue shadows fill the valley of the narrow streets, while the factories and loading docks grow silent.

It's the last day of the job. We've gotten to Lila's early for once, finished sanding and painting, and are cleaning up, putting everything back in place. Around noon, we break for lunch, go out and get sandwiches, chips, and cold cans of soda. Back in the loft, we sit on the floor and begin eating. After we're finished, I pull out a joint, light up, and start passing it around. Johnny picks the diary off the floor and, "for old times' sake," begins reading some of the parts we've liked the best. Virgo lies back on the floor, a joint stuck in his mouth, and stares at the ceiling, like a child listening to a bedtime story.

"Hey," Johnny says suddenly. "Remember that camera we found, you think there's any film in it?"

"I'll go look," I say, getting up and walking to the other room, knowing something good is about to take place.

Virgo sits up, a grin tattooed to his face.

For some reason, which I've never been able to understand, we were all ready to do the same thing.

"There's twelve shots left," I announce in my best Bette Davis voice, sashaying back into the room, camera dangling from my left hand.

"Shit, I got a great idea." Johnny is always having great ideas. "Why don't we jerk off into our last can of paint and touch up the place with it?"

"Huh?" I answer, realizing this is not exactly what I expected to happen, but I was more than ready to do it. I'm looking at the camera, trying to figure out how it works.

Virgo is sitting up and sniffing the last of the smoke. He turns and looks at me. "Hey, that's a great idea," he says enthusiastically. "Let me see that camera. I bet I can set it on automatic so that it will take a picture of us jerking off. Won't that be a hoot?"

After we get everything set up, which we do in a hurry, as if all of us are being pulled forward by some unseen magnet, we jerk off into our last can of white paint, three men in their twenties. It's like the fervent gathering of a prayer group with Johnny leading the way. When we get close, which some-how, miraculously, we all do at the same time, Virgo hobbles over to the camera and pushes the red button down and then hobbles back in time to rejoin us.

"Say cheese," we sing in unison.

Later, each of us has his picture taken holding the vibrator as if it is an ice-cream cone. We sit and stand around like twelve-year-olds: licking our lips, sticking out our tongues, grinning into the camera. Twelve pictures, twelve poses. Then we finish the job, the last of the paint gone by the time we leave Lila's loft, white, shiny, and smooth as a brand-new refrigerator.

Johnny, Virgo, and I sanded more floors and painted more walls, but the job had started becoming a drudge after Lila's loft. We didn't find vibrators or diaries hidden beneath bedspreads, behind books, or in drawers, though we always looked before starting to paint. We didn't learn about other people's secrets, and we remained stuck with our own, the ones we kept telling each other, because to us they weren't secrets, but things other people didn't know or recognize. Worst of all, we weren't painters and sanders anymore. We were voyeurs looking at walls, rather than through someone's window. We were stuck looking at our lives.

. . .

Hey, Lila, we thought we'd leave you a little something to remember us by.

Hey, Lila, we didn't want to just be three shadows passing through your busy, important life.

Hey, Lila, do you ever wake up in the middle of the night and feel like you're stuck inside a giant condom?

Hey, Lila, there's three mongrels out here, somewhere in America, who have drifted into different orbits. But they still have one thing in common, their sperm mixed in the paint covering your walls.

Hey, Lila, it's okay if you went out and hired someone to paint them over. It's even okay if your walls are now blue or pink or gray, because the sperm is still there, beneath whatever you have done.

Yes, Lila, thousands of frozen little creatures surround you and your lover, or whoever is waking up in that sunlit room now. And no matter what you do to them, no matter how many times you cover them over, they'll still be there, burrowing their way to the surface.

I'm sure Johnny and Virgo would understand why you wished those photographs had never left the little black Japanese box they were in, why you wished you never took the roll into the store and had it developed. Did the man say anything to you when he handed you the envelope? Or did he just smile? As if everything was okay.

Yes, the curly-haired garage mechanic's big hands are still preserved like butterfly wings in your diary. It's the place where, each time you remember him, he is born between your long athletic legs. But wishing a person or a thing was never born, that's why Johnny, Virgo, and I did what we did. We wanted a different kind of diary, one that was written permanently on a wall where everybody could read it. It's why we took the pictures. We wanted someone to know who and what we had been.

ACKNOWLEDGMENTS

Grateful acknowledgment is made to the following for the right to print their copyrighted material:

Peter Bacho: "The Second Room" copyright © 1995 by Peter Bacho. Reprinted by permission of the author.

Debra Kang Dean: "Telling Differences" copyright © 1993 by Debra Kang Dean. First appeared in *The New England Review* (Volume 15, No. 3; summer 1993). Reprinted by permission of the author.

Chitra Banerjee Divakaruni: "Lalita Mashi" copyright © 1995 by Chitra Banerjee Divakaruni. Reprinted by permission of the author.

Lillian Ho Wan: "Silence and the Graverobbers" copyright © 1995 by Lillian Ho Wan. Reprinted by permission of the author.

Garrett Hongo: "Kubota" reprinted from *Volcano* by Garrett Hongo, copyright © 1995 by Garrett Hongo. Reprinted by permission of Alfred A. Knopf, Inc.

Jeanne Wakatsuki Houston: "Colors" copyright © 1993 by Jeanne Wakatsuki Houston. First appeared in *The New England Review* (Volume 15, No. 3; summer 1993). Reprinted by permission of the author.

Geeta Kothari: "Where Are You From?" copyright © 1993 by Geeta Kothari. First appeared in *The New England Review* (Volume 15, No. 3; summer 1993). Reprinted by permission of the author.

Geraldine Kudaka: "Bad Blood" copyright © 1995 by Geraldine Kudaka. Reprinted by permission of the author.

Chang-rae Lee: "The Faintest Echo of Our Language" copyright © 1993 by Chang-rae Lee. First appeared in *The New England Review* (Volume 15, No. 3; summer 1993). Reprinted by permission of the author.

Li-Young Lee: "The Winged Seed" reprinted from *The Winged Seed* by Li-Young Lee, copyright © 1995 by Li-Young Lee. Reprinted by permission of Simon & Schuster, Inc.